W9-AOQ-593

EVERY BREATH
SHE TAKES

Suzanne Forster

JOVE BOOKS, NEW YORK

EVERY BREATH SHE TAKES

A Jove Book / published by arrangement with
the author

All rights reserved.
Copyright © 1999 by Suzanne Forster.
Jacket photo by Wendy Schneider.
This book may not be reproduced in whole or in part,
by mimeograph or any other means, without permission.
For information address: The Berkley Publishing Group,
a member of Penguin Putnam Inc.,
375 Hudson Street, New York, New York 10014.

The Penguin Putnam Inc. World Wide Web site address is
http://www.penguinputnam.com

ISBN: 0-7394-0108-4

A JOVE BOOK®
Jove Books are published by The Berkley Publishing Group,
a member of Penguin Putnam Inc.,
375 Hudson Street, New York, New York 10014.
JOVE and the ''J'' design
are trademarks belonging to Jove Publications, Inc.

PRINTED IN THE UNITED STATES OF AMERICA

EVERY BREATH
SHE TAKES

Once she was the loving disciplinarian who sent me to my room, even knowing I would blissfully while away the hours with the books she kept me stocked in.

Now she is my steady shoulder, wise counsel, and true friend.

Always she will be my inspiration, my hero, and my shining example.

This book is dedicated to my mother, Edith-Mary Stephenson Bolster, whose infectious laughter will forever resonate in my heart.

I love you, Mom.

PROLOGUE

It excited him when they screamed. A vestigial quiver of anticipation set his mind atremble. Sweat burned his brow like a fire, and his heart nearly drowned him it pumped so hard. The rush was its own kind of ecstasy, first liquid weakness, then bursting strength. It was the way every man wanted to feel. Powerful. Master of the moment. A god.

Fear made everything more beautiful, he'd discovered. Fear was honest, the only pure emotion. It brightened a woman's eyes and put a tremor in her voice. It made her exquisitely vulnerable.

But sadly fear was never enough. Only terror broke her open. Terror made her sing and the song she warbled was sacred to him, a hymn to all desperate womankind that her captor was strong. Omnipotent. Her whimpers of distress fed his soul like nothing else. But only terror made her scream. And that was what he had to have.

Anticipation brought his head up. He glanced in the rearview mirror at his own darkly dilating eyes. A button opened the console, but as he reached for the phone, a muted sound commanded his attention. The screech of car horns penetrated the bulletproof windows of his Lincoln Town Car, and he quickly changed lanes. There was a logjam on the Harbor Freeway. It was blocked as far as he could see, and he was on his way to the embassy for a meeting with his senior staff. He was already late, but the Third Street exit was up ahead. Meanwhile he had a moment to spare—and an excuse to indulge himself.

He'd begun taking risks to call her, like now. And she was always there, waiting for him, a gasp drowning in her throat. This one sang so beautfully he was already half in love with her. She made him dizzy with her rich, throaty cries. But that hadn't always been the case. Only in the last twenty-four hours had she come around.

He'd been cruel. He regretted that now. He'd stooped to childhood atrocities to get her attention, but that wasn't his style. He was a fair man, honorable. He gave as he got. He would never have hurt her precious house pet if she hadn't defied him. What kind of monster would put a small animal under the tire of a car—chloroform it and tuck it under one of the steel radials, knowing what would happen?

Her shriek was heartrending, anguished. It had shocked him. But it had also filled him like nothing else could. Only now he was hungry again, hungry for the sound of her. Empty.

He turned the wheel sharply, forcing his way into the next lane, and the next. Her number was programmed into his car phone, another risk few men of his stature would dare to take. It pleased him that he could. Everything about his privileged lifestyle pleased him, especially the immunity it afforded.

Her phone had begun to ring. The soft jangle of bells hit his brain just as he reached the exit, and he pressed the accelerator, racing down the empty ramp. Nervous laughter locked in his throat as the phone abruptly stopped ringing. He hesitated, perplexed. What had happened? He couldn't have pressed the wrong button. He never did that.

The moment of confusion was alien to him, unwanted. He'd picked up too much speed and shouldn't have taken his eyes from the ramp. His quick glance at the phone was a reflex action. He couldn't see anything amiss with the uncooperative instrument. But what happened next made him wonder if he was going crazy.

A loud snap broke up the dead air and a scream erupted from the speaker. It pierced his thoughts, his brain. The high-pitched assault sliced its way into his gray matter like Cuisinart blades. It felt as if he was being cut to ribbons.

The pain was excruciating. His head was going to explode!

"No more!" He ripped the phone from its cradle and flung it into the backseat, but it wouldn't stop blaring. He turned on the radio to drown out the noise and the radio erupted, too. Another scream, this one from the depths of hell. It rent him in two, split him apart. He couldn't control the car. As he shot off the ramp and veered across a lane of traffic, horns began to blare. The heavens were shrieking at him and everything sounded the same. The screams of the bereft. Her screams.

He lunged for his briefcase. There were earplugs inside. They helped him sleep when he traveled. But the case was locked and he couldn't manage it at this speed. Enraged, he slammed it down and saw the words painted in red nail polish on the black leather shell: DO UNTO OTHERS AS YOU WOULD HAVE THEM DO UNTO YOU. It was a trap, he realized too late. That very proverb had been smeared across his newspaper when he picked it up this morning. Alongside it lay a bright red snapdragon.

The next eruption was indiscernible to all but him, the searing dog whistle of locked brakes and doomed souls. He was on the wrong side of the road, and the eighteen-wheeler fishtailing toward him was a steel tidal wave. The noise could shatter glass. His neck snapped back as if he'd been hit, and his eardrums began to bleed. His last utterance was a gasp.

ONE

Rio Scott Walker had eyes that looked out on the world like an ancient sage's. He was thirty-seven, but he saw deep. He saw through. And mostly, he saw things others didn't. He gazed at sorrow and saw the truth, gazed at smiles and saw the lies. And when he gazed at a woman, he usually knew what she wanted.

Walker had a gift. Or at least that's what they whispered about him on the backstreets and in the cell blocks of greater Los Angeles. It wasn't just his fellow homicide detectives or the jailers who told the tales. It was the inmates. They were the ones who knew what he could do. A female serial killer on death row was quoted on *60 Minutes* as saying when Walker looked at you for any length of time, you felt like the point of a flame being contemplated by a mystic.

It probably didn't hurt that he was beautiful in an odd, feral way, with his darkly lashed eyes and lean, powerful build. Or that women were immediately given to fantasies of dangerous sex, and men of dangerous quests.

No one claimed psychic powers were involved in what he did, least of all Rio. There were plenty of people who thought the way he worked a crime scene was nothing but smoke and mirrors. But if there was one thing everyone pretty much agreed on, it was that he was unrivaled as an investigator.

He could find shell casings with his eyes closed, literally. He could navigate in the dark like a blind man, without benefit of flashlight, flares, Luminol to bring up bloodstains, or night-vision binoculars. But it was the odd clicking noise he made when he worked that raised considerable speculation.

"Sounds like poker chips," was his captain's comment. "Some shark in a high-stakes game.'' But it really sounded more like water dripping in a barrel, and Rio himself had nothing to say about it except that it helped him focus. His memory for details, even the arcane ones, was well known, too.

Rio had never minded his coworkers riding him about his so-called gift, as long as they didn't cross the line. Had any one of them been rash enough to suggest that it was the ancestral trickle of Shoshone blood in his veins that made him so perceptive, Rio would have backed the sucker to the wall. He was touchy about his past. In fact, he preferred it right where it was. Back there somewhere. Six feet under.

"I see things because I look," he explained, when he bothered to explain at all. "Most people don't."

Right now he was looking at that morning's edition of the *L.A. Times*. He was also drinking Peruvian Bark herbal tea and tapping an unopened pack of Marlboro Lights against the edge of his battered iron desk. He was trying to quit and the tea was supposed to help, according to his partner, Peggy Sykes; a detective third grade who'd become a fish-oil junkie since her bypass operation the year before. Personally Rio thought most of the homeopathic stuff she touted was horseshit, but desperation made people desperate. And he was up to two packs a day.

SHE'S BACK! FEMME FATALE FELLS NUMBER THREE?

The newspaper headline would have held morbid fascination for Rio even if he hadn't been the lead detective assigned to the case. He loved how the usually scrupulous *Times* had joined the herd in assuming the suspect in last night's highway carnage was a woman. The Femme Fatale's MO *was* seductively female, including the calling card painted in red nail polish on the victim's briefcase, but that didn't automatically assign gender. It was the perfect cover for a man.

"Femme Fatale fever," he observed, pivoting in a chair so old and crotchety the wheel guards struck sparks against the axles. "There is no known cure."

It was going on six P.M., and the squad bay was deserted, which was the way Rio liked it. Without Peggy around, he could indulge his lone-wolf tendencies to the hilt. The other detectives mostly regarded him with wary resignation anyway. They might have no idea what the hell he was up to, but they'd seen the results, and somewhere along the line, an unspoken agreement had been reached. They gave him plenty of room, and he returned the favor. It was workable, although lately Rio had been getting pressure to solve the Femme Fatale case.

"Let's bring her in, for Christ's sake," Frank Grover, the division captain, had said when he'd called Rio in last week, "before she becomes a national hero."

"Check out her home page," was Rio's only comment. "She gets more hits than Leonardo DiCaprio."

Rio had already been to the crime scene, gone over the car, and met with the SIDs team and the coroner's investigator. Several witnesses had come forward to confirm what Rio already suspected, that there was no discernible reason for the crash. The deceased's car had suddenly careened across the highway into oncoming traffic and been hit head-on by a semi.

The victim's installed car phone had been ripped from the console, probably moments before the crash. Rio had put in a request for a search warrant, authorizing the phone company to release the victim's records. The phone, along with several other items from the car, including an audiocassette and the briefcase, were now neatly tagged and stashed in the divison's evidence room.

Rio had visited the victim's home and attempted to speak with his wife, but was told she was too distraught. Their Bel Air mansion, which wasn't far from the Reagans', had apparently been bought with the wife's inheritance, which had turned out to be South American sugar-plantation money. Diplomats didn't make *that* kind of money in Rio's experience.

As usual the press had their theories and Rio had his, but they'd scooped him on the flower. Rio was the one who'd fished the still crisp snapdragon out of the undersecretary's trash bin, along with the defaced newspaper. It was part of the Femme Fatale's signature behavior to warn the victim of an impending strike with the bloodred flower, but Rio hadn't bothered to look up its meaning. The *Times*'s crime reporter had.

Besides the obvious resemblance to certain parts of a woman's anatomy, the reporter had written, *the snapdragon also symbolizes vengeance of a particularly female nature. In a nineteenth-century guide to flower symbolism, the message of the snapdragon is this: "Your wanton mischief will be avenged upon you bitterly."*

Rio was impressed, but not convinced. He knew Gabriel Quiñones from years of digging in the same dirt, and the crime reporter had a paparazzo's instinct for a big, sexy story. This story was bigger and sexier if the suspect was a woman.

Rio snapped the paper shut and tossed it on his desk. He lobbed the cigarette pack in the air, aiming at a kiddie basketball hoop that was stuck with suction cups to a bottled water jug. The pack dropped through and disappeared in the wastebasket below.

"Nice shot," he congratulated himself. "Deserves a smoke."

Moments later he crushed the smoldering butt in the Coke can he'd been forced to use since the no-smoking ordinance was passed. No one except maybe Grover cared what he did after five anyway, short of setting fire to the building. Peggy's the one who would have taken him to task. She'd have snapped every one of his cigarettes in half like so many green beans, and worse, called him by his given name, Robert.

Peggy, she was gutsy. No one else would have dared.

Rio tilted back in the creaky chair, his thoughts returning to the case at hand. Call him sexist, but he was betting against a female offender. The evidence pointed in that direction, but how was a woman, maybe a stalker victim herself, managing to upend these guys? Women didn't think like that, like fiends.

Okay, yeah, he was sexist. He tended to idealize women a little, make them purer than they were and maybe less capable of the really heinous shit. But he was also a pragmatist, and in his experience, women rarely got involved in revenge. They might contemplate it, but they didn't do it. They were forgiving. Too forgiving.

Which was why this case had him fascinated. The Femme Fatale's MO was to trap known offenders by becoming their victim. The stalkers were lured by whatever drove them to prey on women, helpless flies to the Femme Fatale's spider. The deaths were all "accidents." But luring dangerous criminals to their deaths was not typical feminine behavior. It was risk-taking behavior in the extreme. Death-wish stuff.

Yesterday's victim was a nasty customer, an undersecretary at some third-world embassy, who used his diplomatic immunity as a shield against the charges of stalking and sexual harassment brought by various women over the years, including coworkers. They claimed in their statements that he was obsessed with the sound of a woman's scream and apparently nothing was too extreme—destroying personal property, mutilating pets, threatening death and dismemberment—the hands-on stuff being untraceable to him, of course.

Plenty of his victims probably wanted to avenge themselves, but not many would have been capable of it after he got done with them. He tended to isolate and slowly drive them to the brink of madness. One had overdosed on tranquilizers. Another couldn't stop screaming and had to be institutionalized. More recently he'd had a victim charged with assault when she confronted him and spit in his face. He was a predator who destroyed his quarry without ever touching them. And now someone had turned the tables on him. Screamed him into the path of an oncoming semi, based on the cassette they found in his radio.

"Good work." Rio didn't know whether to apprehend a chick like that or give her a high five.

Chick. He was doing it, too.

A big, blinking TV set teetered on top of the file cabinet across the aisle from Rio's desk. It ran pretty much night and day, although Rio rarely paid attention unless there was a Mighty Ducks game playing. Once in a while when the thing gave out from exhaustion, he would catch his own reflection in the dull green glass and wonder what it was people saw when they looked at him, women in particular. A few of them were bold enough to look him up and down, but they always stopped when they got to his eyes. Then their expressions changed.

Peggy liked to embarrass him about his eyelashes and his "serial killer" gaze, whatever the hell that was. Rio would not have disagreed that he bore a closer resemblance to a criminal than a cop, especially on those days when he did nothing more in the way of grooming than shower and shake out his hair. He wore the required jacket, but he'd long ago begun yanking the tie free and leaving it to hang around his neck like a noose. And his black trench coat could easily have gotten him mistaken for a government assassin.

To be honest he found it uncomfortable peering at his own image the way he apparently peered at everything else. He didn't want to look too deeply into that black well. No telling what he might find. Even what he knew about he preferred to leave alone.

Now he glanced up, curious about the impassioned voice coming from the TV.

"Never forget the victim's power. The stalker needs her, but she does not need him. She makes him *feel* powerful, and she's the only one who can. He feeds off her fear. It's his oxygen. What victims must do is cut off all contact with the stalker, stop feeding the beast—"

It was *Larry King Live,* and that day's guest happened to be an author who'd written a bestselling book called *Killer Smile.* Her argument intrigued him. Rio agreed in theory that cutting off all contact with a stalker was the best way to discourage him. But there was something familiar about the young woman's intense, delicately chiseled features and burnished wealth of auburn hair. Rio couldn't place her, but she'd made an instant impression on his nervous system.

She came across as knowledgeable and impassioned, as involved with her subject as she was determined to help victims reclaim their lives. If there was a discordant note in the whole package, it was her pale green eyes. They were the color of a daiquiri in a frosted glass, and Rio remembered that chilly gaze from somewhere. But it wasn't until King held the book up and Rio saw the author's name that he knew who she was.

"Jesus," he murmured, and then he said it again, softer. It happened to be his epithet of choice, but not because he got off on being disrespectful of anyone's beliefs. No other word could touch it for slack-jawed disbelief. And no matter how cynical a homicide detective became, he still had his share of those moments. This was L.A.

Rio settled back in his chair, intent on doing nothing more than observing her for a while. It might be the only God-given talent he had, observation. And contrary to popular belief, the tap of his finger against the metal chair arm was not a way to summon supernatural powers, it was a way to focus. He'd picked it up in childhood, the legacy of having been raised by a blind grandfather.

Recognition came in reverse order. It was her backside he remembered first, maybe because that was all he could see the first time she interrupted his line of sight. She was dashing down the hallway of Blue Hills, the Bishop family's mansion, apparently trying to avoid him, although he had no idea why. It was his first visit to the fabled estate and he'd come by on business with her older sister, Virginia "Ginger" Bishop, who'd been busy making a name for herself as the DA office's hottest new prosecutor.

Rio and Ginger had been working together on a case, and he hadn't realized there was a little sister until he'd seen this one scampering out of sight. It hadn't struck him as anything more than odd at the time, but it was to be Rio's first inkling that the Bishop family was unlike any other he ever had—or ever would—encounter in his relatively rocky path through life. They were different. Different and doomed.

It was Ginger herself who first enlightened him that the senior Bishops ranked among the most prominent couples in the land. Both her mother and father were federal district-court judges, and the mother had been a strong contender for a seat on the U.S. Supreme Court at that time. Rio had not been surprised when some years later Frances Stanfield Bishop, of the silversmith Stanfields, won her appointment to become only the third woman in history to sit on the highest court in the land. The big surprise would have been if she hadn't.

The tapping slowed, stopped.

The Bishops were royalty in Southern California, and Ginger was the one chosen to succeed them, their princess. She was anointed, part of some larger destiny and above routine human tragedy, until the unthinkable happened. Ginger was stalked and killed by an unknown assailant.

It had come out almost immediately that Rio and Ginger were more than coworkers at one time. They'd had a brief, intense affair that ended badly when her parents made it clear they disapproved. Maybe Rio should have seen the problem coming, given who the Bishops were. Ginger was a successful professional woman who didn't make a move without Mommy and Daddy's okay.

The woman on the screen, Carlie Bishop, hadn't seemed to approve of Rio either. He could remember the cool touch of those green eyes and the way she'd scrutinized him when she thought he wasn't looking. He'd once studied the progress of a crack in his windshield that way, watching its spiral arms creep toward certain destruction.

He'd dismissed Carlie as a kid at the time, as had everyone else apparently. Ginger had been the pride and joy of the Bishops, as magnetic and brilliant as her mother, but with a warmth that easily won people over. It was clear the family had big plans for their older daughter, whereas the little one had seemed overshadowed and somewhat superfluous. Maybe he had flowers on the brain today, but snapdragons weren't what came to mind when he thought of Carlie Bishop. She was more like a columbine in a garden of prize roses.

Somewhere in the large bay, a phone rang once and went silent. Rio ignored the lonely sound.

Carlie was still a columbine, still strikingly different, but no longer superfluous. The stalk had grown leggy and tall, the crimson flower had opened, and it was a spectacular sight. Less classic than a rose maybe, less perfectly symmetrical, but a hell of a lot more interesting. She was the late bloomer and probably better for it. There was that old adage about some things being worth waiting for.

Rio caught himself counting back, trying to figure out how old she was now, and it hit him that he was interested in more than a professional way. She couldn't have been much more than a teenager at the time, which would put her in her mid to late twenties. Too young to be so knowledgeable about violent men.

Okay, maybe he was being idealistic again, but the longer he listened, the more he was amazed. She had an encyclopedic knowledge of the evil men did to women. The book on stalkers, rapists, and batterers—she'd read it all, cover to cover. She knew these twisted souls better than he did. She appeared to understand every quiver and twitch of their devious neurons, and her advice to the audience on how to spot and deal with them was excellent.

If Rio was impressed, he was also intrigued, and vaguely suspicious. She appeared to be on a crusade, and he wondered about the timing, and how much it might have had to do with Ginger's death. There were other things about her that bothered him, too. Those green eyes, for one thing.

Before the show was over Rio had one of his ideas working. Call it a wild-ass hunch, call it intuition, call it mental telepathy, but the longer he stared at the screen, the more it rose inside him, this river of possibility. He hated to concede anything to the sensation-soaked media, but maybe they were right this time. Absently he tapped another cigarette from the pack and fired up, taking a deep drag before he stubbed it out. Maybe their Femme Fatale *was* a woman.

TWO

"Forget everything Mama taught you about being well-behaved young ladies," Carlie Bishop exhorted her audience. "Mr. Killer Smile is counting on your good manners to get him what he wants. *You.* At his mercy!"

She met the steady gazes of the women crowding the community-college lecture hall. *Stare them in the eye, Carlie,* she told herself. *First one, then the other, look into their eyes and command their attention. Look sharp. You're their mother now. Parent to their child.*

"Be nice, ladies," she warned. "Nice till it kills you. Nice and dead."

Eyes widened. Spines straightened. She had their full attention now. They were ready to listen with more than polite interest. But even so, too few of them would heed her advice, she knew. No one believed it would happen to them. Somehow, tonight, Carlie had to break through the massive denial.

Several hundred women had jammed the hall, and the odds said that a frighteningly high percentage of them would be affected at some point. Statistics revealed that one in five women would be stalked in her lifetime. That was appalling enough. But the fact that they were easy marks because they had been trained to be "nice" was more than Carlie could bear.

"Say no," she urged. Her own sister, Ginger, had died because she was Ms. Congeniality, nice to a fault. "It won't kill you. Saying yes might. Be *rude.*"

A small, shrill voice called back: "How about neutering the bastards? Would that be too rude?"

There was a chain reaction of startled laughter.

"Right on!" someone cheered to a smattering of applause. "The animal shelter will castrate 'em for free."

Carlie laughed along with everyone else, but she raised her hands for quiet. This was her last appearance on a two-month book tour, and she'd hoped to get through the evening without event. The unexpected success of *Killer Smile* had brought pressures she'd never dreamed of, including being taken seriously as an expert in her field. The book jacket described her as a personal-safety expert, and Carlie rather liked that, since she was in the business of teaching women how to be safe, emotionally as well as physically.

"Sorry, no violence except in self-defense," she said.

"A knee to the knickknacks? My daddy used to call that a kindness."

The audience roared. Carlie recognized the first heckler's squeaky southern twang. It was coming from the right side of the auditorium, but Carlie couldn't locate her.

"I'm not sure who needs protection here," Carlie rejoined.

"There's more than one way to swat a fly. I prefer the Cross-Face Chicken Wing."

Apparently Carlie was supposed to know what a Cross-Face Chicken Wing was. "Excuse me?"

A dark head bobbed in the second row. Carlie thought she'd spotted the source of the one-liners, but if this waif was a heckler, then what was the world coming to? Twentyish, slight, and generously freckled, with a rag mop of raisin-black hair, she could have been a high-school cheerleader, except that her features were wary as a defensive child's and her dark eyes were lit with an emotion that bore a strong resemblance to pain.

"That's a wrestling move. I'd demonstrate," the waif volunteered, "except I'm not wearing my kidney belt."

Now the whole place was abuzz. There were whispers, giggles, and gasps. Her edgy humor was infectious, but the lecture was taking on a party atmosphere, and Carlie had a natural instinct for spotting disaster. Risk analysis, they called it in her business. She could see where this was headed, and if she didn't take control, her community-college lecture could turn into a crisis intervention.

The subject matter of *Killer Smile* touched into deeply rooted fears and anxieties. It wasn't unusual for people to react strongly, especially since many of these women were stalker victims themselves, or knew someone who was. Emotions ran high when you were living in fear for your life, and laughter could be cathartic. But it could also touch off the deeper feelings of anger and despair that smoldered just beneath the surface.

"What was your name, miss?" Carlie singled out the heckler with a firm but gentle tone.

"Oh, I'm sorry, did I—" Her tiny shoulder bag had a silver chain strap and she worked it nervously with her fingers. "Jo Emily. Jo Emily Po—"

"That's okay, Jo Emily. First names are fine." Carlie had found that asking people to identify themselves reminded them they were accountable for their actions. In this case it had worked. The young woman looked instantly abashed, and Carlie's heart went out to her.

"I'm not much good at it anyway," Jo Emily admitted with a matter-of-fact sigh. "The Chicken Wing, it requires your upper-body strength."

"I see—"

"Sweet Chin Music is more my speed."

"Actually, I've been looking for a bodyguard," Carlie interjected to the surprise and delight of the crowd. "Could you and I talk after the lecture?"

Jo Emily couldn't hold back a burgeoning smile, but the brightness sparkling in her eyes looked more like tears than excitement. "We could do that, yes."

Carlie had intended to try to catch her after the talk anyway. Hopefully this would ease any embarrassment she might feel and give them a chance to speak privately. She'd been lecturing long enough to know when she had an exhibitionist on her hands, but this wasn't one of those times. Jo Emily was driven by something other than the need for attention. She was also older than Carlie had first thought, probably closer to thirty than thirteen. Those big doe-brown eyes had been lived in a while.

"I'm guessing the rest of you don't know how to do a Cross-Face Chicken Wing either," Carlie said, glad to be back on solid ground as she turned to the auditorium crowd. "So let's talk about how to deal with Mr. Killer Smile, the charming stranger who selflessly takes the time to point out that your car tire is going flat and offers to ride with you to the gas station and show you how to fix it. There are nice people left in the world, you're thinking, right? *Wrong.*"

She went over the warning signs, emphasizing the old adage that it was always better to be safe than sorry.

"To a woman alone, strangers are danger. If you need help, find a woman or a child. Never ask a man you don't know unless he's a senior citizen, and then only if it's a dire emergency. I don't mean to malign all men between the ages of sixteen and sixty. The majority of them are sheep, not wolves, but you don't know that, so the rule is: If they're strangers, they're dangerous!"

Carlie covered the rest of her safety tips in detail, and then finished the way she started, by reminding her audience that it was okay to be rude, something she knew most women abhorred.

"The stranger you meet at noon is just as dangerous as the one you meet at midnight," she pointed out. "If he tries to impose himself on you, look him straight in the eye and tell him no. If that doesn't work"—she winked at Jo Emily—"remember that God in Her infinite wisdom had a reason for giving women knees and men knickknacks."

When the laughter and clapping subsided, Carlie opened the session to questions. As she searched the auditorium for raised hands, she heard a faint clicking sound. Her first thought was Jo Emily, but the young woman hadn't moved a muscle since their exchange. She'd been fixated on Carlie's every word.

The noise emanated from the back of the room, and like a slow drip of water, it disturbed Carlie in some way she couldn't explain. The lights were too bright to see much past the middle rows, but there appeared to be someone standing by the entrance doors, and though Carlie couldn't make out details, she was sure the shadowy form was a man's. It was too big to be otherwise, the shoulders too broad.

She touched her throat, suddenly alarmed.

The audience had begun to notice her staring, but as they turned to see what had transfixed her, the clicking noise stopped. The figure stepped back farther into the shadows, and eventually Carlie realized he was gone.

For some reason she glanced back at Jo Emily and saw the glint of fear in the other woman's eyes. Carlie didn't understand what had just happened, but Jo Emily had felt it, too. There really had been some threat here. She was wondering if she'd imagined the man's presence, but Jo Emily's reaction told her she hadn't.

The parking lot of Von's Supermarket was all but deserted at ten P.M, and the January air held a sharp nip. Worse, Carlie was still in high heels and her black winter silk suit. She'd stayed long after the speech, answering questions and expecting to talk with Jo Emily, only to discover that her heckler had slipped out without anyone noticing.

Carlie had been deeply concerned. She'd called campus security, and while they scouted the grounds, she'd checked the auditorium and the ladies' rest room, but without success. Jo Emily was not to be found, and there was nothing Carlie could do but hope that she'd picked up a flyer at the door and would show up at a support-group meeting.

Right now, her arches aching and bone-tired from the day she'd had, Carlie faced two overflowing cartfuls of groceries. Everything had to be loaded into the back of the Explorer, and it had already taken about as much heft as she had to raise the hatch door. Naturally there wasn't a bag boy in sight. "Tote that bale." Trying not to break nails or anything else, she power-lifted several slippery plastic bags of bottled water, one after another, and reminded herself that tomorrow at this time she would be in her mountain hideaway. She'd had the quiet little weekend trip planned for months now, and just the thought of it had helped to keep the crazies at bay.

The last year had been the most thrilling of Carlie's life, but the pressure had been relentless. Two ten-city book tours alone would have crushed most ordinary mortals, by her estimation, and she'd also had to run her consulting business and contend with the demands of her new post as chair of the Stalker Violence Task Force. She was running on fumes, but wouldn't have changed one overwhelming minute.

She was fiercely proud of the book, and the presidential appointment felt like her greatest accomplishment. At times it was still hard to believe that her goal to see a nationwide support network for victims was actually being realized. The federal program included education, hotlines, and advocacy groups, and Carlie had the chief executive's personal promise of support. However, as optimistic as she was that the program would take many women out of harm's way, she was beginning to wonder if it might put *her* in the hospital.

The muscles of her arms were on fire. She still had half a cart to go, and a dozen bags alone had been bottled water, plus she had groceries for her house in Marina del Rey, as well as the mountain cabin. Fatigue was making her clumsy, but she was too tired to stop, if that made any sense. She just wanted to get home.

"Oh no!" Carlie gaped in horror as the plastic finger hooks got away from her. The bag she'd been lifting hit the cement, and an explosion of yellow-and-white muck sent her moaning to her knees. It was the milk and eggs!

"Not that bag, not tonight," she pleaded, but the gods of overwhelmed women weren't listening. She couldn't even get to her car. The seeping, gelatinous mess had blocked access, and for one horrible moment, Carlie thought she was going to cry. She was actually blinking away tears in a supermarket parking lot. What was wrong with her?

"Your book is at the top of all the bestseller lists," she told herself. "You're not allowed to get emotional over spilled milk."

It had to be stress, of course. Now that the immediate pressure was off, she could fall apart. But as she searched for a Kleenex in her jacket pocket, someone knelt opposite her and offered a white flag of surrender.

Actually, it was a man's handkerchief, and Carlie and her fellow croucher were almost knee to knee.

"Blow?" he said as she looked up.

Eyes that must have seen every heartache known to man gazed down at her from beneath kohl lashes. His irises were deep wells, but that wasn't what made her stare.

"Where did you get those lashes?" she asked. Hers had always been rather stubby and fair. His were the blackest she'd ever seen. Velvet pillow fringe, those lashes. This guy was killer. She didn't know how else to describe him.

"Thrifty Drugs," he said. "Manager's special."

She shot him a look, then laughed. "They came with the package, didn't they? A genetic freebie."

" 'Fraid, so, but it's not a body part a man likes to brag about." He surveyed the glop at her feet. "How about a salvage operation? I think the milk's totaled, but we might be able to save an egg or two."

Carlie wrinkled her nose. "Too slimy."

"Want some help with the rest of it? Maybe we can get the other bags in your car without another casualty. Think?"

"We can try." The right answer was no. No, I don't need your help. I'm a freaking black belt in jujitsu, and I can handle a few measly bags myself. That was what she'd just advised her lecture audience to say. Carlie warned women about these conditions all the time. They were fraught with peril. It was late, the parking lot had emptied out, and her Good Samaritan was the worst kind, a stranger with a killer smile.

All the indicators were there, but for whatever reason, the thought of danger barely registered with this guy. Instead, Carlie was mulling the possibility that he might be one of the most appealing men she'd ever met. And even more improbable, considering her focus on dangerous strangers these days, she rather liked him.

"Let me," he said as she braved the mess on the pavement and reached for one of the bags. He loaded the car himself, all the while engaging her in light conversation. He was especially curious about her dozen one-gallon containers of drinking water.

"You planning to bathe in it?" he asked.

"It's for my tree house." She tried not to laugh as his head swiveled around. There was no way not to explain that her unique mountain hideaway lacked only for piped-in drinking water.

"Family land," she said. "With nothing on it but huge oaks and chestnuts. The conservationists begged me not to cut them down, so I built my dream cottage in the branches. I thought the height would bother me, but I love it up there in the ozone, me and the birds.''

"Ever see that Hitchcock movie?"

She laughed out loud. "I could have written the script. They flock for my burned toast. Got my nose pecked once.''

"Only once?" He gazed at her nose, her eyes, her mouth, lingering. "I'm trying to imagine that.''

Oh yeah, she liked him. Fortunately she caught herself just as she was about to invite him up to check out her mountain retreat, and wondered what she could have been thinking about.

"Chilly tonight, isn't it?" he said. "Perfect weather for a hot cup of coffee.''

Carlie didn't give him a chance to ask. "I really have to get these groceries home,'' she said. "The frozen yogurt will melt.'' Finally, the right answer!

He let her go with nothing more than a friendly admonition to drive safely, and moments later Carlie was whooshing down the street in her Explorer and congratulating herself on a narrow escape.

It wasn't until she pulled onto a little-used side street that she noticed the headlights behind her. It was the way the car hung back as much as the driver's tenacity that made her suspect she was being followed. When she slowed, the car did too.

They were in a residential neighborhood close to her home, where streets were short and stop signs stood at every corner, so it was easy to confirm her suspicion. She negotiated a couple of unplanned turns, saw the lights still behind her, and quickly dug the pepper spray from her purse. She also placed a 911 call on her cell phone.

The intersection coming up was a well-lit street. Carlie's plan was to try to get a look at the car, but it was no longer behind her when she checked her rearview mirror. A couple more blocks convinced her that she'd lost him. Relieved, she headed for home. But as she pulled onto the street where her small gambrel-roofed house was located, she saw a flashing red light.

A police car had driven up behind her.

Carlie pulled over, hoping it was in response to her 911 call, but something bothered her about the car. It wasn't a black-and-white, and from what she could see of the driver, he wasn't wearing a uniform. Unfortunately, she already had the window down before she realized all this, another rule of safety shattered. So far tonight she'd managed to violate almost every word of caution in her own book.

Carlie stared in shock at the man who appeared at her window. It was the stranger with the good eyelashes. He was reaching inside the lapel of his jacket, but she didn't wait to find out why. She grabbed the pepper spray and blasted him before he could get to whatever was in there.

There had been something in his hand, she realized. She'd seen a flash of silver, but the object had already dropped to the ground with a clunk.

"Stay right there!" she shouted, holding him off with the spray while she got out of her car. She knelt to confiscate what she expected to be a weapon and realized it was a detective's badge. LAPD, RHD. She'd heard of the elite robbery and homicide division that dealt with high-profile crime, but she never would have imagined—

"A cop," she whispered. "I've Maced a cop."

THREE

So that's why God made lawn sprinklers, Carlie thought, not daring to smile—or heaven forbid, laugh—as she watched LAPD homicide detective Robert Scott Walker douse his handsome head in the spray. Now she was very glad she'd had the automatic sprinker system installed in her front yard, although it had cost her a fortune. *Don't you just love the smell of freshly watered grass,* she thought ironically.

Walker was a big man. Even bent over that way. A big and probably angry man. Having made that observation, Carlie began to calculate the odds of escaping her predicament alive. She was beginning to wish she'd let Jo Emily demonstrate the wrestling hold. It couldn't hurt to know how to execute a Cross-Face Chicken Wing right about now.

The flashing red light on the hood of his car reminded her that she'd be smart to do something besides stare at him. They were parked in front of her house, on a sleepy side street where there was virtually no traffic at this time of night. Her closest neighbors were senior citizens, and she didn't want them subjected to an embarrassing scene. They thought she was a nice lady, not like the people on the other side who walked naked in front of their windows and let their dogs run loose.

Carlie moved to the middle of the sidewalk. The spray was gently pelting her skirt, and water stains were murder on winter silk. Her rule of thumb in no-win situations like this had always been the lesser of evils, but short of a grown man drowning in a sprinkler, there didn't seem to be any lesser evil.

At least he was legitimate. His relationship with her lawn had given her time to have a look in his car. She'd found his vehicle I.D. number and his business card on the dash. Now she knew why he'd been so gallant about the groceries, but not what he was doing at her neighborhood store. Or here in front of her house for that matter. He was a cop, but sadly, cops could be stalkers, too, often the most successful. She would do well to take her own advice when it came to strangers in isolated areas. Everyone was suspect.

Did that make her paranoid?

Did that mean she didn't trust men?

The answer was yes on both counts. Only in her case it wasn't because of the physical danger any particular man might pose. She'd never been stalked or assaulted, and for that she was grateful. But in matters of the heart she'd been far less lucky. Her dad had been emotionally absent—not with Ginger, of course, *never* with Ginger, whom he adored—but he'd barely acknowledged Carlie's existence.

And Carlie's first great love, the man she had heaped all her hopes on, her adored physical-anthropology professor in college, had turned out to be the worst kind of liar, the worst kind of cheat. A man of varied pursuits, he'd quoted Louis Leakey, Steven Hawking, *and* Robert Browning. He'd also relieved Carlie of her virginity without a qualm, kept her enthralled for months on end, and then abruptly dumped her when she discovered that he lived two lives—one as the brilliant seducer of naive coeds, the other as devoted husband and father of three boys.

Carlie was crushed, demolished. This man had led her to believe he was free to marry her, that he wanted to, but she spotted him with his adoring wife and kids at a faculty function. Even then, she'd tried to salvage what they had, probably because there'd been so little love in her life. She could adjust, she told him, knowing it would destroy her. She would never tell. He'd dumped her anyway, said it wasn't the same anymore.

Carlie had run the gamut of emotions, from abject grief to smoldering hurt and anger. Her men-are-scum period had lasted two years. But she'd come out of it finally, sad but wiser.

A stuttering burst of noise made her flinch and look for cover. It sounded like gunfire, but she could see the detective, and he was still flushing his eyes. The red light pulsed over him as he drew back, shook his head, and spit out what sounded like an obscene comment about the mental state of the entire human race. If he was more specific, she couldn't tell.

A woman's voice broke through the static, and Carlie realized it was a radio dispatcher. What were the odds, she wondered, that this would be a call Detective Walker *had* to answer? She was now officially on tenterhooks. He was back, he was wet, and she was going to have to deal with him.

There was a fabric satchel in the back of her Explorer, stuffed with workout gear in the unlikely event she should ever make it to a gym. She picked her way through the spray, popped the hatch, and wrestled the case out from under the groceries. If she had a plan of action, it was simply to defuse the immediate situation. They were two adults. They could talk about this.

But when he opened his dripping eyes and saw her walking toward him, she wasn't as certain about the number of adults. One of them appeared to have regressed. "Would this help?" she asked, offering a towel from the satchel.

He'd squeezed one eye shut, which could easily have been interpreted as a scowl. Carlie imagined pain was a factor, but the way he was looking at her peace offering made her feel as if she should burn it. Something told her he was not going to be a great guy about this.

"What is that thing?"

A voice gritty enough to sandblast the paint off her house, she thought. Her hopes plummeted further. She should have run. Run for her life when she had the chance. Run screaming.

"It's a towel," she said.

"No—*that.*" Now his scowl was directed at her right hand, where she'd gripped her key chain like brass knuckles, the blades between her fingers.

"My keys?"

He took the towel with a grunt of displeasure, but his focus didn't waver from the keys. Carlie opened her fingers and dangled the chain to make it look less weaponlike, thinking that was the problem. But he was still darkly suspicious, and something about his sudden quiet intensity struck fear in her heart. If she'd been caught with contraband or stolen gems, it might have made sense. But this felt personal.

"Tell me about the charms," he said.

"These?" She tapped the two carved agates that were strung like pearls on the silver links. "My lonely stones?"

The moss agate and tiger's eye were actually gifts from her sister's prized collection. Carlie had been caught playing with them when Ginger was away at boarding school. She'd missed her sister terribly, and had been seeking contact. It was nothing more than a means to stave off loneliness, but her parents hadn't seen it that way. They'd confiscated Carlie's collection of comic books, tossed them in the trash, and forbade her to enter her sister's room again. When Ginger returned, she promptly gave Carlie her two best agates. She'd called them "Carlie's lonely stones," and Carlie had wept as if her heart would break.

"What are lonely stones?" he wanted to know.

"They're . . . these are family heirlooms." It was as much as she was

willing to say. The subject was too personal, and painful, to discuss
with a hostile stranger. Fortunately he didn't press it, but she could feel
the unrelieved tension. It hung in the air like smoke.

"Done with the towel?" she asked, ignoring the fact that he hadn't
used it yet.

"You just happened to have one with you?"

"Part of my workout gear." With a cautious attempt to lighten things
up, she added, "I keep thinking someone will abduct me, take me to a
gym, and force me to exercise. I want to be ready."

"Tried the Yellow Pages under personal trainer-slash-kidnapper?"

"Oh, good idea."

"I might even know one. They should be springing him from Folsom
any day."

She wasn't sure whether to laugh or not. He hadn't, but she had the
feeling they were headed in that direction, and it gave her hope. Curious,
she watched him shoulder out of his trench coat and blot himself dry
with the lining.

"Got a change of clothes with you?" he asked.

"Leotards and tights." Her shoulders lifted in response to his faint
grin. Now they were getting somewhere. "The tights might fit. Some
men like that feeling of being cupp—"

She shut up instantly. The sound he made brought into question the
wisdom of referring to men's crotches, even by implication. She'd been
accused of being too forthright for her own good. Certainly her parents
had thought so. Blunt, her mother had called it. "Not attractive in a girl
of your situation," Frances Stanfield Bishop had cautioned more than
once. At least she hadn't said breeding.

It was probably Carlie's way of rebelling, since she'd never pranced
naked in front of windows or let her dogs run wild. Her parents would
probably have preferred that she had. Honesty was not a virtue in house-
holds where everything was concealed under a high gloss of politeness.
Bad form to point out the cracks in the veneer. Very.

The staticky voices kept crackling from Walker's radio, but he didn't
seem to be paying any attention. Carlie took the opportunity to ask the
question that had been with her since she saw his flashing red light.

"What are you doing here?"

"You put in a 911 call, didn't you?"

"I thought someone was following me."

"Someone was. Me. The way you shot out of that lot, I figured
something was wrong. Do you always drive like that? I could have you
written up for speeding, running a red light, reckless endangerment, and
about six other violations."

Carlie was reasonably sure he wasn't going to write her up for anything, but she knew better than to push it. Still, she couldn't hide the lilt of satisfaction in her voice.

"Where exactly did I lose you?" she asked. "Was it the red light?"

"Just for the record, you *didn't* lose me. I backed off when you spotted me. Better than have you kill someone."

Something about the tilt of his head and the darkish cast of his eyes made Carlie hesitate. She stared at him harder, aware that she was searching for an elusive connection. The line of his body was suddenly familiar and so was the tone of his voice—a rough wood grain, full of slivers if you went against it. Hard to forget, especially for a woman of Carlie's background, where voices and lives were polished to a high sheen. Still, she couldn't place it. She met so many people, and her work included contact with law-enforcement agencies around the country, so it was possible their paths had crossed. But she didn't think so. *He* would have been hard to forget.

"Are you all right?" he asked.

"*I'm* fine," she said, her emphasis reminding him that he wasn't. Maybe it was the sight of male tears, but Carlie felt an unexpected pang of guilt. The sprinklers had gone off, but his long-lashed eyes were still watering. His clothes were wet, and it was cold.

"There's an all-night clinic nearby," she offered. "I could drive you—"

"You're not driving me anywhere. I'm thinking about having your license revoked and your car towed so you can never drive again."

Oh, fine. That's what she got for her guilt. She waved a hand at his car. "Could we turn out that flashing red light anytime soon? The neighbors are beginning to gather at their windows."

"I guess *we* have a reputation to protect?" He swung back to his car, took the light off the hood, and tossed it inside, still flashing. Now the interior of the car pulsed like a red beacon of disaster. "Better?" he inquired sardonically.

Cheeky bastard, Carlie thought. Probably insufferable when he really got going. That was familiar, too. Did she know this guy?

"Detective Walker," she called out. "Could *we* call it a night? I'm tired, and you probably want to slap a raw steak over your eyes and drink yourself to sleep. Isn't that what wounded *warriors* do?"

Carlie knew instantly that she'd crossed the line, though she had no idea what that line was, and he didn't give her time to ask. He lifted his head like an angry god and fired off a thunderbolt that connected with physical force.

If Carlie staggered, it was inwardly. She didn't understand what had triggered the reaction, she knew only how it felt. Like a body slam. One look and he'd sucked the air from her lungs, but she had no idea why. What had she done now?

Carlie was not to have the answer to her question, at least not that night. Walker ducked into his car, switched off the flasher, and the next thing Carlie knew everything was dark and he was pulling away. He whipped the nondescript sedan into a U-turn and drove back the way he came. Without a word. Without a backward glance. And without returning her towel.

"Well, what was that all about?" she murmured.

It was past midnight and the world was silent on Fifty-seventh Street, except for a sound the faint of heart might have found unnerving—the slow tick of Rio Walker's thoughts as he beat out time against the car's console.

Rio had grown up listening to the tap of his blind grandfather's cane and watching the old man perform miracles. There was no better detective. He could find things a bloodhound couldn't sniff out. Like the hunting knife Rio had tried to swipe from the neighborhood pawnshop. Somehow the old man had known it was in Rio's pocket before they left the store, and he'd marched his grandson back to return it. He'd routinely found the dirty magazines Rio stashed, though how he could tell them from the others Rio couldn't figure. And somehow he'd known about the remains of the tomato aspic Rio had flushed down the toilet.

Snick, snick, snick, snick . . .

Steady and slow, the tapping increased only as Rio's thoughts did. There was a map of the black forest inside his head, and when he journeyed there, he was blind to the real world, couldn't see a foot in front of him, and yet he always seemed to know where he was. And sometimes he knew the impossible. Where *they* were.

He didn't think of it as magic or ESP. It was simple concentration, letting your mind operate in the dark, where it did its best work, letting it connect dots and find spaces in need of filling. Certain mental processes didn't like to be observed. They were like cat burglars, sneaking down hallways while everyone else slept. If you could turn down the volume of consciousness and watch, you might catch glimpses of them plying their trade. Thieves in the night. Grave robbers. They could unearth bones and reconstruct skeletons, figuratively speaking.

Sometimes it felt as if they'd created a prime suspect out of nothing, thin air, like Rio's fleeting contact with the TV screen when Carlie was on. But it was much more complex than that, he'd discovered. Complex and counterintuitive. He didn't understand it, but he did know enough to pay attention, fortunately. Like now.

Sherlock Holmes had paced the floor, thought out loud, and called it deduction. Rio tapped and listened. He called it eavesdropping, and he'd come back tonight for that reason. To eavesdrop on his own thoughts about Carlie Bishop. He'd parked down the street on her side, a spot that was hard to see unless you were looking for a stakeout car.

The hunch he had about her was so strong he'd already put a plan into action, something he didn't normally do this early in the game. Her situation had made it easier than she could possibly know. For a personal-safety expert, she was a sitting duck.

Earlier he'd sealed her white terry towel in a Ziploc bag, ready to hand over to a private lab he used. There might be a strand of her hair, a particle of skin to compare against future evidence. Whether or not it would be admissible in court was anyone's guess, but he couldn't pass up the chance. Nor did he want to alert the brass. If they discovered he had Carlie Bishop under surveillance, the sky would start raining politicians. Rio would have to turn over every detail of his investigation, providing they didn't take it away from him.

He had stopped tapping and starting thinking, he realized. It was a miracle he wasn't grinding his teeth. The high-profile cases were hell to prosecute. It was almost impossible to get a conviction with the jury-rigging and the celebrity lawyers.

The media went nuts, too. In this case they could be counted on to reveal things about the Bishop family he didn't want revealed. Plus, once he'd declared Carlie a suspect, he had to treat her like one. He couldn't question her without Mirandizing her. Now he could do anything he wanted, and there was plenty he wanted to do.

Yeah . . . he had to proceed on this one alone for a while.

Just him and the personal-safety guru.

He fished a pack of cigarettes from his dash and tapped it against his lips. It was a different sound, a different thought. Personal.

His mouth curved in a smile and the tap changed, hollow.

He could see in more detail the expression on her face that night years ago. Despite her bouncing copper ponytail, she'd been something of a sharp-toothed, sullen little thing. A fierce glint had lit her eyes as she'd flashed a look at him, like he was a barbarian, invading sacred territory. Later he realized the territory she was protecting wasn't her home, but Ginger, her adored big sister. He assumed the little one hated him, as the rest of the family appeared to. But a few days later, when Ginger introduced them, Carlie could barely look at him. She started when he took her hand. He could feel the trembling, see it. That made him realize she was terrified, probably trying desperately to hide it—and very different from her sister.

Years ago he'd told a friend on the force about his interest in Ginger. The friend had laughed and told him to take a reality pill, he didn't stand a chance with a girl like her.

Men were blunt about those things. But his friend had been wrong. Ginger was easy. Every aspect of her life was planned, every moment accounted for by her parents. She'd loved the fear and uncertainty Rio brought to her world, loved having control wrenched away from her. It had freed her.

But not this one. Carlie had not been cosseted, adored, and protected. Through Ginger, Rio had been privy to some of the Bishops' private matters, enough to know that Carlie was essentially an outcast in her own family, prominent or not. He didn't know why she'd received such cold treatment, but whatever the reason, kids like that were forced to set their own boundaries, even when they were from the upper classes. And in Carlie's case, no one was getting through them, not without a fight.

"We'll see," he said, breaking his silence for the first time since he'd parked. From that quiet place in his mind, he studied her quaint two-story house with its limestone birdbath, gawky sunflowers, and dark green shutters. Odd, he thought, that a paragon of modern womanhood would pick such an old-fashioned charmer of a cottage in this out-of-the-way area. The garden that lined the cobbled walk was overrun with blooming flowers, but there were no columbines as far as he could see. Or snapdragons. It did appear that she was having a fence built around the property by the timber stacked neatly in her yard.

"Build the fence high, Carlie Bishop," he murmured. "And maybe you'd better add a moat and a dragon while you're at it. Because it's going to take all that to keep me out."

Carlie stood frozen at her bedroom window. She'd crept into the darkened room to get a look at the street and make sure he was gone. The spot where he'd parked was empty, but the shimmer of light in her dresser mirror had come from the other window, a small half-moon. And it had riveted her.

Something had moved down the street, out of range of the window where Carlie stood. It could have been a tree branch, an animal, anything. It was too dark to know with total certainty that it was a car. But in matters like this she'd learned to listen to her vital signs. The human body was the world's best security system. It picked up what the mind denied. Even a house pet was smart enough to heed the warnings, while most humans tried desperately to talk themselves out of listening.

"Don't be silly," women chided their pounding hearts when they sensed a threat, "it's nothing."

Right now Carlie's heart was pounding hard enough to tell her it was him. He'd come back.

God . . . he was after her.

He knew something.

Now she *was* jumping to conclusions, and too many for her own good. In a minute she'd have him at the front door with the cuffs, ready to take her in and book her. Vigilance, she reminded herself. Not panic. That was what she counseled. Pay attention to the signals and respond sanely to protect yourself. Her doors were already locked and bolted. She'd had a state-of-the-art alarm system installed. She was safe tonight. Tomorrow when she got to the office she would check him out and find out who he actually was. And more to the point, it might not be him out there. Anyone could have pulled up, and not necessarily to spy on her.

Later, when she was calmer, she began to undress. Her double-breasted black suit and matching camisole sent the message she wanted to convey to women everywhere. Empowerment. You *can* take care of yourselves. Don't let fear rule you. It's your first line of defense. Listen to it. Use it.

Faux-lizard slingbacks were her only obvious concession to femininity, but even those had heels that could be used as weapons. As she sat on her bed and pulled the shoes off, she glanced at herself in the mirror. The sheer white silk of her underwear glowed in the moonlight, making her look slender and fragile. Very defenseless. She didn't like the feeling, and she liked being naked even less.

Was there anything that made a woman more accessible to a man? Naked bodies didn't always mean naked hearts, but in her brief, sad experience with love and sex they had. Normally she would have slipped out of the lingerie and into her red plaid nightshirt in a few stealthy movements. Often she drew the shirt over her head first, then sneaked off the underwear, already surrounded by a changing booth of flannel.

Tonight she did something entirely different. She watched herself furtively, a sidelong glance at the mirror. Shivering, she dropped the bra and rose to step out of the panties. Was this what he would see if he were watching? A moonlit creature with eyes wide and fingers pressed to her mouth, startled at her own desirability, frightened of it?

The pulse in her throat leaped so suddenly it stung. She watched it throb, and felt her body respond to a sharp clutch of longing. He had brought this out, she realized. The sudden urgency she felt. Something about him had triggered feelings she hadn't felt in years, so long ago they took her back—

Robert Scott Walker. Who was he? Why did that name sound familiar? She walked to the window, holding the nightshirt to her body, not even sure she was fully covered. Maybe she wanted him to see her, but why? God, why?

The car was still there.

An impulse drove her to her closet, the smaller locked one where she kept her jewelry, some family heirlooms, and a few treasured things of Ginger's. Inside a padlocked vault, she found what she was looking for. A leather-bound book of poetry with a fake cover, where Ginger had stashed secret notes passed back and forth among girlfriends in boarding school. The gossipy little tidbits about her love life would have scandalized their parents.

Carlie had often wondered if the steamy notes were some kind of outlet for Ginger, because she'd continued the practice even as an adult. After her death, Carlie had found one tucked inside a snapshot of Ginger and a dark-haired man.

Now Carlie stared at the picture, thunderstruck.

He's killer! Ginger had written in an excited child's scrawl. *Don't ask me how, he just is. Some nights he'll call me with a lyric he's heard from a beautiful song or a line of poetry that reminds him of us. Then the next night he's hiding behind the bedroom door like a bad guy. He grabs me, I swear he does, and sometimes it's right there on the floor, before I can even catch my breath. The thing is I never know who he's going to be.*

The man in the snapshot was Robert Scott Walker. The rest of it came tumbling back to Carlie as she stared at his dazzling dark smile. He was Ginger's fatal attraction, the one she dated while she was working at the prosecutor's office. And the subject of ninety percent of her torrid secret notes, only Ginger had never called him by that name. She'd called him Rio.

Carlie closed the poetry book with sweat-slicked hands, knowing she wouldn't get a moment's sleep that night. She was already stressed to the breaking point, but that hardly mattered now. She would be up until dawn, thinking this through.

Rio Walker, dear God.

Ginger had called him something else, too. *Master of the unexpected.*

FOUR

January 9, Midnight

I counted tonight. This is my thirtieth journal entry in less than a month. I'm writing obsessively now, but it's not the release it was. It doesn't exorcise the rage. It whips me, like wind whips a fire. It lays me bare.

Still I keep on, hoping to be understood. What I do needs to be clarified. It has to make sense or we are all, every one of us, in terrible trouble. Because I am a good person. One of millions in this country. I earn my keep, pay my taxes, respect my fellowman, and try to live in harmony with the environment. I have a deep reverence for human life. I eat ice-cream sundaes. I brake for animals, recycle, and buy Girl Scout cookies. But I am doing terrible things.

Some would call me a monster. Many are calling me a killer. The police have an APB out for me, and I am wanted on suspicion of heinous crimes. But to stop now would be like turning my back on a hungry child. There is no other way, and there is no one else but me. I have to believe that.

The real monsters are out there. They're running loose among us, able to operate under the guarantees of our Constitution, protected by law and free to torment the helpless. They stalk their prey with impunity, laughing at us, the good ones, knowing we're bound by the rules, that we will follow them like sheep blindly tumbling off a cliff. It's only when one of us cuts from formation, when we dare go where there are no rules, that we can catch them at their own game. Make them scream.

Sometimes you have to be bad to be good. Cruel to be kind. Die to live.

There is no joy without pain.

No love without hate.

I used to laugh when they referred to me as a serial killer. Me? On death row with John Wayne Gacy and Richard Speck. I'm not laughing now. I have something in common with serial killers, and that frightens me. I hate these men, the ones who torment women. With all my being I hate them.

I want them all in a police lineup, shoulder to shoulder, however many hundreds of thousands there are. I want them to stare, blind as bats, into the glare of the lights, their fate in the hands of someone who despises them as much as they despised their helpless victims.

Then I will decide.

For all the women who've been stalked, raped, tortured, and murdered, I will decide who lives and who dies.

No mercy.

FIVE

Normally Carlie loved going to her office in the morning. The second-story converted artist's loft was a block from the beach, and it sat atop an espresso bar and a Swedish bakery. The smells that perfumed the air at seven A.M. were as heavenly to the senses as they were hard on the willpower. But Carlie feasted on them five days a week, convinced that they fed her soul, as well as her appetite.

Who needs love and sex? she thought. *Just give me a bear claw!* Her favorites were the date-filled. Dense and dreamy, the sinfully rich rolls were drizzled with butter-cream frosting and sprinkled with slivered almonds, which she had to pick off because of her food allergies. However, this morning she'd made do with spartan fare, a grande cup of house-blend coffee and a plain biscotti to gnaw on. Olaf's was out of bear claws, and she was trying to lose a couple of pounds anyway.

Now, enclosed in her sunny nook of a private office, and faced with another monumentally busy day, she didn't know quite where to start. She concentrated on the coffee, eyes closed as she cradled the take-out cup in both hands and sipped meditatively. The encounter with Walker had made it impossible to sleep last night, and her first goal was to clear her head.

Her small consulting company, Safe and Sound, provided education, guidelines for community awareness, and private consultation services to those whose lives had been touched by crime. And while it was gratifying to know that her services helped the plight of innocent victims all over the world, lately the way the phones had been ringing and the demands on her time had increased, every day verged on chaotic.

Ironically the nature of her work called for a serene and welcoming environment, one people could think of as a refuge from their troubles.

She'd had the loft converted into a large, airy workspace, with a reception area and a roomy, comfortable lounge where she could hold her support-group meetings, as well as this glass-enclosed alcove for herself that overhung the street. She'd tackled the decorating herself, choosing a palette of natural colors and elements that were as soothing as they were beautiful—Kentia palms, seascapes on the walls, and cane furniture.

She was proud of what she'd done, and yes, normally she loved coming to work. But serene?

Carlie sighed. "In my dreams."

The release of her book, *Killer Smile,* had hit at the same time that her task force was mobilizing to put together its report on victims of stalker violence. The study's scope was national, and Carlie herself was slated to present the final report to the president and various members of his cabinet at a White House dinner. That she could hardly believe.

Carlie Bishop, the gangly urchin with red pigtails, who was the bane of her dignified parents' existence, was not only invited to dine at 1600 Pennsylvania Avenue, she was to be the night's featured speaker. And to that end she was in charge of coordinating the efforts of professionals and luminaries from all over the country who were involved in a stalker victim's plight, including law-enforcement personnel, judges, ministers, mental-health workers, and people from the private sector.

At times it felt like she was juggling careers as if they were chain saws, and doing it on a shoestring budget. Despite the book's success, she wouldn't see a royalty check for several months, and her consulting work had been put on hold so she could run the task force. Fortunately that effort was funded by a federal grant with a budget that included modest salaries for Carlie and her staff.

But the real problem was that Carlie didn't have a staff. Up to now she'd been managing with one assistant, and that was only because Danny Upshaw was worth five. He was tireless, loyal, and smart, and Carlie couldn't have done any of it without him.

He was also good with women.

Carlie's clientele was primarily female, and many of them were startled when they discovered she had a male assistant. Some voiced concerns, but Carlie had her reasons for hiring Danny and usually her clients' doubts vanished within moments of being around him.

If there were awards for being big and sweet and shy, Danny Upshaw would have had a roomful of blue ribbons. Carlie had often thought the term *gentle giant* must have been coined expressly for the towering ex–army medic. It was hard to believe a black-belt martial-arts expert could blush at anything. Danny blushed the moment a woman spoke to him.

He was a grown man in his late twenties, but a simple "hello" threw him into fits of shuffling aw-shucks embarrassment. A smile could make him stammer, but he always managed to recover enough to shrug off the discomfort and somehow reassure the greeter that it was her presence that had left him speechless. Needless to say, the women involved were totally disarmed, if not downright charmed, by his difficulties.

What a darling, Carlie had thought when he showed up in response to her ad for an assistant. The khaki summer suit he wore was barely adequate to contain his broad shoulders and sandy-haired diffidence. It hadn't hurt that he could type, understood computers, and was qualified to teach self-defense. He was also sensitive to her clients' issues and had lived through as much hell as many of them.

He'd been drawn to the job because of what had happened to his mother. Haltingly he'd explained to Carlie that he'd witnessed her death at the hands of his own father, a truck driver who'd been disabled by a bad back and began drinking his way through the pain and depression. Eventually, soaked in booze and self-pity, his father turned brutal and Danny, only six, was as helpless as his mother to stop the savage attack.

This morning Danny was at his desk in the reception area, busily fielding phone calls and answering E-mail from the task-force Web site. Carlie had her own stack of phone calls to make and several days' mail to be tackled, as well as the latest statistics Danny had compiled on the true incidence of stalking, an historically underreported crime.

"You okay in there, boss?" Danny called from his desk in the reception area. "I don't hear any work noises."

"Thinking," she mumbled.

"Really . . . without moving your lips?"

Wise-ass. Carlie was famous for talking to herself. Such was the curse of an imaginative child raised essentially alone. She had to talk to someone, and who was a better listener?

Danny appeared in the doorway with the coffeepot and an inquisitive look. "What gives? Allergies again? I know it couldn't have been a hot date, because, well, to be honest, Chubbs, there's no evidence you have a social life."

Her eyelids felt like lead weights, but she got them high enough to give him a pained look. She had no idea why he called her Chubbs. If anything she was boringly average at five feet five inches and one hundred twenty pounds. Okay, so maybe she carried a little extra store for the winter in the general vicinity of her stomach, but for that she deserved to be the target of fitness fanatics like Danny? The real problem was that he'd gotten over his shyness with her much too quickly.

Danny Upshaw knew too much about her.

"Work," she said, sustaining herself with a sip of coffee. "Up all night. Secret project. Can't say more or I'd have to kill you."

He clumped into the room and set the coffeepot down on her desk. "Carlie—" Her name came out in a mock scolding tone. "You have to take care of yourself.

A chuckle set Carlie's coffee to slopping. "I'm fine," she said, taking care to set the cup down. "Just tired. And overwhelmed."

The secret-project reference had been a slip. She was glad he hadn't taken it seriously, because she really couldn't discuss it, even with him, and he was probably the man she trusted most in the world right now.

Speaking of men, and trust . . . in a quieter tone, she said: "I need some intelligence done on an LAPD homicide detective. His name is Robert Scott Walker."

"Rio Walker?" Danny barely missed a beat. "He's career law enforcement, but he doesn't fit the mold. Never has. They'd probably love to dump him, but he's got a mind like a goddamn spy satellite. Nobody can figure out what he does, but they can't deny it works. Bottom line? Walker's a maverick with some weird tricks in his bag, and he's heading up the Femme Fatale investigation. Anything else?"

"How do you know all that about him?"

"I'm good?" He shrugged a grin. "The Femme Fatale Home Page. It's one of the hottest sites on the net."

"The Femme Fatale has her own home page?"

"Www.snapdragon.com. Nobody seems to know whether or not she originated the site, but it's maintained by her fan club, which numbers in the millions now."

"Millions?" Carlie's voice was soft with amazement. "Remind me to visit it."

She picked up a pen, but it was a reflex. She was gone from the building. Her mind was elsewhere, circling the grenade he'd just dropped in her foxhole and trying to figure out whether it was live or dead. Danny apparently had information at his fingertips that she didn't know existed. A Femme Fatale Home Page? She had to find out what that was all about and quickly. As for Walker, Danny had just confirmed her worst fears.

"Anything else, boss?"

His question brought her around. Her impulse was to tell him no, everything was fine. Just fine. Instead, she fell back in her chair and swept out her arms to encompass the seven-point earthquake that was her desk. "How about a genie. Someone to wiggle her nose and make it all go away."

"I don't think they have a temp service for that." He folded a pair of brawny, gold-thatched forearms over his chest and gave her a sympathetic nod. "Why don't you let me take some of it off your hands. You can return the police commissioner's call—he's already left two messages—and pull out anything else that requires a personal answer. I'll do the rest."

Carlie reminded herself how lucky she was to have this guy. You couldn't put a monetary value on the kind of support he gave her, but someday soon she hoped to be able to pay him more than a subsistence wage. Meanwhile, she wanted to kiss him, that was how sweet and dedicated he was.

"What planet did they send you from?" she said, marveling. "You must be part of a plot to take over the earth. Otherwise you're just too good to be true."

He blushed, and she was glad she could still have that effect on him. The truth was he didn't have time to help her. He would have to neglect his own work, and he was already putting in outrageous overtime as it was.

Carlie turned to the wall of windows behind her. Gazing out at the boutiques and restaurants across the way gave her a moment to think about the budgeting and workload problems they were facing. Plus Danny needed a break.

Her office was in a good location, not high-end beachfront real estate, but well removed from the county's crime pockets. She'd been lucky to get it, though the rent was high, and she'd had to borrow money for renovations. Her parents had put her through school at considerable expense, but since then she'd been existing on what she made. There was a trust fund, but she wouldn't see any of that until she was thirty-five, and maybe never, if her mother, with whom she'd always had a chilly relationship, decided she wasn't worthy. It wouldn't surprise Carlie at all.

She hadn't spoken with her mother in months, but she couldn't imagine that the newest Supreme Court justice was very happy about her daughter's bestselling book, especially since it had put Carlie in the spotlight and opened the Bishop family tragedy to scrutiny again. If Carlie's father were still alive, he probably wouldn't have approved either. Bernard Bishop had died of a massive heart attack, believing the daughter who would go on to accomplish great things was Ginger. She was the firstborn and named for his devoted mother. He would not have been happy to see how it turned out.

No, Carlie was on her own. There were no parents, no family to turn to in a crisis. She was just about to bite the bullet and tell Danny to call Girl Friday for temp help when the outer door creaked open.

"Hello?" came a small, tremulous voice. "Anybody here?"

Carlie signaled to Danny that she would handle the visitor herself. "I know you're a dear," she whispered as she walked past him, "but whoever's out there doesn't, so let's not terrify her any more than she already is."

The open doorway could have been a picture frame for the slight young woman who stood there. She seemed bolted in place as Carlie entered the reception area, but there was something strikingly familiar about her haunted appearance and round, dark eyes. Carlie knew she ought to recognize her, and the woman actually seemed to be waiting for that, but Carlie'd had too little sleep and not enough coffee.

Still, her heart went out instantly to the waiflike creature. She looked alone and forlorn, Bambi in the blazing forest, and Carlie understood those feelings.

"Can I help you?" she asked.

The silver links on the woman's chain purse were singing out a song of distress. Everything about her seemed frozen except her fingers, which worked like a concert violinist's, madly plucking strings. She'd arranged her shoulder bag in the defensive style common to big cities, the strap over her head, one hand on the bag itself, and the other entangled in the links. She couldn't seem to speak, but she was making wild, beautiful music. And again, Carlie understood.

"It's okay," Carlie said soothingly. "Stay right there if you want. We can talk just fine from here."

She took Carlie at her word and didn't budge. She didn't talk either. There were some brassy red streaks in her dark hair, the mark of a generation Xer, and she looked to be around that age, maybe mid-twenties. But her hip-huggers and cropped sweater were tame compared with the grunge and gothic looks that were popular in L.A. Still, she had an ethereal aspect. She could have been one of those supermodels, all bones and eyes.

"Jo Emily Pough," she said at last, hope softening her faint southern inflection. "Your biggest fan?"

Carlie was supposed to know what that meant. This much was clear. She racked her brain. "Not the Cross-Face Chicken Wing lady?"

A slight smile told Carlie she was right. It was the woman who'd volunteered to demonstrate! The features were the same, but it was hard to believe this tongue-tied waif could have taken hostage Carlie's entire lecture audience. She'd been a fireball that night. But her shrill voice had signaled that she was stressed to the max, the human equivalent of a pressure cooker letting off steam.

Carlie often had that kind of reaction at her lectures. It was easy to be enraged at bullies and terrorists, but as much as she wanted her audience to feel their anger, and their power, the goal was never vengeance. It was safety. Always safety.

"I read this." Jo Emily was digging in her purse and the chains were tinkling like bells. She pulled out the flyer that described the assistance services Carlie was organizing for stalker victims, including her free support group. "I want to join. Please, could I join your support group? Please?"

Carlie didn't answer immediately, and that seemed to immobilize Jo Emily completely. The music stopped. Even her fingers froze.

"Of course," Carlie said. "We'll work something out." Carlie ran the group at her own expense, but through her connections with the local mental-health community, she was trying to get a network of groups started. One of her strongest recommendations for the task-force report would be to allocate monies for support services for victims around the country.

"Are you in trouble?" Carlie asked. A direct question was the easiest way to get to the bottom of things with a highly agitated client, she'd learned. Usually they poured their hearts out, relieved that someone took their situation seriously when even the police so often didn't. But Jo Emily was a safe with a combination lock. Apparently the door had to be blown off before she could express herself.

Her lips were pursed tight and her eyes had taken on the lovely pearl gray cast of a coastal weather front. They got even larger as Carlie studied her, only now she was looking over Carlie's shoulder.

Suddenly Carlie understood. Danny had come through the door from her office. Jo Emily had seen the enemy.

Carlie didn't waste a minute. She went straight over to Jo Emily with one mission in mind, to keep her from running. "It's all right. He won't hurt you, I promise. He would never hurt anyone. I know he's big and scary looking, but he's my assistant and he actually helps me train women in self-defense. So please hang in there okay?"

Jo Emily barely seemed to hear her. Not once did she take her eyes off Danny, and at some point Carlie realized that the tension level in the room had changed. Jo Emily's hands were moving on the chain strap, but slowly, searchingly, and the bells were less strident now. Weirdly melodic.

"Are you okay?" Carlie asked. She was thoroughly bewildered, and more concerned about what was happening now than before. Fear she understood.

"Danny?" She turned to her assistant and saw that he was completely flummoxed at the possibility that he might have frightened Jo Emily

"I'm s-s-s-sorry," he stumbled to get out. About all he could do beyond that was shake his head and mumble. He was already several shades brighter than Carlie's hair.

Carlie wasn't sure which one of them needed her more. Danny was in one doorway, Jo Emily in the other. They were stranded like shipwreck survivors on two desert islands and the sea between them had more dorsal fins than a shark tank. Carlie wanted to rescue them both, but she didn't know how. Besides, there was some new vibe in the air, and she had yet to figure out what it was. Maybe the best move was to step back and let nature take its course.

"I didn't mean to—" Danny shoved his hands in the back pockets of his jeans and began to rock from side to side. His agony was evident. Causing pain to a woman, especially such a fragile frightened one, was unthinkable.

"I shouldn't have barged in," he told Jo Emily. "Please don't go or anything," he implored. "I'll leave."

Jo Emily was shaking her head, a twitchy movement that was neither positive nor negative. "Don't—" she said.

"I need to update the W-Web site," he explained. "Maybe I'll use your computer, Carlie."

"Fine idea." Carlie watched him back into her office, and wondered what he would do when he hit the wall. She could almost imagine him executing a back flip out the window to avoid causing any more discomfort. "Danny?"

"Is that his name? Danny?" Jo Emily had braved the dangerous waters. She was in the room, breathless with concern. "Is he all right?"

"Oh, yeah, sure. Danny's fine. He's a little shy is all."

"Where did he go?" Now she was craning to see in the doorway of Carlie's office.

"I suspect he's giving us some privacy so we can talk." Wasted words, Carlie realized as Jo Emily made her way cautiously toward the office door. The crisis was over, and so was any hope for meaningful conversation with her visitor. Jo Emily had nothing on her mind at the moment save the man who got away. Any hopes Carlie had of finding out what had brought her to the office would have to wait.

Leave it to Danny, she thought. There probably wasn't a man in the world who could have disarmed Jo Emily except one more frightened of her than she was of him. Danny had cracked the combination lock and the safe door was wide open.

Carlie sank into one of the reception-room chairs as Jo Emily inched up to the threshold and peeked in.

"Oh, there you are." Her voice dropped to an anxious croon as she spotted her quarry. "You didn't leave on my account, did you? Because I'm fine. No really, I am. See."

Carlie watched in amazement as Jo Emily stepped over the threshold and presented herself to what Carlie imagined was a mortified man. Jo Emily smiled, nodded, and opened her arms in a modest display of her underfed constitution. A supermodel she wasn't, Carlie conceded. But her purse chains sang merrily.

Carlie couldn't see Danny's reaction, but she could hear him shuffling helplessly. He must be purple by now. He really didn't know what to do with the adoring women who wanted to rescue him, and Jo Emily may already have gone into the mothering mode. If she had, she wouldn't be happy until she had him fed, burped, and tucked in for a nap. Carlie had seen it all before.

"Have I upset you in some way?" Jo Emily whispered. "Oh my, I didn't mean to."

"Oh, no!" Danny could be heard to exclaim. "It was m-m-me. I upset you."

Listening to them timidly wrestle each other for the blame, Carlie had the ironic thought that it was she who should be giving *them* privacy. At some point she would have to sit down with Jo Emily and talk about her ordeal. Painful details would have to be dredged up in order for Carlie to advise her, but for the time being, some information and a brochure of their victims' assistance services would probably suffice. It was important that Jo Emily know she wasn't alone, that help was always at hand.

Meanwhile this budding friendship with Danny might be the best thing that could have happened, Carlie realized. It looked as if Jo Emily had met a kindred spirit, and if that was true, it would undoubtedly be a healing experience beyond anything Carlie could have offered.

The only problem that remained was Carlie's workload. She had plenty to do, but it was all arranged in mountainous stacks on her desk. Her list of phone calls was in there, too, along with her cellular phone.

Funny how she seemed doomed to sit on the sidelines and watch other people have romances. Those magical moments were everywhere. She was always witnessing them, but they never seemed to happen to her. The closest she'd come was the other night, but the guy had turned out to be the law. And the truth was, she'd watched her sister fall madly in love with that same guy.

She felt like the kid riding in the backseat of the car, her nose pressed to the window, watching the world go by. Every once in a while she would see some magical, adventurous thing she longed to do, but knew she never would. Those unexplored opportunities were making her restless.

SIX

As far as Jo Emily Pough knew, she had never frightened anyone in her entire life. Now she couldn't seem to stop. Everything she did set off this Danny person. A smile turned him stop-sign red, a simple question made him hyperventilate. Jo Emily approached and he left skid marks trying to get away. Maybe that's why she was just a little bit confused.

There were guys could make you think twice about saying boo, and this was one of them. He looked like he could put some serious hurt on a person—twirl you on a finger the way those nasty New World Order wrestlers did—and yet Jo Emily had sent him packing with a glance.

The office he'd disappeared into was Carlie Bishop's, by the name plaque on the desk. Right now Danny was hunched behind a computer, tapping away like the machine would explode if he stopped.

"Nice place," she said, eyeing him cautiously while she planned her next move. About all she could see of him was the side of his buzz-cut blond head and his bright blue-and-green plaid sweater. "I've been thinking about getting myself a computer. Don't really need one, though. I do nails at Salon du Soleil in Venice."

He nodded without looking up.

There was sweat beading on his temple. Otherwise Jo Emily might have been wondering about his manners. Poor thing, he wasn't rude. He was milk of magnesia. All shook up, full of bubbles and froth.

For the first time since she could remember, Jo Emily wanted to laugh out loud. To think that she could have this effect when for months she'd been starting at her own shadow and too frightened to close her eyes at night. *She* had rattled a full-grown man. And by God, she wanted to know what she'd done. It might come in handy again.

Besides, she thought, studying Danny's profile—he was cute. Round and golden everywhere she could see, yet sturdily packed rather than soft. Without knowing any more about him, she would have guessed Scandinavian stock.

"Ms. Bishop said you're her assistant," she ventured. "I guess that must be pretty exciting."

Another quick nod.

"You help write her books or something?"

"No, she w-writes the books. I'm updating her Web site."

"*No kidding?* I've never seen a Web site."

Her excitement must have been contagious because Danny Upshaw glanced up at her for the first time, his eyes sky white and blue. His face was lit with an iridescent glow from the screen, and coupled with the light from the windows behind him, he seemed beatified, as gentle and kind as the holy figures in the stained-glass windows of churches.

"Have a look if you want," he said. "I just put up some new animated graphics."

A huge 3-D banner filled the top of the screen, featuring Carlie's book, *Killer Smile*. Below that were endorsements, including raves from the president of the United States and several other dignitaries. But Danny's latest tour de force—the gizmo he pointed out eagerly—was a Jiminy Cricket-like character who beckoned to Jo Emily, urging her to click a button and read about *The Five Things Every Woman Must Know to Save Her Own Life*.

There were other options and other movable parts, all of them enticing the viewer to learn more about Carlie and her work as a personal-safety expert. Danny was listed as her self-defense expert.

"Awesome," Jo Emily whispered. "You did this yourself?"

Danny flushed with pride rather than embarrassment. "I play around. It's not that hard once you know Hypertext Markup Language, hyperlinks, script code, image composing, and stuff like that."

"Cool. Totally." Jo Emily didn't know what else to say. She was impressed as hell, but didn't have a clue what he was talking about. "I'll bet it's great working for Ms. Bishop, huh? She's my hero, you know. Her and the Femme Fatale."

Danny looked up again, this time with new and sharpened interest in his gaze. "You like the Femme Fatale?"

Those blue eyes could be piercing when they made up their mind to be, she thought. "You could say that. You could say I'm her number-one fan."

Jo Emily usually didn't admit to that, but there was something about Danny. She barely knew him, but it felt like she could tell him most anything, and he wouldn't be inclined to judge her. She hadn't run into very many people like that in her life, and maybe she was hungry for the feeling. She could hardly remember what it was like to have a good feeling about someone on sight, especially a man.

"I've been following the Femme Fatale in the news," she told him eagerly. "I probably know every one of her exploits by heart. Don't you think it's cool how she stays one step ahead of even the most devious criminal mind? I wonder how she does that."

Danny began to type rapidly. Carlie Bishop's Web site disappeared from the screen and another page came up. This one was a dazzling red-and-black affair, featuring a large scarlet snapdragon and the image of a dark-hooded woman that was apparently supposed to be the Femme Fatale. Whoever put up the site had listed all her alleged misdeeds, with links if you wanted more information.

Jo Emily clapped her hands together. "Wow . . . oh, wow."

Danny clicked on the first link and waved Jo Emily closer. "You must have heard about this one. It's the guy who picked victims with a certain breed of guard dog—"

"Right! German shepherds, wasn't it?" she cut in. "He poisoned the animals. The Femme Fatale lured him into the hills, where the wild dogs got him and all but killed him."

"The day before it happened a florist delivered a bouquet of red snapdragons and a card that said *Do unto others.* At least that's what the stalker told the police."

Jo Emily nodded, aware that Danny was glued to the screen and couldn't see her. Not that it mattered. They seemed to be in sync where the Femme Fatale was concerned, a couple of the rank and file, cheering her on. Funny how right that felt. Funny how right she felt in this warm sunroom of an office, too. It smelled like coffee and sweet rolls.

"More alleged exploits," Danny said. "Here's the guy who video-taped his victim through a two-way mirror and put the tapes on the Internet with her phone number."

"Yeah, that was tragic. He finally killed her, didn't he? What happened to him?" She knew exactly what had happened, but she didn't want to come off sounding like one of those nuts who was obsessed with every detail.

"He got blinded by mirrors and stepped into the path of an oncoming bus. Interesting that the bus driver was a woman."

Jo Emily shivered, horrified and excited at the same time. "My favorite is the E-mail Stalker. He got his kicks spamming elderly women with obscene E-mail, and now he's in a straitjacket in Camarillo. He claims the Femme Fatale sent a pulse through his computer that nuked his brain!''

Danny glanced around at her and grinned.

Jo Emily hadn't realized she was touching his shoulder until she felt muscles bunch beneath her fingers.

"I don't believe what they're saying about her, though, do you?" she interjected. "That she's a sadistic man-hater? I read that in the paper just this morning. Some reporter for the *Times* is doing a series, and he claims she likes causing her victims unbearable pain rather than simply killing them.''

"Wrong. Dead wrong. She's a humanitarian, trying to help people who can't help themselves.''

Jo Emily's sentiments exactly. This was great. She could feel the fire in Danny, his passion for justice, and it fed her own. She didn't feel awkward anymore, and he didn't seem to either. They were sparks from the same hot blaze.

"The best part,'' she enthused, "is how she uses the stalker's own perversions against him. She gives him a taste of what he hungers for, and he can't stop. 'They are the weapons of their own destruction.' That's what Diane Sawyer said on *PrimeTime Live*. Did you see it?''

Danny nodded. "Like that last guy, the diplomat who loved hearing women scream.''

"Excuse me—''

Jo Emily looked up to see Carlie Bishop knocking on the door of her own office. "Sorry to intrude,'' she said. "I just wanted to be sure Jo Emily got a brochure and that she knew about our services. If you'll take care of that, Danny, I'll just grab my messages and my cell phone and be gone.''

Jo Emily stepped back apologetically. "Oh, sure, thanks,'' she said, thinking this had to be one of the most beautiful women she'd ever seen with her hot red hair and her cool green eyes. Jo Emily probably felt as tongue-tied around Carlie Bishop as Danny did around her.

"Hold on, Carlie.'' Danny pointed to the screen. "Come have a look at this first.''

Carlie came over, but she didn't seen to share Danny's enthusiasm for the site. "Good God,'' she breathed, sounding faintly horrified. "What's that?''

"It's the Femme Fatale's home page.'' Danny wheeled back so she could get a look. "I told you there was one.''

Carlie moved in closer, studying the screen with a mix of disbelief and suspicion. "Would you look at that,'' she said after a moment.

"They're even predicting who she might go after next. Mike Tyson? Do they mean the boxer?"

Jo Emily sensed that the other woman was uneasy about something. "I guess you don't like the Femme Fatale, am I right, Ms. Bishop? Do you think it's wrong what she's doing?"

"No, please, call me Carlie." She rifled through the papers on her desk, apparently looking for her phone messages, but she still seemed troubled.

Jo Emily wished she hadn't brought it up. "Danny thinks she's a humanitarian," she blurted.

"What do *you* think of the Femme Fatale, Carlie?"

It was Danny who'd asked, but instead of answering, Carlie flashed him a chilly look. "I don't really have an opinion."

Her comment was brusque enough to plunge the room into silence. She slipped some papers, along with her cell phone, into her purse and was halfway to the door when she took a huge breath and halted. After a ten-count she came back around.

"Okay, look," she said with a resigned tone. "You have to understand my position. Somehow I don't think the president or his cabinet would like me to publicly declare myself a Femme Fatale fan. But among the three of us, let's just say if she runs out of victims, I could give her some names."

"I've got one for her!" Jo Emily applauded.

With that, and a quick smile, Carlie was out the door. "Going out for coffee," she called back. "Take your time."

"Good woman," Danny said as the outer door closed.

"The best," Jo Emily agreed, wistful all of a sudden. Carlie was good. She went out of her way to help people, and now that Jo Emily might be lucky enough to be one of those people, it saddened her that she was not going to be able to tell either her or Danny the whole truth about her situation. There was no way she could reveal what had brought her here to this office, where she felt so safe and sound.

Jo Emily's purse had gotten twisted and she pulled it around, preparing herself. She had the feeling it was time for her to go, too. She'd disrupted Carlie's lecture the night before, and now she and Danny had driven her out of her office.

"Think you could get me one of those brochures she mentioned?" Jo Emily ticktocked her head. "And would you ask Carlie about the support group for me? She never did say whether I could join."

"Not to worry." Danny pushed a pad and pencil her way. "If you don't mind leaving your number, one of us will get back to you. Carlie won't keep you hanging. That's not her way."

Under her number, Jo Emily scribbled a note of encouragement that said *Call anytime!* and gave Danny back the pad, wondering if he would get the hint. "Thank you," she told him, her hopes creeping into her voice.

"It's nothing." He rose from the chair, accentuating the difference in their heights. He was a good deal taller, but Jo Emily smiled up at him anyway, still feeling warm and safe in his presence.

"No," she said softly, "I mean for being frightened of me."

Red crept up his throat, heating his ears and the tip of his nose. His blond hair tossed back and forth. "Aw, no—I wasn't—you don't think—"

She touched his hand to stop the sputtering. "I know, I do. But thanks anyway."

Carlie loved hideaways. She had several of them, squirreled away all over the city like caches of golden acorns, each one replete with the little touches of ambience that calmed her spirit when nothing else could. The hideaway she most often escaped to during the workday was a quaint, French-style outdoor café down the street from her office.

She could relax on the patio at the Harp Inn, shaded by a droopy green umbrella, and watch the world at work and play. Surrounded by hanging baskets of red and pink geraniums, she had the sense of being removed from the bustling street traffic, but not totally isolated from it.

Today she had the patio all to herself, with only a small swarm of white butterflies to keep her company. Even better, she'd dropped the messages she planned to answer in the chair next to her and not looked at them since. The question most pressing on her mind was whether or not to have another cup of frothy cappuccino. She sank back in the creaky wicker chair, glad she'd worn her jeans and could be lazy.

Danny and Jo Emily had given her an excuse to get out of the office, and she needed this break. She'd been trying for weeks to steal away for a weekend at her tree house, which was not the backyard clubhouse that came to most people's minds when she mentioned it, but a spacious aerie with two bedrooms and a wraparound deck, nestled in the branches of a massive century-old oak. But the way things were turning out, her trip would be for work more than rest. It was crucial that she carve out some time for her new project, and that meant privacy.

The pressures of her schedule began to crowd her thoughts again, and she closed her eyes, determined to push all the obligations away for a little longer. Every moment, she thought. Every moment of her life felt so squeezed, so rushed. All the breath jostled out of it . . .

Carlie's lids blinked open at the sound of laughter. She hadn't even

realized she'd been dozing, though it could have been only a few moments or her waiter would have been by. There was a couple at a table
across the way and for some reason she thought they were Danny and
Jo Emily.

When she sat up, she realized how wrong she'd been. The man was
lean and dusky, the woman rounded and fair. Carlie had no idea who
the couple was, but it was their excitement that had caught her attention—the soft throaty laughter of discovery, the electricity they gave
off when their eyes connected. A touch, even accidental, sent internal
thermostats soaring. Carlie could see it in their flushed faces and sense
it in the fever glow of their body heat. Infatuation, love, lust, whatever
it was that generated enough energy to light up a room, these two
had it. No one in the world existed except them.

Carlie still had the patio to herself, she realized ironically. It was just
her, the butterflies overhead, and the restless twinges in her chest.

After a while she began to watch the couple more openly, leaning on
the table, her chin cradled in her palm. She wasn't intruding on their
privacy. They didn't even know she was there. Maybe she was trying
to understand the soft ache that had crept into her throat.

They seemed happy, giddy in fact.

So why were they making her miserable?

"Rude," she murmured into the deep well of her hand. There was
no other word for it but that. They were falling in love in plain view
of everyone on the patio, never mind that it was just her. If the place
were packed, they'd be doing the same thing, she knew, and right in
front of everyone's noses.

"Clearly they have no idea how demoralizing it is for those less
fortunate," she grumbled to herself, "like most of the population. And
especially to the wretched few of us who can't seem to manage to fall
in love anywhere, even in private."

The couple leaned across the table toward each other as if drawn by
atomic fusion. Their hands touched, entwined. Their chairs creaked out
sweet, sexy sounds.

Carlie's chair creaked, too, sharply, as she dropped back. It wasn't
like her to succumb to self-pity. Her whole life had been about squaring
her shoulders and getting on with it, but something had overwhelmed
her today.

Look at that, would you? she thought, her despair evidencing itself
in a soft groan of disbelief. They were having a "thing." What could
compete with that? A presidential appointment? *Hah.*

"Nothing can compete with a thing," she declared softly, knowing they couldn't hear her. Especially when you couldn't manage to have one if your life depended on it.

Carlie wanted her check, but her waiter hadn't put in an appearance in some time. He probably didn't want to intrude on the lovebirds. She hadn't finished her cappuccino, but it was no good trying to regain her earlier state of mind. That had vanished with the twinges in her chest. Her havens were being invaded. First her office, now this. It didn't make sense that she should feel this way when everything was going so well in her career, but none of that seemed to count right now. There was no avoiding the fact that she was approaching thirty, had no personal life, and if this morning was any indication, was destined to be the last single female on the planet.

"So what is it?" she asked the chair arm she was drumming. "What's wrong with me?"

Another couple meandered onto the patio from the street. The girl's hip nestled gently against the boy's, their fingers entangled in the sweetest kind of love bondage. Carlie couldn't not watch. It was the car-accident syndrome. You didn't want to see it, but you had to look.

Carlie Bishop counseled women on living alone. She advised them how to create full, happy lives for themselves, with or without men. Most of them had fallen into a pattern of bad choices. They picked controlling, abusive men because that was all they knew. On their own they could discover their inner strengths and learn to take care of themselves.

Carlie was intimately familiar with the process because she'd picked some questionable men herself. She wasn't the Queen of Bad Choices. Ginger had taken that crown, but Carlie had given her a run for it.

She was also fuzzy on the etiquette of courtship these days. She hadn't dated much since the college debacle, but the experience had taught her that with love came vulnerability. And with vulnerability came fear. Carlie had been frightened for as long as she could remember, maybe since childhood. It had started with the very first boy who liked her back.

I hope he doesn't see it, whatever's wrong with me. . . .

Carlie wasn't sure what it was herself, but she had no doubt it existed, some horrible, hidden stigma. Otherwise her parents wouldn't have treated her like a leper, would they? It probably went without saying that she wasn't pretty or talented enough to suit them, but that couldn't be the only reason. Maybe she had a disease that would manifest itself later in life. Or maybe she'd done something unforgivable, like being born when they didn't want any more children besides Ginger. Maybe it was that.

She'd done battle with her fears in all the years since, and excelled at everything she'd tried, but the feeling of accomplishment was fleeting. It seemed she was always having to start over, to prove herself again, which made her wonder if the real goal was some unconscious need to hide "it" under the bright sheen of success.

Futile, she knew. No amount of varnish could hide a deep-set crack, which was probably why she felt a tiny quiver of terror whenever a man returned her interest. Even now. How long until he discovered the flaw? How much could she reveal of herself before he saw whatever it was that had repulsed her own flesh and blood. And then leave, of course. How could he not?

Sadly the one man she'd opened her heart to had never been in love with her at all. She'd been the quarterly booster shot to his ego, the proof that he could still seduce dewy coeds with a smile and a few serious discussions of preferential mating and genetic drift.

"Men are scum," she pronounced aloud, declaring it with finality to the unhearing, uncaring world.

The waiter wandered by and Carlie waved, but he didn't seem to see her. "Attention deficit disorder," she intoned.

"Wrong."

The remark came from someone behind her, and Carlie nearly sprang out of the chair. Her heart hit bottom with a resounding thud when she saw who it was. She wasn't alone on this patio. Maybe she never had been alone. Rio Walker was sitting at a table in a small alcove to her left, and he was close enough that he'd probably heard every word she'd said. She couldn't imagine how she'd missed him when she sat down, unless he'd sneaked in when she shut her eyes.

"Wrong," he repeated.

"What is that supposed to mean?"

"Men." He pointed to himself. "You know, us scum? We don't all suffer from attention deficit."

Carlie's first thought was to excuse herself and go crawl out the ladies'-room window. She could feel herself turning as red as the geraniums. Luckily she'd spent enough time with reporters and talk-show hosts to understand the concept of damage control. "Then what is it?" she asked.

He answered her with a small, shrewd grin. "I'll be happy to explain the mysteries of the male gender, but you'll have to come over here if I'm going to reveal my deepest, darkest secrets."

Oh, sure, now that you've just eavesdropped on mine. "I'm honored," she said, "but I need to get back to the office."

"Is *that* what you need? Didn't sound like it to me."

He had overheard. *This is what you get for being a one-woman chat room, Carlie. When will you learn?*

She strolled over to his table, plunked down in a chair. "So, how much did you hear?" *Enough to blackmail me with, I'll bet.*

He lounged back, enjoying himself but trying not to show it. He was wearing a suit jacket and an open-collared blue shirt with a dark tie hanging around his neck, undone. It was a great look for him, especially with the riptide of sable-black hair that rose from his high forehead and came tumbling down the back of his neck in waves. It reached all the way to his shoulders, she realized. She'd thought the LAPD had regulations about that.

"I didn't hear anything," he said. "Nothing at all."

Oh, you liar! Just look at those scheming brown eyes and lying black lashes. "What are you up to, Detective Walker? Is this how you shake down your suspects? Make 'em sweat?"

"Carlie Bishop sweat? Now there's an item for the tabloids." He tilted back in his chair and casually rearranged the one next to him with the toe of his well-worn Adidas.

Must be a guy thing, Carlie thought. *Rearrange the furniture, and you've established a claim.* Some subtle form of ownership had taken place.

"Maybe I was being gallant," he said. "Or honest. It could happen."

"Maybe I knew you were there, and I was making up stuff as I went along."

He grinned. "Wish I'd heard the stuff you were making up. Sounds like it might have been good for something, a chili dog at Tommy's at least."

He was playing with her right now, but he held the advantage and was making sure she knew it. "What are you doing here?" she asked. "And don't say the ambience, because that won't wash."

"The view? Okay," he conceded as she glared sharp objects at him. "I'm here to check on Jo Emily. Do you mind telling me how she's doing?"

"How do you know Jo Emily?"

"I referred her to you. She came to me with a story about a guy who's been stalking her."

Carlie bristled. "Why do you assume it's a story?"

"That's cop jargon. Everything's alleged until proven. I don't doubt someone's giving her grief, or I wouldn't have sent her to you."

Carlie nodded, pleased that he'd done it. It meant he must take her efforts seriously, and that was more than some of the others she'd dealt with. Also, he was heading up the Femme Fatale case, which technically

put him on the other side. Ironic that Jo Emily was a huge F.F. fan.
Carlie wondered if Rio knew.

"She seemed to be doing fine last time I saw her," Carlie said.
"She'd comandeered my office and was working her wiles on my assistant."

"That support group of yours must accomplish wonders. Got one for
men?"

"Jo Emily hasn't been to the group yet," Carlie explained patiently.
"We're meeting tomorrow night."

"I can hardly wait to hear what happens."

So that was how he planned on keeping tabs. Carlie only wished she
knew whom he was keeping tabs on, her or Jo Emily. "I really should
go," she said. "My assistant might need me."

She rose and Rio did, too.

"Go ahead," he said. "I'll get the coffee."

Something stopped her from protesting. "Thanks."

"Thank you, for taking on Jo Emily. She seemed pretty lost."

Carlie nodded and turned away, aware that he said her name as she
moved to leave. She hesitated. There was a resonance in his tone that
made her think she should keep walking, straight out the gate and down
the street to her office. Not possible, though. Not possible. His voice
had the kind of energy she'd been picking up all morning. Physical
energy. Sexual energy. Atomic.

"Carlie, did you hear me?" he said, loud enough for everyone to
hear. "There isn't a man breathing who wouldn't want to have a 'thing'
with you. Publicly, privately, anywhere. Trust me on this."

She wasn't looking at him. Thank God for that because she couldn't
have. There was no way to respond. No way to shrug it off. He'd made
it clear what he meant. If there wasn't a man breathing, then he'd included himself. He was breathing. He was a man. And she was
astounded.

SEVEN

Contrary to popular wisdom, the United States Supreme Court hasn't always deserved its stuffy reputation. If written accounts can be believed, one of the first justices openly imbibed, gambled, and enjoyed the company of saloon-hall girls. A nineteenth-century dandy secretly enjoyed the company of bathhouse boys, and who could forget the infamous confirmation hearings that involved pubic hair, Coke cans, and male anatomical nicknames?

Frances Stanfield Bishop didn't approve of such nonsense, either in the court's personnel or its rulings. She might be the newest member, but in her opinion, the Supreme Court had been grievously derelict in its duty. They'd let the federal government run amuck, and if anyone needed clarification on that point, Frances could cite the 1994 act that forced reductions in the size of toilets to 1.6 gallons, with fines of up to $2,500 for buying a larger tank.

"Water conservation?" she'd snapped within earshot of the delighted media. "Why not attach a meter to keep track of how many times we flush? Make it a capital crime. Invoke the death penalty."

She'd had the bad timing to make the remark during her confirmation hearings, and it had almost cost her the appointment. The Senate committee expected more discretion in its nominees, and they were wary of activist judges.

But Frances had friends in powerful places, a family history of stellar public service, and a personal life that was squeaky-clean compared with some of the other justices. She was confirmed by a majority vote and had kept her guns holstered since. There were no more outbursts for the media to overhear, and if she had strong feelings, she conveyed them with her voting record and her written opinions.

Such was the public Frances Stanfield Bishop. Privately she was as sharp and prickly as ever, and her personal agenda had never wavered. She wanted the government to mind its own business. United States citizens did not need bureaucracies keeping tabs on their bathroom habits, and who else but the highest court in the land could—and should— rein the pencil pushers in?

This morning, in the mahogany-paneled splendor of her private chambers, Frances pored over a stack of folders marked CONFIDENTIAL— JUSTICE BISHOP'S CHAMBERS ONLY that contained drafts of upcoming decisions. They'd been left by her clerk, along with several memos reviewing cases that were seeking a writ of certiorari, which simply meant that they were asking the Supreme Court to review a decision of a lower court. If four justices were to grant "cert," the case would be accepted and put on the docket.

A speed reader, Frances leafed briskly through the document in front of her, turning pages with her left hand, smoothing them with her right. But the material didn't have her full attention. The image in the back of her mind was of a sitting justice, solemn and regal in her black robes, posed against a backdrop of slanting light and grandly set off by a gold-leaf Venetian frame. Frances planned to sit for such a portrait that coming weekend.

An "official" photograph of all nine justices had already been taken to include her as the new appointee, but Frances had never thought of herself as one of the gang, even when the gang was the Supreme Court. She was having this painting done on her own, and it would reflect exactly what she wanted seen and known about herself. That she was going to be a powerful agent for change.

She'd heard the murmurs. They'd already dismissed her. Beyond improving gender equity on the court, they expected her to be quiet and accommodating, to play the traditional woman's role. But this court would not be the same when Frances Stanfield Bishop was done with it. If she had her way, it would go down in history . . . and so would she.

A scratching sound broke into her vision of the future. Someone was timidly knocking at her door, and her secretary was out sick today, which left the law clerks. Each justice was allowed two, but Julie, Frances's newest clerk, didn't seem to have her bearings yet. It had to be her.

"Come in." Frances waited patiently for the door to open, wondering how a brilliant twenty-something Stanford Law grad could be so hesitant. The young woman had sterling credentials, but sadly, seemed to lack confidence.

"Sorry," Julie said breathlessly, poking her head in the door. "Your daughter's on television. It's the *Sally Jesse Raphael* show, and they're talking about Carlie's new book. I thought you'd like to know."

"I'm afraid you thought wrong."

"Ma'am? I just . . ." The clerk faltered, obviously startled.

Priorities, Frances lamented. This child was woefully ignorant of the essential order of concerns for a woman in Frances's position. A television talk show did not outrank God and country. Corny as that sounded in the nineties, it was true. Especially a show featuring Carlie Bishop's personal crusade. It wasn't her daughter's stand against stalking that Frances objected to. It was the way she'd hung the family laundry out to dry. Why couldn't she leave the tragedy alone?

The notes in front of Frances blurred. The wetness stinging her eyes was so sharp she fought not to squeeze them shut. She plucked at the sleeve of her gray turtleneck sweater, refusing to be blindsided by emotion. She would not cry. That was unthinkable, and not just because a law clerk was watching. Ginger was gone now. Her eldest was dead, and so was any hope of carrying on the family tradition beyond Frances herself.

Her forebears had made their fortunes as silversmiths, but in later years the Stanfields had served their country in the military, in Congress, and in its courts of law as attorneys and judges. Her late husband's family, the Bishops, had been landowners who distinguished themselves as mayors, governors, and diplomats.

Now there was only Carlie to represent the next generation, and she couldn't be counted on to carry the torch. She'd always been a strange and difficult child, but Frances would never have predicted this turn of events. This media campaign of hers was dangerous in ways she couldn't possibly know.

Carlie was struggling to deal with her grief by striking out against all stalkers. Frances understood that impulse. No grief, or rage, could have been greater than her own, especially when she'd learned what had really happened to her daughter. There wasn't a psychopath in the country safe against Frances Stanfield Bishop. But she wouldn't have dreamed of taking her outrage to the public arena. These things needed to be accomplished quietly and efficiently.

Meanwhile her law clerk was still hovering at the door, waiting for some sign.

"It's all right, Julie." Frances waved the clerk into her chambers. If she was going to let the girl go, she couldn't do it over a television show. "Come in. I have a question for you."

Julie looked like a feather afloat in the large baronial room. She seemed to be drifting rather than walking toward Frances's desk.

Frances rose, aware of how stiff and traditional she must seem to this young thing in Calvin Klein jeans and a black blazer. Frances still wore the pearls and cashmere of her college days. A skirt and sweater were as casual as she got in the office, and when court was in session, she wore a suit beneath her robes.

"I've gone through your memos," Frances told her. As the new appointee, Frances had the responsibility of evaluating and recommending cases for review, but no justice could possibly keep up with the flood of petitions. It was the clerk's job to go through them first, and make recommendations as to whether they should be heard.

"I'm puzzled that you so strongly recommended *Ramirez* v. *the State of Oregon*," she said, "given the gravity of the others. Would you please explain that, Julie."

"Well . . . it deals with race relations."

"I know that." Now she was sharp. "So do a hundred others. The court actually heard three last year. Don't you think some of these other cases deserve our attention? What about religious freedom? Assisted suicide? Gun control? I fail to see how those things are not just as urgent and possibly more timely."

Surprisingly, Julie stood her ground. "With all respect, ma'am, I would argue that they're neither."

"Excuse me?" Frances tilted forward on her fingertips. She was playing devil's advocate. "Are you suggesting that the other cases aren't timely? The court has been dealing with race relations since the Civil War. That's over a century."

Julie wet her lips. "That's exactly why we have to deal with it again, ma'am. *Now*. After more than a hundred years it's about time we got it right. Race is still the most divisive issue in the country, maybe the world. But it's timely because the pendulum has swung both ways. We've had slavery *and* affirmative action, which was our attempt to compensate, however ineffective. We've seen the extremes. It's time to see where the middle ground is. I think we have to deal with it now, because it may be the only time in history that we have this unique perspective."

Frances was impressed. Whether or not she agreed was irrelevant. The young woman had an opinion. She might be quiet, but she could also be eloquent. *I still can't imagine that she's tough enough*, Frances thought, *but I hope I'm wrong. I was wrong about Carlie.*

Again, Julie seemed to be waiting anxiously for some sign of approval, and Frances was determined not to give her one. The young woman needed a crash course in the realities of a complex legal system, and that started at dealing with ambiguity.

"Thank you, Julie," Frances said. "I'll keep that in mind. Now you need to get back to your work and so do I. Go." She waved her out. "Go!"

Once the door was shut and the clerk gone, Frances clapped softly. "Brava," she whispered. She swiftly brushed away the hint of moisture that had returned to her eyes. "No time for that, you old biddy," she chided.

Her chambers contained an adjoining room where the basic creature needs could be met. There was a television hidden in a cabinet among the kitchen appliances, but Frances had always grumbled that operating the remote required a degree in engineering. You could probably fly the Concorde with this thing, she thought, squinting at the fancy array of buttons and arrows and acronyms.

She set it aside in frustration and turned the set on manually. The station was in the midst of a newsbreak, and the commentator was going into great detail about the president's allergies and their possible treatments, which included a cortisone shot.

Frances watched with great interest, smiling as the woman remarked on the chief executive's aversion to needles. There was a men-are-such-babies subtext that Frances found amusing, particularly since she and Johnny Addison went back to their college days, and Frances knew it to be true. It was also true that everything seemed to be newsworthy where presidents were concerned. Reagan's colon polyps had dominated the media for a week.

"There she is," Frances murmured, going quiet as Carlie appeared on the screen. The talk-show person, Sally something, was holding up the book that her daughter had authored and that Frances found so offensive. She would never understand how Carlie could have exposed her own family that way. The very fact that she continued to rake up the nightmare surrounding Ginger showed her lack of respect for everything Frances held dear.

She'd raised her daughters as she'd been raised, to honor the family name and jealously guard its privacy. And for the good of all concerned, that was how these things needed to be handled—privately. But Carlie was too stubborn to see that, and now Frances was going to have to find a way to make her daughter back off before it was too late.

The smile had long since disappeared when Frances turned off the TV. Now there was a hard set to her mouth, and a sparkle of painful resolve in her eyes. *Carlie, Carlie,* she thought, *my strange misfit. What am I to do about you?* It was her youngest daughter's sad lot in life that she was born to a mother with a higher calling. And sadder still that Carlie could never be the one to succeed her mother in this work. *That is* my *lot,* Frances acknowledged.

This time Frances didn't brush away the tears that welled in her eyes. She wasn't even aware of them. She was lost in thoughts that were virtually unimaginable. Was she the only mother in the world who wished a child had not been born? Was she the only monster?

Rio Walker hadn't been this caught up in a case in years. Maybe the work had been getting stale lately, and he hadn't realized it. It was well past midnight, and his thoughts were coming so fast, they were jostling each other for space. The department's shrink would probably have cautioned him about becoming obsessed. And there *was* that little question of his motives that remained unanswered. Did he want to break the case? Or did he want to break her?

A sharp click resonated from the pencil he was tapping against his teeth. He'd propped his feet on the edge of his desk and rested a yellow legal pad against his bent knees. Not the pose of a man staring at the answer to the mystery of the ages. In fact, all Rio was doing was making a list, but the longer it got, the more he knew he was onto something. Huge.

He glanced around the squad bay. When he'd assured himself that no one was coming up behind him, he reviewed what he'd written, looking for omissions and making notations.

1. Orderly and efficient.
2. Workaholic. Type-A personality with obsessive-compulsive tendencies.
3. High-minded idealist. Passionate about causes; champion of truth, justice, but selectively applied.
4. Achievement-oriented; strives for excellence in all things. Extremely image conscious.
5. No social life unrelated to work.
6. No men in her life.

He underlined number six and added a note. *Appears to maintain good working relationships with the opposite sex, but does not trust them on a personal level.*

7. Subject to great pressures in both professional and personal life. Outwardly composed, inwardly volatile.
8. Difficulty accepting loss of loved ones.

9. Tense, troubled relationship with mother.
10. Principled, but secretive; high probability of cover-up.

He put another question mark after number seven, but it was number ten that had him hooked. Beneath it he wrote: *May be connected to Ginger Bishop's death.*

That was the last personality trait on his list, but there was more, a great deal more, that he knew about her. He'd had her investigated so thoroughly he could have run out and bought her groceries for tonight's dinner. He knew her bra size and the brand of feminine hygiene products she used. But this was enough to deal with for now.

He tossed the notebook onto his desk and dropped his feet to the floor. He would have killed for a cigarette. He'd smoked his last the day he spotted Carlie Bishop on television. Stupidly he'd vowed not to light up until he'd cracked the case, and that was going on forty-eight hours ago.

Hell of an incentive. You could say he was anxious to clear this baby. You could say that.

The folder lying open on his desk was a criminal profile of the suspect. He studied the label and almost smiled. It was a name that would have rocked the entire country, maybe the world.

FRANCES STANFIELD BISHOP. Not Carlie. It was her mother he was investigating. On a hunch he'd decided to double back over some old ground—the Ginger Bishop case—a trail that had grown cold over the years, but still bore several sets of footprints, including his own.

He'd been curious about the family's reaction to Ginger's death, but it was Frances in particular who'd caught his attention, perhaps because their paths had crossed more than once in the legal arena. He'd heard complaints from defense attorneys that crucial evidence was not being allowed in her courtroom and witnesses weren't called. Her sentences were harsh, too, especially in stalker and sexual-assault cases. She was always within the law, but there was speculation that her rulings were an outlet for the pain she couldn't, or wouldn't, express.

It had hit him as eerily coincidental that her nomination to the high court and the first Femme Fatale strike had occurred on the same day. It was either the perfect diversion or the mark of a classic megalomaniac, but he also knew he'd be laughed out of RHD if he named her as a suspect. Still, he'd called in a favor from a private-detective buddy who provided him with what amounted to a deep background check.

The guy was a magician. He'd come up with things on the Right Honorable Frances Bishop that would have cost her the appointment if they'd been revealed during her confirmation hearing. Nothing really juicy, like sex, drugs or rock and roll, but there were strong indicators of a cover-up during the investigation of her daughter's death.

That news hadn't surprised Rio either. He'd long suspected that his own relationship with Ginger had been swept under the carpet, along with a few other aspects of her private life. The department could easily have considered him a suspect. He'd had the motive and the means, but they'd never questioned him, not even unofficially. And when he'd inquired about the case, he'd been hustled off to Quantico, Virginia, for an FBI training seminar, one that he'd requested and been denied the year before.

It was almost as if they were afraid to question him because they didn't want to deal with the possibility that he might have done it, or more to the point, that he knew something they didn't want to know about the nature of Ginger's life and death.

If they'd bothered to check—

Rio leaned forward and turned off the halogen desk lamp, melting into the peaceful silence around him as he rose from the chair. Now he was alone, inside. He preferred it this way, still and dark. The facets of his personality that revealed themselves only when it was dark were stirring now.

His mind reached. Touched.

If they'd bothered to check, they would have found out they were right. . . .

She preferred it dark, too. It was one of the few things they'd had in common. She had a penchant for it. And for fantasy. She loathed weakness in men, and loved power. Raw power. Physical domination. Her dreams were so dark they would have terrified most women. But not Ginger.

If they'd known what he did, he would be in jail now.

Somewhere a pencil began to click against a desktop. Rapidly. A drumbeat. The sound brought Rio out of his reverie. He looked around the squad room, thinking someone was tapping on a window. But it was merely a precautionary move. He knew that no one was there but him. The tapping was so instinctive he hadn't realized he was doing it. Strange how it had become his signature, the way serial offenders left trademark clues that linked their crimes.

Another phone ringing, lonely in the night. It reminded him of a voice calling out as he continued to ponder the seemingly irresistible power of darkness to the curious female psyche, the luminous female spirit. . . .

Sometime later he switched the light back on, turning away from its brightness. He leaned over the folder, buttressed by his forearms, and returned to the work on his desk. To Frances Stanfield Bishop's vaunted ideals, and to her surprisingly sordid secrets.

The PI had come up with some background data on the "varied and interesting" social life Frances had enjoyed in her salad days. The names mentioned were of people destined for high places, the same dizzying heights Frances herself now occupied. If the report was true, Frances hadn't always been the high-minded idealist her personality type indicated.

But what struck Rio now was that her list of character traits could have been Carlie's. Mother and daughter shared many things in common, including the emotional makeup and the intense pressures that could drive a law-abiding citizen to acts of vigilantism. Carlie had the motive, too. They both did. It wasn't clear whether either of them had the cunning or the technical skills the Femme Fatale had demonstrated, but technical skills were for sale. If you had the money you could have the pope taken out.

The department had its own criminal profiler who'd been called in on each of the alleged Femme Fatale strikes. The forensic psychologist's analysis had dovetailed with Rio's, except for one crucial detail. Based on crime-scene evidence and the offender's modus operandi, the profiler had predicted the Femme Fatale to be a status seeker, the kind of personality who was motivated by a desire for self-glorification. He cited the prominent victims and the sensational situations, as well as the way she linked her acts with the ethical tradition of the Golden Rule; leaving the erotic flower was another symbol—a real attention getter.

But Rio saw the Golden Rule as the Femme Fatale's mission statement. He, too, thought of the flower as a symbol, but saw the suspect as a reformer rather than a status seeker, one who wanted to save the innocent, punish the guilty, and change the world. Frustrated reformers would go to any lengths. No sacrifice was too great, even if it meant sinking to the stalker's depths, luring him. If she sought publicity, it was for her cause, not for herself. It was all a means to an end. And who better at espousing self-righteous causes than . . .

The name in his mind was Frances Bishop. But the one on his lips was Carlie. It all came back to her.

"Jesus." Rio threw back his head and breathed out the word with as much reverence as frustration. A moment later he was eyeing the pack of Marlboro Lights he'd impaled on the metal spike that was his note holder. How many hours now since he'd lit up and flooded his brain receptors with what they were screaming for? Too many. Too goddamn many. But there was no point in going home. He wouldn't sleep tonight.

Staring at the ceiling, he gave in to another powerful urge, and let his thoughts run amuck. It all came back to her. *It did.* Criminal mind or not, Carlie Bishop was the apex of the triangle. She was the crusader, the self-proclaimed savior of the downtrodden, and Rio had had enough experience with character analysis to know that those traits, subjected to building pressure, could erupt in a quest for vengeance.

Reformers-gone-bad weren't glory seekers or thrill killers. It wasn't a twisted need for sexual or ego gratification that drove them to violence. It was justice. Their cause was the greater good. They believed fervently, and had no qualms about taking the law into their own hands if they judged it wrong or inadequate, as she clearly did in this case.

Carlie Bishop. Green-eyed do-gooder.

Aspiring ax murderess?

Rio laughed, but he couldn't rule it out. No competent investigator could. She was beautiful enough to catch any man's eye, but once she had that eye, she was as likely to spit in it as anything else. Lots of chilly attitude on that one, and yet a total paradox. Maybe it was her vulnerability that was driving him nuts. Her main concern that morning was why she couldn't seem to have a "thing."

What's wrong with me? she'd asked, imploring some higher power for understanding.

Rio hadn't doubted her anguish for a moment. He'd heard it in her voice. Nor did he doubt what was happening to his gut at this very moment. He could feel the deep stirrings in his groin as he remembered her throaty anger—and her righteous indignation—at the couple making out across the courtyard from her.

He'd been waiting for her to go over and accost them, as any true reformer would have. And then he'd blown it. He hadn't given her a chance. He'd spoken up, let her know he was there, and then, for Christ's sake, he'd responded to the melting pain in her lime-green eyes, and told her that any man would be crazy not to want her.

Any man. *Me, baby, me. If you could see what's going on inside me.*

With a heavy sigh, he picked up the Marlboro Lights, walked to the basketball hoop on the watercooler, and slam-dunked the pack. *Worried about motives, Romeo? Maybe you'd better watch your own.*

Whatever he couldn't have was exactly what he wanted. A cigarette, or twenty of them. Her. Christ, he wanted her, and that surprised the hell out of him. He hadn't wanted a woman badly enough to fuck up a case in years. Maybe never.

"You can't have her," he said, staring at his surly expression in the dead television screen. "Get it straight, asshole. She's your prime suspect, the kiss of death."

What he could have, if he could distance himself enough and recover his detachment, was a high-profile female serial killer. A conviction. Success would have to satisfy his soul. As for his body . . . hell, maybe he'd start smoking again.

He closed the file, aware that he was dangerously close to making the fatal mistake of trying to prove his own theory. He had the suspects, two of them with almost exactly the same personality type and motive. And if he wasn't careful, he would soon be attempting to make the crime fit the person. That was backward. It was wrong. Peggy would have kicked his butt if she'd caught him doing that during his training days. You started with the crime scene, the physical evidence, and from that you inferred behavior.

But this case was different.

Rio closed his eyes, blocking out the light. He let himself breathe with the energy running through him. It *was* different. He knew that in his gut. There was no "right" way. There was only what he felt, what he knew. He'd always worked like this, in the dark of his mind. He'd never followed any traditional method of investigation, and it made no sense to start now. He was considering it *only* because she'd thrown him off base, confused his instincts.

He was onto something. He had the scent, only it was two suspects instead of one. Two Bishop women.

Life was interesting, wasn't it? he thought. Time did mete out its own kind of justice in its own way. What went around, came around. The family that had deemed him not good enough for their daughter were the ones in trouble now, and he was holding the whip hand. He was their judge and jury, just as they'd been his.

Rio Walker was plenty good enough now, it seemed.

There was just one question that remained in his mind.

"Mother or daughter?" he asked himself.

EIGHT

"My insurance company dropped me." Jo Emily's voice seemed trapped somewhere within her tangled body.

"He smashed the windshield of my car so many times they let me go," she said. "My friends, too. He broke their windshields whenever they came to see me, so they stopped coming over. Even my family was afraid—"

She was laboring for breath. Carlie recognized the symptoms of panic, but had to let her go on. Victims tried to deny their fears. They thought ignoring them would make them go away, when just the opposite was true. Once it was out in the open, Jo Emily could let go of the burden. The support group would carry it for her. Shared fear was manageable, Carlie had found.

"I still had my job at the beauty shop," she told them, "but it didn't take him long to fix that. I got fired after he took a baseball bat to the owner's van. That's when I prayed to God to have him die in some horrible, painful way. I just wanted him *dead*."

A quiver of rage shook through her. "It was the stalker who heard my prayers, not God. He called, laughed at me. Then he busted out my landlord's window and went after my neighbors. Everyone was terrified, but not of him, of *me*. I got evicted and ordered to stay away from the building. They wouldn't even let me get my things I had in the storage shed."

"So you bought a bus ticket and came to Southern California," Carlie said. It was time to give Jo Emily a break, and clarify things for the rest of the women, who were gathered in a circle around Jo Emily. "How long have you been here?"

"Going on a year now. He hasn't found me, yet."

One of the members spoke up. "Did you change your name or do anything to hide your identity?"

"I couldn't see how." Jo Emily shook her head. "I needed a letter of recommendation to get another job. The shop owner mailed me one, but even with that the best I could get was part-time work. I don't use my credit cards anymore, and I'm unlisted now, so he can't trace me that way."

Carlie had heard a thousand such stories, but the suffering made it new every time. New and painful. It still infuriated her how effortlessly these brutal cowards could destroy lives. And get away with it.

"Did he ever say anything or identify himself to you in any way?" It was the woman who spoke earlier.

"Have there been threats?" another asked.

Carlie wasn't surprised at the way the group was reaching out to embrace Jo Emily. They could do more than just empathize, they could help her with ways to protect herself. It was a sisterhood bound by common terrors, and when they looked to each other for understanding, it was there.

"No, nothing like that," Jo Emily answered, "which is why the police, they couldn't help. When he called he'd mostly laugh and sometimes he'd say the words from that song, you know—'Every Breath You Take.' I guess that was so I'd know he was watching me."

"Aii!" Hot coffee slopped over the Styrofoam cup, burning Carlie's fingers. The cup hit the floor with a sharp splat, spewing the white tile with mud-puddle black.

Jo Emily stared at Carlie with huge eyes. "Did I say something wrong?"

Every breath you take.

"No, no, of course not!" Carlie hurried to the sink and turned on the water. The group had congregated in the coffee lounge of her office tonight because of the smaller turnout. The refrigerator was handy and there was a picnic-type table they could all sit around. It had a kaffee-klatsch feeling the larger lounge lacked. Fortunately there was also cold running water.

Every breath . . .

"I wasn't paying attention," Carlie said. "The silly cup slipped right through my fingers. Sorry."

"That's okay." Jo Emily forced a smile.

. . . you take, Ginger.

Carlie could do little more than smile back reassuringly. Her heart was hammering so hard she could barely manage her hands. But it had nothing to do with the burn. She was intimately familiar with that lyric.

It was the same threat Ginger's murderer had used, the man who'd stalked and killed her. The exact words. Carlie's parents wouldn't discuss the case, but Carlie had read about it in the newspaper.

She tried to compose herself as the rest of the group rallied to clean up the floor. They were laughing and ready to resume by the time Carlie had finished with her hands. Even Jo Emily seemed reasonably settled, but Carlie wasn't sure she could go on. Ginger's stalker had never been caught, and the possibility that this was him was monstrous. She could barely think what to do.

"Am I interrupting?"

A male voice startled Carlie's heart into another burst of gunfire. Her hand was still under the water as she twisted around, undoubtedly expecting it to be Rio Walker. He'd shown up everywhere else. Why not here? But she was wrong.

A pleasant-looking man, perhaps in his mid-thirties, stood in the doorway, wearing a khaki trench coat over his jeans and white dress shirt. His olive skin and dark eyes were vaguely familiar, but Carlie couldn't place him, and had even less idea what he was doing there. It was lucky that he seemed to. He rapped lightly on the door frame and grinned.

"Gabe Quiñones, the *L.A. Times*," he said. "I was supposed to come by tonight, wasn't I?"

"Quiñones?" Carlie had barely recovered from her first shock. She'd never met Gabriel Quiñones face-to-face, but she knew who he was. This was the investigative reporter who'd done the in-depth series on Ginger after her death. It was in one of his articles that Carlie first heard the line Jo Emily just mentioned—every breath you take. Carlie would have known next to nothing about what had happened to her sister if not for Quiñones. She owed him a huge debt of gratitude.

She shook the water off her hands and dried them with paper towels. "I'm sorry," she said, thrown by his presence as much as her own confusion. "There must be some mistake. I have a group in session tonight."

"Right," Quiñones said. "That's why I came by."

Carlie was at a loss. She'd had a message from Danny that Quiñones was doing a series on stalker victims and wanted to interview her, but since she'd been "run" out of her office that morning, there'd been no chance to get back to the reporter. It wasn't like Danny to make an appointment for her without telling her, but that must have been what happened.

"You *are* Carlie Bishop, aren't you?" Quiñones said. "I recognize the green eyes from your book-jacket photo."

"Guilty." Carlie smiled to cover the awkwardness. Even without talking to Quiñones, she'd recognized the value of a feature series. It could be a huge boost to the cause of increasing public awareness and encouraging the passage of stronger stalker laws. She was in the middle of a session, and it was a crucial one for Jo Emily, but she couldn't leave the man standing there. And she didn't want to pass up an opportunity that could benefit them all.

"I'll be right with you. Dorrie?" she said, appealing to one of the veteran members of the group. "Could you take over while I talk to Mr. Quiñones? I won't be long."

Carlie waved Quiñones with her into the hallway. It was important they talk in private and without alarming any of the members. She wanted to know how he'd tracked her down as much as why he was there. And she had her answer to the latter question almost immediately. Quiñones had already begun to plead his case before they reached Carlie's office.

"Listen," he said as they walked together down the hallway, "I overheard that woman's story, and it's incredibly compelling—a stalker victim in flight, every waking moment spent looking over her shoulder, waiting for the bogeyman to show up and shatter her car windshield, and her life."

"Well, yes, but that's the problem—"

Quiñones touched her arm, clearly excited about the possibilities. "Ms. Bishop—is Carlie all right? If we can believe Jo Emily, then the man who's stalking her is using the same signature behavior as the one who stalked your sister. Or at least he's using the same line. What are the odds of that? It's incredible."

Now Carlie stopped him. Obviously he'd had the same thought she had. "Are you thinking that it's a coincidence? She couldn't have heard him wrong, not if he said it every time he called."

"True," Quiñones agreed, "but it's possible the stalker read my series. It went out on the wire and several big papers picked it up, including *USA Today*."

There was no way to know, Carlie realized, *unless* the stalker was caught. If he was Ginger's killer, then this could lure him into the open and let the police apprehend him. But it could also put Jo Emily in danger.

The cable-knit fisherman's sweater Carlie had worn over her jeans was meant to ward off the evening chill, and she could feel dampness ring the base of her neck. She was sweating.

"Are you okay?" Quiñones asked.

Carlie didn't want him, or anyone, to know how badly this had shaken her. "How can you feature Jo Emily in a story without blowing her cover?" she asked. "Won't that tell him right where to find her?"

"There *is* that possibility, but it could also scare him off. And there are ways to protect her identity, if that's what she wants. I certainly don't have to use her name, and I could alter the stalker's signature behavior."

He held up a hand as if he were taking an oath. "You have my word that I will protect her in every way I can. I'd go to jail before I'd reveal her identity to anyone. If you know anything about me, you must believe that."

What she knew about Quiñones was that he'd forged ahead with a series on Ginger even after the police had backed away from the case. He hadn't bowed to whatever pressures had been brought to bear, and Carlie assumed they were considerable. He'd also received a Pulitzer nomination for the series, and Carlie was sorry he hadn't won.

But he was giving her an impossible choice. Lure the stalker back or scare him off? Both situations held risks that Carlie didn't know how to calculate. And those risks had to be weighed against the importance of the task force's mission in getting the laws changed. Ultimately it wasn't up to Carlie. She would have to talk to Jo Emily.

"If I do feature her," Quiñones added. "I'll need to talk to her myself. An interview, and maybe more than one. Can you arrange that?"

Carlie would have preferred to play it safe and say no, but that wasn't fair to Jo Emily or the group. The publicity would certainly help Carlie's cause. It was difficult to get media attention on any but the most sensational cases, which led the public to believe that it was only celebrities who were stalked. They didn't understand how the life of the average citizen, who didn't have the resources to hire bodyguards and round-the-clock security, could be left in shambles.

There was even a chance Jo Emily's situation could be improved by the publicity. It wasn't a risk Carlie wanted to take, but some stalker victims went public, revealing their stories and showing pictures of their stalkers on national talk shows in the belief that massive exposure was a deterrent.

Moreover, Quiñones was right about Jo Emily. Her desperate situation was a perfect human-interest piece. Every man she encountered, every face she looked into, triggered the same terrifying question: was he the one?

Was he the one? *Did he kill Ginger?*

Those were the questions that terrified Carlie. "I'll talk to Jo Emily," she promised the reporter.

"And the group?" he pressed. "I can't do a series without talking to several victims. They *are* the story. I'll protect them, Carlie, I promise."

"Okay, but let me think about it."

He caught her hand and shook it as if they had a deal. "Any chance that I could sit in on the rest of the your meeting? How about it? I promise not to use the group or Jo Emily in my story until they've had time to think about whether they want to be involved. But how could it hurt if I introduce myself to them and explain what I want to do? Maybe they'd feel safer about talking to me."

Carlie's stomach was churning, but she would have been hard-pressed to say exactly why. There were so many possibilities, so many question marks and amorphous fears. It wasn't Quiñones who concerned her. It was the possibility that saying yes would unleash something she didn't understand. Something in her gut told her that she shouldn't let a newspaper reporter into the circle.

Still, who knew better than she that there was no gain without risk? And the least she could do was speak to the group on Quiñone's behalf and let them make the choice about whether or not he deserved a hearing. "I'll do it," she said.

Carlie awoke the next morning to a voice-mail box full of messages. When she'd come home the night before, bleary-eyed with exhaustion, the red light had been blinking madly, and her reaction had been instantaneous. She'd grabbed a pillow and attempted to smother the phone machine.

She'd even begun muttering to herself. "He was right. Whoever said anyone who owns a telephone is at the mercy of any damn fool who knows how to dial one was right."

It was probably just exhaustion. The support-group meeting had run very late with Quiñones there. He'd been a huge hit, and not only had the members agreed to let him sit in, they'd volunteered to stay afterward and be interviewed. That had given Carlie a chance to speak with Jo Emily alone, and she'd surprised Carlie by being as eager as the other members to be featured in the reporter's series. Carlie had insisted that Jo Emily's name not be used, but other than that, it was clear that she could set aside her fears and give everyone the green light.

Carlie had also offered Jo Emily a part-time job working at Safe and Sound, which had resulted in much joyous whooping on Jo Emily's part and a prayer for earmuffs on Carlie's. Carlie was fairly sure the joy had more to do with Danny than with the job. But hey, Jo Emily needed the money and Carlie needed the help.

Suzanne Forster

Everyone left the meeting happy, and Carlie was pleased about that, but it was midnight before she got home and crawled into her flannel pajamas. She'd slept like the dead until the alarm went off moments ago at six-thirty. Now, still in her pj's and barely conscious, she picked up the bedside phone, tapped in her code, and hit the speaker button.

This was not going to be a day of boundless energy, she could tell. Usually she was brushing her teeth by now, foaming at the mouth as she massaged her gums the way the hygienist told her, and making mental notes about the calls she had to return.

She rose to stretch while the messages started playing back. A throaty sound slipped out as she reached high above her head and twisted her torso. It was her poor stiff body moaning. She was tight all the way to her toes, but every inch of muscle resistance felt good, especially around her shoulders.

"Carlie, this is your mother calling. . . ."

"My mother?"

Carlie listened in shock to the soft, but commanding voice. It *was* her mother. She was asking—well, demanding—that Carlie be good enough to return the call at her earliest convenience. Other than saying she would be in her chambers, she gave no clue what the call might be about.

Carlie hadn't heard from her mother in months. They didn't talk on a regular basis. In fact, they barely spoke at all unless they had to, which meant this was important. Still, the steel in her mother's tone gave Carlie pause, and she could feel herself going into an avoidance pattern. Maybe she'd return the call when she got to the office.

A slow rotation of Carlie's head triggered all manner of crunches and cracks. She closed her eyes as the rest of the messages droned on. The majority were about the upcoming task-force meeting at Carlie's house. There were some invitations, mostly to charity and speaking events, which she could have Danny answer, a call from her editor, her publicist, and one from her agent, who jokingly referred to her by a pet name.

"What have you done, Bellissima," he wanted to know, "run off to Brazil with some Argentine tango master named Ramon?"

"I wish," Carlie murmured.

She would have loved to have run to anywhere with anyone, but she was bound to the mast and lashed by guilt. Her to-do list was endless. There was no way to get through it except to prioritize and that meant bumping her new project down the list. She'd already started the research, and it was really just a matter of getting something down on paper, a rough proposal to send to her agent. But before she could direct her energies to that, she had to finish putting together her portion of the task-force report, and she hadn't even plowed through Danny's latest bunch of statistics yet!

With a promise that she would let nothing impede her progress today—not her lovelorn office staff or some nosy sneak of a detective with Elvis eyelashes—she wandered into the bathroom and studied her rumpled reflection in the mirror. Red-gold locks defied gravity, sticking this way and that. It was not unlike the new "straw cap" look for spring she'd seen in *Mirabella*. Maybe she could spritz it and say she just had it done.

"Hey, Chubbs, call me when you get back from the meeting tonight. I'll probably still be here. I've got a new batch of data, and it looks good."

It was Danny on the machine. Another call Carlie was glad she missed. At least she'd hired him some help, although she had qualms about what sort of team he and Jo Emily would make.

The messages ended after Danny's, and Carlie went back to making herself presentable. She had the faucet running and her toothbrush loaded with paste when something stopped her, a frisson of awareness that was more sensation than sound. Carlie hesitated. She glanced at herself in the mirror, brush poised, wondering what she'd heard.

Unless she was imagining it, there was a faint clicking noise coming from somewhere in the house, like a finger tapping on a counter or a key turning in a lock. Her blood ran cold until she realized it must be the machine. The tape had run out. She quickly rinsed her mouth, but by the time she got there the clicking had stopped and another message was playing.

"They say there are two ways to make someone be-have . . . just two. Do you know what they are, Carlie?"

Carlie's heart went weak. It sounded like Rio Walker.

"Love . . ."

She waited for him to finish, say the other one, but the silence burned on until she imagined she could hear him breathing.

". . . and fear."

Fear? What did he mean?

Again the line slipped into silence.

"Do you think they're right?" he asked at last.

It was him. She couldn't imagine why he was posing the question, unless it was to frighten her, and it had worked. Her strongest impulse was to back away from the machine. What he'd said insinuated all kinds of things, but the tone of his voice was unmistakable. It alerted every nerve ending. God. Any woman would have known what that kind of whispering meant. It was grainy and intimate, a male in the early stages of arousal. Maybe the late stages, but undeniably a man with a woman on his mind.

Carlie hit a button to shut off the machine and heard the tape go into rewind. In frustration she yanked the cord from the phone jack. She didn't care if she lost the other calls, she didn't want to hear his voice or that message again. It had raised the hair on her arms. Something was going to have to be done about Rio Walker. He was getting too close, and it was more than an invasion of her physical space. He'd insinuated himself into her consciousness. She was even beginning to associate certain sounds with him.

Carlie lectured on listening to one's intuition. Hers was telling her to get dressed and get going. Danny should be at the office by now, and he was a good sounding board when she needed to talk. It was her habit to map out the day's schedule while she applied her makeup, but there was precious little time today as she scrubbed at her face with a Buff Puff, dabbed some moisturizer around her eyes, and turned on the shower. Halfway out of her pajamas, she realized she didn't want to be naked in the shower, not even for a moment. It would make her feel too vulnerable.

"Just wash and go," she told herself.

A shadow fell across her arm as she was searching through her makeup bag for her lipstick, and she glanced up instantly, wondering if the lights had flickered. She'd meant to change the bulbs above the vanity mirror. The whole row had begun to go in and out, flaring and dimming as if something were wrong with the wiring.

After a moment she realized she was staring at her own reflection, trying to understand what was wrong, what she was feeling. Because something *was* wrong, and that was when she heard it again. The tapping. It was the same sound, only hollow and sharp now. Nearer.

Not the phone machine. It was the sound he made. He could have been in the bathroom with her. He *was*.

No! Her heart began to race as fast as her thoughts. The sound might be real, but the rest was her imagination, a fantasy. She knew that because it had happened before, many times . . . and yet she stood there, staring into the mirror and waiting for it to happen again, for a man to step out from behind the door.

The lights flickered wildly. The bulbs were going out. Suddenly they flared, hot and wiry, washing the room in brightness. Carlie was blinded for a second, and then she heard a caustic pop. The smell of burned filaments hung in the air, but everything was plunged into shadows.

Was that movement behind her?

Her head lifted, frozen. Her pupils shrank to pinpoints. All she could see in the mirror was her own startled expression. Fear had locked her into her own image so tightly she couldn't move. The incessant tapping grew louder, echoing in her temples like firecrackers, like lightbulbs.

A white spot burned her focus as she forced herself to turn toward the door. She could see nothing. The room was a shadowy void, but she could feel the presence of someone else. She knew he was there.

Crazy, she told herself. This was crazy. She was remembering what had happened to her sister, how he'd come up behind Ginger in the darkness. Carlie had read about it in the notes, and then she'd fantasized it herself. If she hadn't been able to escape to the thrilling places her imagination took her, her childhood would have been unbearable.

"What are you doing?" she whispered.

There was a quick scrape of footsteps, the hush of breath, as something came up against her, all cool heat and force. A hand slipped around her back and another clamped over her mouth.

"Love or fear," he said, "which is it?"

Shock vibrated through Carlie. Cold shock. It imprisoned her as effectively as his low, whispering voice. Shock had paralyzed her. She couldn't have escaped if he'd let her go.

"I've been watching you all night, watching you sleep . . ."

She didn't believe it. If he'd been watching her, then he must have broken into her house.

". . . watching you breathe."

No!

"Do you know how beautiful you are that way? How vulnerable? Do you know what it does to a man, watching you?"

He held her so tight she couldn't move. His mouth grazed her hair and she could hear the groan in his sharp intake of air.

"I wanted to slide inside you while you were sleeping, Carlie, let you feel what you do to me. Feel it."

She tightened, unwilling to feel anything, and somehow created more sensation than her body had ever experienced in one jolt. It was electricity. Caustic burning current. Her rigid muscles were the filament, overburdened and sparking to every signal. She was going to flare and burn out!

She sank back with a helpless sob. *Don't,* she thought, not sure who she was pleading with, him or herself. *Please don't.* This was what she was afraid of, that she would react to him like this. Her lips had parted against the heat of his palm, and the scream that welled up in her throat was not one of fear. It was some other deeper, wilder utterance.

He heard it, too. Heard it and released her mouth with one shaking word on his lips. "Yes."

She gasped for air. Her neck arched, and her head fell into the hollow of his shoulder. All she could do was roll back and forth. All she could do was feel.

"Fear," he whispered. "You've chosen sweet, wild fear. I can give you that. I'm good at that." His fingers slid down her arms. They raked her shivering flesh.

Such passion Carlie barely knew what to do. Such passion she hated him for triggering it. Hated and *feared* him. She had always feared him. The sound in her throat changed. It broke with anguish, helpless despair. On impulse she whirled and struck out, her only thought to make him understand what he'd done. But there was nothing there.

She struck at air.

Carlie rushed to the door and turned on the overhead light. She stared at the empty room in horror, confused for a moment, then realizing what she'd done.

"Oh, God," she whispered, ducking her head. Now she couldn't look at herself. Fiery heat crept up her throat, and she wished it would burn her to ashes. Apparently she hadn't outgrown her adolescent imaginings. She hadn't had a Rio Walker bathroom fantasy in years, but this was definitely one of her more lurid ones.

In boarding school she'd secretly dreamed of being an actress. Eventually she'd worked up her courage and joined the drama club, where she'd excelled despite her shyness. Often she'd run lines from the plays by herself, taking all the parts. She'd loved the romantic scenes best, thrown herself into them. But this was ridiculous.

Now she walked to the shower and pulled open the door. The tapping sound had come from this stall. She hadn't turned the water all the way off. That's what had triggered the episode, but understanding did nothing to ease her chagrin.

She wasn't kind to herself. Not kind at all.

"Change the lightbulbs in the vanity, Bishop," she said scathingly. "And while you're at it, change the one that's gone out in your head."

NINE

A quip, a joke, a snappy one-liner. Anything.

Danny Upshaw would have given his left lung for a clever comeback. If he'd thought there was any chance that God was in a sporting mood, Danny would have rolled the dice and risked it all. *Just let me say the right thing for once, give me some words that will warm her sad eyes and make her smile. Danny's a pretty cool guy once you get to know him. Couldn't you just whisper that in her ear, Man? Huh?*

But God had never been in a sporting mood as far as Danny could tell. Otherwise, why would one poor jerk have been blighted with so many social handicaps? Tying a man's tongue in a thousand knots and cursing him with the ability to turn ten shades of red—that stuff did not qualify as a running start in Danny's book.

A whistle as squeaky as her voice sailed the length of the conference table. It brought Danny's thoughts to a halt and his head up. Jo Emily sat at the other end, a look of weary triumph about her. They'd been doggedly stuffing envelopes all morning with brochures for free victims' assistance services, and Jo Emily had just finished off a box.

"One down," she said with a thumbs-up. Her black denim mini skooched upward, flirting with her panty line as she pushed back the chair and pulled over another box. Long shimmery dark hair ebbed and flowed with her movements. There were several more boxes to go, and at this rate, they had a long day ahead of them.

Danny racked his brain for something to say. Envelope stuffers rule? No, that was stupid. So many envelopes, so little time?

Jo Emily glanced at him with a cautious smile. Everything about her was sweetly cautious, Danny thought, except when she lost her cookies, like at the lecture.

"Now, I could be all wet," she conceded. "It would not be the first time. But I do believe they have mailing services for this sort of thing."

"Joe, the Postman. It's down one block and over. We've used them before, but the budget's tight this month, so I volunteered to do the mailing."

"Aren't you the nice one," she said softly.

She gave him a little beam of a smile, and again Danny prayed to that Blackjack Dealer in the sky. *Surely You could keep my ears from turning red, couldn't you? How much time could that take in the overall scheme of things?*

Danny wasn't taking any chances on a response. He shot Jo Emily a nod and went back to stuffing. It was easier dealing with people when he had a computer in front of him and the wonders of the Web to talk about. He could point to the screen, explain things, and divert attention from himself. He managed to instruct people in self-defense, too, and not be overly self-conscious. But let it be about him and he turned into a colossal fumblebutt. He sometimes wondered why Carlie kept him around, inept as he was with people. He worked hard, trying to make it up to her.

"Know why I chew Dentyne?" She stopped long enough to dig in the shoulder bag that was hanging over the back of her chair and pull out a pack. "Sure, it cleans my teeth, that's what you were thinking, right? But it calms me down, too."

She held out the pack. "Want some? No? Sure? Well, I hope you don't mind if I do."

It would have taken more than gum to calm Danny down. But his silence didn't seem to discourage her from enjoying its therapeutic benefits. She unwrapped a tiny stick and popped it in her mouth.

After another short while she asked: "How's the weather down your way?"

She was trying to keep the conversational ball rolling and Danny didn't want to let her down. "Have you . . ." he started.

"Have I what?"

He cleared his throat. "Have you ever taken a self-defense class?"

"No, but I watch wrestling." She snapped her gum.

Danny contemplated her crooked grin with a sense of wonder. Jo Emily Pough, angel or tramp? You couldn't tell by looking, and if he thought about it, he probably didn't care. His heart was already trying to negotiate whatever land mines lay between them.

"There are some basic self-defense moves that just about anybody can do," he told her. "Gouging the eyes and going for the groin are no-brainers."

"Really?"

"You can damn near neuter a guy if you do it right."

They'd both stopped stuffing envelopes and Jo Emily was gazing at him expectantly.

Offer to show her, you blockhead. It's what you do!

"Do you think *I* could neuter someone? Me?"

"Yeah, sure. You could do it. Easy." Danny crossed his arms, uncrossed them, then rolled up the sleeves of his watch-plaid shirt. He could feel his mouth going dry and his tongue swelling up. "Wa-want me to show you?

"Please!"

She was eager. He let go a sigh of relief. He liked that in a pupil.

As it turned out, she was good, too. Danny'd never had his eyes gouged and his groin kneed by anyone quite so tiny or fierce before. Her spirit made up for whatever was missing in the way of muscle. He hadn't bothered with padding. He hadn't expected to need it, but to be honest, she'd given him a bad moment or two. The odd light that had come into her eyes as she prepared to turn her bony little knee into a battering ram was a terrifying sight.

"Could we try that again?" she asked afterward, flushed with victory and tugging at her formfitting top to get it tucked back into her skirt. He'd been trying all morning not to notice how the black and gray stripes clung to her slender ribs and molded her breasts.

"It's only a demonstration," he reminded her.

"Oh, did I—" She glanced at his crotch in horror. "Did I hurt you, Danny Upshaw?"

"Nah! Hell, no." But he pretended to buckle at the knees, and they both laughed. That rusty-hinges voice of hers drove him nuts.

"You know what I'd love?" she said, her dark eyes glowing. "I'd love to flip a great big guy like you. Wouldn't that be fun?"

"Fun?" Danny was halfway convinced she could do it, but it wasn't physical damage he was worried about. Up to now he'd been in the teacher mode, thinking of her as a pupil rather than a woman. If he had to come up behind her and put his arms around her, he wasn't sure what mode that would put him in. It could trigger the uneasiness he had about getting close to people, especially a woman he was attracted to.

"We could save that for another lesson," he suggested.

"I s'pose we could."

She was trying to be a good sport, but she looked so crestfallen he didn't have the heart to try to talk her out of it. Maybe he didn't want to anyway, not once he got the idea in his head. It had been a long time since he'd been near a woman with any thought other than teaching her to defend herself. He usually didn't allow himself to have those thoughts, but this felt different.

They'd already come out to the reception area. All he had to do was move a couple of Kentia palms into the hall and get Carlie's Chinese porcelain vase out of the strike zone. Once he'd created some maneuvering room, he didn't see what harm it could do to show her how it was done.

"The trick is to throw your attacker off balance," he explained when they were ready. "You could flip Hulk Hogan if you caught him off balance. Picture the guy coming up on you from behind. The minute he grabs you, you drop to your knees and he pitches forward. See . . ."

He demonstrated several times while she watched, wondering why he'd made it sound so easy. Flipping someone took skill, dexterity, and timing.

"I'd prefer to picture Randy 'Macho Man' Savage. He's one of those no-good New World Order hooligans."

Danny thought about smiling and decided against it. She didn't seem to be kidding. "Let's just go through the moves," he suggested. "Don't actually throw me."

He did have to smile as he soundlessly approached her from behind. She tensed up like a cornered mouse, waiting for the cat to pounce. If anything, he was too gentle in his demonstrations for Carlie's lectures. For as long as he could remember, he'd worried about losing control and hurting someone. Men his size didn't realize their own strength, and the thought of causing pain was intolerable.

He hesitated behind her with his arms outstretched, rehearsing what he was supposed to do, and wondering why she smelled so damn good, like warm gingerbread. At last he sucked in a breath and swept her into a choke hold. He had to fight the desire to apologize.

"Not a word, lady," he warned. "And you won't get hurt."

She made a mewling sound and pulled forward. But it was the wrong move. *Drop*, he thought. *Drop to the floor!*

"Jo Emily?" He couldn't figure out what she was doing. Not only didn't she drop, she began to wriggle and squirm, twisting her hips until finally she'd managed to work herself all the way around and face him dead-on.

"What are you doing?" he asked cautiously. "This isn't what I showed you."

She stared square into his blue eyes. "I know, Danny. I was going to drop, honest. But then I got to thinking that it might be nice to do this."

"Do . . . what?" He could feel himself heating up.

"This. What we're doing."

What were they doing? They were toe-to-toe, but those weren't the only places they were touching. He could feel her knees and her belly and the velvety warmth of her breasts. They could have been dancing, or something even more intimate. She was so close he could smell the cinnamon on her breath and see the darkening desire in her doe-brown eyes.

This was more than Danny had bargained for. It was more than he'd dreamed of, to be honest, and probably more than he deserved. He knew he was supposed to say something, but he hated the sudden silences that announced it was his turn. Talking was difficult enough anyway. It was impossible when someone was hanging on the words, waiting.

There had to be something he could do.

"Th-this?" he said. He touched her hair and his heart bucked like a frightened horse's.

"Oh . . . that's nice."

She nestled her cheek against his hand, and chimes peeled throughout the office, sharp and silvery.

"Listen to that," she exclaimed, marveling. "Bells are ringing."

Danny heaved a sigh. His ears had not turned red. He wasn't stuttering all that much. So, of course, the phone had to ring.

"It's Ma Bell, Jo Emily." There was despair in his voice. "And I have to answer it. Sorry."

Prepared to be curt with the caller, he picked up the phone at his desk in the reception area. But it turned out to be Carlie on the line, and he could tell by the sound of her voice that something was wrong. She didn't want to talk, even when he pressed. She would say only that she had some things to do at home and might not get in that day.

Danny hung up the phone, vaguely disturbed. He was familiar enough with Carlie's business concerns that he should have been able to puzzle out what was bothering her. But he didn't have a clue this time. This was about something else, something personal.

He couldn't concentrate anyway. Jo Emily's presence made that damn near impossible. He was sitting on his desk, and she was standing right beside him, close enough that their thighs could have brushed. Any other man would have reached out and pulled her into his arms, right back where she'd been a moment ago. She was probably expecting that, too. There wasn't any reason she shouldn't be, given what they'd been doing, and what she knew about Danny Upshaw. She clearly thought he was like any other guy she might be hugging, a little shy maybe, but once they got around that—

If only the phone call hadn't burst the bubble. If only it hadn't given him time to think.

"Danny?"

Her voice wavered sweetly, but he couldn't look at her. He was trying to gather his nerve and find the way to make contact again, but something inside him was paralyzed. It wasn't her fault. In fact, it had nothing to do with her. It was about life, about timing, about some goddamn trick of fate that made it impossible for him to pursue what he wanted most.

"That was Carlie, right?" she asked. "Is something wrong?"

"I'm not sure."

She touched his arm and her petal-soft fingers made his jaws ache. It was a child's touch, light and hopeful. God, how he wanted to touch her back.

"There is something wrong," she said after a moment. "Can you tell me about it?"

No, I can't, Jo Emily, he thought. *Not ever.*

The pain that rose in his chest had nothing to do with Carlie's situation. It was the pain of not being able to share himself with anyone. He couldn't tell Jo Emily what was stopping him from taking her into his arms because she would never be able to accept it. He couldn't accept it himself. For one crazy moment he'd thought something good could happen between them. What was even sadder, he'd allowed her to think so, too.

He didn't see any way to get back to where they'd been, and he couldn't even tell her why. But she must have spotted it in his face when he looked up at her, because she stepped back and sucked in a breath. A wary child, she knew the signs. People were inexplicably cruel. They dangled the prize, then snatched it away when you reached. They played games with your dreams like kids playing pass-off, tossing the ball to someone else every time you got close.

Her eyes had gone tight and sad, as if she were expecting to be hurt. But this had not surprised her, Danny realized. She went through life expecting this kind of treatment.

"I guess we should get back to the envelopes," she said. "Maybe we can get them done before Carlie gets here."

Danny watched her walk away and wondered if he had the strength to join her. He was possessed of a body that could wrestle giants to the ground, but those places inside him that were weak could drain every drop of life out of him. Like hidden sinkholes, they lay in wait to suck him under, to swallow him whole and leave him fighting for breath.

He didn't want to hurt Jo Emily. He didn't want to hurt anyone.

*   *   *

Like most cops, Rio hated hospitals. On the street you dealt with life
and death on a daily basis, and you took it in stride or you cracked.
This was L.A., land of televised car chases, where reality exceeded the
movies. Nobody died here but the bad guys. But hospitals put the lie to
that macho illusion.

There was no reason to be in one unless you were cheering up a
wounded buddy or identifying a dead one. There were cops shot full of
holes in hospitals, and every time you visited one of them, you knew
your turn was coming. The odds shortened with every day you stayed
alive.

One foot in hell, Rio thought as he jogged up the steps to UCLA's
medical center. There was only one person in his life who could have
induced him to come here on this bright, crisp, nearly smogless morning,
and that was his partner, Peggy Sykes.

She'd taught him how to be a detective, and she was still teaching
him, though he doubted he would live enough years to learn everything
she knew. She was a good cop, inside and out, and there weren't enough
of those around. That's why it tore him up to see her flat on her back
in a bed with bars, reduced to the indignity of wearing gaping, string-
tied gowns and sipping water through a flex straw.

He was sure it got worse, like bedpans, enemas, and needles jabbed
in vulnerable places, but he didn't want to know about that. She was
running a fever, suffering from fatigue and night sweats. Because of her
bypass, they were concerned about infection, but the tests were inconclusive. A few days had turned into a week, and they still didn't know
what was wrong.

Rio was getting worried, but if Peggy shared his concerns, she didn't
let on. He had the feeling she was still clinging to the illusion of in-
vulnerability. There was an unwritten code among cops that said you
perpetuated the lie at all costs. You never admitted the gut fear and
despair you felt. You never admitted the hopelessness of cleaning up
the mess that was out there, because to do so was to break the back of
every cop you knew. Peggy put most men to shame in honoring that
code. She might be killing herself to honor it.

Six fast flights of stairs left Rio huffing, but his partner looked surprisingly chipper as he entered her room. She was watching a steamy
soap opera, propped up by pillows and the adjustable bed back. She'd
exchanged her hospital gown for a terrycloth wrapper in violent pink
that lit up her eyes and her military-short, salt-and-pepper hair.

"Sneaking cigarettes again?" She looked Rio up and down, apparently referring to his labored breathing.

"Where you hiding *your* Joe Camels these days?" She was always bugging him about his smoking, the little hypocrite. She usually kept a pack of unfiltered Camels under her pillow, claiming it was a test of her willpower. At least they were both trying to quit and could keep each other reasonably honest.

"Isn't it a little early for hot-tub love?" he asked her, referring to the seminude couple on the screen, who were stalking each other in a bubbling Jacuzzi.

Peggy jetted nasal laughter. "Maybe for you, Don Pardo."

"I guess *we're* feeling better."

She ignored the comment and zapped him with a look. "I hope you've come to tell me that our beloved Captain Frank is doing cartwheels in the aisles of the squad room because you finished the sixty-day report on the freeway sniper case, which you really should call the hundred-and-twenty-day report, since by my count it's at least sixty days overdue."

"There's a better chance of the *Titanic not* sinking."

"That he's doing cartwheels or that you finished the report?"

"Either," Rio said dryly.

Frank Grover was not a member of the Rio Walker Fan Club. Peggy had always maintained it was because Rio never filed his "damned" reports and the department had been known to fire detectives for less. Rio could have come up with lots of reasons for the animosity between him and his superior, but report writing wasn't high on the list. Their styles clashed.

Grover was by the book, and he wanted his star players to be a reflection of him. He had his disciples, but Rio with his mysterious "mojo" wasn't one of them. They'd been at odds since Rio started with the division, and when Rio began to receive departmental accolades and, worse, media attention for his work, the tension increased.

Privately, Rio suspected that the captain was threatened by more than his investigative style. It was Grover who'd blown smoke at him during the Ginger Bishop case. Rio'd had his own reasons for standing off to the side back then, but that didn't mean he hadn't been biding his time, waiting, watching, ever since.

" 'Never put off until tomorrow,' " Peggy intoned.

She was as big on proverbs as she was report writing. "Ever heard this one?" he fired back. " 'The sooner you fall behind, the more time you have to catch up'?"

Rio remained standing through the withering glare he'd provoked. Motherly scorn, he thought. If he didn't love her . . . well, it was a good thing he did.

"Do you ever tie that thing?" she grumbled, referring to the crumpled length of black silk hanging around his neck that was supposed to be a regulation tie. Grover had a dress code, and this was Rio's interpretation—jeans, a white dress shirt, and an unknotted noose around his neck. One more reason they weren't good buddies.

"Sure, but not on me," he said, checking her out with a wink. "Looks like it would just about fit your skinny neck."

Before she could retort, he filled her water glass and handed it to her. "Drink this and calm down, doctor's orders. I'm here to check up on you, babe. Make sure you're taking your medicine, minding your manners, and not frightening the nurses. Drink."

He might as well have been offering her poison. "And?" she said as she took the glass. "The reason you're really here? I know how you love hospitals."

Rio was hard-pressed to hide his admiration. He'd met his match in Peggy Sykes. She could spot an ulterior motive in a newborn infant. "I need your take on something," he admitted.

Peggy was drinking from the glass as he added, "There's been a break in the Femme Fatale case."

She nearly lost the water. "A break?" Catching the dribble with the sleeve of her wrapper, she said, "What does that mean?"

"I'm onto something, Peggy, but I can't go to Grover with this. I can't go to anyone. I need more time, something solid. It's all inductive bullshit at this point, and you know Grover, Christ. He thinks we're dealing with Helen of Troy."

"Helen of Troy?" She sniffed her disapproval this time. "The Femme Fatale isn't that big a deal, is she? If you ask me—and you *have*—I think the woman should be left alone to do her work. We can't seem to stop the bastards, so let her do it."

Rio had pulled his tie free and now he was tucking it in the back pocket of his jeans. Peggy's attitude came as no surprise. She'd worked with stalker victims in the Hollywood crimes-against-person section before she'd been transferred to RHD. No one knew the frustrations of trying to bring the offenders to trial better than she did. Still, Rio had to impress upon her that this case wasn't typical.

He lowered his voice and moved closer. "The 'her' you're referring to could be Carlie Bishop, daughter of Frances Stanfield Bishop. Name ring a bell? *Either* name?"

Now she stared at him in wonderment. "Big whoop," she murmured softly. "What have you got on her?"

Rio quickly ran down his investigation, sorry as it was. He described the criminal profiling he'd had done on the Femme Fatale and the char-

acter typing of both Carlie and Frances. Since the strike zone was Southern California, he was focusing on Carlie, but the timing and location
of the strikes didn't rule Frances out, because the Femme Fatale was
never on the scene. So far she'd picked male offenders with little of
significance in common except their penchant for terrorizing women,
and she'd prearranged the hits.

Peggy was nodding as he finished up. "You're right," she said. "It's
all bullshit. Grover would laugh you out of the office with that."

"How do I hold him off?"

She grinned. "You could have sex with him."

"Hey, I might. It's been that long."

Rio left the bed and walked to the window. Peggy wasn't telling him
anything he didn't know. Maybe he'd hoped she'd come up with a
miracle. It wouldn't be the first time, but she wasn't going to be able
to help him on this one. She had her own problems to deal with, like
staying alive in this Palace of Death by Medicine. Rio would have to
dig himself out.

He tapped the windowpane, thinking.

She spoke from the bed. "You're hunting an endangered species, my
friend. You bag a baby Bishop and there'll be hell to pay. Even if you
bring her in alive and unmarked, there'll be hell to pay. She might as
well be Chelsea Clinton or Amy Carter, Rio."

Rio stared out the window at the maze of streets, buildings, and parking structures that was UCLA's medical complex. Designed, he believed, to keep you driving in circles until you voluntarily checked
yourself into the neuropsychiatric unit. Today the scenery matched his
convoluted thoughts.

A knock at the door ended his brown study.

"We're scheduled for a transphageal echocardiogram, yes?"

Rio turned, immediately uneasy at the chirpy inflection of a woman's
voice. A warden in white bustled into the room, carrying a tray of
suspicious-looking medical hardware.

God, he hated hospitals. And cheerful nurses.

"I've got a little something to relax you," the nurse told Peggy. She
set down her tray, pulled on a pair of sterile gloves, and picked up a
syringe with a wicked-looking needle.

Sunlight struck silver, glinting brightly. Rio felt his stomach do a
back flip. On his list of preferred company, mass murderers would have
ranked higher than nurses with needles.

"Later, Peg," he said, giving the interloper a wide berth as he made
his way to the door. "Thanks for the ear."

"Where you going?" Peggy cried. "She'll only be a minute. Hang around. I could use the moral support."

"Uh . . . to write those reports."

Peggy laughed. "What? No way!"

"Enjoy the echo-whatever," Rio said, and disappeared through the door.

"You're afraid of needles, aren't you?" Peggy shouted after him. "A great big guy like you?"

Beads of sweat cooled Rio's brow as he headed for the stairway he'd come up. Of course he wasn't afraid of needles. It was too close in that room, was all. They kept this place about ninety degrees, and the way he understood it, germs proliferated in warm environments. It was a miracle every patient in the place wasn't dead.

He was still moving at a good clip by the time he reached the ground floor, but he'd had some time to think, and he realized that Peggy may have helped him more than he'd thought. She'd been right about hell to pay. He had to get his hands on something tangible, hard evidence.

But first he had to get closer, inside access.

A smile flickered as he pushed through the exit door into the bright sunshine. Inside access, he liked the sound of that.

TEN

She wanted it dark. The need for caution felt imperative. She'd told no one what she was really doing today, which made the mix of dread and excitement brewing inside her all the more potent. It also made the secret all her own. And she meant to guard it jealously. She was filled with possessiveness and purpose.

This was going to be good. The best thing she'd ever done. But first she had to light candles and call up the spirits, so to speak.

She patted around the cluttered surface of her desk with her fingertips, feeling her way. The light was dim, but the gadget she sought was hiding somewhere in the stacks of research material she'd organized around her like a paper bunker. Except for a sparkle of gold light from the hallway and the green glow of a banker's lamp on the credenza behind her, the small book-lined room she worked in looked more like a defense-industry black vault than an office. Louvered windows were shut tight against the afternoon sunshine, and the curtains were drawn.

She wanted it dark. Secrets were dark things. They were all your own, hidden where no one could take them from you. In a world where people confessed their sins on television and your privacy was compromised every time you used a credit card, secrets were power.

"There it is," she said under her breath.

Her fingernails clicked against something cool and smooth as she moved a pile of newspaper clippings. The TV remote felt alien in her hand, like a weapon. But that could be her mood. Maybe she wanted the potency of a weapon. A television set only slightly larger than a makeup-case mirror was wedged in the crowded bookshelf across the room from her. She aimed the remote and the screen crackled.

The image that appeared startled her. It wasn't the segment of tape she expected. Perhaps she hadn't hit fast forward, or the equipment wasn't working. There was no audio either, but oddly, that only made what was happening on the screen more compelling to her. She walked around the desk and stood alongside it, drawn by the silent movie, and entranced by a woman who was far too radiant and assured to be Carlie Bishop.

She was dangerously close to charismatic, that woman. She reached out to the audience with her eloquent plea for understanding. Some would have said she was too impassioned to be thought of as composed. But she was good up there, good in a public forum. It couldn't be Carlie.

Only it was. Not Ginger, not Frances in her gilded youth. This was the youngest Bishop, the "other one," as her parents had called her.

Tears filled Carlie's eyes. "Idiot," she said, but that didn't stop the flow. It always happened, this surge of emotion when she watched the tape, and it made her feel foolish. It was her first national television appearance, and the clip signified a milestone. Carlie Bishop's accidental career had brought her to a turning point, and maybe it was as simple as being accepted.

Children who grew up feeling shunned often came to expect that treatment from the rest of the world, even though they'd done nothing to deserve it. Sadly, they blamed themselves. Carlie had kept her fears to herself, but she'd actually expected disapproving stares and damning silences when she went public with her book. She'd been in utter shock when, instead of condemnation, the world had opened its arms and embraced her. She still was.

Even so, the transition had not been an easy one. For someone who'd felt invisible most of her life, it was an unnerving experience being catapulted into the spotlight. On the first round of outings, she'd been struck with paralyzing self-consciousness. She'd been unable to eat, and had actually developed a nervous tic in her lip.

She'd managed to hide the turmoil, but only because she'd been something of a natural actress in her younger years. She'd briefly turned to drama in boarding school and found it wonderfully freeing to play the part of someone else onstage. Her teacher had taken notice and encouraged her, but neither of her parents had ever come to the plays, and Carlie knew they would have been embarrassed if she'd pursued an acting career. Eminent civil service was the only appropriate path for a Bishop.

Carlie almost certainly would have quit making public appearances if it hadn't been about Ginger. She owed her sister so much, and in a way, Carlie's own transformation was part of that debt. As time passed, it was less and less an act, and eventually Carlie Bishop became the woman on the screen—one of the foremost experts in her field, respected and admired by presidents and the populace alike.

Carlie still couldn't fathom how it had all come about, unless she had a guardian angel. But Ginger would have been proud, she knew.

Carlie's pain turned bittersweet as she imagined her sister's reaction. "Look at you, Red!" Ginger would have cried, ruffling Carlie's coppery curls and hugging her breathless. "Didn't I tell you you were going to be smashing someday. Didn't I predict you'd show them all."

Ginger had said those things, repeatedly. She'd been the dreamer of the two, but her dreams had always been for her little sister. Carlie had often wondered if it was because Ginger's dreams had been determined for her before she was born. Ironically there were times when Carlie had suspected that Ginger was envious of her in some wistful way, probably of her freedom, and it had made Carlie feel sad. She hadn't known how to help her sister, and Ginger, with all her gifts, had never been able to bring herself to admit needing help.

Carlie's key chain lay in a tray lined with burgundy felt, where she also kept her watch. The facets and grooves of the carved stones had always evoked memories of her sister, some so poignant Carlie could hardly bear them. They stabbed her, but they also reminded her what she had to do. The stones were her scales and fasces, symbols of justice. A promise to bring meaning to Ginger's death.

But today the image in her mind as she picked them up was of Rio Walker's icy glare. She hadn't understood his reaction that night, and she still didn't. It could have been rage, revulsion, even fear in his eyes. But in the dark of this room, one thing was clear. He knew something about her sister, something Carlie was afraid to know.

He harbored some secret about Ginger's life and death. He might even know who killed her and why. Or think that he did. But Carlie didn't want to hear Rio Walker's secret, his confession, or whatever it was. Ginger had been the only good thing in her life, and Carlie was fiercely protective of her memory. She wouldn't allow it to be tainted by an ex-boyfriend who undoubtedly bore a grudge, maybe against the entire family.

Someone had taken her sister. All Carlie had was memories. No one would take those. No one would touch them.

She pressed the stones between her clasped palms and felt their gathering energy. Odd that Ginger had been the forager for stones when it was Carlie who'd majored in archaeology. Carlie had been gone during the months before Ginger died, away on a dig in Central America, trying to salvage her own life after the disastrous affair at college. She hadn't been there to help her sister, and unbelievably, no one in her family had told her what was going on.

Flickering lights brought her back to the present. The talk-show segment was over. Carlie picked up the remote. There was something else recorded on the cassette, a scene she'd forced herself to watch several times, almost ritualistically. That was why she'd stayed home today. Why the lights were off.

It was time to put herself through that hell again.

The tape hissed as she hit the fast-forward button.

A moment later she hit stop, then play.

The noise and gaiety of a garden party filled the screen. It was Ginger's sweet-sixteen birthday celebration, and she was surrounded by rapt teenage girls as she opened her gifts. The small white box in front of her contained a delicate gold locket, glowing with sunlight as Ginger picked it up. Delighted, she called a very shy Carlie over to help her put it on and thanked her sister profusely for the "perfect" gift.

Ginger rose from her chair to give her a hug and tell her how much she loved her. Tears sparkled in both girls' eyes. But Carlie's were dry now as she stared at the screen. She knew what was coming next.

The final shot was of Ginger's face. Flushed with pride and pleasure, she held up her locket and smiled at the camera. The image was so vivid it lingered in Carlie's mind, even as another one replaced it. This was of a terrified, disheveled woman, one Carlie hadn't recognized when she'd first discovered the segment on the tape.

The woman was bound hand and foot and lying on her side on a bed stripped to the mattress. Her hair was tangled, her eyes pleading, and her cries were cut off by the thick cloth gag in her mouth. Carlie wouldn't have recognized it as her sister if she hadn't seen the gold birthday locket around her neck.

When Carlie found the tape among Ginger's things, she'd become physically ill. She'd barely had the presence of mind to realize the police must have missed it because of the birthday-party sequence. She'd taken it to her mother, but Frances had forbidden her to call the detectives who'd investigated the case. Carlie had thought her mother was in denial. If Frances were forced to deal with Ginger's case, then she would have to deal with her death. But it had turned out to be more complicated than that. Frances had just learned she was a top contender for a Supreme Court nomination, and she feared the media frenzy she knew the tape could cause.

The prime suspect in Ginger's death had been a man Ginger herself prosecuted on charges of sexual assault and battery. When that lead didn't pan out and no other suspects surfaced, the investigation was put on hold. Frances wanted it to stay that way. Ginger was gone, and Frances didn't want her daughter's memory tainted with sordid details. He'd be caught, she'd promised Carlie, caught and dealt with harshly, but she would say nothing about how that was to be accomplished.

Carlie watched until the images dissolved in gray fuzz.

She bowed her head, listening to the static. Sick inside.

Losing Ginger was painful enough. Being forced to deal with her suffering was unbearable, and the cassette showed that someone had made Ginger's last days on earth an agony of suffering. There were newspaper articles, too, the series by Gabe Quiñones, which turned out to be a scrapbook of atrocities. Carlie forced herself to read every word. She didn't want to bury her grief, as Frances seemed willing to do. She wanted it alive, burning.

Ginger's first contact had been a whispered phone call. Four words. "Every breath you take." He'd ended every subsequent call that way, right up to the moment when he took her last breath. He'd also tormented Ginger with lines from the fables she loved. Toward the end he'd started breaking into her apartment while she slept and taking pictures of her, only he'd altered them to look as if she were in bondage, including the suspension device she'd died in. Smothered.

Carlie knew all that and more about the man who'd killed her sister. She'd subjected herself to the horrific details in order to make sense of what happened. But she hadn't succeeded. The Executioner, as he called himself, was a total enigma because Carlie couldn't understand how anyone could hurt someone as good as Ginger. Her only consolation was that one day he would have to explain the unexplainable, because she intended to find Ginger's killer if it was the last thing she did in this life, and then she was going to give him a chance to tell her why he'd hurt her sister.

It would be the last thing he would ever say.

Carlie set down the key chain, shaking. Nausea forced upward, spilling into the basin of her throat. The bathroom next to her office was pitch-black, too. She touched the walls and fixtures with her trembling fingers, feeling her way. But she didn't turn on the light.

She wanted it dark.

When the sickness went away, there would be rage. The white light that burned through her would hurt as much as the tears. But there wouldn't be any more crying. Only certainty. Purifying certainty.

Carlie wrote with the fury of a possessed poet, dashing down thoughts as they came to her, regardless of order or logic. It felt as if she were purging her soul, and she wanted to capture every word. They were tumbling through her head and out her pen, writing themselves. She could hardly keep up with them.

If the greatest crime is unnecessary pain, as Shaw said, then these bastards are criminals of the lowest order. They do violence to the mind as well as the body. They reduce their victims to hunted animals, and for that alone, they deserve—

A silvery peal of chimes interrupted her momentum, but Carlie didn't even glance up. It was the front doorbell, and she had no intention of answering it. It was almost always someone trying to sell her something, or ask directions. If she stopped writing, she would lose the flow. But the chimes sounded again and again, making it impossible to ignore them. Someone was either rude or very determined.

In her frustration Carlie hit the button on her desktop intercom. As she glanced at the clock, she realized there was a meeting of the local task-force members at her house that night and she'd ordered in dessert. It was supposed to be delivered by three!

"Chocolate to Go?" She spoke into the receiver.

"Yes, ma'am," a boyish voice came back.

"Hang on, and I'll buzz you into the foyer. Just leave the delivery there, and I'll take care of it. Thanks."

Carlie figured she had about five to ten minutes before the frozen grasshopper mousse pies started to melt. It might be enough time to recollect her thoughts. But considering the pace at which she'd been writing, there was a good chance she wouldn't be able to decipher her own scrawl.

She was reading the material through and making notes when she heard the floorboards squeak. Her hand froze on the pen, and she looked up, shocked to see someone coming down the hallway that led to her office.

"The foyer's fine," she called out. "Leave it there, and I'll come get it."

She'd thought it was the delivery boy. But when Detective Rio Walker materialized in her doorway like John Law himself, Carlie's shock turned ice-cold. She flipped shut the notebook and pulled open the center drawer of her desk to put it away.

Warning bells rang in her head.

No, Carlie. He'll think you're hiding it!

There was a tiny canister among the pens and pencils. She had it in her hand as she sprang out of the chair. Her knee hit the drawer and slammed it shut with a bang.

Rio's hands flew up defensively. "No more pepper spray! I'll go quietly."

"You got that right." Her finger was poised on the button, but he was out of range. Giving him a defiant stare, she pivoted the can, opened her mouth, and squirted. The burning sensation made her gasp. It felt as if her throat had caught fire.

He stared at her in disbelief. Only gradually did his handsome brow unknit. "Breath spray?"

"Peppermint," she informed him sweetly. "Care for a pop?"

Carlie didn't wait for an answer. She kicked back her chair and breezed right past him out the door. Her leopard-print shift blew in the gust she created, and the tendrils from her upswept hair fluttered around her face. *Draw his fire, Bellissima,* she thought. *Lure him away from the treasure map.*

It was pure bravado, a brazen bluff. She was headed for the kitchen, and if he didn't follow, Bellissima was meat sauce.

She had to get him out of that office.

Her kitchen was all buttery pools of afternoon sunshine and flowery touches, a refreshing contrast to her tomblike office. Her potted African violets were heavy with pink and purple blooms and she'd gone out that morning and cut some sunflowers for a breakfast-table bouquet. Their huge, droopy faces lit the entire room. She loved sunflowers. They were wistful, yet optimistic. Sure things are tough right now, they seemed to be saying, but they're going to get better. How can they not?

She'd brightened the room up intentionally, hoping to distract herself from the bizarre experience she'd had that morning in her own bathroom. Ironic that the fantasy had been about him, and now she was hoping her cheery little kitchen would distract him, too.

Get him in here, Carlie.

She heard another creak and turned, purposefully. "Hard to sneak up on someone who lives in an old house, isn't it?" she said.

He gazed at her from his superior height with that mystical look in his eyes she'd heard people talk about. Far away and yet right there, contemplating the flame. The flame being her.

Carlie reminded herself to breathe, much as a sculler would have chanted "pull" with every stroke. This was the very look that triggered fantasies, and she didn't want to go to that wild, desolate place again. She couldn't even ask him about the message he'd left on her machine. Love and fear were not safe topics, no matter how curious she might be.

"Not that hard," he said.

"Excuse me?"

He didn't smile, but she had the feeling he was smiling, somewhere she couldn't see.

"Sneaking up," he said. "It's not hard if that's what you want to do." He took several steps backward into the hallway, then walked toward her. Neither trip made a sound.

"Think air," he explained. "There's lots of it between us and the ground. The trick is to create a bubble."

He demonstrated again, and she was aware for the first time that his black trench coat was almost duster length and his denim jeans rode narrowly over a pair of black Adidas. The only other staple of his wardrobe was the tie, she realized. This time he wore one made of a material that was as velvety dark as his eyes, and it hung around his neck as if he'd just wrenched it loose.

Did he know? she wondered.

She didn't care about muscles or Tom Cruise grins or even great buns. But give her an unbuttoned shirt and a tie hanging loose, as if the guy wearing it was getting ready to shuck the trappings of civilization and free his soul, and she was in trouble. It was her one weakness.

Who did it?

Who sent her this man?

Someone was responsible.

"It takes a little coordination," he was saying. "The important thing is the way you place your foot."

"Fascinating." Loose tie or not, she had no intention of being taken in by Rio Walker and his sleight of foot. She couldn't even afford to like the man, although admittedly, some weak-kneed, spineless part of her wanted to. Where in the annals of law-enforcement training did it say that personnel were required to know the finer points of air-bubble espionage? Was this the new LAPD?

She thought not.

She discouraged his quizzical expression with a sharp look. He was not going to shuck that shirt and free his soul in her kitchen. He could just get used to the shackles of civilization, like everybody else. "If it's not too much to ask . . . what are you doing here?"

"The delivery boy let me in. I guess he thought I was the man in your life."

No shame. Of course he didn't have any. Why should that surprise her? If she was going to play games with this one, she would have to cool down, create that air bubble he was talking about, envelop herself with it—and let him bounce off it like a crash-test dummy.

"I use Chocolate to Go all the time," she said. "They know I don't have a man in my life. You bribed him."

That brought a wry look. "Chocoholic, hmm? We all know what that means."

She tweaked her shift, making sure the scoop neckline hadn't dropped too low. "We do not *all* know what that means. Some of us do not believe chocolate is a substitute for sex."

The *mmmmm* sound in his throat rippled with nothing but male perversity.

"Some of us think it *is* sex," she said.

Oh, baby, his rich laughter responded.

Carlie gave him a so-there tick of her head. Time he knew she wasn't born five minutes ago. She had a trick or two in her purse that even the great Rio Walker probably hadn't seen.

"Did we ever determine why you're here?" she asked.

Something about the way he hesitated told her she wasn't going to like the answer. He wandered over to her kitchen window garden for a look around. "Guess you must like flowers."

"Guess I must."

"Any of these going to be snapdragons when they grow up?" he asked, inspecting the pots of violets.

"Snapdragons are outdoor plants."

She was so cool with that one he turned around for a look at her. She gave him a wink. *Totally out of character, huh, Rio? Just keep that tie on, copper, and we'll do fine.*

She strolled over to the kitchen table, pulled out a chair, and sat down. She wasn't budging until he told her why he was there.

Apparently sensing a standoff, Rio leaned against the counter and tucked his hands in the pocket of his jeans, which made his coat flare out to the sides.

The Marlboro Man, she thought. *Who did this to me? Who sent him?*

"I'm here because of the task force," he told her. "Jim Plunkett is retiring as your law-enforcement liaison, and I'm taking his place."

"You? On *my* task force?"

"Is that a problem?"

A soft, frantic beeping sound echoed the flutter in Carlie's breast. She reached for her beeper and realized it was in her purse, which was in the office. Rio had already pulled his beeper out of his pocket.

"Can I use your phone?" he asked. "It's the department."

She nodded to the decorator "pay" phone on the wall by the door and got up to leave the room. She was going to give him some privacy, but before he was two minutes into the conversation with whoever had called, Carlie realized that it was something important. It actually sounded as if there'd been another strike by the Femme Fatale.

"South Beach, Florida?" Rio turned around to study Carlie. "That's not her zone," he said. "She's never struck outside L.A. County. Who was the victim, and how'd he die?"

Carlie was uneasy with the probing depth in Rio's gaze. She was on her way out of the room, but something in his silent expression told her not to move.

"You're kidding me. Leroy Studebaker, the world heavyweight champ? And he drowned in a Jacuzzi full of laundry detergent?" He turned his back to the wall, his legs splayed, and faced Carlie dead-on. If she'd tried to run he would have caught her before she reached the door, of that she was certain.

"And she left her calling card written in dried foam on the terrace bricks?" Rio's laughter was quick, cold. "That sounds like our girl." He glanced past Carlie at her African violets. "What about the snapdragon?"

He seemed to be repeating the details aloud in order to remember them. Or was he doing it because he knew she was listening? Carlie busied herself with unloading the dishwasher so he wouldn't see how nervous she was. Now she understood why he'd been closing in on her and trying to block all the exits. Up to this moment he had really believed she was the Femme Fatale, and this latest strike had not seemed to dissuade him.

From that realization, her mind took another turn, sharp enough to make her dizzy. Did that mean he'd been pursuing her only because she was a suspect? It had nothing to do with personal interest? That felt intolerable to her, and obviously she was crazy as a loon.

"I can't get a flight out until tomorrow," he was saying. "I've got to be in court in the morning to testify at a prelim."

Carlie could see enough of his reflection in the kitchen windowpane to know that he'd pulled a black book from his trench coat and was checking his schedule. South Beach, Florida? And he couldn't get out until tomorrow?

A dangerous impulse overtook Carlie as she listened to his travel arrangements. It was an idea so fraught with risk she could hardly believe she was considering it, but it might be the only way to accomplish her goals and offset his suspicions at the same time. Maybe Detective Walker wouldn't be the only one flying off to the Sunshine State. . . .

She was weighing the pros and cons of that possibility when another realization hit her. Her grasshopper mousse pies were melting in the foyer.

ELEVEN

Jo Emily Pough picked and sorted folks by the state of their fingernails. It was only natural given her profession. She was a manicurist by trade, and she'd learned a lot about human nature in the beauty biz. Mostly she'd learned that when hands were your livelihood, you had better heed them in the ways that counted. She didn't read palms or predict futures, but she liked to think she could read character in the condition of a cuticle or in the amount of moon showing at the base of the nail. The fuller the better, in her opinion. And she wasn't wrong all that often either.

Some of her observations were just plain common sense. Strong, well-shaped, shiny nails usually signified good character as well as good health. Moon color was important, too. White was showy, but then you had your temperament to deal with. Those clients could be difficult and demanding. Unpredictable tippers, too.

Shell pink or flesh tones were the best. A warm glow meant a kind heart, even if the nails themselves were under endowed. Jo Emily preferred that term to stubby, and in fact, stubby did not equal stingy, as some of your bow-teek manicurists thought. The blunter, rounder shapes almost always belonged to well rounded personalities, who understood the importance of good grooming and appreciated Jo Emily's efforts.

She was also the unhappy proof of her own theory, because if well-tended nails told the world how you felt about yourself, then she ought to be sitting on hers. She hadn't given herself the works, as she called a full manicure and pedicure, since she left Tennessee. She hadn't had the heart or the energy to deal with her appearance. Mostly she'd wanted to disappear.

But today all that was going to change. She had out her tools of the trade, primed and ready. She was partial to French manicures on both fingers and toes. The works. When she was done with that, and whatever other dolling up she decided to do, she had an appointment to meet that reporter fellow, Gabe Quiñones, at a nearby coffee shop and give him the interview of his ever-lovin' life.

Jo Emily had decided to tell all. Well, not quite all. There was that one thing she couldn't tell a living soul, not even Carlie Bishop or Danny Upshaw. Especially not them, though it pained her to be deceitful with folks who were being so kind and helpful to her. Still, the way she saw it, she hardly had any choice in the matter. None at all, really. Not if she didn't want to get herself in a shitload of trouble.

Meanwhile, her miracle makeover was set to take place at the kitchen table, which was actually white plastic patio furniture, complete with a bright blue sun umbrella she'd bought at a garage sale. It made her feel like she was having lunch at the beach, but that wasn't why she'd settled herself and all her paraphernalia in here today. It was the only flat surface in her studio apartment that wasn't piled high with clutter.

She'd always liked to do her thinking while she clipped and filed. Unless you had a talker for a client, it was like meditation, doing nails. One part of your mind worked on your client's problem, and the other part worked on your own.

Interesting that Jo Emily's only real problem at the moment was Danny. He'd turned back into the tongue-tied lion from *The Wizard of Oz*. She couldn't get him to talk for anything, and when she asked him outright if something was wrong, things got worse.

"Hell, no," he'd mumbled, turning as red as Congo Flame, her brightest nail polish. He'd avoided her the rest of the day, and was probably relieved that she had an interview this morning and couldn't come into work. She hadn't talked to him directly, but she'd left a message at the office.

Such a perplexing man . . .

By the time Jo Emily had reached the top-coat stage, she'd decided Danny had woman problems. Not that he didn't like them. She was pretty sure that wasn't it, based on his reaction when she was in his arms. A man's body didn't lie, and his had taken a shine to hers, no matter what he might say about it. No, there was something else bothering him, and whatever it was, he had her going. He sure did.

She grinned all over the place as she sank back in the rubbery patio chair and lifted her hands and feet in the air for inspection, as well as to let the paint dry.

"Well, if that isn't just a beautiful thing."

Naturally she'd saved the nails for last. Any self-respecting professional knew that. Otherwise you'd mess them up doing your face and hair. But Jo Emily hadn't messed these beauties up, not one little bit. They glowed with pink and white perfection. Looking at them made her feel even better than she'd thought, like a new woman, inside and out. Her hair was pretty, too. It swept around her face to her shoulders in soft, dark wings that curled forward. An egg yolk in her shampoo and the white added to the rinse had tamed its wispy fineness.

Luckily, loose jeans were in, because she'd lost weight from all the stress, and there wasn't money for new clothes. Her black cotton turtleneck was still snug and her suede boots were properly scuffed. She didn't have a full-length mirror, but she could get a sense of things by holding her makeup mirror at arm's length and tilting it up and down.

It was a good look. It worked.

"Come get me, cowboy," she whispered to no one in particular, although she was probably thinking about Danny. "I'm ready."

She removed her car keys from her purse, then fastened the latch and checked the various zipper compartments to make sure everything was secure. When you were being stalked, you started doing things like that, checking locks and latches. Through the bag's leatherlike softness, she could feel the outline of a miniature weapon. It wasn't a can of Mace or a pair of brass knuckles. It was something much worse, to her way of thinking. Jo Emily had always been terrified of guns, but she'd bought the purse-size revolver herself back in Tennessee, and then taken a course to learn how to use it. That's how desperate she'd been.

She'd waited until she got out here to buy a car, and the best she could afford was a black Camaro with gold pinstriping that was nearly twenty years old but still ran strong. She kept the car in a covered carport behind the building, but she didn't much like the setup because it was poorly lit at night and even in the daytime it was hard to get a good look around without going inside the structure.

Today she had her keys hidden in her fist with the notched end sticking through her fingers the way Danny'd been teaching her. Probably all the little precautions made her feel safer, but she couldn't imagine herself actually slugging anybody.

"Would you look at all that dust," she said, bewildered as she came up on the stall where her car was parked. She'd been assigned the space closest to the wall and there was barely enough room to get her door open, but she could see the roof and part of the hood, and it was covered with a strange, sparkly coating of silt. It was almost pretty, like fairy dust.

For some unknown reason, Jo Emily's stomach turned over, rolling with the motion of the key as she rotated it in the lock. The click of metal latch bolts made her insides jump.

Old fears were stirring in their graves, the ones she thought she'd left back in Tennessee with all her belongings and her former life. She couldn't explain it, but she didn't seem to want to open the car door. It felt as if something awful might happen if she did.

Her French manicure gleamed, each fingernail a pearl.

Carlie had told her to listen to her feelings, to take precautions if they told her she wasn't safe. Right now they were telling her to run. But something held Jo Emily there, maybe the sight of her hands, maybe her dread. Whatever it was, she couldn't run away from her fears anymore. This was supposed to have been her new start, her new life.

She squeezed the door handle. There were two more clicks, like gunshots being fired, as she opened the door.

"Oh, my God," she whispered. The fabric seats were covered with broken glass. The front windshield had been smashed in.

Jo Emily backed to the wall of the carport.

Light pierced her eyes, sharp as the shards of a shattered mirror. It pierced her memory. Someone was wailing, and the noise was awful. It sounded like the chains of her purse clanging together, but it couldn't be. Nothing could make that loud a noise. Nothing but ghosts rising from their graves.

He'd found her. He was here.

It was Gabe Quiñones who found Jo Emily Pough, and the sight of her frozen against the wall of her carport gave him a bad moment. He might be a reporter, but he was not the heartless scavenger the public had come to associate with media types. Thanks to the paparazzi, all reporters were now seen as craven and unprincipled, willing to sacrifice newborn lambs, bleating for their mamas, at the altar of a sensational story. But Gabe was honestly torn. Jo Emily *was* a sensational story, but she was also in a bad way.

"I can't stay here," she kept whispering into her cupped hands. She looked over at Gabe. "Help me, please. I have to get away from this place."

"I will," he assured her. "But I can't unless you tell me what happened."

She shook her head, unwilling—or unable—to talk. Gabe continued his cautious approach. It was going to take some time to win her confidence and get her to open up, he could tell, but he had the feeling it could be done.

When she hadn't shown up at the restaurant, he'd called and then come to her place for a look around. You never knew with a subject as jumpy as she was. Sometimes they were hiding out, half hoping you'd find them so they could unburden themselves. Most troubled souls blurted out stories that sounded like pleas for help, but Gabe had always thought of them as acts of confession. Once it was out there, and the world knew their secret, good or bad, they felt absolved and could get on with their lives. It was like a fresh start, and in that sense, he'd always thought of the story as doing a service.

Still and all, nothing got in the way of his professional instincts for long. His first reaction when he saw Jo Emily was a flash of concern, but his second was to slip his hand in his pocket and turn on his tape recorder. Only then did he approach her and ask what had happened, knowing she was in a vulnerable state and might say things she would later regret.

Gabe knew a great story. He lived for that. He knew people at their weakest and their worst, and that was when the truth came out, however sad and sordid it might be. He went after the in-depth stories of human frailty that couldn't be done on the five o'clock news.

He wasn't the flashiest writer around, but no one reveled in the hows and whys of aberrant behavior like Gabe Quiñones, and if anything explained his rapid climb up the food chain at the *Times*, it was that. He was getting accolades, but as gratifying as the recognition was, it didn't satisfy him. Nothing ever seemed to satisfy him for long. He lived with an existential ache for validation. It kept him up at night, sleepless, plotting strategies, and he blamed his restlessness on the one award that had eluded him. He hadn't bagged a Pulitzer yet. But he would. It was coming.

Gabe Quiñones's time was coming. He'd promised himself that, and as he stared at Jo Emily's pale horror in the face of her stalker's return, he knew this could be the story that would put him over the top.

He said her name when he was close enough to touch her. "Jo Emily? Are you all right? Can you talk?"

She shook her head in a tight little arc. "Not without Carlie. Could you get her for me?"

Gabe didn't want Carlie Bishop around right now. Jo Emily would undoubtedly open up and tell her everything, but Carlie, being who she was, would have the presence of mind to set some limits. She would inform Gabe it was all off the record, and he couldn't chance that.

"Hang on a minute," he said, giving Jo Emily's arm a reassuring pat. He pretended to have a look around, but it was more for show than anything else. He already knew what had happened. Any reasonably observant investigator would have spotted the glass on the floor near the front tire. The windshield had been broken out, smashed into the next millennium by some nut wielding a baseball bat.

When he turned back to her, she'd crouched in a huddle.

"Your stalker is back, isn't he, Jo Emily?" He crouched next to her, gentling his voice as if he were talking to a child. "That's who smashed in your car window." If she wouldn't open up to him, then he might get her to confirm or deny it by asking the right questions.

"He found you, didn't he? He found you and did this terrible thing. Am I right?"

Her sigh was full of hopelessness, but she nodded her head, and he took it as a sign that she might be ready to talk.

He sat down opposite her and crossed his legs. She had one leg drawn up to her body and the other folded under her, and she was wrapped around herself in a very odd way. Their knees bumped like two kids who were sharing frightening revelations and trying to comfort each other.

"Tell me about it, Jo Emily. Not what he did today. I can see that for myself. I want to know why you had to run for your life. I can help you. I *will* help you. Tell me, and then I'll call Carlie."

He reached out his hands, and after a moment she stopped clutching herself and extended hers. Her fingers were cold and stiff as icicles, but once he took hold of them and pressed them between his, she began to thaw. She didn't move or speak, and Gabe had no idea how long they sat that way. He couldn't see his watch because of the way his arm was turned, but the cement was stone cold against his ass and the garage stank of motor oil, and it felt like a damn long time.

"Help me stop him." He tried gently to break through to her. "If you tell me your story, the whole story, we can expose him for what he is. There won't be anywhere left for him to hide."

"But that's how he found me—"

"Jo Emily, it's too late. He has found you. He's here. Now help me stop him . . . please."

She began to shake. She began to cry. "I *will* stop him!"

The burst of vehemence came out of nowhere and left her white and trembling. Gabe was astonished at how strong she was. Her grip tightened on his hands until they hurt. His circulation was being cut off, but he couldn't free himself. When she finally did release him, a line of foam had formed at the corner of her mouth, and she couldn't stop the shudders that racked her.

Gabe could tell when a subject had cracked, and this one was split down the middle. She was getting ready to tell him everything. There was just one problem. He wasn't quite so certain he was ready to hear it.

* * *

Danny Upshaw had his hands full. His knee was wedged in the front office door, holding it open, his arms were piled high with boxes of brochures, and the damn phone was ringing. Normally he would have let the message center get it, but he'd been waiting all morning for a call from Carlie, and if he missed it he would be kicking himself all over the office.

She'd stayed home the day before, and there'd been a message from her when he got in this morning saying she would be out of the office the rest of the week. She'd given no explanation, except to assure him that she was fine, had "tons" to do on her new project, and would be checking in with him. Danny had been trying to reach her all morning, but she wasn't answering her phone, and that wasn't like Carlie. Worried? Yeah, he was worried.

Somehow he got his leg out of the door and made his way back to the desk, where he juggled the boxes around just enough to free his right hand and punch the speakerphone button. "Safe and Sound."

"Carlie Bishop, please."

The man's voice was vaguely familiar, but Danny was too hassled to play guessing games. "Carlie won't be in the rest of the week. Is there something I can help you with?"

"There's been an emergency."

"Just a minute!" Danny nearly dropped the boxes trying to set them down. "Is it Carlie?" he said as he punched a button and picked up the receiver. "Where is she?"

"Sorry, I don't know anything about Carlie. This is Gabe Quiñones, and I'm calling about Jo Emily Pough."

Danny fought to quiet his pounding heart and reorient his thinking. Jo Emily? The office was suffocatingly hot, and the back of his neck was wet, but he couldn't spare the concentration to wipe it away. She'd called in earlier saying she had an interview that morning. She hadn't mentioned who with, but it must have been Quiñones.

"Somebody smashed the windshield of her car," Quiñones went on. "She's pretty upset about it, and I don't think she ought to be alone."

"Is she all right?" Danny's voice fell so low it could hardly be heard over his breathing.

Quiñones assured him she was fine and went on to explain that someone had vandalized her car and that he'd found her in the carport in near shock. By the time he was through, Danny's chest was a vise grip. "Who did it?" he asked.

"Dunno. She thinks it's the same guy who was stalking her back in Tennessee." Quiñones paused, sniffed. "Looks like he found her."

Sonovabitch, Danny thought, meaning Quiñones. Sonovabitch! If the reporter had been within reach, Danny would have snapped his skinny neck. Normally Danny kept his temper on a tight leash, but this time the violence felt good. It felt right. It made him insane to think that Quiñones could be so fucking casual about something like this.

"Tell her I'm coming over," Danny told the reporter as he hung up the phone. *And you, mister, had better be good and goddamn gone by the time I get there.*

Danny was still smoldering as he closed up the office and got ready to leave. He wanted to hit somebody, shake some teeth loose, do a little damage, maybe a lot. He was in a rage, and he wasn't even sure why. He'd already done the math. A romantic relationship between him and Jo Emily was about as likely as the sun going out. Maybe this was about his frustration as much as it was about her safety. He didn't know. The only thing he was sure of at the moment was that he didn't want her having to depend on that cocky bastard Quiñones for anything.

TWELVE

"Oh, you *are* a policeman. And just look at that badge. What a wicked piece of jewelry that is."

The hotel clerk glanced up from his inspection of Rio's credentials with a smirk that was vaguely startled.

It was Rio's business to be good with details, but it wasn't the clerk's plump, cherubic features or even his shaved head and heavily plucked eyebrows that registered. It was the jewelry he wore. A narrow gold bar engraved with the word TRAINEE, was pinned to the khaki pocket of his official Hotel La Trouvaille jacket.

Rio hadn't decided whether that was good news or bad.

"I'll only need a few minutes in the room," he assured the kid, who was already shaking his shiny bald head.

"I'm sorry, sir, I thought you understood."

"Understood what?" Rio wasn't trying to book a room. This was one of Dade County's most expensive hotels. The main lobby had enough marble on its floors to have emptied Europe's quarries and as much crystal in its chandeliers. Big words like opulent wouldn't have covered it. And neither would his paycheck for the next two years.

Rio had known he was in trouble when his taxi pulled up at a block-long crimson canopy and a team of liveried doormen had appeared. Not that he had any choice in the matter. He was here to investigate the alleged South Beach Femme Fatale strike, and while the hotel had not been the scene of the crime, the victim, Leroy Studebaker, had been booked in its Presidential Suite.

"That room has already been searched and cleared for occupancy, sir. I can't let you up there now."

"Five minutes," Rio said. "It's official police business."

"Sir!" The clerk was getting exasperated. "The suite has a waiting list. The South Beach police and the FBI were here *yesterday*. They released the rooms at our request, and we booked them immediately."

"The suite is occupied?"

"There's someone in there, yes."

Rio should have expected this. He'd been notified of the body's discovery yesterday while he was at Carlie's, but he'd had a court appearance this morning and hadn't been able to catch a flight until after lunch. He'd coordinated the trip with the South Beach detective assigned to the case, and should have asked him to hold the room open another day. He could have brought some official pressure to bear, if he'd thought about it. But there'd been other things on Rio's mind. Other things being Carlie Bishop.

"Is there a problem?"

Another clerk came over, properly imperious, and clearly intending to make short work of the ruffian with the undone tie. The gold bar on his chest said MANAGER, and Rio was half tempted to give him something to manage. Police matters tended to make hotel guests nervous, so naturally the brass tried hard to keep that kind of unpleasantness under wraps. The irony was that most of the hotel's customers probably weren't aware of the crime, much less that the victim had been staying there. But Rio could change that. Fast.

"Be a shame to cordon off the entire ground floor of this hotel," he said, glancing around the place as if he were measuring it for yellow tape.

The manager struck like a snapping turtle. "And what *is* your point?"

Rio shrugged. "The way I hear it the victim was seen right here in this lobby with a prime suspect. They hit the restaurant, the bar, the gift shop—"

"Who told you that?" The trainee pointed at himself in mock horror. "I never said that!"

"What's your point?" Rio ground out through clenched teeth, aware that a curious crowd was forming. "Police get tipped all the time. There's a Femme Fatale hotline going around the clock."

The manager worried his tie at the knot. He pulled the trainee into a huddle, whispered something, and then sent the kid back to deal with the ruffian.

Rio had them. They were going to give him access to the suite, but ironically, he no longer wanted it. He'd already begun formulating another plan of attack when he saw there was going to be trouble. Door Two was risky as hell, but could pay off big if it worked. Besides, he was in no mood to play any more games with these bozos.

"We could call the guest," the clerk offered with a small sigh. "If you insist—"

"Forget it, cue ball," he told the kid, then fished a twenty from his pocket and tossed it onto the counter. "Rogaine. Grow some hair."

He tucked his badge in an inner pocket of his coat and cast the two of them a look that put their membership in the human race into question. Apparently they shared the sentiment. They were staring at him like he'd just landed an alien spacecraft on the roof of their multi-storied hotel.

Rio refrained from shouting "Drop to the floor and kiss marble!" as he walked through the crowded lobby. However, he did find the need to adjust his shoulder holster, which caused quite a stir. One of the security guards panicked and drew his weapon, and there was little Rio could do at that point but pull out his badge and identify himself.

"Police?" a fashionably dressed woman said faintly as she hugged her purse to her breasts. "I didn't know they allowed them in here."

Like big hotels the world over, La Trouvaille had more than one entrance, as well as a service elevator nearby, hidden away from public view. Rio made quick and dirty use of both. It took a special key to get to the penthouse floor, but he'd come personally equipped with an unusual way to pick locks.

He used a tactical knife and a technique called echolocation that he'd picked up from years of living with his maternal grandfather, a cabinetmaker who lost his sight to diabetes and ended up on disability while still a young man.

In order not to be dependent on either canes or Seeing Eye dogs, Rio's grandfather had learned to find his way around and locate objects by using clicks of his tongue. The sound waves he created bounced off objects and resonated differently depending on how close the object was. This uncanny ability to see things by "hearing" them had so captured Rio's imagination that he'd spent a good part of his childhood wandering around in the dark, practicing.

He'd gotten good enough to own the blindman's bluff title, and it had made him an oddity as a kid and a legend as a detective. His other senses had been enhanced as well. He could identify fibers and foreign substances by touch, and blood by its smell. But those abilities he'd kept to himself. The echolocation was more difficult to hide.

The first case that earned him national notice was the sensational broad-daylight kidnapping of a movie producer's daughter. Rio was part of a multiagency task force, composed of the very best investigative minds. He was the rookie, but when all the traditional efforts had been exhausted, it was Rio who found the child, buried alive in her own backyard.

Subsequent cases brought Hollywood on the run with offers. His Indian heritage was touted in the press, much to his displeasure. First, they wanted him to star as himself, and when he'd said no, they asked him to consult. He hadn't said no to some of the starlets that came his way. Maybe he should have.

That period of his life was fast-lane stuff—flashy, fleeting, and ultimately unsatisfying. He couldn't work, or live, in a fishbowl, and he sure as hell couldn't explain what he did. He didn't understand it himself. He'd quickly realized that where show business was concerned, detective work was safer. He still believed that, except for situations like this when it seemed the only way to enforce the law was to break it.

Rio didn't know exactly how echolocation had worked for his grandfather, but for him it was like ultrasound, creating pictures on some inner screen of his mind that no one else could see. As in the kidnapping case, he'd been known to find hidden bodies, dead or alive, stashed murder weapons, identifying objects, even shell casings.

He could also pick locks. With the frequency and amplitude of the sound he made, he could often "see" the internal workings of the mechanism. That told him what kind of device it was and how to free the bolt.

Elevators and locked suites were no-brainers. The risk came once he got inside. There was no way to know what he'd be dealing with, and in this case, it didn't seem likely the occupants would be in bed at nine P.M., unless they were newlyweds, in which case he could use a battering ram and they probably wouldn't notice. He doubted he would get that lucky, but there was always the possibility they'd gone out.

The hotel was old but elegant, with sky-high ceilings and hallway floors as creaky as Carlie Bishop's. Rio felt like he was in an English garden maze as he took corridors that intersected at odd angles with no apparent architectural logic. Even his internal guidance system was scrambled by the time he found the suite.

Luckily the rest of it was clockwork. In fact, the lock opened so easily that he hesitated, suspicious. It wasn't the sense that he was walking into a trap as much as that someone was waiting for him. Maybe they even knew he was coming. It seemed unlikely, but the management could have notified the occupants that someone wanted to search their room.

Rio was going in regardless. The department would be yanking him back to L.A. in the next day or two, and this was his one shot. Frank Grover had surprised him by doing an abrupt about-face on the Femme

Fatale investigation. The captain was now suggesting that Rio back-burner it.

"She's *already* Helen of Troy," Grover had said when he dropped by Rio's desk that morning. "Let's wait this out, give her enough rope to hang herself."

They'd both laughed as if he were joking, but Rio knew he wasn't. Law enforcement was the convenient whipping boy when high-profile cases were perceived as bungled, and LAPD had taken its hits. If the Femme Fatale tripped and fell into their laps, it took the pressure off everyone.

The Presidential Suite was dark when Rio entered, and there didn't appear to be anyone in the narrow foyer as he moved through it into the living room. He hesitated, listening with his eyes closed, letting the pictures form in his mind. There was nothing but shadows at this point.

Human movement was different. The weight of their bodies and the warmth of their breathing created perturbations not unlike the ticking of clocks and the pop of expanding or contracting natural objects like wood or metal. A sense of satisfaction crept into his mood, mixing with the anticipation he felt. It was almost sexual, definitely male in nature. Maybe he *was* going to get lucky. He was picking up nothing that said he wasn't alone, at least in the immediate area. He began to navigate the spacious room, knowing he had to concentrate totally and move decisively. If the guests were out, they could come back at any time.

Normally he picked up on hidden weapons, personal objects, contraband, anything that might have been stashed or left behind by accident. But this wasn't a crime scene, and the place had already been searched by the SID unit and cleaned by the hotel housekeepers. The best Rio could hope for was that they'd missed a clue that would tell him something about the victim's contacts and any visitors he might have had.

From what Rio had been told, the champ, as the press was now calling the slain boxer, was a notorious ladies' man. But he was also a health nut who avoided alcohol and "toxic" foods, which probably ruled out a drug-related death. Tomorrow Rio would meet with the investigative team and go over the crime scene. An autopsy was still in progress, but a visit to the medical examiner could yield some information.

Rio hesitated in front of a cloth-draped occasional table. He crouched down and swept the area with his hand. It had felt as if he were about to step on something, but there didn't seem to be anything on the carpet but folds of heavy cloth, the tapestry that covered the table. What he was "seeing" looked like a solid object that was caught within the folds.

A moment later he was holding the unlikely looking "weapon" in a piece of tissue and studying its narrow, cylindrical length. Heavy drapes blocked the light, but Rio's eyes had already adjusted, and there was enough illumination to see that it was a tree branch or a flower stalk.

Interesting, he thought. Echolocation had its limits. The technique required a certain amount of mass or a metallic substance to bounce the waves, and small porous objects like branches tended to absorb sound. But something had stopped him.

Cold steel dug into the back of his neck, and a woman's voice hissed at him.

"This isn't pepper spray, asshole. It's a fucking gun barrel! Don't move unless you'd like a bullet through the brain."

"Thanks for asking nicely."

A hollow pop echoed in his ears. Light seared his retinas and every nerve ending in his scalp caught fire. Not a gunshot, he realized. A spotlight in the ceiling had come on. Several more pops flooded the room with color and detail.

He could see his assailant in the gilded mirror that hung above the table. She'd meant it about the gun. Carlie Bishop had him dead to rights. He could forgive her for that. He could even admire her for that. But she was going to pay for scaring the bejesus out of him.

"Put that goddamn thing away." He stared her straight in her frosty green eyes, drilled her until she blinked. At the same time he set the flower stalk alongside the table where it couldn't be seen. "You're making me nervous."

"That is the point," she informed him.

She tossed her head, silky hair flying, and Rio thought of wild horses—beautiful, wild, untamable horses. An entire fantasy in living color passed before his eyes as he stared into hers. He'd never broken a horse, but he'd seen enough westerns to know the concept, and he would have loved nothing better than to break this one for riding. Every sweet and nasty thing a man could do to a tempestuous woman, he would do to her. Twice.

He saw her blink, and knew that she knew. If she thought for a second that he couldn't knock that gun out of her hand, send it flying, and pin her to the wall with his body—for a second that he couldn't handle her. Well, she thought too long.

Tame her? Maybe not, but he could handle her. He could do that just fine.

"Turn around," she said, taking a couple of steps away from him. "I don't like the idea of shooting a man in the back."

"That's a comfort."

She jabbed him with the gun.

Pushing your luck, sweetheart, he thought.

But he turned. Taking his damn sweet time about it, he turned and saw the black satin nightshirt she was wearing, and the long, sleek palomino-gold legs it revealed. Letting his eyes drift down to the floor, he also saw the bare feet and hot red nail polish. Sexy.

Could be his heart was beating a little harder. Could be, but he didn't want her to know it. Could also be there was that deep gush of feeling in his groin that tells a man he's not going to get much sleep that night, unless . . .

"What are you doing here?" he asked her.

"Getting ready to ask you the same question."

This was a woman who could piss a man off. "Let me be more specific. I'm here on a murder case. What are *you* doing in Leroy Studebaker's room?"

She seemed to be taking a deep breath and thinking. Thinking and breathing.

"Question too tough?" he asked.

She chilled him with her eyes. Chilled him like the frost in a lime-green Sno-Kone.

"Okay," she said at last. "I want to tag along while you investigate the Femme Fatale case." Ignoring his grunt of surprise, she plunged right ahead. "I won't get in the way or ask questions or bug you. I just want to observe."

"Why?"

Like a clever politician, she didn't answer. She pressed home her point instead. "If you agree to let me observe, I won't report you for breaking and entering. Deal?"

"Report me? For breaking and entering?"

"Well, you did, didn't you? I don't remember letting you in. And when I realized there was someone in the suite, I pressed the panic button. Hotel security's probably on the way right now."

"Jesus—"

She spoke the truth. Rio was cut off midstream by a half-dozen very officially uniformed thugs, who didn't bother to knock. The doors crashed open and they barged in, all of them carrying weapons.

At a command from their leader, they spread out in something resembling SWAT formation and started to close in on what must have looked to them like an ugly scene. The only thing that stopped them was the sight of Carlie's gun.

"Which one of you called security?" a burly guard with gray buzz-cut hair demanded. He was the one barking out the orders.

"I did," Carlie said. "But it's okay now. I know it doesn't look okay, but it is."

Not terribly persuasive, Rio thought. She was going to have to do better than that.

The big guy wasn't buying it either. "Are you sure, miss?" He gave Rio a look that pronounced him the worst fiend of the twentieth century. "Did he try to hurt you?"

Carlie set the gun aside, and then she gave Rio a look, too. This one said, Make up your mind, buddy. Do we have a deal or do I turn you over to these ex–death-row guards, who already think you're a rapist and worse?

She had him by the short ones, Rio conceded. The boys downstairs weren't likely to cut him any slack after the little contretemps at the desk. They'd probably call the South Beach police and demand he be picked up like some delinquent kid. That was assuming, of course, that Carlie didn't press the breaking-and-entering charge. If she did—

Rio gave her one curt nod. Deal, it said. You've got your frigging deal.

"I'm fine!" Carlie trilled to the squad leader. "Really, it's just a little game we play. Sorry you had to come all the way up here."

"Game . . . ?" The leader looked perplexed, then suspicious.

Rio saw his chance for some payback. "My fiancée," he said, strolling over to Carlie before she could object or otherwise do anything to stop him. "Gotta love the little fiend." He slipped an arm around her waist and hugged her close.

Carlie stiffened, but didn't say a word.

Several of the men were trying to hide smiles. The leader seemed to be waiting for Carlie to confirm, which, of course, she had to do. "Gotta love me," she said through clenched teeth.

She broke away from Rio and walked to the double doors, beckoning the guards to follow. "Thank you for responding so quickly," she said, her fingers at the lapel of her nightshirt, fluttering, checking buttons. For the first time she seemed to be aware that she was wearing sexy lingerie for an audience of highly appreciative men.

"I feel much safer now," she told them, "but I really am fine. *We* really are fine, and—"

"We'd like our privacy," Rio finished for her.

She glared at him, smiled at them, and swung open the double doors. Her meaning was obvious. The guards filed out and she waved good-bye as she closed the place up behind them, then immediately secured the bolt lock.

Rio was still across the room, and the branch he'd set down was on the Oriental carpet near his feet. Only it wasn't a branch, it was a flower stalk. Snapdragons. Red ones.

Carlie collapsed against the door, her head falling back. "You can go in a minute," she said, allowing herself only a brief respite. With a sigh of relief, she opened her eyes. "Give them time to get back to wherever security goes in this hotel."

But Rio had already taken off his coat and thrown it on the nearest chair. Now he was loosening the buttons on his shirt. He didn't have to mess with his tie. It was already undone.

"What are you doing?" she asked.

"Staying," he said in an ultrasoft voice.

"No—"

"Carlie," he said with such authority she hushed. "Don't ever think those guys aren't keeping an eye on this place. As we speak they're gathered around a video monitor, glued to the screen, and the hidden security camera they're watching is trained on this suite. Yeah, I can just see them now, grinning like a bunch of guys at a stag party, hoping they're going to get a show."

She knew immediately that he was telling the truth. She didn't claim to be a security expert, but she was supposed to know about personal safety.

"You sleep out here on the couch," she said.

He just grinned. He had her, and God, how he loved the feeling. It was his turn. She'd come after him with pepper spray, breath freshener, and now a gun. "I think you and I have some negotiating to do."

He stepped back and offered the couch with a wave of his arm. "Maybe you'd like to get comfortable? I'm going to."

She crossed her arms and gave him the eat-dirt-and-die stare.

"And by the way, care to explain this?" he said as he reached down and picked up the foliage lying at his feet.

"I don't care to explain any—" And then she saw what he had in his hand.

Earlier that morning . . .

"En garde!" Frances cried. Sensing weakness, she took the offensive and launched a direct attack. Her partner tried desperately to parry her cuts and slashes, but he was clearly outmatched. Frances fenced as she did everything else—to win. With sabers it was a game of attack and counterattack in furious succession, and she gave no quarter. She wasn't clever or elegant. She was aggressive, fast. It was all she needed to be to quickly eliminate the flagging opponent who'd been foolish enough to take up a saber against her that morning.

Lights flashed and buzzers sounded as the winning touch was made. Frances pulled off her mask and her opponent did the same, saluting her with his weapon. His bowed head conceded her superior skill, but Frances wouldn't hear of such humility. She generously congratulated him on a great game and insisted on a rematch when he was in fighting shape again, implying that his recent bout of flu must have dulled his reflexes.

After all, he was a United States senator.

Frances often invited Washington's elite to thrust and parry in the small gymnasium she'd had built into the ground floor of her Georgetown brownstone. She didn't always beat them so soundly, though. She and Jack Grant went back a long way.

"Fran, you're wasted on the Supreme Court," he told her as they removed their protective gear. Sweat glinted off his lean, patrician features, confirming that he was still a handsome man in his sixties. "Quit that silly job and run for president. We need you in the executive branch."

"I'd make a terrible president, Jack, and you know it! I'm an outspoken old bag who never learned to lie. I doubt certain members of Congress would like having their heads bitten off and spit out before breakfast."

Ironically, it was all true except that part about the lying. She'd had to tell some whoppers in her time in order to save her career and her reputation, and Jack had been there for the worst of it. Her very way of life had been at stake, and it was this man, the senior senator from California, who had come to her aid. The third woman to sit on the Supreme Court might have been sitting in jail now, if it weren't for Jack Grant.

On the other hand, Jack most certainly would not be a senator if it hadn't been for Frances Stanfield Bishop. She'd used her influence as well as her name to get him out of some nasty scraps, including sexual-harassment charges brought during his first mudslinging run for the Senate.

The two of them were former law-school cohorts and lifelong friends. Frances had known Jack since their carefree earliest childhood days, when he'd been the Stanfield's paperboy and a charmer of an English lad, bent on being president when he grew up. She'd been a gawky dreamer, whose idea of perfect happiness was to navigate a river on a raft, like Huck Finn. Obviously, neither had seen their fond visions come to life, but they'd formed an unspoken pact along the way, based on admiration for each other's spunk and determination.

Frances had once wondered how a romance might have changed things between them, but their relationship had never taken that turn. She'd fallen madly in love with someone else in college, and Jack had been there to help pick up the pieces when it fell apart. Eventually Jack had married his campaign manager, a rather strident woman, in Frances's opinion, but one who, nevertheless, loved him dearly.

Sadly, these days Frances's relationship with Jack seemed to be based on mutual need as much as friendship. But if she trusted anyone in Washington, it was he. She'd turned to him when the investigation of Ginger's death went awry, and he had brought his considerable influence to bear. But even Jack didn't know the real reason Frances had wanted the case quietly shelved rather than solved. There was no one she would have trusted with that information. No one. Not even Bernard.

Her late husband's death had been tragically premature. He'd been cut down in his mid-fifties by a massive heart attack, but Frances was actually grateful he hadn't lived to see what had happened to Ginger. Better a heart attack than to be destroyed by the thing you loved best in life, and Bernard had loved his daughter without reservation.

He wouldn't have had the stomach for it, Frances knew now. Bernard couldn't have endured the horror of Ginger's ordeal, or what Frances had had to do to salvage the Stanfield-Bishop name in the aftermath. Bernard had never had her drive, or her nerve. Not that he wasn't a good man in many ways, but all of his hopes had been pinned on Ginger, as had Frances's at one time. Now Frances wondered if that wasn't where the very seeds of destruction had been sown, their grand dreams and schemes for Ginger's future.

Yes, Frances was glad Bernard was gone, but sometimes she did regret that her husband of thirty years hadn't lived to see her sitting on the high court. That might have pleased him. It might have pleased him very much.

Frances was going gray. It had come as quite a shock when she stood in front of the vanity mirror that morning, readying herself for the match with Jack. She hadn't known quite what to make of it, so she'd tucked the graying strands of her dark hair back into the sleek bun she always wore and forgotten all about it. Now she smoothed back those same strands, aware that Jack was studying her.

"The gray is striking, Fran," he said. "You know that, don't you? It makes you all the more remarkable."

Gratitude rose so swiftly it hurt her throat. Her voice thinned as she spoke. "And you know that I'm indebted."

"For the compliment?"

"For everything, Jack. My God, what would I do without you?" They both knew what she was talking about. She'd had to call on him again last week with another request to pull some strings, and as always, he hadn't refused her.

Now they were about to part ways, he to the gymnasium's shower, she to her own bathroom upstairs, and he reached for her hand with genuine affection. It should have made her feel as if someone cared after all these years. She'd had little enough of that in her life, but oddly, it made her feel terribly lonely. Nostalgia washed over her in soft waves, not for the way her heart had gone, but for the way it might have gone. She hadn't felt anything quite so poignant in years. She wouldn't have indulged it this morning, except that it was more comforting now than hurtful.

Comforting? She wanted to laugh. She could remember when these same feelings had felt as if they would destroy her, though it hadn't been Jack who'd triggered them then. Maybe that meant she was getting old. Certainly it meant she could never go back. Bitterness had been her mainstay all this time, and the emotion she was most comfortable with. Not the deep, acrimonious bitterness that turns a woman into a shrew. Hers had been the spur that drove her in another direction, away from the pitfalls of emotional involvement. Experience had taught her there wasn't a man living who deserved her tender feelings, certainly not the one she'd loved in vain all those years ago. Not even Bernard, her devoted mate.

Life was simply safer when you stuck to business, she reminded herself. How many people ever had the opportunity to have an impact on millions of lives, *hundreds* of millions? This was hers.

"Is there something wrong, Fran? You seem pensive."

"I'm fine, Jack," she said. "You know me, always writing the opinion that will secure my place in history."

His expression was fondly tolerant. He knew better than most about her visionary goals. At least she'd never had to keep those a secret. Shared priorities was one of the many things they had in common, that and a belief that ends did justify means when there was some greater good involved.

"You would tell me if something was wrong, wouldn't you? Is it Carlie?"

She dismissed the question, only now the bitterness rose to the surface. It was evident in her voice. "What could be wrong with Carlie? She's a bestselling author now, didn't you know?"

"Frances—" He sounded beleaguered, perhaps because he'd made this argument before. "You have to let kids go their way, even if you don't approve. Carlie's in a position now to do a lot of good, and you're partly responsible for her being there."

"Don't I know," she snapped. "And don't I regret it."

Not all of Frances's string pulling had been on her own behalf. She'd known for some time of Carlie's desire to start a task force, and Frances had been trying to help the cause by discreetly taking it to the top, to the people who could get something done. The result had been the presidential appointment, although Carlie knew nothing about Frances's involvement.

But Carlie's book hadn't come out then, and Frances hadn't realized there would be such a fuss over it, or a national media tour. Frances had watched the talk shows, probably all of them thanks to her clerk, Julie, and she had cringed at the questions about Ginger's life and death, and of course, the inevitable questions about Ginger's mother, who sat on the Supreme Court. And there was Carlie, herself, baring not just her own soul, but the collective family soul. Where was the Stanfield sense of dignity and propriety? Carlie had been taught better.

"Such a strange, difficult child, that one," Frances murmured. "Not at all predictable."

Jack sighed. "What's the poor kid done now?"

"Oh, nothing, nothing." She waved him toward the shower door, knowing they would argue if she continued. "Go make yourself presentable, Senator. Don't you have a *Meet the Press* taping this morning?"

He checked his watch, thanked her for reminding him, and headed off to get ready, leaving Frances alone with her worries. It would have sounded trivial to him, but she hadn't been able to reach her daughter, and that had her greatly concerned. Carlie hadn't returned her calls, and it was imperative that Frances speak to her soon, before Carlie blundered into things she knew nothing about. Potentially deadly things.

The solution came to Frances on her way upstairs. It was very simple, really. If Muhammad wouldn't come to the mountain, then the mountain would get herself on a plane.

The morning papers were waiting for her when she got to her bedroom on the third floor. She'd planned to take a shower before she did anything else. Fencing was a vigorous workout and she was still overheated, but one of the newspaper headlines caught her eye. FEMME FATALE K.O.S WORLD CHAMP?

Frances sat down at her desk, aware of the drone of her housekeeper's television playing next door. Louise was addicted to soaps and game shows, which Frances didn't wholeheartedly approve of, but given the dearth of good help, anything short of heroin addiction would probably have been acceptable. Frances had asked Louise specifically to pick up *The Miami Herald* for her this morning, and it was sitting on top of the pile.

Frances read the Femme Fatale article with interest. The writer gave herself away as a fan when she praised the perpetrator's "poetic cleverness," and Frances quite liked that reference.

She went through the rest of the papers quickly, stopping only to read the *L.A. Times*'s feature article about Carlie's support group. She didn't disapprove of Carlie's work. It *was* an important service, and in that respect, she was proud of her daughter, but that was no reason to involve the family.

She was putting the paper away when she noticed a sidebar article about one of Carlie's group members. It was a horrific story about a young woman who claimed she'd had to go on the run to escape her tormentor. But it wasn't that aspect of the story that caught, and held, Frances's attention.

"What is this?" she whispered, reading on.

Frances was going to be late for that morning's conference with her colleagues. Normally she would have been in her chambers by now, preparing, but she hadn't even begun to dress yet. The paper was on her lap, crumpled under her hands, but the words raced madly through her head. The victim wasn't named, but her story was uncannily familiar.

" 'Every breath she takes.' " Frances's voice was hushed with disbelief. It was, word for word, what Ginger's stalker was supposed to have said. How could that be possible?

It wasn't possible.

Sounds of laughter and applause came from the next room. Some call-in contestant had answered the trivia question right and won a ridiculous prize. Suddenly that was all Frances could hear, braying laughter and clapping hands.

Deplorable, the lack of goals, the shoddy work. No one cared about anything anymore. Where were the standards, the values? What was happening to this country when its citizens aspired to nothing more than winning trivia contests?

Staring at the newsprint crumpled in her hands, Frances wanted to shake her head in despair. She had a couple of choices, but she couldn't seem to bring herself to do anything. She could call Carlie and rail at her for exploiting her sister's death to sell books. Surely Carlie would stop then, whether the accusation was true or not. Or Frances could call the man who'd written this story and reintroduce herself to Gabriel Quiñones. He couldn't have forgotten her. They'd had quite an intense relationship once. He was, after all, the one who'd done the investigative piece on Ginger's death.

It took her some time to snap the wrinkles out of the paper, fold it, and drop it into a file for safekeeping. She would read it again, later, and commit every word to memory. Every vile word. Meanwhile she had a phone call to make.

Danny found her in the bedroom of her apartment, but she was sitting on the floor, hidden behind the open door.

"Joey?" he said. He knelt beside her, not sure why he'd called her by that name, just heartsick at the sight of her.

"I'm all right," she insisted. She even raised her hand as if to stop him from making a fuss over her.

Danny wasn't sure what to do then. He couldn't help but notice the polished nails and the softly curled hair. She looked beautiful. Shell-shocked, but so beautiful he was at a loss, especially if she didn't want him near her.

"Why are you here on the floor?" he asked.

"I don't know—" She looked up at him in confusion, perhaps noticing where she was for the first time. Now she was fighting not to cry, and the whimper that caught in her throat cut through any prayer he might have had of holding back.

"Come here," he said. "Just come here, dammit."

He scooped her into his arms and she fell against him in a sighing heap. He could feel her desperation, but there was relief mixed in, too. She might not trust him totally—and maybe she had reason—but for now he was all she had.

All she had. His heart ached as he held her. He was all she had in the world. He would have bargained his soul for that to be true.

She tried to tell him what had happened, how she'd found her windshield shattered, but it wasn't coming out right, and Danny couldn't concentrate on the details anyway. All he could think about was how good she felt in his arms. And how much it hurt him to acknowledge that. It wasn't right that he should let himself need this. It wasn't fair to either of them. That's why he hadn't wanted to come over here. But of course he'd had no choice.

"He f-found me," she said. "He hunted me down and now he's going to kill me, just like it says on those awful bumper stickers. You seen those s-sicko things?"

Danny shushed her, fighting a despairing grin. Who else could have made him smile in a situation like this, and she didn't even realize she'd done it. "Maybe it wasn't him. Kids smash car windows all the time."

She looked up, her face streaked with tears and blinking disbelief. How could you be so silly, Danny boy? she seemed to be saying. "There aren't any kids in this complex."

"No kids?"

"Says so everywhere you look. Big ol' signs."

"Oh, Jo—" He couldn't get out the rest of it. He wanted to tell her how funny and precious she was, but this wasn't the time. And even if it had been, there wasn't any way to do it without sounding ridiculous. He'd never met anyone like her, so full of hope and hopeless at the same time.

His shirt was a wrinkled mess from all the crying she'd done. He was wet everywhere, but he couldn't remember feeling anything sweeter than her tears.

"I brought you something," he said, fishing a pack of Dentyne gum out of the dampness that was his chest pocket. "I thought it might help."

"Oh, would you look at that. My brand."

She plucked it from his fingers, struggling to get the tightly wrapped package undone. For someone in her state it was like peeling an onion with boxing gloves, so Danny did it for her. He broke open the pack, unwrapped a piece, and popped it into her mouth.

"Thank you," she said between blissful chews. Her gaze was adoring. "This is just the sweetest thing, your bringing me gum. You know that, don't you? I don't know how to thank you."

She quickly thought of a way. She threw her arms around his neck and gave him a gentle, cinnamon-sweetened kiss, not quite on his lips.

The brush of her mouth made Danny feel as if he were in outer space and his stomach was hurtling toward Earth. He wanted this so badly, this kiss, this woman.

His sigh was hard and quick. And painful.

Why was God tormenting him like this, sending him something he could never have? He took her arms from around his neck and gave them back to her, then pushed himself up from the floor. When he was on his feet, he offered her a hand.

"Are you going somewhere?" she asked.

It didn't seem to occur to her that she'd been rejected again, and he was grateful for that. No one rejected an injured bird. His heart tugged at the thought. Certainly not one with such lovely dark plumage and bright, sad eyes.

"I was going to get you something," he said.

"What?"

"Some tea, maybe? Hot tea? I'll see what's in the kitchen. Why don't you curl up over there in that blue comforter with the clouds on it."

He was pointing to a full-size bed with more clothing heaped on it than he had in his entire closet. A sky-blue comforter afloat with fluffy white clouds could be seen peeking out from under the piles.

"I'd rather stay down here," she said in a small voice.

There was a tug on his hand. Apparently she wanted him to stay down there with her, too.

"Sure thing, Jo Emily, I'll get the tea and we'll have it on the floor."

There was a booby trap behind Danny, but he didn't see it until he turned and nearly fell into the overflowing laundry basket. The only thing that saved him was quick footwork and the rubbery plastic material, which *boinged* back from his assault and then bounced away like an inner tube, spilling towels, linens, underwear.

"Are you all right?" she asked as he peeled a pair of her panties from the leg of his jeans and bent to pick up the rest of what had flown from the basket.

"I'm fine, but what happened in here?" For the first time Danny looked around and saw the condition of her apartment. Apparently she'd never unpacked and was living out of boxes, but it looked like the boxes had been upended and emptied on the floor, if there was a floor. It was hard to tell.

"Did he vandalize the place?" Danny asked, meaning her stalker.

"No, of course not." She seemed genuinely surprised at his question as she glanced around the room, and finally she dismissed it with a perplexed shrug. "I guess some of us weren't born with enough of the 'Tidy Bowl gene.'"

She was the vandal. He should have known. "Will you be okay while I go to the kitchen? I won't be long."

He was freed by her nod, but didn't make it out the door. Her soft, inquisitive twang stopped him on the threshold.

"Know what I need, Danny?"

"Tea?" he asked hopefully.

She was clutching herself as if she were cold, so he went to get the comforter, wondering why he hadn't thought of it before.

"Not that," she said as he began to dig through the layers on her bed. "I'm frightened. Still."

Her back was pressed to the wall and she'd drawn her legs up. Now she began to inch upward, wobbly but determined, and still tightly holding herself. He felt compelled to help her, but something told him not to. This was a test of some kind, and she wanted to do it on her own.

Her struggles pained him, especially when he saw that she wasn't going to make it. Halfway up the wall, her knees buckled and she slid toward the floor.

"Goddamn him," Danny whispered as he caught her. Afraid he might crush her, he braced her with his arms and steadied her on her feet. Who would want to hurt someone like her?

"I don't know what I'll do if he comes back," she whispered.

Rage burned through Danny. He hated the asshole, whoever he was, ached to kill him with his bare hands. But only after the bastard had felt fear. Real fear. Let him drop to his knees and beg. Let him sob until his nose ran like a snotty kid's. Only when he'd lived through what he'd done to this innocent woman, who'd done *nothing* to him, would he be allowed to die.

"Did he ever hurt you before?" Danny asked.

"No, but he kept saying he would."

Danny held his fury in check, but just barely. His first concern was quieting her. He thought about stroking her hair, but it seemed too much, and his hands were shaking from the anger. He hoped she could feel his strength and take some comfort from it. He had so much of it, and little else to offer her but that.

She rested her head against his chest and seemed to fill up with a sigh. He couldn't tell if it was pressure or relief.

"I liked it when you called me Joey," she said after a minute. "I liked that a lot."

He felt a warming glow. She liked his pet name for her. Therefore she liked him.

"And one more thing, Danny? Could you stay?"

"Stay here?" He couldn't have heard her right, or if he had, she couldn't have meant *stay*.

"Gabe Quiñones said Carlie's out of town," she explained. "I know she'd help, but she's gone, and I don't want to be alone."

He *had* heard it. She had meant it. Whoever was running things—that Great Closet Organizer of Life—had a warped sense of humor. Danny had always known that, but nothing drove it home like this situation. Normally he would have turned to Carlie, but Jo Emily was right. His boss was in Florida.

What the hell she was doing there he didn't know, but he'd checked messages on his way over here and there'd finally been one from her, leaving her hotel and room number. He'd called back, but hadn't been able to reach her, so he'd left a message telling her to get her butt home, and why.

Meanwhile he had to figure this out on his own.

Jo Emily tilted her head back and looked at him. "Should I be getting my hopes up or not?"

"Okay—yeah, I'll stay."

She began to cry again, and then to laugh and shake and hug him. "Thank you!"

"You are cold," he said. "Come on. Let's get you wrapped up in that comforter."

As they made their way to the bed, Danny had a ridiculous thought. He would have killed himself before making light of her fears, but he didn't think she'd have anything to worry about as long as she stayed inside. The stalker wouldn't be able to hurt her unless he could find her, and there wasn't much chance of that in here.

FOURTEEN

Carlie considered the wilting flower stalk he held, with its velvety red blossoms. She knew what it was immediately, knew she was in trouble. She glanced at the gun she'd left on the cherrywood bureau.

Rio smiled darkly. "Race you there," he said.

She had visions of a steamy struggle, arms entangled, much gasping and grunting, bodies bumping and sliding as intimately as if—no, uh-uh. Not going there. Not as long as she had a functioning brain cell, although it was clear he'd love to.

"Are those flowers?" she said, pretending to look around for a vase. "How thoughtful of you. I'll just see if there's something to put them in."

"Carlie!"

"Yes?" She was sincerity itself.

"What the hell are you up to?" He wouldn't let her evade him this time. Imposing in his half-buttoned dress shirt and his towering suspicion, he started toward her, each step a warning. "Why are you staying in this suite and what were these snapdragons doing under the table?"

She reached in the pocket of her nightshirt and pulled out the remote with the panic button. "Those guards would be back in a flash," she warned him. "They didn't *like* you."

That slowed him up, but not enough. He was aroused now, nostrils flaring with the scent, on the prowl. His head cocked at a suspicious angle and his ebony hair gleamed, catching beams from the chandelier. He moved to her left as if he were intending to circle, but it was the gun he was going after.

"That won't do you any good unless your goal is to get me wet." Carlie was about to explain what she meant when she realized what she'd said.

His mouth formed the word "wet?" and he looked at her.

"No, not that—"

But the spark that lit his eyes was quite terrifying. It was hot with curiosity, dark with carnal knowledge. Carlie had triggered images no adult man should ever have. He was obviously thinking it was some secret kink she harbored, that she was turned on by guns.

"Check it out," she implored him, waving toward the table. "See for yourself."

He traded the flower stalk for a nine-millimeter Beretta-type automatic. Turning the gun in his hand, he checked the clip, popped it back in, then squeezed the trigger and sent a jet of water across the room.

"Jesus," he muttered. "A squirt gun?"

"See? You were never in any danger." She thought that might help, but it only seemed to make things worse.

"I can see that you're *nuts*," he said under his breath. "Is this what you're telling the women of the world to do? Brandish fake guns? Do you know how fucking dangerous that is?"

She was intimately familiar with the dangers of handling a weapon, fake or otherwise, but perhaps it was just as well not to mention that, especially after the way he'd *brandished* the F-word.

"I don't advise the women of the world to do anything," she said with what she hoped was exquisite calm. "I teach them to analyze, avoid, and evade."

He rolled his eyes, and the gun hit the tabletop with a clunk. "Evade this, Ms. Bishop. No more squirt guns. No more games. I want answers, and I want them now."

Carlie still had the remote in her hand.

"Ditch it," he warned. "You bring those guards back up here, and they're going to find you swinging by your ankles from the balcony. Me? I'll be holding a knife to the rope."

He wouldn't do it. No way was he going to let her swing from a balcony. But he would do something. She could see the evil intent written all over him. Besides, she didn't want the guards up here any more than he did. That would only complicate things.

"All right," she said once she'd made the short trip to the bar and set the remote there. "What now?"

He looked her over, mulling the possibilities. "Why is personal-safety expert Carlie Bishop staying in the late Leroy Studebaker's suite and why were these flowers under the table? Let's start there."

The suite he spoke of was decorated in the grand style of a French country estate, and Carlie had used her only unmaxed credit card to pay for it. Lustrous golden oak marquetry and eighteenth-century landscapes covered the walls. The windows were richly draped in ruby silk and the tables scented with sprays of fresh-cut yellow roses and feathery greens.

"I told you why I took the suite. I'm interested in the investigation. As for the flowers—" She shrugged. "The Femme Fatale must have left them. That is her calling card, isn't it?"

His tie slithered from around his neck like a snake and ended up tucked in his back pocket. Apparently he wasn't going to strangle her just yet.

"You've heard that old saw about the perpetrator returning to the scene of the crime?" he said. "It's true. They're either motivated by guilt or by glory. The really sick ones come back to gloat about how clever they are."

His pregnant pause said, You don't look very guilty to me.

"Rio, I was with *you* when it happened."

"You were with me when I got the call. The time of death hasn't been determined yet. They don't know when it happened."

"But I haven't been out of Southern California in days, weeks. Ask Danny. Ask anybody."

He wasn't impressed with her passionate denial. "The Femme Fatale can strike from anywhere," he pointed out. "She plays mind games. She doesn't get near her victims, or won't get near them. It's like they're beneath her contempt."

"How do you account for the snapdragons?"

"They show up before a strike, like a warning. How do you account for your interest in the Femme Fatale? Or did you travel across the country to be with me?"

You wish, she thought. Now Carlie had to decide how much to reveal. She had always believed that secrets were power, probably because of the way she was raised. The secret world of her imagination and her desire to be an actress were the only things that made her feel special as a child. But she would have to trade something for his cooperation, and information seemed the safest route.

"If I tell you, you'll have to self-destruct," she said. "I'm starting a new book, and it's top secret."

"And that brought you here?"

She stepped aside as he went to the bar and poured himself a Scotch. "Do I have your word that you'll keep this confidental?" At his nod, she said, "This is a research trip, and my book is about the Femme Fatale."

I want to vindicate her, she thought. *I want people to see that anyone could do what she's doing under the right circumstances.* But she didn't say any of that.

"Will you help me?" she asked.

If he was surprised he didn't show it. "Any reason why I should?" He lounged against the bar, drink in hand. The clicking sound he made set Carlie's nerves on edge. It was his fingers, she realized, tapping against the rim of the highball glass.

"Because we already have a deal?" she ventured. "Because I might discover something you can use? Because I'll put you in the book?"

"I've had my fifteen minutes of fame, thanks. All it got me was a bad rep. And, no offense, but I have a hard time imagining you're going to uncover anything vital."

Carlie bristled. "Don't be so sure," she told him. "I've been here since yesterday. I may already have discovered something vital."

"Are you drinking?"

She wasn't sure if he was insulting her or offering her some Scotch. When he raised his glass, she realized it was the latter.

"Here's to deals made at gunpoint with women in black silk nightshirts," he said.

Too easy, Carlie thought, quite certain she hadn't convinced him of anything. This was not a man to wave the white flag, especially considering his ethnic makeup. He had some ulterior motive and any number of possibilities occurred to her. Most likely he wanted to keep an eye on her. Or maybe it was about what he had planned for the long night that lay ahead of them. Sleep, she hoped, and lots of it. But there was a dimmer switch in the bar and he adjusted it, lowering the brightness of the spotlights to a warm golden glow.

Carlie tugged at the lapel of her nightshirt.

"Isn't it a little late to get self-conscious now?" he wanted to know. "You've been prancing around in that thing all night."

"I'd hardly call it prancing."

"I was being polite, Carlie. 'This isn't pepper spray, asshole. It's a fucking gun barrel.' Out of the mouths of presidential appointees? Where'd you pick that up?"

She flushed. "Hanging around with homicide detectives?"

"Touché."

He was nursing the drink, and Carlie was counting every sip. It was time for them to say goodnight and lock themselves in their separate rooms, but she didn't know how to bring it up. The only thing he seemed interested in was her nightshirt and her foul language.

"You've been on talk shows across the country," he said. "Aren't you concerned about being recognized by the guards? At least one of those guys has got to be on some tabloid's payroll."

Carlie had already taken that into consideration. "I'm not registered under Carlie Bishop. And besides, I'm hardly a household name. Occasionally people say I look familiar, but they can never seem to place me. Probably because I'm out of context.''

His range of interest had widened. The body parts her nightshirt *didn't* cover were gaining in popularity as the moments ticked by. Namely, her bare legs.

"We need to decide who's bunking where." She scoped out the living room, official counselor for the camp-out.

"What are my choices?"

Thinking to appease him, she offered the master suite. There were two guest bedrooms at the opposite end of the place, with a library, a living room, dining room, and kitchen in between.

"Where are you sleeping?" he asked.

"Anywhere," she threw out casually. "I'll take one of the guest rooms."

"Are the guest rooms side by side?"

"No."

"Close?"

"They're connected by a bathroom."

"Close enough," he said, and smiled.

Danny couldn't sleep. Jo Emily's floors were cement under the meager carpeting, and even with a layer of laundry under him, it was like sleeping on the sidewalk.

He sat up and rolled his shoulders, suppressing a deep-throated groan. As long as he was up, he might as well be all the way up. Somebody had to be night watch.

The room was bright with moonlight filtering through the thin window curtains. Danny could see Jo Emily sound asleep on the bed. Correction, he could see a lump. She was barely visible under the comforter.

At least she was sleeping. He was grateful for that. Poor kid had wanted him right there next to her as she dozed off, insisted he sit on the bed and hold her hand. That was all it seemed to take to calm her, and he was glad to do it, although the sense of regret he felt was familiar. Would that his needs were as simple.

He made it to his feet without waking her, and as he was looking around the room for a place to sit, an idea came to him. Maybe he could quietly clean things up a little. It was going to be a long night, and he might as well make himself useful.

Roll up your sleeves, Danny boy. There has to be a chair hidden around here somewhere.

His smile turned ironic as he estimated the damage. It would be simpler to have the place declared a disaster area and request federal cleanup funds.

He started with the floor because that's where most everything was. Silently he folded laundry into the night, pleased with himself as he built one neat stack after another, creating a skyline of towels and clothing. He wasn't sure what was clean and what was dirty, but she could take it from there. At least the place wouldn't be a fire hazard.

Gathering up what felt like fifty pounds of magazines and catalogs, he sorted them by date. He made a small tower out of her romance novels, smiling at the passionate couples on the covers. One of the guys looked a little like him, he decided optimistically. He put that one on the top.

The chains jangled on her mood-music purse as he picked it up and set it on the dresser. He glanced at Jo Emily to make sure she was still asleep, but his mind was on the small, hard object he'd felt inside the bag. He would have bet it was a revolver.

That thought stayed with him as he noticed that the bottom drawer of her dresser wasn't closed. There was a discount-store scrapbook wedged in there, and it was so fat with pictures and clippings it had jammed the sliding mechanism.

It was Femme Fatale stuff, all of it. Danny couldn't help but notice as he tried to get the drawer unstuck. Ragged newspaper articles were haphazardly taped to some pages and crushed between others. Someone had scribbled notes all over the margins. Furious notes, full of rage and spleen.

They were barely legible, but Danny could make out names like *coward pigs, bastards,* and *sick fucks.* There were threats of violence, too, some of them incredibly bloodthirsty. It must have been Jo Emily who'd written the notes because she'd scrawled *castrate him with a telephone cord* at the top of one page, and then at the bottom, *gut him with broken windshield glass and leave him to bleed.*

But most of it read like a manifesto. There were pages of pain, describing the torment that stalkers inflict on their victims. The way they systematically destroyed lives. But there were more pages filled with thoughts of unbridled vengeance. It was one woman's sworn vow to turn the tables on her stalker, or perhaps all stalkers, Danny couldn't tell.

He was blown away.

He'd known Jo Emily had a streak in her. He'd seen evidence of it when she broke up Carlie's lecture, but he had no idea it was this dark. It was normal for victims to feel rage, but few were so graphic or detailed in their plans for revenge.

He looked over at the peacefully sleeping woman, the fallen angel, with one question on his mind. Who was she?

A hunted woman, he told himself, and that was all there was to it. She would have cracked under the stress if she hadn't relieved it by making the scrapbook. But the longer he watched her, the more he believed there might be something else going on.

His gut was churning as he went through her purse and found the gun inside. It was a real weapon, loaded and lethal. Now he had no choice. He had to leave her for a while. He didn't want to, but there was something he had to check out, and it couldn't wait. She was sleeping, he told himself. She wouldn't even know he was gone.

FIFTEEN

Things didn't get really bad for Carlie until she heard Rio turn on the shower. Of course the obvious question was why he required a shower at this time of night. It was past twelve, and she'd been in bed for two hours, trying not to think about him, but she'd heard him in his room, knew he was in there, maybe mussing the sheets and thinking about her.

That was bad enough. Then she had only to wonder if he slept nude. Now she *knew* he was nude. Guys didn't shower in their shorts.

What would those curly eyelashes look like wet?

Cords tightened in Carlie's shoulders, and she dug her toes into the sheets. Tension. She always felt it at the extremes of her body before she felt it inside. Sometimes her fingers cramped, but tonight it had cinched up the laces of her backbone like an old-fashioned corset.

She would not allow herself to apply the wet-eyelash question to the rest of him. She'd made a conscious choice not to go there, and had been fighting to honor it. But her mind was turning her into a Peeping Tom.

Even with her eyes closed she kept seeing visions of legs, lean and straight, fluidly muscled like a runner's. They were coppery in color and made for powerful movement. Never-ending. These were legs so long she couldn't see all the way to the top. And it was giving her whiplash trying not to.

She twisted to look at the clock, wondering when he was going to get out of the shower and go to bed. She was quite sure that there was no sleep to be had until he did. Finally she switched on the light and sat up.

Eyelashes be damned. What would he look like wet?

There. She'd done it. She'd owned up to the question. Now maybe she could obsess about something a little less stimulating, like sleep? Silly, silly notion, of course. Her mind was a cassette on fast forward, and the tracks were all the same. She'd never felt less sleepy, or more stimulated.

The Aubusson carpet was thick and cushiony under her feet as she rose from the bed. There was icy marble tile everywhere else in the room, and it sent a chill up the back of her legs as she stepped on it. But Carlie needed space.

Killer, of course.

With a sound of despair, she reminded herself never to think out loud when he was around. How else would he look *but* killer?

He was tall and broad-shouldered and wore his black trench coat like a damn spy provocateur. In other words, with fabulous sinister grace. The list went on, except that she hadn't come here to admire the man. She'd come to throw him off the track and salvage her project.

This is the wrong fight we're fighting, Carlie. There is a larger problem here. Your little principality is being invaded by land, sea, and air, and you're worrying about a leak in the plumbing. Deal with reality, not bare legs and eyelashes.

You're the Femme Fatale.

She stopped pacing and breathed deeply. An immediate sense of calm and purpose spread through her. When she could take on that role, she felt powerful. Centered. She'd put on a good performance tonight, but the show wasn't over. The woman who'd held the gun to his head had been cool and fearless. Somehow Carlie had to sustain that composure through the entire trip. Keep the charade going. She couldn't let him see the tightly coiled spring that lived inside her.

She was still breathing deeply when the shower stopped.

He was done. The roar of the pipes and the drumming water had ceased. Everything was silent. Deadly silent. Her hand crept to the neckline of her shirt as she stared at the door, waiting. She'd already imagined it coming open and him standing inside, water sluicing down his limbs. Another one of her absurd fantasies, but the way her spine had locked her in place, it felt like anything could happen.

She could feel her brain wanting to race with the possibility, and it brought to mind the surreal moment in her bathroom when lightbulbs had started popping and the room had gone dark. She'd been staring at the door one minute and the next she'd felt a man slam her up against the wall with his body. He'd imprisoned her arms above her head and leaned into her with such hungry force she'd been knocked breathless. She'd felt shocked, horrified—

Thrilled. Thrilled nearly to death.

Carlie, stop!

God, her heart was breaking the speed limit. It was sprinting as fast as her mind. It made no sense that she had these persistent, maddening fantasies about a man who seemed determined to put her on death row. But she knew why. She knew the reason, and if anything doomed her, that did.

He was her first. The first man who'd captured her imagination, and once he had that, her heart and body were quick to follow. Rio Walker was her first imaginary lover, and since then, she'd never been able to separate reality from fantasy. It wasn't about what he looked like or even what he might do to her as much as about who he was—or who she *wanted* him to be. She'd created an ideal, the kind of man a woman longed for, strong and smolderingly passionate and yet, hidden somewhere in that crazy mix, trustworthy.

Carlie could imagine him whispering the words so many of her sex wanted to hear when things seemed hopeless: ''Let me hold you and everything will be all right.'' She could imagine that so easily because he had that quality about him, too, the quiet power of a man who could make everything all right just by taking her in his arms. And much as she hated to admit it, that possibility undid her. It just did. Maybe it was what she'd responded to the night he'd come to her rescue in the parking lot.

Rio Walker was nothing like the glib talkers who traditionally preyed on women's needs. There was strength to him. There was depth, or the appearance of it, and that was the danger. He was the kind of man you trusted when you shouldn't.

Trusted when you shouldn't, Carlie.

It would not be wise to forget the impact he'd had on Ginger. He'd seduced her sister within an inch of her life, and maybe that was part of the reason he was attracted to Carlie. Certainly he wanted to bag the Femme Fatale, but why not bed Carlie Bishop while he was at it?

Carlie looked down. She'd twisted the top button off her nightshirt. She had to remember who he was, a detective who seemed determined to pin her with the Femme Fatale strikes. And who she was. His prime suspect. Lifting her head, she swung back her hair and glanced at herself in the mirror, a witness to her own green-eyed turbulence. She was trying hard to make herself dislike him. She couldn't tell if it was working or not.

Rio leaned against the bathroom countertop, one leg hooked over the edge. His arms were casually folded against his chest, and he gazed at

Carlie's bedroom door as if he could see through it. He'd just searched the entire suite, but had found nothing of interest. What interested him was on the other side of that door. He wouldn't mind going through her things.

He was fully dressed, totally dry. The shower had been a ruse. He'd turned it on so she wouldn't hear him prowling around. Now water dripped from the showerhead, a steady tap that focused his thoughts. But it didn't bring the answers he wanted. A clever story, that business about her top-secret book project. In some ways it was the perfect cover, which didn't mean it was true, of course.

Right now his head was spinning where she was concerned. He didn't know whether the hell she was guilty or not, but his body was certain of a few things. There was a beautiful woman in the room next door, just beyond his reach, and he wanted to feel her quiver, hear her breathe, and know what it was like to break her reserve just a little.

A sensation flashed deep in his jaw. He told himself the red-hot cinder meant he wanted a cigarette. *Had to have one.*

He rose from the counter in an attempt to release the pent-up energy. Nothing had changed, he reminded himself. Nothing could change. He was going forward with his plan. The trap was set and waiting for her to blunder into it. If she was the Femme Fatale, she would be caught red-handed, and once that had happened, they would all be forced to come to terms with it.

He would be forced. He'd told himself she had to be stopped before she took out any more people. That they were bad people was beside the point. Carlie Bishop wasn't above the law. That's what he'd told himself. Christ, he was a cop.

He already knew she wasn't in South Beach when Leroy Studebaker drowned. He'd had her under surveillance for some time. That didn't mean she couldn't have been the mastermind, but Rio had his own theory on how the boxer had died, and the snapdragon he'd found actually added weight to it. Tomorrow would tell.

He unkinked his shoulders with a rolling stretch, then walked into the bedroom, unbuttoning his shirt as he went. He'd be damn lucky to sleep tonight knowing she was in the bed next door, with that black nightshirt of hers probably hitched up to her golden butt and those beautiful legs all over the place.

Now he did want a cigarette. The red-hot spark had dropped. It was searing his groin.

Those green eyes made him weak, especially when they frosted over. Not much of anything else did that to him anymore.

He stopped in front of the armoire mirror and took a look at himself as he finished with his shirt and pulled it off. His jaw was set like stone, and his eyes had a wildness that shouted of physical hungers. It wasn't food he wanted.

There were two doors between him and her. To walk through them would be to sacrifice his case. That was almost certain. He couldn't touch her and then charge her for a crime or expect to be a credible witness against her. He couldn't even put her on a list of suspects. It was something to think about.

The clock radio said six A.M. when Carlie opened her eyes. The phosphorescent green numbers were the first thing she saw, the only thing that could be seen in the pitch-black room. It was still dark outside. Not even a glimmer of daylight had seeped beneath the opaque window curtains.

Right here it was, she thought. This was the reason she'd never liked hotels. It could have been midnight, and except for the miracle of electricity, she wouldn't have known. She felt as if she'd been sealed in a vault and dropped to the bottom of the sea, it was so dark. Hotels provided their guests with endless night and her with endless insomnia.

She rolled to her back and yawned. Better that than weep. The cocoon she'd formed with her covers was warm with the heat of her body and fragrant with the rose they'd laid out on her pillow at turndown. But there was no point in trying to go back to sleep now, which was not quite accurate anyway, since she'd never *been* to sleep.

There were hints of impending daylight by the time she'd gathered herself together and was padding silently through the suite in her bare feet, headed for the kitchen. Rising early had certain advantages, she admitted. It would give her a chance to have some coffee, clear her head, and think through the day before she had to deal with Rio.

She felt like a ghost, whispering through the manor halls as everyone slept. It was a rather nice feeling, like *being* a secret as opposed to *having* one. But she slowed up upon entering the living room, or "salon," as her mother would have called it. Something had caught her eye, a suggestion of movement. She'd thought she was the first one up, but it looked as if she had company outside on the balcony.

Him, she realized when she was near enough to see in the low light. He seemed to be staring down at the awakening city from the railing as if he were the one responsible for its shadows. He was shirtless and barefoot, and the jeans he wore accentuated the extraordinary length of his legs. Not something she wanted to be reminded of at the crack of dawn, particularly since it had kept her awake all night.

He must have heard her tiptoeing.

"Up so early?" His voice carried through the open doors.

"Brrrr." She shivered and clutched her arms as the outside air touched her. The sky was just beginning to color, but not enough to warm things up.

She wandered onto the terrace anyway, curious. "Aren't you freezing?"

"Not a chance," he said. "I'm burning up."

It was probably sixty-five degrees, she realized. Not cold enough for her to be chilled or hot enough for him to be ablaze. Something else was going on here.

When he turned full around, she saw the flower stalk in his hands. Apparently that was what he had on his mind, that and Carlie Bishop.

"Your sister got off on danger. Maybe you do, too?"

Carlie was stunned by the remark. Perhaps he didn't realize he was trampling on sacred ground. "My sister is not up for discussion here," she answered, flaring. "And don't you say anything about her. Ginger was an angel."

The way his body blocked the glowing shoreline made Carlie think of omens, bad ones.

"Maybe she fell from grace, and you didn't notice?"

"No, she was perfect. She was good." And she was the only one who'd ever cared about Carlie, so if Ginger was bad, then what was she? Ginger's love had made her worthy. There had been times in their early years when Carlie felt like a card-carrying member of the human race only because her sister had found something of value in her, something to care about. "Ginger was good, dammit."

His lashes lowered, velvet tracery. He gave her a look. "I'm not questioning that, but she also had her hang-ups."

"Not until she met you." Carlie ducked her head and whispered the next, fiercely: "You corrupted her."

Laughter? Was he laughing? There was a suspicious rustle in his breathing. "You find this entertaining? How nice for you," she said.

"I'm sorry. I know you loved your sister."

He actually sounded contrite, which surprised Carlie, and gave her some time to compose herself. It probably wasn't smart to let him see her get this emotional, even about Ginger. She rarely flew off the handle unless it had something to do with her sister, and then mother lionesses had nothing on her. She could attack with frightening ferocity.

"You give me too much credit," he protested. "No one can be corrupted without their cooperation. Ginger wanted out of the glory game your parents created for her. She existed to fulfill their vision of greatness and for no other reason. On some level, she knew that, and it destroyed her.''

''She told you all that?''

''She didn't have to.''

''What do you mean?'' she pressed. But he'd already turned back to the view. Apparently that was all he was going to say, and his cryptic comments left Carlie in a quandary about his relationship with Ginger. She didn't know if they were that close or he was just incredibly perceptive. But she was reasonably sure he was on the right track.

She hadn't been with Ginger the last months of her life, but they'd spoken on the phone, and Ginger had seemed different at times, almost desperate, as if she wanted to escape something and didn't know how. But if Carlie understood now that it was her own image Ginger was trying to escape—as created by her parents—she hadn't realized it then.

Rio seemed to read the situation with more clarity than she did. He was bent over the railing now, intensely absorbed in some thought process that made her wonder if she was at the eye of his hurricane. But it was the way he tapped his finger against the wrought iron that made her uneasy. She hated that sound. There was something eerie and sinister about it.

''I'm going to make some coffee,'' she said. When he didn't answer, she stepped back into the house, but continued to watch him. It had been her plan to get here a day before he did and do some nosing around on her own, and the advance work had paid off. She'd picked up some fascinating hearsay about Leroy Studebaker, but revealing it now seemed risky. It might make Rio wonder about her motives and lead him to think she was trying to cover her tracks.

What concerned her at the moment was what she'd already revealed. She'd told him everything she could about her project, but she had the feeling he hadn't believed a word of it. Detective Walker had not yet taken Carlie Bishop off his suspect list.

It was the middle of the day in halcyon South Beach, land of bronze flesh, turquoise waves, and pink beaches. An ideal time to catch some rays, except that Rio was on his way to a nightclub called the Courtesan, a private enclave created exclusively for the entertainment of wealthy straight males.

It was the first real break in his investigation of the Studebaker case. Unfortunately the information had come from Carlie, and in exchange for the tip, he'd had to bring her along. Not that she wasn't hot enough for an all-male club. Her midriff-baring shorts outfit was worthy of a runway model. Those golden legs of hers were getting more exposure than they had in the nightshirt. Maybe that was what bothered him.

His first appointment that morning had been with the detective heading up the South Beach investigation, who'd briefed him on their progress to that point. Carlie had begged him to take her along to the meeting, but Rio had drawn the line at having to explain her presence to the South Beach squad. Instead, he'd met her at the crime scene, a luxury condo where the body was found.

It still hadn't been proven conclusively that Studebaker was murdered, which was typical of the Femme Fatale's MO. She made it look like the deaths were either accidental or self-inflicted, but she wanted credit or she wouldn't have left her various calling cards.

"They're not going to let us in without some fast talking," Carlie warned as Rio drove the rental sedan up to the gleaming gold facade of a Moorish building. Flamboyant would have been Rio's word to describe the place. The exotic structure reminded him of the palace described in "Kubla Khan," with its graceful gilded domes and lacy minarets.

"We could tell them you're looking for work."

"Excuse me?" She seemed more startled than offended at his suggestion, which, in fact, had been intended as a compliment.

Rio seriously doubted they'd get past the guard at the parking lot. He'd done some checking. This place had better security than a military installation, and any attempt by Rio to finesse his way in would be seriously hampered by having Carlie along. But this was their deal, and she was the one who'd come up with the lead that had brought them here.

She claimed to have spotted the owner of the condo at the crime scene and pretended to be a neighbor. Her friendly, gossipy questions had coaxed information out of him that the police, in their official capacity, had missed. She'd learned the boxer's newest hangout was this private club, and that he'd been here earlier the night he died. That this information had not already been leaked was one more indication of how tight the Courtesan's security was.

Rio pulled up to the gate and hit the button to lower the car window as the guard sauntered over. He was a stocky older man with slick gray hair and heavy muscles that had gone mostly to fat. Rio took him for an ex–weight lifter, which meant he probably wasn't much of a fighter. Muscle men let their bulk do the talking.

"The club doesn't open until eight," the guard said, giving both Rio and his gleaming black Infiniti the once-over. "And it's members only. Have you got a card?"

"I have an appointment with the manager," Rio said. "He's expecting me. Tell him it's Rio Walker, and I've got good news." Rio gave him a smile meant to blind him with reflected sunlight. "He's sole heir to a sweepstakes fortune. His deceased cousin John won the Lotto."

Carlie kicked him with her foot, probably to shame him. But Rio had used all kinds of ploys to gain entry, and this one usually worked, greed being the universal character flaw.

"Yeah? How much money?"

Bingo, Rio thought. The guard's eyes had turned Andrew Jackson green. "I can't reveal that to anyone but the heir."

"Can't help you, then, the manager's not here today."

"When's he coming in?"

"Could be a while. He's on vacation."

"Then why is there a car in his reserved space?" Rio could see through the bars of the gate. The manager's parking space was marked, and sitting pretty just inside the lines was a big black Lincoln Town Car.

The guard glowered and Rio flashed his badge. "Tell him it's Detective Walker, and he can talk to me now, in the privacy of his office, or I can drag his ass down to the station."

The guard returned to the booth, made a quick phone call, and hustled back with a nasty grin. "You better have a warrant on you, flatfoot. The boss said you ain't getting in, even if you're *Pope* Walker."

Rio had about as much chance of getting a warrant as this cretin did of having an IQ higher than his belt size. Rio considered his options and went straight for the one that involved blood and screaming. One strategically placed blow would wipe the smirk off the cretin's face. And Rio wanted to do that. Bad.

His problem was Carlie. She was still kicking his foot and trying to get his attention. Plus, what would he do if more guards showed up and things got nasty? The club probably had a security force the size of a third-world army.

"Let's go," Carlie urged. "I've got a better idea."

"Better than what?"

"Could you take me shopping?"

The guard forgotten, Rio cranked around to look at her. He couldn't have heard that right. He was supposed to relinquish his macho fantasy of mopping up the parking lot with this bozo to take her where? *Shopping?* There was no longer any doubt. They could put it in the encyclopedia under Well-Known Facts of the Twentieth Century. Somebody in this car was nuts.

"Over there!" Carlie pointed to a grouping of arty boutiques clustered on one of the four "hot" streets in the buzzing beach city. "Let me out on the corner by those shops, Rio. Do you see them?"

What Rio saw was a woman having a breakdown right before his eyes. First, she'd concocted some nutball plan she wouldn't tell him about, and now she was trying to open the car door of a moving vehicle. He could only assume that she planned to stunt-roll to freedom if he didn't pull over and let her out.

"Hang on," he growled.

He grabbed her by the wrist to stop her from flying out the door as he double-parked the car. "You're not going anywhere until you tell me what's going on. How is this 'shopping trip' of yours going to get us into the Courtesan?"

"I'll explain later."

"I've heard that before."

She tugged. He tugged. "Rio, there isn't time to explain! Please, just trust me. Everything will be fine. Go back to the hotel and wait for me there, okay?"

"You want me to sit at the hotel and wait? Wait for what? I don't think so."

"Okay, then, follow a lead. Do whatever detectives do. I'll get in touch with you when I'm ready."

"Ready for what?"

"You'll see."

She patted his knee and Rio felt the muscles ripple pleasurably. Still skeptical, he let her go and watched her dart through a crowd of tourists and into a boutique that looked as if it specialized in women's underwear by what was displayed in the window.

Shopping. Great way to solve a murder. He was tempted to follow her and *make* her tell him what she was up to. He liked the way her pulse had been hammering under his fingers, and he knew some interesting ways to make people talk. But he did have something else to do. Something detectives did, as she'd so sweetly put it. He had a date with the coroner. A few questions about the condition of the body when it arrived, and the odds were good that he could solve this case, in which event Carlie's little shopping spree would be superfluous.

Pleased with himself, he wheeled the car back into traffic and headed for the morgue. She probably didn't think he knew words like superfluous.

SIXTEEN

Rio was angry, and he tended to break things when he was angry. That was why he hadn't finished the glass of Scotch he'd left on the fancy French commode by the windows, even though his hand twitched every time he walked past it. If he picked it up, some very expensive Baccarat crystal was going to take a trip across the room.

It was seven P.M., and he still hadn't heard from Carlie.

The living room's spacious windows framed a seascape as enigmatic as the woman who kept him waiting. On one side they looked out over the Atlantic, and all he could see were the stars sparkling in the sky and the silvery lace of ocean waves. Beautiful and enticing, but revealing nothing.

"Where the hell is she?" His question was lost in the soft crash of breakers as Rio walked out to the balcony. The night sky glittered with stars. It had been dark since five, which only increased his concerns. There'd been one ambiguous message from her when he got back, saying only that "Phase One" was successful and she was starting "Phase Two." Before hanging up, she asked him to wish her luck and pleaded with him not to do anything until he heard from her.

Wish her luck?

That was four hours ago. There'd been no word since. He had no way of knowing if she was delayed—or dead. And if she wasn't dead, maybe he would kill her himself.

"Jesus." He hated the helpless feeling that overwhelmed him when a woman or a child was in jeopardy and his hands were tied, and this felt like one of those times. Police training had taught him to assess the situation quickly and take action. His intuitive approach allowed his instincts to take over and apprehend what his senses couldn't. But neither approach seemed to work where she was concerned. He had plenty of reason to think she could take care of herself, but none of that calmed him. The image in his head was of a woman in distress, a woman who needed him. And he didn't know how to get to her.

The back of his neck was damp with perspiration. The cooling air should have helped, but it was still heavy and humid from the heat of the day, and he wanted the rest of that goddamm Scotch.

It disappeared in one gulp.

On fire, Rio slammed the glass down. He blamed himself. He should have known better than to let her out of that car without knowing what she had planned, and shopping was the least of it, he was sure. Phase Two? What else could that be but a solo attempt on the Courtesan? She was going to try to finesse her way in, and he could hardly imagine anything more dangerous. They were pros at that place, with celebrity clients and possibly even crime czars to protect.

He ripped off his tie and glanced at the clock. Fifteen more minutes. Enough time to shower and change. If he hadn't heard from her by then, he was going over.

He was still toweling off, beads of water on his legs, when he returned to the living room in search of his wallet and car keys, and saw the envelope that had been slipped under the entry door. It was a formal, engraved invitation. He knotted the towel around his hips and bent to pick it up. The Courtesan's return address was printed in the upper left-hand corner, and inside was an invitation to the club that night, addressed to him.

My apologies for the incident at the gate today, it said. *Please be my guest for an evening of sensory delights at the Courtesan. Come and enjoy all our amenities.* It was signed by the manager.

Rio gazed off into space and smiled. She was good.

When the locals described it as a cross between an imperial palace of the czars and an Arabian Nights theme park, they were referring to the exterior's Moorish tracery, soaring arches, and golden spires. Few had ever seen the interior's celestial glass domes, green copper cupolas, crystal chandeliers, and nude frescoes. Or ever would.

Unlike Disney World, this theme park was dedicated to a very privileged few with enough money to buy their whims and wishes outright, no matter how self-indulgent.

There was no sign of the offending guard at the entrance gate when Rio drove up. The one who'd taken his place looked like a young military officer. He did everything but salute as he waved the rental Infiniti into the parking lot.

Rio gave his invitation to a woman seated at an antique desk in the reception hall. She welcomed him with a gracious smile, pressed a button on the phone, and a trio of young women, all exotic, dark-haired beauties in flowing Indian silks and a deferential manner, appeared.

"This way?" one of them said, linking her arm in Rio's. Her voice was as breathy and soft as her outfit, and the question seemed to imply that if he'd wanted to go some other way, any way at all, she would have been happy to oblige. The others followed behind, and though Rio was tempted to ask what was on the menu in the way of "amenities," he decided to let the girls surprise him.

Their first stop was a room the size of a bedchamber with rococo mirrors for walls, velvet couches thick with tasseled pillows, stools cushioned in antique needlepoint, and in the center, a stagelike pedestal, mounted with a lighted three-way mirror. The crowning touch was a multifaceted crystal chandelier.

It was pretty much what Rio would have expected a luxurious changing booth in a couture salon to look like. As it turned out, he was right about the changing part. He was politely requested to undress in preparation for the grooming rituals that were to come. But to his surprise none of the women left. Instead they shut the door and proceeded to do the job for him.

He didn't have to lift a finger as they unbuttoned, unsnapped, and unzipped. It looked like he was going to be relieved of every stitch of his clothing down to the skin, which made him damn glad he hadn't worn his shoulder holster. Rio was the only one who seemed to feel even slightly awkward about the unveiling. Clearly the women had done this before, and their lack of self-consciousness made him wonder why suddenly he could sympathize with an adolescent boy who was terrified of getting an erection. Maybe because he'd never been undressed by three women before? One was the optimum number. And he usually did the undressing.

Yeah, this was awkward, he thought as one of his beautiful escorts elected to help him out of his briefs while another quickly snapped the wrinkles out of the shirt she'd just removed and then slipped it on a hanger. She returned to massage his neck and shoulders.

"Step?" the girl at his feet requested. She glanced up with a polite smile, waiting for him to comply. He did, and she had the decency to suck in a little breath at the sight of his naked male splendor, so to speak.

This girl was going to get a nice tip, Rio decided.

The whole routine was a clever way to disguise a strip search. That was another of his thoughts when the Del Rubio Triplets finally took mercy on him and gave him a monogrammed terry robe to put on. The next stop was the masculine equivalent of a beauty salon, where he was shaved and plucked of hair from tender extremities, like his nose and his ears. The smiling attendants would never know how relieved he was that they hadn't asked him to open his robe.

Finally he was bathed by a second crew of women, all blond and pink-cheeked, who scrubbed him up and down and forward and backward with great soft brushes while they sang what sounded like Ukrainian folk songs. They also clipped and manicured everything that could be clipped and manicured. He couldn't wait to tell the guys back at RHD about this.

When all the cleanup work was done, Rio was escorted to a perfect square of a room, draped like the ceremonial tent of a nomadic sheikh, where he was left to his own devices. There were trays of fruits, dates and sweetmeats to nibble on, as well as carafes of ice water and spiced spirits to drink. The only furnishings were circular bedlike mounds of velvety pillows with red-and-gold canopies, tiny inlaid tables, and richly textured tapestries.

The ladies had begged his permission to be dismissed after the bathing, which he'd magnanimously given, aware that he was starting to enjoy this lord-of-the-domain-and-all-he-surveyed stuff. But before the last one had vanished with the others, she'd pointed out a pair of black silk lounging pajamas and explained that everything in the room had been left expressly for his use. When he was ready for the next event of the evening, he could pull the tasseled cord, and an escort would come for him. Meanwhile he could rest himself as long as he liked on the beds of velvet pillows. And if he preferred anything else to eat or drink, two pulls of the cord would bring a waiter to take his order.

Rio was not going to eat dates or nap. No telling what they'd do to his unconscious, defenseless body. The pajamas felt like he imagined clouds would feel if they were spun into clothes. Weird. They were so light they seemed to float around his legs, but they were totally opaque. Lounging outfits were not a fashion statement any self-respecting tough guy wanted to make, but these were narrow-legged and only marginally embarrassing, he acknowledged. And there was always testosterone therapy.

He caught a look at himself in the room's only mirror and wanted to laugh at the pained expression on his face. If he was lucky no one would mistake him for Hugh Hefner. Otherwise, he'd have to kill himself.

Speaking of that, where the hell was Carlie?

He pulled the rope once, half expecting her to appear. Instead, it was the Del Rubio triplet who'd linked arms with him in the lobby.

"We go to the Galerie des Beaux Arts now?" she said, seeming to gasp out the words.

No, we go to the doctor now and get that breathing problem fixed, he thought sardonically.

The exhibition hall she took him to lived up to its name in every way. Brilliantly designed and lit, it had the feel of an old opera house as much as a gallery. The walls were hung with lifelike three-dimensional paintings. The gleaming parquet of the hardwood floor was dotted with graceful statuary and tableaux vivants, which his escort explained were meticulous recreations of historical scenes.

But Rio noticed the motif immediately. All the figures were women. They were in period costumes ranging from ancient to futuristic times, and stunningly beautiful. Saint Joan writhed on her funeral pyre, her lovely features contorted in pain and her ragged chemise exposing a breast a little too plump and perfectly shaped for the likes of a starving martyr. Lucrezia Borgia, infamous daughter of the Roman pope, looked more wistful than wicked as she reclined on a chaise with her robe open, perhaps waiting for a lover. There was a female archer in a skimpy tunic, probably the Huntress, Diana, and a Barbarella look-alike.

"Do you notice anything unusual about the collection?" Rio's escort asked. Her smile was vaguely wicked, and that alone intrigued him. "Other than the obvious, of course."

By obvious he took her to mean their gender and seminudity. He turned slowly, letting his gaze brush over the various pieces. He was known for seeing things others couldn't, but he honestly didn't realize he wasn't looking at actual art until one of the figures appeared to move.

Had Joan blinked?

Rio honed in on her, and then on several of the others. He'd been picking up some vibe he couldn't identify since he walked in the room. Not a sound, it was more like warmth; invisible waves of it. It could have been a breeze, but this was internal. Metabolic. Body heat.

"They're alive," he said, "all of them."

"Flesh-and-blood women." She turned in a circle, her arm extended. "Do you see anything you like? As a guest you're invited to choose from among them and pick a companion for the evening. Go ahead," she urged.

She must have seen the disbelief on his face. Rio walked among the figures, impressed by how still they were. If he focused, he could spot the breathing, but only by the quiver of hair in their nostrils. But they still resembled consummate works of art more than women, except one.

Directly ahead of him was a scene that appeared to be an ancient

Roman slave auction with a captive girl bent in supplication. He noticed the figure wasn't just breathing, she was trembling.

A card titled it *The Torching of Rome* under the reign of Nero Claudius Caesar. The figure was described as a young Christian acolyte, claimed as spoils of war. She was on her knees with her hands tied behind her back and her head bowed. Her face was hidden by a veil of mahogany hair.

But when she looked up, Rio saw that it was Carlie.

His breath caught hard in his chest. Maybe he'd known it was her before this, but the sight of her still shocked him.

She had the look of a desperate waif, her eyes pleading with him for mercy, and for a moment he wondered if this woman *was* Carlie. The wild dark hair must be a wig. But when she spoke, her voice was familiar. Beneath the pleading tone, she had the same clear timbre as Carlie.

"My lord Nero," she implored as he approached her, "take my life if you must, but please, I beg you, spare my aged father. He has committed no sin except to have sired me, a professed Christian."

The escort touched Rio's arm to get his attention. "Is this one your choice?" she asked. "You picked well. She's new, untried."

Rio hesitated, mostly out of confusion, but Carlie, the slave girl, seemed to take it as rejection.

"Please!" she moaned softly. Rio's silence prompted even more extravagant pleading. "I will not run away, lord," she promised. "Untie me and I will do anything you wish. I will renounce my own beliefs and serve only you, wise and gentle Nero."

From what Rio knew of Nero, the "gentle" part was highly optimistic of her. She was utterly convincing, but his primary concern was how she'd gotten in the place, and how he was going to get her out.

"This one will do," he told the escort.

The woman nodded and stepped back, but did not leave.

Rio hesitated. Carlie writhed and moaned beautifully. Rio had never seen such unbridled passion, and he wondered if they'd given her something. It wouldn't have surprised him if they drugged the girls to slow their breathing, but Carlie had to be on uppers, maybe a hallucinogen.

"She is yours," the escort prompted, "to do with what you wish."

Rio's answer was a lame "thanks" as he stalled for time. He had no idea what the gentle Nero would have done, but his first thought was to get her out of those ropes.

"Are you all right?" he whispered as he bent to untie her. "Did they give you something? Drugs?"

"Drugs, lord?" she cried out. "No one has touched me, I assure you.

I am undefiled. I come to you of my own free will to beg for my father's life. Please, please free me so that I can prove myself to you.''

When he released her hands, she fell forward in sweet supplication, her arms questing for him, or for something. Her breath came in sobs. ''I will do anything,'' she pleaded.

Rio wanted to clamp a hand over her mouth and tell her to chill, but that wouldn't be very lordly. The escort was still hovering, possibly waiting to be dismissed.

''Be gone,'' he told the woman, doing a credible Richard Burton. ''I wish to be alone with the sniveling wench.''

The escort's eyes gleamed with approval. ''She does seem to require discipline. I leave her in your hands, sire.'' She bowed several times as she backed to the door.

Rio waited for her to make her protracted exit, aware that the other works of art had already left. At some point they'd come down from their various perches and pedestals and stolen away.

When he was sure he and Carlie were alone, Rio bent over her prostrate form. ''Carlie, it's me,'' he told her.

She continued to sob, even when he lifted her up by her arms, stared her in the eyes, and gave her a gentle shake. ''It's me.''

She shook her head, desperate. ''You must not, lord! You must not pretend to be familiar with me. They will kill me.''

Casting about, she twisted to see behind her as if there were demons on her heels. ''It's only because they believe I'm a virgin and will bring a good price that they didn't throw me to the lions.''

''It's all right,'' he assured her. ''They're gone.''

But Carlie gripped his arms, and he could feel the sharpness of her fingernails through his robe. ''No, no! They are everywhere. They see everything.''

It had occurred to Rio that there might be hidden surveillance cameras. Now he was reasonably certain that's what she was trying to tell him. They were being watched, if not for security reasons, then for someone's prurient pleasure.

That left Rio with very few options. He still couldn't tell whether Carlie was drugged or up to something, but she was playing her role to the hilt, and it looked like he was going to have to play along.

''Untie my feet, lord,'' she begged, ''and I will repay you a thousandfold. You will cry out your pleasure to the angels. Your body will tremble and your heart will shudder with joy.''

Rio wouldn't have bet against it.

He liked her auburn hair fine, but she was approaching vixenhood with that exotic raven mane tumbling around her shoulders. Unfortunately, no body parts were on artistic display beyond the honeyed thighs, but he would have sworn she was nude beneath the draped cloth she wore. Her breasts bounced and swung invitingly.

Despite Rio's best efforts, the sleeping beasts were awakening. He could almost hear the low growls of satisfaction deep inside. Muscles rippled and stretched. Limbs unfurled in sinuous movement. The wench was getting to him with that tremulous voice and those melting green eyes. It didn't help that her flesh shivered like satin with every move she made.

She caught hold of his hand, and for a moment he thought she was going to kiss it. She *had* to be drugged. This was not the woman who said hello with pepper spray.

"Be seated, wench, so that I can untie those filthy feet of yours. Sit!"

She scrambled to obey and, in doing so, plopped her filthy feet in his lap. He gave her a questioning look, and she brought her arms up prayer-fully. "I beg of you, lord," she said, her voice throaty with contrition, "do not punish me for my eagerness to please you. I live for that alone, lord."

Rio's stomach tightened pleasurably. He could almost hear the gears grinding and the wheels locking as he tried to put the brakes on the physical sensations that were unfurling inside him.

Totally into it, he thought. She's totally into this.

"Your hands are so strong and beautiful, lord, these hands that will free me." She dared to run her fingers lightly over his, and he could feel them shaking.

She hesitated as if waiting for him to reprimand her. When he didn't, she seemed almost giddy with relief. Piped-in music jingled like silvery bells, accentuating her breathlessness.

She didn't stop stroking and fondling him the entire time he worked on the ropes that bound her ankles. She caressed his arms, swirling the dark hair with her fingers and emitting excited little kitten whimpers. She played in the waves at his nape, and her breath brushed the lobe of her ear as she bent forward, exposing her liquid bosom to his view.

"Nero's hair is as dark as a raven's and your eyelashes, lord. So long and curly."

Rio freed the last knot and wondered if it was possible to get an erection from untying a woman's feet. He'd never been into bondage games, but this slave-fantasy stuff was hotter than hell. The lights in the room dimmed, apparently on a timer, but for a moment Rio thought he'd blown the circuits. Sweat cooled the heat of his brow.

He pulled her to her feet, and she came up against him eagerly. "Thank you, lord, oh, thank you! Let me repay you now."

Rio was no longer sure if he wanted to talk her back to reality. "Carlie—"

Her fingers silenced him. "Shhh, I have no name."

She rose to her tiptoes, replaced her fingers with her lips, and brushed a lingering kiss across his mouth. "I can make you happy, sire, if only you would let me." Whispering, she kissed a moist, steamy path to his ear.

Her hands fluttered up his thighs and lightly grazed over his fly, promising, promising.

Rio stifled a groan.

A bell sounded, causing Carlie to hesitate, and Rio to think he'd been saved. The bell chimed again.

"The feast is ready, lord," she told him. "We must go to the Grand Hall."

Luckily the hall was close, because Rio was having trouble walking normally. The huge, circular room they entered looked like another tableau vivant on a larger-than-life scale. A statue of Nero himself, garbed in official robes, stood near the head of a large banquet table. An exotic perfume misted from pipes hidden in the gilded ceiling and serving girls carried in trays of food and wine, a bacchanalian feast.

Rio and Carlie were the only ones seated at the table, and the moment the servers were gone, Carlie was at him again, a clinging, murmuring, nibbling nymph. She plied him with fruit and wine and fed him slivers of roasted meat with her fingers. When he insisted he'd had enough, she popped a grape in his mouth and brushed the crumbs from his lap, arousing him with delicate touches.

By the time she suggested they visit the royal bedchamber, Rio was painfully ready.

She led the way to a vaulted room with a canopy bed of shimmering gold cloth and a Grand Cascade fountain studded with marble statuary. It was about as royal as anything Rio had ever seen. But the moment she shut the door behind them, she transformed into Carlie, the personal-safety expert. The desperation and drugged bliss were gone.

"I have the name of the woman who killed Leroy Studebaker," she said, linking her arms around his neck and drawing him close as she whispered the name. "She was one of the hostesses here, his favorite until he decided to trade her in."

The detective in Rio was damn impressed. The man was too far gone to care. He buried his hand in her fiery hair and pulled her head back, thankful for his lordly privileges. "She's a copycat killer, right?" He mouthed the words against her lips. "Not the Femme Fatale?"

"Yes, lord, oh, yes!" She gasped as he kissed her, gasped and whispered the question, "How did you know that?"

"I went to the morgue after I dropped you off. There were marks on Studebaker's body, signs of a struggle. The Femme Fatale doesn't touch her victims."

Rio was far more interested in Carlie's MO than the Femme Fatale's. He was ready to carry on from there, but she caught hold of his roaming hands and held him off.

"You have to go," she told him under her breath. "Pretend to be ill and leave at once."

Rio was no longer in any hurry to go anywhere. He wanted to finish the bedchamber scene. Wanted that like hell.

"You could make me better," he said, dragging her up against him. But she was quietly adamant, and when he wouldn't let go of her, she reached behind him and grabbed a tasseled pull cord. The damn things were everywhere.

Two thugs dressed in Shazam costumes appeared instantly.

"I fear m'lord has eaten something that didn't agree with him and would like to leave," Carlie told them. "Would you kindly show him the way to his car?"

Rio had enough testosterone flowing to back off both of them, and he might have if he hadn't known it would endanger Carlie. He was going to have to leave peaceably, but he was damn glad the pajama top was long. He was beginning to wish the legs had been looser. Hell, let them mistake him for Hef.

SEVENTEEN

Rio woke up thirsty, and with a nagging stitch in the center of his forehead. Two A.M.? He picked up his watch and shook it, wondering if the numbers on the luminous dial could be right. He'd dozed off on the living-room couch, fully dressed, sitting up, and waiting for Carlie to come in.

She hadn't. If the door had opened or the phone had rung, he would have heard it. He pressed his fingers to his eyes and massaged to clear the cobwebs. He needed to think this through. Maybe she couldn't call. Clubs like the Courtesan stayed open all night. Still, he had a bad feeling in the pit of his stomach, and it wasn't only about her welfare.

Soft chandelier light bathed the room, but it might as well have been police-helicopter spotlights. Squinting, Rio rose from the couch. There was a dimmer switch by the bar, and while he was there, he poured himself a glass of water. The sensation of thirst was overpowering. His mouth tasted like fireplace ashes from all the food and booze the little wench had forced down his throat. He finished the glass in one throw and poured another.

It pained him to admit it, given the switch she'd pulled on him—slave girl to Mata Hari in sixty seconds or less—but he didn't like the idea of her trapped in a club that existed solely to entertain horny men until all hours. He didn't even want to think about the trouble she could get herself into in a place like that.

On the other hand, some instinct told him Carlie Bishop could take care of herself just fine. He wouldn't put anything past her, given what he'd witnessed—and experienced—at her hands. She had the drop on just about any female he'd come across in his time, even some of the dedicated criminals. This one knew how to work it. She could turn it on and off like a faucet. And had. He being the faucet.

If he hadn't been concerned about her, he'd be happily plotting how to even the score. Nasty stuff, revenge. And he was going to love every second of it. But that would have to wait. He had to make sure she got out of there safely first, and without knowing what she was up to, saving her sweet ass was going to be a bitch.

He settled himself against the bar and nursed the next glass of water, wondering if they stocked the bathrooms in this place with aspirin. He was tempted to go back down to the club, but given his history with their security, he'd be spotted immediately. Even phoning seemed dangerous since the calls were probably monitored.

The breath he took was hard, but resigned.

He finished the water and headed for the bathroom. Hanging in was hell, but it was the smartest course right now. He could put her at risk by going after her, and she might panic if she called and couldn't reach him. Meanwhile at least, he could clean up and get rid of the headache.

By three A.M. he was eyeing the Scotch bottle and craving a cigarette like it was dope. A drink would calm him down, but it would also dull his senses. And he'd vowed not to smoke until he'd cracked the Femme Fatale case.

He couldn't believe how she'd gotten to him. He was going insane imagining that she might be in trouble. Given the situation, it was hard to imagine anything else. She was clever, but the club's clientele were wealthy males, used to getting their own way. Could she fend off spoiled, self-indulgent celebrities? Mobsters?

The thought of some guy pawing her made him sick.

He started to reach for the booze and his hand curled into a fist. If he didn't slug something, he was going to explode. It was a stupid, primitive impulse, but he was in a stupid, primitive mood.

Not five minutes later he had on his shoulder holster and trench coat and was walking out the door. Nothing could have stopped him—except the phone. Its shrill report sent him spinning back into the suite. His heart was in his mouth when he snatched up the receiver. "Carlie?"

"Rio?"

It was Carlie's voice, but the noise on the line was so thick he could hardly hear her. "Are you all right? Where are you?"

"Yes, I'm all right. I didn't want you to worry."

Relief made him shake. "Are you at the club?"

She didn't answer right away, and the static was bad, but Rio thought he heard her say she was on a plane.

"What did you say? A plane?" he shouted over the noise.

"I have to go back," she told him.

That time she came through as clear as a bell, but Rio could hardly make himself believe it. "Back to where? California?"

"Yes, there's a problem—"

"What problem?" *I've got the problem.*

Static drowned her out and no amount of shouting got through. Finally the line went dead, and Rio stood there, the phone in his hand, thunderstruck. She was on a plane to California, but the real mystery was why he didn't heave the receiver across the room. Christ, he could have crushed it in his hand. Some other options flicked through his thoughts, all gratifyingly violent, but he didn't act on any of them. Instead, he set the phone neatly in its cradle, stepped away from the thing—and his impulse to annihilate it—and with a slow, savage effort of will, turned the violence back on itself.

It was like turning an avalanche around.

His jaw flexed. Bones locked in their sockets, and the taste in his mouth was metallic. Another ounce of pressure and it felt like something would dislocate. He could remember only one other time he'd been this bent on destruction, and it had not been pretty. If he didn't get control, somebody was going to get hurt.

In his mind a row of cellblock doors clanged shut, one by one. The noise was thunderous, but the louder it got, the more it soothed and quieted him. He wasn't locking himself away, he was caging the demons, and when the last door handle had slammed shut, he wasn't violent anymore. He was something else. Deadly calm.

He was going to have that Scotch now.

As he drank it, one slow sip at a time, cradling the fire in his throat before he swallowed it, Rio wondered if she knew how lucky she was. There was only one thing in the world he wanted more than a cigarette right now, and that was to get his hands on her.

Jo Emily stirred sleepily inside her cozy mountain of covers, cherishing the feeling of warmth and safety that enveloped her. She didn't want it to change, ever. This was the sweetest kind of nice she'd felt in a long time, and if she moved or opened her eyes, she might chase it away.

She was just drifting back to sleep when she remembered, and a smile flickered through her thoughts. There was something she had to see . . . had to . . . just a peek.

She felt like a turtle, poking its head out of the shell as she inched above the covers and lifted drowsy, sleep-cemented lids. The room was bright with moonlight, but it was also as black as shadows in places.

And either she was dreaming or she wasn't focusing quite right. But she couldn't pick out Danny anywhere. He didn't seem to be there.

Okay, she had to be dreaming. He'd stayed the night with her. He was right there when she fell asleep. The last thing she remembered was him sitting beside her and holding her hand. She hadn't expected him to sleep with her or anything. He was too jumpy, poor guy. But she also knew he would never leave her in these circumstances. Danny wouldn't do that. He might be frightened of her for some reason, but he wouldn't run out on her when she was in trouble. She would have bet her tools of the trade on that, even her faux-marble nail-polish caddy.

Something didn't make sense. Maybe she was too groggy to figure it out, but she was pretty sure she'd seen him stretched out on her floor. He'd made a bed out of a pile of her laundry and he was lying on his side, facing her. He'd reminded her of a cavalry officer, dozing by the fire, but primed to spring up at the first snap of a twig.

Could be that was the dream. If it was she liked it better than the one she was having.

She burrowed under the covers, hoping to recapture the coziness. But the image of her moonlit bedroom stayed with her, even as sleep tugged at her, fuzzing and distorting her thought processes. There'd been something other than Danny out of place. One of her dresser drawers had looked as if it were hanging open, the one where she kept her scrapbook. She knew she ought to rouse herself, find out if she was right. Important that she go check, but it was too late. Sleep was weighing her down, pressing on her shoulders like heavy hands.

Her last thought before she succumbed was that her bedroom had looked clean.

Clean? That was less likely than Danny being gone. But that's how she remembered it. The place was all tidied up. Her clothing was folded, magazines had been stacked, and the carpet was empty of Fig Newton packages and other debris.

Now she knew she was dreaming.

Danny double-clicked the mouse impatiently. It was the middle of the night, but the article he wanted was taking forever to download. All the major papers now had Web sites where you could pull up stories, often before they hit the streets, and whenever there was big national news being covered, the traffic on those sites got heavy.

Danny preferred virtual newspapers over the real thing because he could go right to the source, which in this case was *The Miami Herald*. He was looking for updates on the South Beach Femme Fatale strike.

The hourglass icon on the screen was slowly sifting sand, telling him what he already knew, that his machine was still trying to download.

Danny's impatience made every grain seem like an hour. He checked his watch again and drummed the glass face with his fingers. He'd been here a half hour already, sorting through the junk on the Femme Fatale site, and he wanted to get back to Jo Emily before she woke up and realized he was gone.

He just needed to do this one last thing.

A cup of coffee sat on the desk beside his keyboard. He grabbed it without thinking and took a swallow.

"Arrrgh!" Battery acid filled his mouth. He came close to doing a David Letterman spit-take, the stuff was so disgusting. It was cold, yesterday's, maybe the day before. Carlie had coffee detail this week, but she hadn't been around to pick up supplies. Danny hadn't had time, so he was reduced to drinking dregs.

Cup in hand, he rolled out of the chair and headed down the hall to dump the stuff and rinse the bitter taste from his mouth. He was used to holding down the fort alone, but it was the middle of the night and the scrape of his footsteps in the narrow hallway had an empty sound.

At least he knew Carlie had gotten his message about Jo Emily. She'd left word on his voice mail that she was on her way back from Florida. Of course things were more complicated now. Danny hadn't known about the scrapbook or Jo Emily's "dark" side when he'd left the message about her windshield being smashed. He'd thought he was dealing with a stalking victim. Now he wasn't at all sure that Jo Emily's situation was that simple.

Normally he would have confided his concerns to Carlie, but as close as he and his boss were, he'd decided not to do that this time. It felt like information he should keep to himself for a while, until he had a better idea what was going on.

The coffee, cup and all, got deposited in the lounge's trash masher. Danny enjoyed the crunching and snapping noises it made while he gargled a full glass of water. By the time he got back to his desk, his machine was beeping at him.

"Yes!" The article had come up, and Danny had most of it read before he landed in his chair. It was a rehash of yesterday's account, except for a brief reference to a tip the police had received. It said the boxer had been seen leaving a private club with one of the hostesses on the night of the crime, and that they were now seeking that woman for questioning.

" 'The police have not yet ruled out the Femme Fatale as Studebaker's killer,' " Danny read aloud, wanting to laugh. As always, they were a full one-eighty off target. He could have told them it wasn't the Femme Fatale, and after he'd read the first account of the crime, it had taken some self-control not to pick up a phone and do just that.

"Idiots," he breathed, sighing.

There was nothing in the article that answered his questions about Jo Emily, but there were some interesting posts on the Femme Fatale Home Page from South Beach fans. One of them claimed Rio Walker had flown in to investigate the alleged strike and predicted that Walker would be her next victim. Someone else thought the pie in Bill Gate's face had been an FF strike.

Danny fell back in the chair, but not to relax. His mind was spinning. Everybody was acting oddly lately. Carlie had never explained her sudden trip to South Beach, and he had a feeling she wasn't going to, but he would have been willing to bet it was about the Leroy Studebaker case. She'd been secretive lately, but he hadn't wanted to add to the enormous pressure she was under by probing.

And no one knew the pressure she was under better than he did. Sometimes it felt like his mission in life was to protect Carlie Bishop and keep the wolves at bay so that she could do her work. Right now there was only one wolf who had him worried, and that was Walker.

Jo Emily was another puzzle. There was too much about the girl that didn't jibe with the typical stalker victim. She seemed a wistful kid on the outside, but there was a tough edge to her, and based on the notes in her scrapbook, it was probably fueled by rage. Everybody had different sides to their personality, Danny certainly did, but hers seemed opposite in the extreme. He didn't question that she'd been stalked, but he was back to wondering if she'd cracked under the stress.

Was his fallen angel really an angel of death?

Danny shook his head at the thought. Laughter erupted from somewhere in his gut, bursting out of him so suddenly it sounded like a shout for help. He bumped the desk, and his keyboard crashed to the floor, but he still couldn't stop laughing. Nothing could have stopped him.

God, it felt like he was going insane.

Jo Emily couldn't be the Femme Fatale . . . not unless there were two of them.

E I G H T E E N

"Hell of a patient you are," Rio quipped as he walked into Peggy's hospital room unannounced.

She was out of bed and sitting in a chair by the window, reading something she apparently didn't want him to see by the way she clapped the book shut, slipped it underneath her, and actually sat on it. Her pink chenille robe was the perfect camouflage. It would have made Richard Simmons a good pup tent.

"Don't you ever knock, Detective?" she snapped, clearly pleased to see him, despite her annoyance.

"Never give away the advantage," he reminded her. "You taught me that yourself, *Detective*." He pretended to try to see what she was sitting on. "What you got under there, some steamy sex novel?"

She gave him a shake of her salt-and-pepper head. "I make it a point not to read about people having more fun than I am, which would be just about anyone these days. How about you, Don Pardo? You have any fun in sunny South Beach?"

She smiled at the sound he made. Even the most euphemistic soul would have called it a snarl of animal rage. He couldn't remember when he'd slept last, and Carlie's phone call had left him with enough adrenaline to fly home on his own. As it was, he'd caught the first flight out that morning and arrived at LAX at nine A.M., roughly an hour ago, which was the amount of time it had taken him to catch an ice-cold shower and fight the traffic to get over here. Having fun yet?

He snarled again, louder, and jerked at his tie.

"Guess not," she said. "Want to talk about it?"

That was a big negative. Rio couldn't have discussed it calmly if he'd been on Thorazine in massive doses. Besides, he and Peggy didn't have that kind of relationship. They'd never discussed their sex lives in any detail, probably because both of them were compulsive workers and didn't have much to discuss.

He knew she'd been married briefly when she was young, and that she'd lost a baby, which may or may not have contributed to the divorce. Afterward, at the advanced age of twenty-seven, she entered the police academy. Other than that, he knew almost nothing about the real Peggy Sykes.

"I guess your Femme Fatale turned out to be a copycat?"

Her question surprised him. Rio had been looking around the pale green room, trying to decide what it was about these places he liked least, the chalky color or the antiseptic smell.

"How'd you hear that?" he asked.

"Saw it on the news while I was having green Jell-O for lunch." A remote was hidden among a pile of newspapers on the windowsill next to her chair. She picked it up, clicked on the wall-mounted TV.

"The South Beach police apprehended a woman who worked at a club where the champ hung out," Peggy explained as she surfed through the channels. "She cracked like an egg under questioning and confessed to the whole thing, including trying to make it look like the Femme's work."

Rio didn't bother to mention that he'd given South Beach the lead, maybe because it was really Carlie who'd given him the lead. And a headache. And blue balls. And—

"As far as I'm concerned, the more FF clones the better," Peggy announced. "But then you know how I feel about that. I think we ought to recruit her for our stalker unit."

"*Et tu,* partner? Now even Grover's pressuring me to back off and give her a clear field. Next he'll be asking me to fax her our ten-most-wanted list."

"Maybe there's hope for that man."

Rio heard Peggy mutter, but he was tapping his lip with his finger, thinking. "Why is everybody so sure it's a she?"

Peggy squirmed a little, as if she were trying to reposition the book. "Aren't you? The last time you paid me a visit, you'd fingered Carlie Bishop. She's a *she,* right? Unless you know something I don't."

Interesting point. Rio wondered why he didn't feel that same degree of certainty now. Carlie had admitted to writing a book, but that could be a ruse. She'd sure as hell proved she could be cold, calculating, and devious enough, and he wasn't letting her off the hook for a hot second. No, he had plans for Carlie Bishop, but that was personal.

Meanwhile the copycat situation had reminded him that he needed to keep his options open. He'd always thought it was the perfect cover for a man, but the motive eluded him. Why would a man have a vendetta against male stalkers exclusively, unless he'd lost a loved one to one of them? Or been a target himself, which brought up the question of sexual preference.

"You've got a thing for Ms. Bishop, don't you?" Peggy was peering at him, motherlike in her knack for cutting to the chase.

Thing? Interesting she'd picked that word. You could say thing. You could say major fucking thing. "Maybe I have an *issue* with women arrogant enough to think they can take the law into their own hands. Don't you?"

He returned her piercing stare, and watched her squirm. What the hell was she sitting on? He was about to ask her when she plucked a newspaper from the pile next to her and thrust it at him.

"Did you see this?"

The paper's Metro section had been folded open and an arrow drawn to Gabe Quiñones's byline. Rio could feel another snarl coming on. He'd been avoiding the reporter's column. Quiñones had the mind of a hungry ferret. He was razor sharp, but Rio had always considered him too flashy with his facts, the Geraldo Rivera of investigative print journalists.

"What do you think?" Peggy asked. "Was it her stalker?"

"Jesus," Rio whispered as he saw the headline. HARMLESS PRANK OR HAS HER STALKER RETURNED? The story was about a woman whose car windshield had been shattered. She wasn't named, but it was a member of Carlie's support group, and that could only have been Jo Emily. Rio skimmed as much as he could stomach, aware that he was crushing the paper in his hands.

The flash of guilt he'd felt when he saw the headline had twisted into something much darker, a mix of dangerous impulses. Peggy was watching him, but Rio couldn't have explained the conflict churning inside him without triggering suspicion, and he sure as hell didn't want his partner going there.

"Rio . . . ?"

She was waiting for an answer. "I think Quiñones would do anything for a story," he said, not bothering to hide his rancor toward the reporter. "I think he lured Jo Emily into this one, hoping for something sensational, something just like this, and he got it."

The tattered article fell to the floor as Rio released his fists. He was once again in a mood to smash something, anything that looked at him, and that was a damn difficult thing to hide. A snarl of rage would have sounded like a hymn compared with what was going on inside him.

"Hey!" Peggy bent over to save her paper, but as she made a grab for it, something else hit the floor with a soft thud.

"Oh, shit!"

It was the book she'd been incubating. It had slipped out from under her, and she nearly fell off the chair, trying to get to it before Rio did.

"*Blessings in Disguise?*" Rio read the title as he snatched it up. A quizzical smile flickered. The tiny, flower-choked volume was not the secret vice he'd been imagining. He'd been thinking sex, or maybe blood-soaked gore. But this was worse. No self-respecting cop would ever be caught with something like this in his or her possession. No wonder Peggy had hidden it.

Shaking his head, Rio leafed through page after page of proverbs and inspirational verses, each one bordered with a profusion of butterflies, picket fences, hand-holding children, and impossible as it seemed, more flowers.

" 'It's always darkest before dawn'?" He read one of the platitudes aloud and gave Peggy a look. "What *is* this?"

She struggled out of her chair and snatched the book away from him with such force that Rio thought she was going to order him out of her room. It wouldn't be the first time. He expected her to say the book was a gift and she was looking through it to be polite. But to his utter amazement, she did none of that. Her eyes welled up, and she turned away.

"Peggy, what is it?"

"None of your business, that's what it is," she snapped, and made a great fuss of tucking the book into the sleeve of her robe, where it couldn't be seen by his prying eyes, or anyone's.

"No, I mean you." Rio was genuinely concerned now. He would never have done anything to hurt Peggy. He would have given his life for her. She was his partner. "What's wrong? And don't tell me it's nothing."

She seemed to be trying to collect herself, and the last thing he wanted was to embarrass her any further, even to attempt an apology before she was ready to deal with one. He waited quietly while she went to her bed and got in, wondering if this could have something to do with her physical condition. For all he knew, she'd had bad news and was using the proverbs to boost her spirits and strengthen herself for some upcoming ordeal.

The chill that passed over him had to be fear.

"Are you feeling all right?" He started toward her, angry at himself for not asking before. Maybe it was the robe, but she'd looked in the pink of health when he'd walked in the door.

She didn't seem in any hurry to answer, but when Rio began to fumble with an apology, she gave out an exasperated sigh and cut him off at the knees.

"Don't bother, Walker," she bit out in her own inimitable Peggy Sykes style. "You never could apologize worth a shit anyway."

Rio barely felt the pain he was so relieved. "So put me out of my misery. Tell me what's going on. Are you okay?"

"I'm feeling fine," she insisted. "Probably better than you are right now. But that doesn't seem to matter around here. The latest batch of tests was inconclusive. Actually, they were worse than that. They were contradictory, so I get to play lab rat and run the maze all over again."

Rio poured her some water, which she brusquely refused. He asked, "They still don't have any idea what's causing the fevers and the abnormal blood count?"

"Oh, they've got lots of ideas. The cardiologist thinks my heart's inflamed and wants to put me on intravenous antibiotics. The neurologist thinks I'm nucking futs and wants to send me over to the psychiatric unit for evaluation. So if I'm not here the next time you visit, try me there. I'll be the one in the padded cell."

"Your heart's in flames?"

"Might be a 'blessing in disguise' if it were," she said sharply. "They could turn the hose on me."

By the way she was bristling at him, Rio knew she was as concerned about the situation as he was. She had no family in the area, and no regular visitors other than him as far as he knew. He'd spoken to one of her doctors on an earlier visit, a woman blood specialist who'd seemed genuinely baffled, and not afraid to admit it.

"There are no incurables," she'd told him, probably paraphrasing some scientific great, "only things we haven't found cures for *yet*."

Rio had appreciated her candor, and despite his famous phobia of hospitals, he was grateful his friend was at UCLA, one of the finest research facilities in the world. He took some comfort from that, even if Peggy didn't.

He just dammit wished she would get well. And that she had someone who could care for her halfway decently, instead of an emotional recluse like himself. He wasn't any better off in the family department than she was. He had no close living relatives either, and like Peggy, he'd devoted so much of himself to his work, he'd developed few close relationships over the years. Peggy was the only lasting one. If he lost her—

Rio couldn't let himself think about that. The barren landscape that stretched before him was uninhabitable. He might as well be the last man left on the moon. He hadn't realized how much he counted on having Peggy around until this very moment. Hadn't realized how empty his life was of human contact.

He gave the sleeve of her bathrobe a tug, the one where she'd hidden the book of verses. "What's your favorite saying?" he asked. "Read it to me."

Peggy looked at him, aghast. "I don't have a favorite saying, Walker, and don't you get sappy on me now, or I'll call that nurse up here, the one with the big needle."

Rio laughed, glad he could.

Jo Emily was hanging up the phone when Danny came into the bedroom, carrying a cup of tea and a plate of banana-nut muffins. He set the stuff down on the nightstand on the other side of the bed and stared at her as if he'd recognized the light sparkling in her eyes for what it was. Fear.

"Was that him?" he asked.

He meant the stalker. She knew that because his voice had gone cold and the hair at his nape had bristled as if he'd sensed an enemy. Jo Emily shook her head, not wanting to tell him who'd called, not sure he would believe her if she did. But her hand had sprung back from the receiver as if the phone were a chunk of ice, and he must have seen that.

She'd begun to think that Danny harbored a deep hatred of men who abused women, and though that comforted her, it made her uneasy, too. Every once in a while she caught a glimpse of another man, an explosive man, trapped inside his efforts to be good and gentle.

They'd agreed this morning that he would answer the phone, because Jo Emily jumped two feet off the floor every time it rang. All she'd meant to do just now was call the salon and let them know she wouldn't be in for a couple of days, but when she picked up the receiver, Detective Walker had been on the line. She wouldn't have touched the phone if she'd heard it ring.

"Do you want some tea?" Danny asked. He was still watching her like she was glass about to shatter, and he'd been at it all morning, watching her. She figured it had to be the scrapbook making him act so strange. He hadn't said anything, but the drawer was shut tight when she woke up, and *she'd* never been able to get it shut. She hadn't been dreaming about the room, either. It was brand spanking clean. *Where'd you up and disappear to last night, Danny Upshaw?* She wanted to ask him that, but if he had any doubt he was dealing with a nutcase, that would remove the last speck of it.

"I made orange spice," he said. "The kind you like."

When he brought her the cup, her hands were unsteady.

"What's wrong?" he asked. "It *was* him, wasn't it? Why didn't you tell me?"

"No, really, it wasn't." She thought about saying it was a wrong number. It would have been so much simpler that way, but Walker had said he was coming over to see her, and she didn't want Danny around when he showed up. The detective knew too much about Jo Emily Pough, things she didn't want anyone else to know, awful things.

The tea was good, steaming hot against her parched throat. The pungent spices soothed her, and when she'd taken several sips, she felt more capable of talking.

"It was Detective Walker who called," she told Danny, knowing he was waiting for that news. He'd gone back to the nightstand and was busying himself buttering the muffins.

"Rio Walker? Is everything all right?"

"Sure is. He was just checking on me, is all." Jo Emily wasn't entirely sure why Rio Walker scared her. Maybe it was that dark horse he rode like some messenger of doom. Sometimes she wondered if he'd eaten of the Tree of Good and Evil and could see whichever one was lurking inside you. Or maybe she just didn't like the police. She'd had plenty of bad experiences with them, starting with the first time she ran away from home when she was a kid. But none of that had anything to do with Walker. The truth was she owed him, and he wasn't about to let her forget it. That's what had her scared.

"One muffin or two?" Danny asked.

"One'll do fine." She wasn't hungry, but didn't want him to worry that she wasn't eating.

"What did Walker want?"

"Ummm—" She held up a hand, calling time until she could deal with a gulp of tea. "He was just saying I should come down to the station and fill out a police report. He thinks I should get myself another apartment right away, too, and of course, he's right about that."

"I'll go down to the station with you," Danny offered.

"Oh, no, no! You're not going down anywhere with me, Danny Upshaw. You're going to report for duty. Things must be piled up to the rafters at Safe and Sound since you've been playing bodyguard around here. And don't ever think I don't appreciate it. I am grateful—most grateful, as we say down south—but I'm worried what Carlie thinks."

Danny'd slid the plate of muffins across the bed to her. But meanwhile he was wolfing one down himself, and it took him a moment to finish it off. "Carlie's fine with it," he insisted. "She wants you to feel safe. She wants you to *be* safe, Jo Emily. That's all she cares about."

Jo Emily couldn't argue with him on that. Carlie had called first thing to see how she was holding up, and to remind her about the support-group meeting that night. Danny'd picked up the phone, but he'd put Jo Emily on the line, and she and Carlie had chatted awhile, long enough for Jo Emily to convince Carlie she was fine. Now she had to convince Danny of that.

"How could I not be safe down at the station house, silly?" she wanted to know. "I've got the rental car that nice insurance man brought over, and when I'm done with the police report, or whatever it is Walker wants, I'll come on over to Safe and Sound and pester you. That way I won't be alone in this place any longer than it takes to brush my teeth and get my cruddy self cleaned up."

She still had on the big T-shirt she'd worn to bed.

Danny didn't seem too sure about her plan, but Jo Emily was sure enough for both of them. She had to get him out of there, and quickly, so she took the initiative. She marched right around the bed and took hold of him by his husky blond arms, undaunted by the fact that he towered over her. She wasn't such a puny little thing that she couldn't take on just about anybody when she set her mind to it. Anybody. Even Rio Walker.

"You go on now," she insisted. "Take yourself some more of those banana-nut muffins and eat them on the way. Carlie needs you more than I do this morning."

It took her some powerful talking and tugging to get Danny to her front door, but once she had him there he gave in to the inevitable and went peaceably. Maybe it was the business about a woman needing her privacy that convinced him. Most all men were nervous about the things women did in the bathroom.

Jo Emily watched from the safety of her window, but as Danny drove away she was gripped with a feeling that nearly shook her to her knees. She couldn't tell if it was fear or relief, but something tore through her bony frame like a tornado through a rickety lean-to, and there was nothing she could do but hang on and wait for it to pass.

Raw nerves, Carlie thought, taking a sip of the nonfat latte she'd picked up on her way to work this morning. That's what she was running on, raw nerves. But at least she was running. She'd caught a little sleep on the plane the night before, but hadn't closed her eyes since. There'd been no time for anything except unpacking and readying herself to face a staggering backlog of work.

At least she was too busy to think about anything else, like how Nero was going to feed her to the lions when he caught up with her. There wasn't any time for that kind of nonsense. This slave girl's to-do list was a mile long.

The coffee was scaldingly hot. She could take only tiny sips or forfeit her taste buds, but the cinnamon-sprinkled foam was delicious. Her first priority was the task-force meeting later this week. She was scheduled to present her portion of the preliminary report. It was only a dry run, but she'd barely had time to look over the statistics Danny had compiled.

"The chance of being stalked in your lifetime is now one in five," Carlie murmured as she skimmed the material. Surprised, she read on, highlighting salient points and making notes in the margin. "One million women and three hundred thousand men are stalked in the course of a year."

The numbers were high. Either the incidents had increased dramatically or they were being reported more accurately. Whichever it was, this was good news for her report and disturbing news for the public, because according to Danny's figures, eighty-five percent of all cases involved average citizens, not celebrities.

And there was more, pages of it.

"Welcome back, boss."

Carlie was so engrossed she hadn't heard Danny come in. He was standing in his usual spot, not three feet from her desk, but for a moment she wondered if he'd been fighting. Purple bruises underscored his pale blue eyes and his naturally ruddy skin had a gray cast. Fatigue, she realized. Apparently no one had been getting much sleep.

"You have no idea how good it is to be back." She was delighted to see him, no matter what his condition. She almost got up and hugged him, except that his shyness had never allowed her to be that demonstrative.

"How's it going?" she asked him. "Is Jo Emily okay?"

"Fastest recovery on record."

His quick smile didn't convince Carlie. He looked worried, and a little confused. They'd run out of coffee-room supplies, so she lifted her cup, offering him a sip of her latte. It was part of the sign language they'd developed over the last few years of working together.

He took her up on it.

"Where is Jo Emily now?" Carlie asked him as he swigged from the tiny raised plastic piece in the cup cover.

"She went down to the police station to fill out a report."

"By herself?"

"That's the way she wanted it. But it was Rio Walker who called her, so I guess she'll be okay."

Rio? Carlie tried not to show her surprise as Danny returned the cup. If Rio had called, then he must be back from South Beach already, which meant—She didn't know what it meant. But depending on his mood, she might need to refill her pepper spray canister.

She put the cap on her highlighter, sealing it tight as she stood up. "Jo Emily probably needs to feel independent," she said, moving around her desk to sit on the edge nearest him. "I know it seems soon, but it's always better when victims want to reclaim their lives, as long as they do it safely."

"Carlie, do you think she's all right? Mentally?"

The question caught her off guard. It frightened her. "Why? Don't you? Has she done something?" Carlie was hesitant to say what she was thinking, but it had to be done. "Do you have any reason to think she might hurt herself?"

"No, nothing like that." He seemed vaguely flustered and unable to explain himself. "I was just wondering what it would take for someone like her to, you know, snap."

Now Carlie had an inkling of how deep his concerns ran. "I'll talk to her tonight," she promised. "We'll have to find a place for her to stay, maybe a safe house. And if she needs treatment, I'll arrange for that, too."

She rose from her perch, thinking only that it might help both of them if she gave Danny a pat and told him everything was going to be all right. But as she reached for his hand, he caught hold of hers and pulled her into his arms.

Carlie hugged him back, startled. Danny shaking? He was her rock. She caught a breath and held on to him, wanting to be there for him in whatever way she could, and aware that she needed that, too. She hadn't realized the strength she took from him, or the part it played in her ability to cope.

She'd had a frightening premonition after agreeing to let Gabe Quiñones do his series. As silly and unfounded as her fears had seemed at the time, now it felt as if they might be coming true. This was no time to panic, she knew. Jo Emily was fine and for all they knew the broken windshield could have been a prank.

Carlie told herself all that, but she was finding it much more difficult this time to shake off the feeling that something, somewhere, was spiraling out of control. Of course it didn't help that she was exhausted and her own personal world was in chaos. Maybe she was projecting that feeling onto the entire planet. She hadn't had time to open her mail, hadn't returned her phone calls in days, including the one from her mother. And she had probably made herself a lifelong enemy in Rio Walker.

That last thought brought a little shudder all its own, and she clutched Danny tighter. Maybe she would join Jo Emily in that safe house.

"Happy birthday to you, happy birthday to you, happy birrrrrthday, dear support group . . ."

The Osmond family we're not, Carlie thought as she joined the mem-

bers in song. They were celebrating the support group's third-year an-
niversary, which would have slipped past Carlie altogether if Dorrie,
one of the charter members, hadn't remembered and brought a decorated
sheet cake, which was now ablaze with candles.

Carlie was trying hard not to get weepy, but she was touched by the
gesture, and proud. A dozen laughing faces turned her way as the song
ended. It was their way of acknowledging that this was her group, the
one she'd founded three years ago, and in all that time she'd never
missed a meeting. Nothing had come in the way of their weekly ses-
sions, even if it meant cutting short trips and other obligations. Her
commitment, and her deep personal ties with these women, had kept
her in touch with her reasons for starting Safe and Sound.

"Let's cut that cake!" someone shouted.

Carlie pretended to duck for cover as a dozen sugar-starved women
rattled their flatware in readiness. A group "blow" extinguished the
candles, and a moment later Carlie was handed a big chunk of carrot
cake with cream-cheese frosting. The only thing she loved better than
a piece of carrot cake was two pieces, but tonight she could do little
more than pick at the rich, moist dessert.

Jo Emily hadn't shown up yet, and the group was already halfway
through its meeting. According to Danny, she was supposed to have come
by the office that afternoon when she finished with Rio. By two o'clock
Danny was too antsy to wait any longer. He stopped by her place when he
went out to get the coffee-room supplies, but she wasn't there.

Since then both he and Carlie had tried to reach her by phone, but
there was no answer at her apartment. Finally Danny called Rio and
was told he was "in the field," whatever that meant. Just before tonight's meeting started, Danny had taken off again to go check on her.

Carlie was torn. She'd considered notifying the police, but it was too
soon for Jo Emily to be declared a missing person, and there was nothing they could, or would, do. Carlie was still holding out hope that she
would show up. Otherwise she would have no choice but to contact Rio,
since he was the last one who'd seen Jo Emily as far as she knew.
Carlie had no idea what frame of mind the detective would be in, but
surely he could put petty grievances aside in a situation like this.

"Where's the reporter?" one of the members asked as the women
ate their cake and caught up with the more mundane details of each
other's lives. Carlie hadn't given a thought to Gabe Quiñones that evening, even though one of the topics of conversation earlier had been the
series he was doing about the group.

"I don't know," she said. She'd set down her cake and was warming
her hands on a mug of hot tea. Gabe's latest article had been the broken-

windshield story, and naturally everyone was asking about Jo Emily. Carlie hadn't wanted to send up a flare until she knew what was going on, so she hadn't mentioned her latest fears. But by the time the break was over, and the group was ready to resume, she'd made a decision.

"I'll be right there," she said as the women began to file back to the conference room. "I need to make a phone call."

She headed straight for the phone in her office. Her gut was telling her something was wrong, which meant she wasn't the only one who needed to put petty grievances aside. This was an emergency. She didn't have Rio's home number, but she would tell the dispatcher it was an emergency and ask her to page him.

A shrill scream drowned out the women's friendly chatter. The phone tumbled out of Carlie's hand, and she rushed down the hall to the conference room. By the time she got there a crowd was clustered around a quaking figure, huddled against the wall. Carlie couldn't see the woman's face, but she knew it was Jo Emily. Odd that what gave her away wasn't the long, dark hair, or the nasty bruises on her legs, or even the torn denim miniskirt. It was the purse jangling on her shoulder.

"He tried to d-drag me out of my car," Jo Emily was saying, in between gasps. She appeared to have been running for her life. "But I fought him off and ran away. I lost him, I think."

"Who?" one of the women asked. "Your stalker? Was it him?"

Jo Emily shook her head. "I couldn't see him. He had on a black hood."

Carlie was filled with rocketing despair. He might not be Jo Emily's stalker, but he *was* Ginger's, and Jo Emily was his new target. The police had to be notified now, and Carlie knew what that meant. They would bungle it just as they had before. They would never catch this man. Never. He was too clever for them.

She couldn't let that happen. He couldn't escape twice.

Gabe Quiñones came in while Carlie was trying to talk Jo Emily into reporting the incident. She was in a state of abject terror and convinced the stalker would retaliate if she spoke to anyone. Most of the group had gone silent, not knowing what to do, but Quiñones joined the two women on the couch and began gently to coax Jo Emily, too.

"He can't have gotten far," Quiñones told her. "If he's in the area, they'll find him."

"Time's running out," Carlie pressed. "Whoever it was, he's getting away."

And finally Jo Emily relented.

Carlie put in the call, and requested someone from the stalker unit, who was trained in dealing with victims, but she was told the unit consisted of one man and he wasn't available that evening. It would be one of the officers on night watch.

"Why couldn't they have sent a woman?" she lamented under her breath to Quiñones as a husky thirtyish patrolman questioned Jo Emily. Maybe she was being unfair. He was not unsympathetic, but he was frankly discouraging about the possibility of catching and prosecuting the stalker. And Carlie had heard it all before. She knew the laws were still inadequate and virtually unenforceable. That's what her task force was all about, but the ambivalence on the part of law enforcement disturbed her.

She had enough experience to know that most officers would rather deal with gang disputes, partly because stalker victims rarely followed through on the charges they brought against their harassers. Time and again officers waded through paperwork only to have victims get frightened and drop the charges. But Carlie feared it was a deeper issue, a fundamental lack of understanding about victims that mistook their fear and vulnerability for "weakness."

"You sure you want to go through with this, ma'am?" the officer asked Jo Emily as he finished up with the questioning. "Odds are we won't get this guy, but if we do, you'll have to go to court and testify against him."

Carlie couldn't hold back her frustration. She'd just come back with a fresh pot of coffee, and she set the tray down on the conference table. Gabe touched her arm as if to stop her, but it was too late. There were some things that had to be said.

"I don't understand." She splashed some coffee in a cup and offered it to the officer with a politeness she didn't feel. "Why does law enforcement seem so reluctant to go after stalkers, but you'll relentlessly pursue the one brave soul who's trying to stop them?"

He took the coffee and set it down, untouched. "And who would that brave soul be, ma'am? Are you talking about the Femme Fatale?"

Carlie admitted that she was, and to her surprise, the group members who were left broke out in applause. But the loudest clapping came from the doorway, where Danny was standing. Breathing hard, his clothing disheveled, he surveyed the scene. Carlie hadn't heard him come in, but she was grateful to have him there.

The officer rose and closed his notebook. "I'm going to do everything I can, ma'am," he assured Carlie. "But the lady hasn't given me much to go on."

"What more could I tell him?" Jo Emily wanted to know. Her voice faltered. "I didn't s-see the man's face. I've never seen his face."

Carlie sat next to her and took her hand. She didn't want her to regret what she'd done. Filing a report was crucial. Even if the stalker wasn't caught, it was important to have the assault documented if the case ever came to trial.

"She's going to need protection," Carlie told the officer. "Can you provide her with that?"

He shrugged apologetically. "There's not much I can do along those lines, unless you're thinking about a restraining order. I could give you the names of shelters in the area. She'd be safe enough there."

"Jo Emily's not going to a shelter. I'll take her to my place before I'll let her do that."

It was Danny who spoke up. Jo Emily seemed startled, and Carlie was surprised at her own reaction. She'd been about to offer Jo Emily the use of her home, but there were many reasons why that would have been difficult. This at least solved the issue of Jo Emily's housing, but Carlie had concerns she hadn't even recognized herself until now.

There was a budding relationship between Jo Emily and Danny, but Carlie would rather have seen it progress in a more normal way, for both their sakes. They were adults and could make their own decisions, but she felt protective, and honestly, there were things about Danny's background that worried her a little, even though she'd never been able to put words to her concerns.

There hadn't been any women in Danny's life that Carlie knew of, and she was aware that he'd witnessed the death of his own mother at the hands of his father, an alcoholic and a brutal batterer. Danny was one of the sweetest men Carlie'd ever known, but sadly that was what women always seem to say of the men who lured them into vulnerable situations and attacked them. Still, Carlie couldn't imagine him as anything but a gentle soul, and she was pleased that Jo Emily seemed willing to trust a man.

Danny was watching Jo Emily as if waiting for an answer. Everyone seemed to be waiting for that. She was clearly the shy one at this point.

"Would you rather go to a shelter?" Danny asked. His hands had balled into fists at his sides.

She swallowed so hard it was audible. "No, I want to go with you."

Carlie half expected the room to break out in applause again. For herself she breathed a sigh of relief and felt a pang at the same time. There was a lump in her throat because she did want these kids to be happy. Right now it felt like she wanted that more than her own happiness. But she had to admit that when it came to love, it was safer to let others do the falling. If there was a "thing" going on, Carlie Bishop was sure to be there to watch it.

NINETEEN

"Got any Dentyne?" Jo Emily asked as Danny bustled around, picking up his living room. His place was spick-and-span compared with hers, but he didn't have the look of a man used to overnight guests, not by the way he was speed-stacking computer magazines and muscling his set of barbells into a closet.

"Dentyne," he said, stopping to dig in the pockets of his hooded windbreaker. "I stuck that pack in here somewhere."

She liked his jacket, especially the way it felt when he accidentally brushed up against her. The silky fabric was warm from his big, male brick oven of a body, and as blue as the cloud coverlet she was wrapped in. They'd stopped by her apartment and picked up her comforter, along with some of her other things, including the humongous red T-shirt she had on.

The first thing she'd done when they got here was clean herself up in his bathroom and cover all her various wounds with Band-Aids. It was stupid of her to have gone out by herself, but the meeting with Detective Walker had left her shaken, and she'd wanted a safe place to think, anywhere but her apartment with its jangling telephone. She'd driven to a neighborhood park and sat on a bench for a long time, watching the kids fly their kites and turn their Levi's green doing cartwheels on the wet grass.

She hadn't sensed anyone lurking around until she went into the ladies' room and heard the door creak behind her. It was dark by then, and if the bathroom hadn't had another exit, she would have been trapped. She caught a glimpse of a man in black as she ducked out and made a run for it. God, she'd run for her life, but the car door had jammed. Damned rentals anyway.

Her shrieks scared the assailant off before he could do any real damage. But he chased her down in his car, forcing her to drive all over the road, which terrified her. When she finally got to Carlie's place, she tore out of the rental and never looked back. She'd imagined him right on her heels, a snarling black beast, everything but his slitty yellow eyes hidden behind a ski mask. Coming up the stairs, she'd tripped and banged up her knee.

She hadn't stopped shaking until moments ago. But now, curled up on Danny's couch, she felt like she could take a deep breath, maybe drop her guard for a short while. More than anything, she was just wanting to feel safe again, and this was the closest she'd come.

His apartment wasn't much bigger than hers, except that he had a second bedroom and probably paid a lot more rent. He was in a better part of town, and she'd noticed the guard gate they drove through had a real-live person inside. That cost money, though she doubted he made much at Safe and Sound.

What furniture there was in his living room looked pricey, too. The couch had a real leather smell to it, and the shiny entertainment unit against the opposite wall was wood and black Plexiglas. There was strip lighting on the ceiling and an Oriental-type carpet under the coffee table.

Maybe he was independently wealthy.

She smiled to herself. Such an imagination she had.

"Can't seem to find that gum," he said, shucking his jacket. "How about something to eat instead? I've got ice cream. Vanilla, okay?"

He seemed extra nervous tonight, but Jo Emily had decided to ignore that. He was doing his level best to make her comfortable. "I love vanilla. Got any chocolate sauce?"

Moments later he was back with the biggest bowl of ice cream she'd ever seen. Where she came from it could have fed a church picnic. She smiled at the huge serving spoon he'd stuck in one of the chocolate-drenched scoops.

"I'm glad you're okay." He handed her the bowl and sat on the coffee table, facing her, his expression as intent as a life-size worry line. "But next time call me before you take off, okay? I went a little nuts when I couldn't find you. I must have called every half hour."

Jo Emily had heard the phone ringing, but she'd been afraid to pick it up. She'd been trying to pretend the stalker hadn't found her, that he wasn't even real. A silly game, maybe, but that's what she needed to keep from losing it. She couldn't get it out of her mind that if she heard his whispery voice again, even once, she would shatter, just like her windshield.

"Sorry—" Now she was torn. She felt awful that she'd frightened him, but she couldn't help being happy that he'd gone a little nuts, as he put it. "I really am sorry, Danny. I won't do it again."

"Meltdown," he warned, pointing to her spoon.

Jo Emily quickly licked the back of the utensil before it dripped. "Mmmmm," she said with a smacking sound. "Want some?"

He smiled at her efforts, but shook his head.

"Did you go somewhere last night, Danny?" she asked him when she'd finished the cleanup detail. "I woke up and you weren't there."

He didn't seem to know what to say. "I was just wandering around. I couldn't sleep." Blushing, he tugged on the comforter that surrounded her. "Sorry if I scared you. Does that make us even?"

Who could figure this guy out? He was as sweet as a big ol' bug. She wanted with all her heart to trust him, maybe she wanted that more than anything else. Danny would have made a great knight in shining armor, and who needed one more than her? But something was holding her back, and that something was him, she realized. Maybe he wasn't any different than anyone else. Everyone had stuff they kept to themselves. God knew she did. But without having any idea what Danny's stuff was, she sensed it was trouble.

What's your problem, Danny? She'd been wanting to ask that since she met him, but she hadn't had the courage. And she couldn't bring herself to do it now because of the way he was looking at her. Like she was the Christmas present he'd been waiting for all year.

She must have smeared some chocolate sauce because he reached up and rubbed at the corner of her mouth with his thumb. Jo Emily gasped inside. She saw it coming, but it startled her anyway, as did the charge she felt come barreling up from the vicinity of her thighs. It could have lifted her right off the sofa. As it was, she did something plumb crazy. She sprang up, caught his face, and kissed him.

He pulled back in surprise, and within seconds he was as bright as her T-shirt. Damn, she was always going too fast!

"I'm sorry!" she exclaimed.

"No, hey, that's all right. That's fine."

But he made a pretty big deal of getting the chocolate off his face, and then he stood and tucked his banded-collar shirt into his jeans. Watching him made Jo Emily feel as if she'd molested him in some way.

The comforter slid down around her waist, and she tugged it back up. She couldn't pull it over her head because of the ice cream, so she sank down, wishing she were a magician's assistant and could disappear.

"How's that ice cream?" he asked.

"Good, real good." She began to eat, even though she could hardly taste it. That made her sad, too. Melting vanilla with Hershey's sauce was one of her favorite things in life.

She had a big mouthful when he sat down again, exactly opposite her now. Their knees could have touched if she hadn't been so heavily bundled. He was smiling like a man who'd embarrassed himself and wanted to put it behind him.

"I guess—" He cleared his throat and started over. "I guess you're feeling okay now?"

She wondered if that's what he'd intended to say. "I guess."

They were both quiet for a while, and she began to play with the melting mounds in her bowl, making dark swirls through the white.

Finally he gathered up his courage and reached over. His hand hovered in the air like a leaky helium balloon. Jo Emily couldn't begin to guess what he was about to do, and when at long last he stroked the cotton sleeve of her shirt, she froze.

"Looks comfortable." His voice was husky with nervousness. "Is that your favorite thing to wear to bed?"

Was he talking about her *T-shirt*? Jo Emily could not believe her ears. It couldn't have been anything else, but she just wasn't able to get her mind around the idea. She was astonished he'd mentioned the B-word, but she didn't want to read too much into that either. Keep quiet, Ms. Pough. And do *not* kiss him. She wasn't falling on her face again, not with Danny Upshaw. He was too damn confusing.

"Oh, sorry," he said. "I shouldn't have—"

She waved off the apology. "I guess it *is* my favorite," she admitted. "But I like silk and such, too. You know those gowns with lace where the straps are supposed to be? I like those, too."

He nodded, assuring her that he did know. But his throat struggled with a swallow, and his Adam's apple wobbled.

"This just didn't seem like the night for it," she said. "You know, for silk."

"No, no—'course not."

Somehow the bowl landed in his hands, and Jo Emily found herself wriggling out of the comforter. "I probably look like one of Santa's elves, huh?" She lifted the T-shirt by its shoulders to let him see how big it was.

A grin warmed his blunt, blond features. "Yeah, you do." His voice softened with admiration. "And I've never seen a cuter one."

"Cute?" she squeaked. "I probably scared the damn stalker off with this hair of mine!"

She shook her head, scattering dark locks to the winds. Jo Emily didn't take compliments well, and besides, he was making her head hurt the way he was looking at her. God, he was so sweet.

She kept thinking he was about to apologize again, and she didn't want him to do that. She didn't know what she wanted him to do. Everything in her pulled to be close to him, to hang on and never let go. But that always seemed to backfire. Dealing with Danny Upshaw was like being allergic to something you loved. Chocolate. You had to have it or die, and then, bam, you broke out in hives.

Jo Emily was suddenly ravenously hungry. Grateful she wasn't really allergic to chocolate, she reached for her ice cream. But Danny was already up and heading for the kitchen with the bowl.

"Where you going with that, mister?"

"It's melted. Want some more?"

She shook her head, just as glad he'd taken it away. It wasn't ice cream, she wanted, not really.

When he came back into the room, he stood apart from her, by the stereo. "I just want you to know that you're a beautiful sight, Jo Emily Pough, even with those bandages all over you. And I would like very much to be right there next to you—all over you, to be honest—but I don't think that's a good idea. I think it might be too soon. You need to let the cuts heal, and everything else, too. Don't you think?"

She moved her head, pretty sure she was nodding in the affirmative. Either she was still suffering from shock, or he'd said he wanted to be all over her. *All over her.*

"You can take the bedroom," he offered. "How's that sound? I'll stay out here. And if it makes you feel better, put a chair up against the door."

Oh, Danny, Danny, Danny. She sighed inwardly. Chair against the door? What did that mean? Was he warning her he might lose control of his primitive self, break the door down, and have his way with her?

"Sure, I'll take the bedroom," she said.

"Okay, then . . ."

He disappeared again, leaving Jo Emily dizzy enough to pass out. It could have been simple physical shock. She'd been through enough for that to be the reason, but she didn't think so. Danny Upshaw had just made a pass at her. It wasn't important that he hadn't followed through. He was holding off for her sake, and that was the noble thing to do. She glanced at the bedroom door, hiding a smile, and not at all sure which one of them needed the protection. Maybe *he* should put a chair to the door.

*   *   *

Rio *and* her mother? Carlie had been up since dawn and mentally circling the telephone on her desk for close to an hour, plotting strategies to deal with her messages. There were only two, but they were from the people she least wanted to talk to on the face of the earth.

Carlie hadn't yet returned her mother's first call, and Her Justiceship didn't relish being kept waiting. The message had instructed Carlie to call back the moment she got in. It would have been easier to outrun a bullet, Carlie thought ironically. Rio's message was even less subtle.

"You owe me an explanation, slave girl. Call me back, or *gentle* Lord Nero is coming over there to extract the truth from you with cudgels, iron claws, and pincers."

The call had come in yesterday afternoon, and it was now seven in the morning. She was surprised he wasn't "clawing" on her door already. "Get some clothes on," she mumbled. "That will make you a fraction less vulnerable to the one-eyed Gorgon. And maybe by then you'll have thought of something."

She hadn't. A half hour later she was dressed to stop traffic in glen-plaid wool slacks, a black turtleneck sweater, and her faux-alligator boots, none of which made her feel any less vulnerable. She had now stalled as long as she could. She had to answer those messages. The only remaining question was, which one first?

"Justice Bishop's office," a cheerful voice announced after just one ring.

Justice Bishop. Her mother. Given a choice of calling anyone in the world, including Saddam Hussein, Carlie had called her mother. Okay, maybe that wasn't a sign of the apocaplyse, but it was a pretty good indicator of her fear level where Rio was concerned. Better the devil you knew than the one you didn't. Whoever said that could take the credit for this move.

"Hello? This is Justice Bishop's office."

The voice was a little less cheerful now, and Carlie had visions of not saying a word, of sitting there like an awestruck kid who couldn't quite bring herself to make that first prank phone call.

"Hello? Is anyone there?"

"Is Justice Bishop in?" Hope not. Hope not. *And how old are you now, Carlie? Twenty-seven going on five?* "This is her daughter calling from California."

The digital readout on Carlie's phone said it was seven A.M., which meant it was ten in D.C. Unless her mother was in session, there wasn't much chance of missing her. She was probably still in her chambers.

"There's a rumor that my daughter is calling me. . . ."

The ultracool voice on the line was Frances Bishop's. And the rumor reference was her idea of humor. Carlie's key chain lay in the tray where she kept it. She rested her hand on the stones, curled them into her fingers.

"Hello, Mother," she said. "How are you?"

"Other than wondering what's happened to my erstwhile daughter, I suppose I'm fine."

"I just returned from Florida on business," Carlie explained. She refused to apologize. Silly, maybe, but she felt as if she'd been apologizing since the day she was born, mostly for being alive.

"Don't forget that you and I are the only Bishops left, Carlie," her mother chided. "We're all we've got now."

There were actually lots of Bishops and Stanfields left standing, but her mother seemed determined to ignore that, most likely to make Carlie feel guilty. It never bothered her that they were the only ones left until she wanted something, like now.

"Is everything all right, Mother?"

Frances came right to the point. "I've been reading the *L.A. Times,* Carlie, the article about your group and that poor creature who's being stalked. I understand that publicity is important, but do you really have to talk about your sister? She's gone, Carlie. Couldn't we let her rest in peace?"

The burning sensation in Carlie's throat was anger. She'd always felt like an embarrassment to her parents in some way. Even as a kid, when she brought her papers home from school they'd reacted as if her projects were odd or not quite acceptable, and what praise she got seemed forced. Her reaction may have been hurt and bewilderment then, but all she could feel now was anger.

"That poor creature you mentioned—" Carlie's voice was sharp. "Her stalker may be the same man who killed Ginger. He says the same things to her. He wears a black hood."

"Don't you *dare* involve yourself in this, Carlie," Frances warned. "You are not to do anything reckless, do you understand?"

Carlie was startled at the force in her mother's voice. If they'd had a different kind of relationship, she might have thought it was parental concern. "No, I don't understand," she said, quietly defiant.

"That man is not Ginger's stalker. I'm certain of it. But even if it should turn out that I'm wrong, that he is the one, then he will be dealt with, and dealt with severely. But not by you. I'm not going to lose another daughter in such a monstrous way."

For a moment Carlie actually thought the crack of sound she heard was her own heart. It was beating so hard she wasn't aware the stones had fallen to the floor. She could almost believe from the passion in

Frances's voice that her mother did care, and if that was the case, then maybe she would listen to reason.

"No matter who the stalker is, Mother, I have to be able to talk about Ginger. She's the reason I'm doing this. The book is because of her. It's about her."

"You can't." Frances came back hard. "When you talk about Ginger, you are talking about me and your late father. You are talking about all of us, and these are private family matters. I refuse to let you rake them up. It's difficult enough having you out there on television and everyone knowing who you are. Don't you see?"

Yes, Carlie did see. And the disappointment she felt nearly knocked the wind out of her. She'd been wrong, foolish. It was a mistake to expect any kind of support or understanding from her mother. Frances was concerned only about her position and her image. She seemed to think of Ginger's death as a failure, probably on Ginger's part, and she didn't want there to be any reminders that would reflect on her or the family.

Maybe Carlie was being harsh, but that's how it looked to her. "No one was more devastated over Ginger's death than I was," she said stiffly. "Early on I suppose I talked about her because it was part of the grieving process. Now I talk about her because it helps me relate to the women I work with. Many of them are in grave danger, Mother, and they're more willing to trust someone who understands what they're going through."

Frances was quiet for a long time. "You've styled yourself into some kind of safety expert. Isn't that enough?"

Carlie found it hard to believe that she could still be hurt this badly. It seemed there was nothing she could do to end the everlasting disdain her mother felt for her. Carlie was ready for the conversation to be over, but Frances wasn't.

"I have to go now," she said, "but we'll talk about this again, and maybe then you'll see the damage you're doing. Our family's tragedy should not be used for publicity, Carlie. I don't care to be part of a campaign to sell books."

The click in Carlie's ear sounded like a gunshot. It felt like a shell had impaled her heart. She hung up the phone and stared at the key chain on the floor. No wonder she hadn't wanted to call her mother back. Nearly every word out of her mouth was an outrageously hurtful one. Carlie's throat felt like she'd eaten fire. She was angry enough to strangle someone with her bare hands. But she'd hardly had the strength to hang up the phone. And she still had Rio to deal with.

TWENTY

January 20, 10:15 A.M.

I don't kill them. They kill themselves.

What amazes me is how easy it is. All I do is give them what they want. That, I have come to realize, is the quickest way to destroy a man, especially a greedy one.

Give him what he wants.

Fill his need.

Whet his appetite and he'll come back for more. He can't help himself, can't control the urge to control. He can smell weakness. It's his aphrodisiac. He can taste fear. It's his liquor. But what he needs is power. Never forget that. It's the only way to destroy him.

He is the most feared of all predators, yet the most vulnerable. Obsessed with his prey, he's blind to danger, blind to anything other than bringing her down. The power he craves, the absolute control, is what makes him vulnerable—

But only to her, his prey.

That is my power.

He can't conceive of my luring him, trapping him, stalking him. He's blind to the snare. He sees only my helplessness, not his own. So while he feeds on his power, and becomes more and more vulnerable, I will insinuate myself into the very fibers of his being.

I'll be the shadow that flickers in the corner of his eye, the creak of floorboards in the hall, and the silence at the other end of the phone when he picks it up. I'll be the fear whistling through his wind-

pipe, the fist that locks his gut muscles, and the acid frothing in his throat.

I'll be his prey.

I'll play his game.

To the death.

TWENTY-ONE

"The state of our courts is deplorable," Carlie told the task-force members who'd gathered in her living room. "Roughly half of first-time offenders get probation or a fine. The rest typically get less than six months, serve sixty days, and are out on good time.

"Now, I ask you, is that a deterrent to an obsessed stalker? The answer is no. Emphatically not. It's a joke, and sadly, the joke's on us."

She took a moment to gauge the reactions of the small, distinguished group. Some of the most prominent people in the southland were gathered in her modest home, enjoying refreshments.

Johnny Lawford, a young man widely believed to be Billy Graham's successor, represented the religious community, and Barbara Harper, a former state's attorney general represented the legal. Other members included one of the area's most successful businesswomen, a national women's-shelter director, and a dowager philanthropist, who was a friend of Frances's.

Carlie had tried to ensure that every part of the community that dealt with victims of stalker crime had a voice on her team, and her goal tonight was to convince them to *use* their voices to support her tough enforcement policies.

"Roughly a million women and three hundred thousand men in this country are stalked every year," she said, tapping on the blackboard she'd set up. Carlie used a pointer to draw attention to the numbers. "If just ten percent of those are killed by their stalkers, that's one hundred thirty thousand deaths. And yet we don't consider stalking a 'dangerous' offense.

"Any questions?" she asked with a searching glance around the room. "I'd be happy to clarify anything I've said, so please don't hesitate."

Carlie meant every word of it. The members had been quiet all evening, probably because stiffer penalties was a hotly debated topic. It was difficult enough making the lenient ones stick, since the very constitutionality of the stalker laws was constantly under attack by defense lawyers. She couldn't tell if the group was simply deferring to her or if she'd shocked them speechless by the toughness of her earlier recommendations.

"Can I presume you want tougher penalties for violating restraining orders, too?"

The group's judicial liaison had asked the question. A spherical Humpty-Dumpty of a man, Judge D. Bart Holgren was wedged into her American willow rocker and testing its holding power with his girth. He'd served with her father on the superior court, and Carlie had always liked him for his basic fairness and integrity. But she knew he wasn't going to approve of her answer.

"Make it a felony," she said with total conviction. "With a maximum sentence of five to ten years for the first offense, no bail, and no chance of probation."

There was an audible gasp. "Ten years?" Flora Bryce, from the police commission, spoke up. "Aren't we asking to get shot down with a sentence that severe?"

"Not asking," someone else chimed in, "begging."

"Those penalties would be limited to stalker cases, of course," Carlie explained. "I'm not talking about throwing a journalist in jail because he pursues someone for a statement. I want to go after the offenders who systematically terrorize their victims and make a mockery of *all* of our constitutional rights. Our current laws are inadequate. They still protect these monsters—"

That was as far as Carlie got with her impassioned plea. Her gaze snagged on a dark form in the hallway. The man who was posed there, like an assassin planning his shot, had undoubtedly heard everything she said.

Rio Walker flashed Carlie a lethal look as he came forward. He might as well have pulled the weapon from his shoulder holster and let her have it with that. Still, she could hardly believe her good luck that he hadn't shown up at the beginning. She'd hoped to get through her talk, betting that he would oppose her every step of the way, just on principle. He didn't care about stalker legislation. He wanted revenge, but she wasn't going to let that happen, not at the expense of this year's one-million-plus victims. He would have to find some other way to get back at her.

She returned his glare, unconcerned with what the others might think. He was about to be introduced to Carlie Bishop, mother lioness. They all were.

"How nice that you were able to make it, Detective. We're discussing stiffer penalties for stalker crimes, but I'm sure you'll understand if I don't stop to recap. The meeting *is* nearly over."

"I thought you wanted feedback." He pretended innocence, but the edge in his voice was honed to cut. "Did I misunderstand or weren't you pleading for that a moment ago?"

He was about to undo everything she'd done, and if that should happen, Carlie was prepared to loathe him for the rest of her life. Her heart was bursting with readiness. There wasn't a heart big enough to contain all the enmity she felt.

"I'd welcome more discussion," Flora said. "Let's hear what he has to say."

Carlie shoved a hand in the pocket of her black blazer and felt the material tighten against her shoulders.

Several others agreed with Flora, and that was all the encouragement Rio needed. He moved into the center of the circle, Carlie's territory. She was waiting for him to try to take the pointer away from her. He would have had a battle on his hands. It was only with great reluctance that she moved aside and gave him some room.

"In general, stiffer penalties aren't a bad idea." He gave Carlie a nod, conceding that much to her campaign. "But clearly Ms. Bishop doesn't understand the concept of due process *or* the mind-set of a stalker."

"And you do?" she rifled back.

"I understand that most stalkers are obsessed and rejection is intolerable to them. For a man like that, a temporary restraining order isn't a deterrent, it's a provocation. It's public rejection. It requires the stalker to save face. He has to retaliate. The victim would have a better chance with a red flag and a bull."

Carlie had heard that argument, and she'd seen some evidence of it with her support group. They were almost always cases of spousal stalking, and Carlie not only explained the risks of restraining orders, she suggested alternatives when she dealt with such situations. But for other types of harassment, TROs could make the difference between winning and losing a case. The California statute still required proof of a "credible threat" by the stalker in order to convict him, and restraining orders were one way to prove intent to harm on the stalker's part.

"TROs aren't silver bullets," she admitted. "But what is? If we don't strengthen the laws we have and make them more enforceable, we're left with no protection at all."

She turned and appealed to the group. "If the stalker violates the order, he cools his heels in jail for a long time. That gives the victim a chance to put her life back together, to relocate if she chooses. It ends the cycle of violence and allows some healing to take place, perhaps on both parts."

"Or the opposite," Rio countered. "He's incensed by the order, violates it, and by the time the police get there, she's already dead."

Carlie's head snapped around. If you were smart, *you'd* get a restraining order, she warned him with a look. "The goal of this task force is to create solutions, not more problems. We were discussing crime *prevention*. Do you have anything constructive to offer on that score?"

"Just one thing." He took off his trench coat and her blackboard became a coat tree. "Your tough penalties aren't going to prevent anything if you can't get them adopted. Flora's right. Ten years is too severe. Five is too severe for a first offense. You couldn't push that through with a bulldozer. I know you're trying to make a statement, but it will be a hollow victory if you lose the war."

The other members were nodding, but Carlie wasn't ready to give up the fight. "Sure, ten years is tough. But how else do we make people understand that stalking is a heinous crime and won't be tolerated?"

His coat landed on the floor and the pointer cut the air dangerously close to his head as she brought the group's attention back to the figures on the blackboard. "Our goal is to educate people," she told them. "Kidnappers get life, why not stalkers? Do they violate a victim's constitutional right to liberty any less? No, they violate it more. They isolate and terrorize their prey in their own homes. They make every second of the victim's existence a living hell. Why isn't violence to the mind and the spirit a capital crime?"

"Because that kind of violence can't be photographed and submitted as evidence," Rio said. "Our primitive brains need to see blood and gore, and most stalkers never touch their victims. Argue until you're blue, but you aren't going to get a bunch of reactionary politicians to equate stalking with kidnapping, rape, and murder."

"Of course we won't," Carlie acknowledged, "not with that kind of negative thinking. You want us to give up without trying, to admit defeat before we start. I say we have to try."

Rio just shook his head and sighed. "It's a great speech, Carlie, but it's not going to get you what you want, unless what you want is to make speeches.''

God, she could have killed him. He had no soul. She turned to the others and saw that they had reached the same impasse that she and Rio had. It was a proverbial catch-22, and no decision was going to be made tonight.

Flora popped up with a conciliatory smile. ''I suggest we table this for now. What do the rest of you think? It's been a marvelous debate, but I don't believe any of us are ready to make a decision.''

Carlie was more than ready, but she'd already gone as far out on the limb as she dared. She was younger than almost everyone here, and she didn't want to totally shake their confidence in her as their leader. Rio had just done a good job of that for her.

''We all need some time to think about this,'' she agreed. ''But I hope by the next meeting we can reach a consensus and be ready to move forward. Please remember that we are working against a deadline.''

Everyone seemed anxious to leave, so she thanked them for coming and led the way to the door. Rio was at the end of the line, and not by accident, she was sure. She had no idea what he was doing back there, probably making air bubbles.

Her plan was to say nothing as he left. *Let him go. Do nothing to encourage him to stay . . . like yanking that jaunty tie from around his neck and throttling him with it.*

She felt as if she'd summoned enough mind power to achieve cold fusion. But her supreme indifference deserted her when he walked by and flashed her a look of triumph. He actually did seem to be leaving, him with those street-sweeper eyelashes and that insufferable smirk. Everything about him issued a veiled sexual challenge. *You want to play with the big boys? Eat your Wheaties.* That's what he seemed to be saying.

Carlie let him get just out of earshot. ''Don't ever fuck with me like that again, you—''

He stopped at the door and she sucked the rest of it down her throat. ''You what?'' he said, turning.

She could easily have denied saying anything. She could have ended the pissing contest right there, because for him that's all it was. A game. He was pushing his weight around, paying her back for South Beach. She had people all over the country depending on her. She was responsible to others, responsible for their lives, and that's why she *couldn't* let him fuck with her, dammit.

''I'm serious, Detective Walker.'' Her voice was faint but firm. ''You don't want to mess with me. Obviously you've forgotten that I'm a presidential appointee. With one phone call, I could—''

Carlie knew how haughty that sounded. She intended it to. Attitude was the only recourse she had at the moment. Not that it seemed to be backing him off. On the contrary, it was more like waving a restraining order in front of a stalker.

Fortunately the others were out the door and gone before he backed her to the wall.

"You could what?"

The wood grain of his voice made her want to shiver. It was thrillingly low and splintery. She could feel it pricking her senses, roughing them up. . . .

"Run home to Mama and tell on me? Is that what you could do?"

His knee brushed her leg, and she kicked at him. "Get away from me, Rio. I warned you—''

"That sounds like a threat. And I tend to get serious when someone threatens me." He forced her chin up and stared her straight in the eyes. "I tend to get in their face."

Carlie stared back, defiant. God, how her heart was pounding. She would have been smarter to concede, laugh it off, and get him out of there, but something wouldn't let her. He was too close, especially his mouth. She could smell wintergreen on his breath and hints of the rich black coffee he must have had with dinner. Even stronger was the scent of her own perfume, rising off overheated skin.

She thumped him with a shoulder, and he retaliated by pressing her to the wall with his hips. She fought not to gasp, but the violation of being held that way surprised her. It was like having sex with your clothes on. He'd cornered her as if they were lovers. His bones were high and hard, curved against hers. Dominating.

She went still. There was little she could do that wouldn't make things worse.

"You *can* behave," he observed softly. "That's encouraging."

"Don't get your hopes up." Behave. What had he said about making people behave? *There were two ways. Just two.*

"It isn't my hopes you need to worry about."

He'd tilted his head and was studying her with a scorchingly hot stare, as if he were harboring all kinds of dark notions, including what it would be like to press his advantage and thrill her into submission. Carlie dared him with a sharp breath, but it had little effect, except to incite him.

She couldn't remember the rest of his telephone message, but she knew it was important. Somehow, now, it seemed very important.

"Hey, come back!" he said as she ducked away.

Before he could get his hands on her, she dipped under his arm and fled down the hallway. The floor tiles were slippery under her heels, but she moved fast, determined to escape. She made it all the way to her office.

"Damn jacket," she muttered as he seized her by the coattails of her blazer and dragged her back.

"You're pretty slick," he said, sounding slightly breathless. That gave her some satisfaction.

She relaxed for a moment, hoping he would too. Let him think she'd given up. Please. "This is so silly," she said, laughing. But when she wrenched away from him, the jacket snapped tight. Her own clothing had become a tether.

She wasn't a match for him physically, but luckily her arms were free, and the adrenaline was flowing like wine. She slipped out of her coat in a maneuver worthy of Houdini. But the blazer hadn't hit the floor before he had her hands behind her back, locked at the wrist.

"I was going to suggest you take that off," he said.

His breath was fire on the back of her neck. A tug on her wrists informed her that he could get physical if it became necessary. She steeled herself for more rough stuff. But suddenly she was spinning. Somehow he'd turned her around as if they were dancing.

Two ways to make people behave . . .

The grainy texture of Rio's voice drowned out all Carlie's other thoughts. But he hadn't spoken. It was the telephone message he'd left her, playing in her head.

Just two.

What were they?

The answer eluded her, and suddenly there was no time. She was backed to the edge of her desk so thoroughly and decisively she thought he was going to pick her up and set her down on it.

He wanted that leverage. His thighs were crowding hers, and they were as hard as the oak desk. His body was hot from the chase, and his mouth was so close she could have nipped him and drawn blood, if she'd had the nerve. He didn't press his advantage this time either, but there wasn't a doubt in her mind that he intended to.

Her only thought was to thwart him, but something was making her body shake. She couldn't control it at all. The sensation in the pit of her stomach was like falling in a dream, a sheer drop that left her floating inside, weak.

The feelings were intolerable, too sharp and bright. Her only thought now was to stop *them,* and the touch of his lips galvanized her. He bent to kiss her, and she actually grabbed a handful of his hair. Danny would have been proud.

"Hey, let go!"

"You let go!" All bets were off now. Her feverish grip told him she would pull the crowning darkness out by the roots if she could.

He let out a snarl of anger that frightened her half to death. He couldn't move his head without risking partial baldness, but he groped until he had her free wrist cuffed behind her back, and then he grabbed a handful of *her* hair.

"Ouch!" Carlie cried as he gave it a yank.

"That was nothing," he warned.

She tugged back. "So was that."

Her head was arched backward and his forward. Neither of them could move. It was absurd, but she had the advantage now, and she wasn't giving it up.

"Love!" she whispered.

It was like a word uttered in church. It crashed, boomed, banged, in the quiet cathedral.

His fingers released. They fell away from her hair, and he stepped back, searching her expression. Strange the effect of that utterance on him, on both of them. Her hair had fallen in her eyes. He might even have been smiling as he brushed it away and peered at her. Except that he wasn't. He was looking for something.

The mystic now. The flame.

"You never answered my question," he said.

"I don't know the answer."

"That is the answer. Not knowing means you're afraid to know."

There are two ways to make people behave. Love and fear. Which is it for you, Carlie?

"Then it's fear," she said defiantly.

He touched her. Carlie flinched away from him, bewildered. The lightness was bizarre compared with how heavy his touch had been moments ago. She was a butterfly in flight, fluttering to catch the wind. And he was that man her sister had spoken of in whispers, a master of the unexpected. This was the last thing Carlie would have thought he'd do.

"There isn't a man breathing—"

"Stop that," she whispered. His voice seemed to have been affected by the sudden force of some emotion inside him. His touch was searingly tender. If they didn't keep fighting, she was dead. She ducked her head again, refusing to look at him.

"Stop me," he whispered back. And then his lips were on hers, hard and soft, swollen with lust. He dropped her hands and gathered her into his arms. God, he was strong. Carlie heard a rumble of desire rising in his throat, and she sank into the kiss. Sank up to her eyelids and wondered how long before she drowned.

Love and fear. Which is it for you, Carlie?

Even through the heavy mist that was clouding her thoughts, she heard the answer to his question, and knew she should have stopped him when she could. Because this was what she *feared* more than anything else. Love. She feared love. This sweetness could kill her.

She reached out, only not for him. Perhaps subconsciously, she reached for the tray behind her. There was a thunderclap of sound as it crashed to the floor. But Carlie's senses resonated to another sound, muted, yet painfully sharp. The impact of two small stones hitting the hardwood floor. Lonely stones.

Rio stepped back and looked down. He saw immediately what had fallen. And then he saw the look in her eyes.

What Carlie saw was black water, icy and deep.

She knew it was over.

She knew he would leave now, that he hated those stones.

She even thought she knew why.

TWENTY-TWO

Danny probably wouldn't have gone into the lingerie shop at all if the young female clerk hadn't seen him lingering at the window and come out. He'd been there about twenty minutes when she opened the door and angled her head out.

"Can I help you?"

Flowery incense and soft pop music wafted from the interior.

"No, thanks." Embarrassment burned Danny's ears as he shoved his hands in the pockets of his windbreaker and shuffled his feet. She probably took him for some kind of pervert, maybe a Peeping Tom. "I was just leaving," he explained.

"Really? Are you sure?"

"Oh, yeah, absolutely." All Danny could see of her was jet-black bangs that looked as if they'd been blunt-cut with garden shears, and a perplexed red heart of a mouth. In contrast, the rest of her features paled to the point of invisibility.

"I'm on my way," he assured her. "Nothing to worry about."

Her inquisitive expression blossomed into a smile. "Of course there's nothing to worry about. I'll bet you wanted to buy a gift for your girl-friend, right? And you don't know what she'd like?"

Danny nodded. "Something like that, yeah."

It seemed to please her that she'd figured him out. "I can always tell when a guy is in the mood to buy pretty things," she said. "He gets a certain look on his face, kinda lost, kinda tender. I can't resist that look. Come on!"

She propped open the door of the shop, a Kewpie doll in a black angora sweater with a lace collar, and waved him in. "I'll help you find something."

The tiny boutique was crowded with rack after rack of sheer frilly things, mostly in white and black. Expressionless mannequins sat on glass shelves, their upper halves swathed in lacy bras and silk teddies. Their lower halves seemed to be missing in action, or so Danny thought until he saw several sets of legs kicking up in the air in a display by the nylons counter.

Something smelled good, too. Like baby powder. He couldn't decide if it was the clerk or the shop.

"Not such a bad place, is it?" She gave him a wink.

"Not at all." Danny had a good feeling about her, despite how young she was, early twenties at most, and he was usually uncomfortable around women his age. She seemed kind and there was something soothing about her voice.

"See anything you like?" She held up a violet-sprigged silk chemise. "If you don't I could make some suggestions."

But Danny had already spotted a diaphanous red gown and robe hanging on a wall hook, high above their heads.

"You like that peignoir set?" She pointed to it. "We have our own line of lingerie, and that's our brand-new color, snapdragon red. I have some over here."

She disappeared down an aisle and was right back again with the set. The neckline, hem, and sleeves had a feathery boa effect, à la Marilyn Monroe, but Danny was struck by the color.

"Did you say snapdragon?"

"Yes! Just a minute—" The clerk disappeared again. When she came back this time, she had the Living section of the *L.A. Times*. Danny was immediately drawn to a splashy article on the Femme Fatale that took up the entire front page. Its vibrant graphics featured the sinister silhouette of a woman and a huge red snapdragon.

"In honor of the Femme Fatale," the clerk explained. "You must have heard of her, the masked woman who's making it safe for the rest of us to go to the mall again. She's the inspiration for the peignoir. . . ."

She continued talking as Danny skimmed the article. He scratched a little spot by the tail of his eyebrow, as amazed by what he was reading as by what he was hearing.

"All the girls in the shop just love her," she exclaimed. "I guess it's a chick thing. Isn't that article great? They're saying since the strikes happen like, you know, once every month, the Femme could be a housewife with PMS. Or maybe a frustrated actress who wants to get caught, thrown in jail, and have a movie made about her. Personally, I think it's like, you know—a rogue FBI agent or something—because who else would know how to do all the stuff she does, like rigging car radios to scream?''

Danny emitted a surprised chuckle. He couldn't help himself. The clerk looked a little crestfallen, but he wasn't laughing at her. He was impressed with her ingenuity. It was a damn good guess.

"Great," he said. "The article is great."

"Who do you think it is?"

"A frustrated FBI agent with PMS?"

They both laughed and the lingerie fluttered as if a breeze had blown up. "So, do you like the peignoir? Isn't it cool? I heard that we may be doing an entire Femme Fatale line. Like that would be *so* cool."

Danny felt weird and tight inside he liked it so much. He gingerly touched the boa material and wondered if he'd ever felt anything as soft. Maybe dandelion fluff, but he wasn't sure. And there were parts of a woman—He cut off the thought, aware of the stirring in his groin.

"What size do you need?" She checked the tag. "It's a medium. That should fit her if she's about my size."

Danny wasn't prepared to look at the clerk that closely. He hadn't blushed since he'd come inside the store, and he didn't want to start now. "She's about your size," he said.

"Well, then, we'll just give her this one." She fluttered the peignoir again. "If it doesn't fit, she can always bring it back, lucky girl. She *is* lucky, you know."

"Yes, ma'am—" It was all Danny could manage. The grace period was over, and he'd been banished to the Valley of Blushing and Stammering again. A look had come over the clerk that seemed reserved for him and chubby infants, that ooooo-isn't-he-the-cutest-thing look. He often saw it in women's eyes and it always made him feel like he *was* a chubby infant.

If only they knew, he thought.

If only they knew.

Rio grabbed the View section of the morning paper as he let himself out of his Chevy sedan and slammed the door behind him. Rolled in his hand, the newspaper rustled against his trench coat as he strode across the gravel parking lot toward the two-story cedar-shingled building.

A sign by the side entrance said SEAGATE PLAZA and listed the businesses housed inside. It wasn't more than a couple of blocks from the beach. Rio ought to have been able to smell the brine and hear the ocean waves. But the crunch and grind of rocks beneath his feet was the one sound he registered against a backdrop of muted traffic noise.

A January chill bit at his bare hands and his face, but he barely noticed the cold either. He'd had a nasty run-in with his boss earlier that morning, and the newspaper now rolled in his fist had triggered it. Frank Grover had dropped the Femme Fatale article on Rio's desk and asked Rio who *his* suspects were. He wanted to be brought up-to-date on the case, but Rio hadn't been "cooperative," according to Grover, and what started out as a casual inquiry turned into a near fistfight. And then it got worse. Much worse.

That's why Rio was on his way up to Carlie Bishop's office to ask the personal-safety expert a question or two. He'd gotten good and side-tracked the last time he was with her. But if anyone's toes were getting tromped on today, they were hers.

He spotted Carlie in her office on the telephone. She was turned in the executive chair, half facing the windows, and tilted back slightly. Red-gold hair was scattered over the black leather headrest like a fan, and one of her hands was raised in the air above her head.

Rio smiled at the tick-tocking yellow number-two pencil in her fingers. Either she was counting off points as she made them or conducting some invisible orchestra. There was no one at the reception desk to stop him, and her blond thug of a bodyguard didn't seem to be around anywhere, so Rio walked right in.

Carlie looked up, startled, as she spotted him in her doorway. She came around in the chair and gestured for him to wait outside, but clearly didn't want to interrupt her conversation to order him out of her office. So he stayed. And made himself at home.

She held promise as a slob, he decided. She favored piles, lots of them. They cluttered every flat surface in the room, most of them anchored by paperweights. A crystal obelisk on her desk caught his eye, but it wasn't until he picked it up and tossed it from hand to hand like a piece of fruit that he saw the engraved family crest. He heard a little sound of displeasure, and the next thing he knew an angry demigoddess in a black turtleneck had risen up and snatched the sacred object away from him, the impertinent mortal.

He grinned, surprised she could reach that far.

"Thank you, Congressman." She spoke into the phone, clutching her prized paperweight to her breast and holding Rio at bay with a hail of visual arrows. "I appreciate your support on this. I'll pass it along to the rest of the task force—"

Turning her back on him to finish her remarks, she unknowingly exposed to his view one of the loveliest rumps Rio had seen in a while. The subtle curves that flared from her narrow waist looked succulent enough to warm up for dinner.

God, how I'd love to fuck this woman, he thought.

His fist crushed the newspaper, but it was nothing compared to what was going on in his groin. He wanted to take her right there on that messy-ass desk of hers, the phone in her hand, her hair aflame. There was so goddamned much he wanted to do to her it was ridiculous, including watching her try to carry on a conversation with the congressman while she was being ravished—

"I hope they'll be encouraged to support stiffer penalties when they hear about the amendments you have planned to 646.9," she was saying. "If we can't deter stalkers with this legislation, at least we'll keep them off the streets, right?"

She turned back to Rio with that, faintly smug.

You want stiffer? he thought. *I'll give you stiffer.*

"How about the death penalty?" He mouthed the words and got himself another warning glare for his trouble.

"I will, Congressman. When I talk to my mother, I'll tell her you asked about her, I certainly will."

She said her good-byes, dropped the phone in the cradle, and cocked an eyebrow as if to say, So there.

Rio let her have her moment. Poor kid was going to be picking up her marbles and wanting to go home soon enough.

"Let me guess," he said, "the congressman's in favor of the guillotine for repeat offenders?"

She took a sip from her coffee and all but smacked her lips in satisfaction. She was not only going to have her moment, she was going to stretch it to the end of the week if she could.

"He thinks a life sentence might be a little harsh," she conceded, "but in theory, he's a strong proponent of hard time."

"And in practice?"

She laughed merrily. "A strong proponent of hard time."

"One bloodthirsty politician does not an amendment pass," he pointed out.

She turned her coffee cup into another paperweight, setting it down on the closest pile of papers, and then she gave her chair a little spin and sat down. From that vantage point, she looked him over quizzically. "One would think you didn't want the bad guys punished."

"I want their balls cut off, but there's a difference between what I want and what I'm likely to get." He snapped open the rolled newpaper and dropped it on her desk, already bored with the subject. "You know where I stand," he said.

Carlie glanced at the article, taking in the stark red-and-black graphics. "I've read it," she informed him. "So?"

"As of this morning, I'm off the case."

"The Femme Fatale case?"

She seemed so genuinely startled that Rio was tempted to take her off his list of conspirators. Someone with some clout wanted his investigation shut down, but maybe it wasn't her. Or if it was, maybe she hadn't gone about it this way.

"Who did it?" she asked. "*Why* did they do it?"

"Because I refused to turn over my notes and reveal the names of my suspects. You could say my boss is unhappy."

She stared at him for several long, blinking moments. The only thing she didn't do was ask the next question out loud. They both knew why Rio hadn't named his suspects.

As the silence lengthened, it felt as if some unspoken alliance had been formed without their knowledge, a bond between enemies. And maybe one had, Rio realized. He did know his reasons for refusing to open his files were incredibly complicated, yet very simple. And they all had to do with her.

She broke the spell by casting down her wide green eyes, by avoiding him, and for some reason he found that irresistible. She began to work a lock of her hair that was clinging near her mouth. Rio vaguely remembered her doing that as a kid, and he felt the pressure of an inward sigh. It was a strangely painful thing taking shape inside him, this need to reassure her.

There isn't a man breathing . . .

Christ, Walker. Zip your pants, man. Keep them zipped.

With some effort he got his juvenile-delinquent mind back to the matter on *top* of her desk. He'd marked up the article, highlighting various quotes that came from an unidentified "expert." The source had done what amounted to a personality profile of the Femme Fatale. It was the kind of information only a biographer, or the subject herself, would be able to supply, and where the Femme Fatale was concerned, Carlie Bishop was the next best thing to an official biographer.

"What do you know about Quiñones's 'anonymous source'?" he asked her, tapping one of the marked items with his finger.

"I know it's not me," she said. "Quiñones called me about the piece, but I wouldn't grant him an interview."

Rio could think of several reasons why she wouldn't. He could also think of a few why she would, like generating some advance hype for the book she was working on.

He flipped the paper over and jabbed the sidebar that described Jo Emily's latest attack in gruesome detail. "You didn't have any qualms about being interviewed for this one. Looks like you gave Quiñones total access to your group and carte blanche on his series. Didn't you think that was a little dangerous?''

"I had my reasons.''

"I'll bet.''

She flared, clearly defensive. "Jo Emily wanted to be interviewed. The whole group did.''

"Where *is* Jo Emily?'' The cold question reflected Rio's anger. Carlie was playing guardian at the gate, and he wanted to know why she'd denied him access and granted it to Quiñones. She didn't need to know anything about Rio's true concerns. He was a cop and he'd referred Jo Emily to her group. That was enough reason for him to be asking questions.

"Jo Emily doesn't want anyone to know where she is right now.''

"Was that your idea?''

"No, it was her choice.''

"She hasn't returned my calls. Is that her choice, too?''

"I have no idea why she isn't returning your calls. Do you?''

"I believe that was my question.'' He stared long and hard into her cool green eyes, not looking for a crack in the facade as much as hoping to put one there. Her surprise still seemed genuine, but she was a damn good actress. No one knew that better than he. His powers of observation didn't work like they should with her. They required a cool, detached focus. Not the laser she provoked.

Several service awards cluttered a credenza behind Rio. He'd seen them during his look around. Now he turned and picked one up. "Woman of the Year,'' he said. "And here I thought these were bowling trophies.''

She didn't seem to appreciate the irony, especially when he continued down Trophy Row, reading the inscriptions to himself. By the time he turned back to her, she'd come out of her chair and was watching him like a cat would its natural enemy, a too-inquisitive dog.

"I didn't realize you were so celebrated.'' Impassive, he met her narrowed gaze. In his circles this was known as a fake-out, and Rio took a certain predatory enjoyment from it, depending on who his opponent was. He was going to love faking this one out.

"You must be proud,'' he said, "especially of those thespian awards in boarding school. Drama club, wasn't it?''

Her arms were folded, her brow furrowed, and she'd begun to tap her foot.

"There aren't any thespian awards on that table,'' she said.

"None? Are you sure? The Sarah Goodall Academy? You played Jane Eyre and won the Meryl Streep Creative Arts Award.'' He grinned. "Named after one of the school's famous alumna?''

She marched around the desk and inspected the awards herself. He tagged along, and when she got to the end of the credenza, she swung around, ready to take him on.

"What are you up to?" she demanded. "There aren't any drama-club awards here. I keep those at home, and you couldn't have known about them, unless you've been talking to my mother, which I sincerely doubt. Or . . ."

Recognition began to dawn. She stared at him as if he'd grown horns and a tail. "Or you've done a background check."

Interesting that she seemed stunned by the realization. He'd made almost no attempt to conceal his suspicions about her, yet she was acting like a wife who'd just found out her husband was having her followed. Maybe it was the bond he'd sensed earlier, the element of trust that existed even between enemies. Some lines could never be crossed, but apparently in her mind, he had just crossed one. He'd betrayed her.

"Is that it?" she demanded. "You've been snooping in my private life, eavesdropping, spying on me?"

It's my job. What do you want from me? If she was trying to make him feel like a jerk, it was working. Still, he'd be lying if he said that her reaction didn't give him some gratification. She'd faked him out royally in South Beach. This was child's play compared to that. What was a little background check between friends?

She was quiet for so long it began to concern him. He knew it was a mistake going over to her. The more distance the better with this one, but finally some impulse got the best of him. He wanted to think it was curiosity.

"Carlie?"

She didn't respond except to shake her head. He heard a sound and thought she was crying, but when he touched her shoulder, she whirled on him.

"You're not a detective," she said vehemently. "You're a voyeur, a disgusting Peeping Tom!"

She slapped away his hand and shouldered up to him like a guy about to take a swing. "Am I under suspicion, Lieutenant? Are you here to charge me with something? And who, might I ask, authorized that background check?"

Rio had to give her credit. She'd taken the offensive, and it was a gutsy move. Wrong, but gutsy. With every question her voice got raspier.

She poked his shoulder, demanding his attention. "Then either produce some evidence and press charges against me or back off, Detective. Do you hear me?"

He did hear her. He felt her, too, drilling a hole in his shoulder with her diamond drill bit of a fingernail. Yeah, he heard her, loud and clear, and it was a damn good idea.

She was right about his voyeuristic tendencies. He had a better time than detectives were supposed to have going through her underwear drawer. After leaving her office, Rio decided to conduct his own private tour of Carlie Bishop's tiny castle in Marina del Rey. She'd challenged him to produce some evidence. He was just trying to oblige.

She hadn't built her fence yet, not that it would have stopped him any more than her security system. She had the basic photoelectric and infra-red sensors, which detected motion and tripped an alarm. He had a personal fondness for ultrasonic systems, probably because they operated much the way he did, by generating sound waves that bounced off objects. But none of it was hard to beat if you knew what you were doing.

Once he was inside, he'd done a routine check that turned up nothing unusual besides some nylons stashed in her freezer. And then he'd gone quiet, tuning in. The windows were locked and shuttered throughout the house, but fortunately he'd never needed light for what he did. That had always come in handy, especially on illegal searches. Echolocation had picked up a golf club slipped beneath the dust skirt of her living-room couch, probably meant to be used as a weapon. He also found a crowbar and flashlight under her bed.

Pretty primitive stuff, but not incriminating. None of the Femme Fatale's victims had been taken out with a golf club, and if he remembered correctly, Carlie had a chapter in her book on self-defense where she recommended simple household items.

Rio sought a light switch. He wanted to see more than shape. He wanted to see color, texture. It was the bed that got him thinking about her underwear drawer. The swirls and flourishes of the wrought-iron headboard were inlaid with diamond shapes of emerald-colored glass that immediately brought her eyes to mind. And there were so many pillows heaped against the headboard, the lace quilt was smothered.

It looked like a bed meant for sleeping alone, for dreaming. He wondered what personal-safety experts dreamed about. Life sentences for stalkers, if he knew this one at all. She was tough, in his face every chance she got, and he was supposed to be one of the good guys.

Sweats were what he found in her underwear drawer. Several pairs of them, well-worn and faded from washing. Rio had a thing for women in sweats. He loved wondering what the soft folds concealed, and it wasn't hard imagining Carlie Bishop, naked and tender as a baby, inside one of these feathery fleece cocoons.

The thought of cotton clinging caressingly to her breasts did inde-
scribable things to his gut, especially because it surprised him. Maybe
he'd been expecting the black satin nightshirt she wore in South Beach.
But that was just for show, he realized. This was who she was.

Her bedroom personality revealed some secrets, but so did the overall
condition of the rest of the house. It was meticulously clean and orderly
everywhere, except her office, which looked like a family of raccoons had
just moved out. If you were patient, you could spot her system of organi-
zation in all the chaos. It was the same one she used at Safe and Sound.
Piles.

He began carefully to sift through the ones on her desk, aware that this
was the room that had been on his mind. She'd been too anxious to get
him out of here the other day, and he'd been curious about it ever since.

There was nothing remarkable on the desktop, except that one of the
shorter piles was a stack of literature on the joys of tree-house living.
Apparently she'd been serious the night they met. All that water *was*
for drinking, and not to drown one of her targets.

Rio sat down in her chair. He did his best thinking with his feet up,
but given the state of her desk, he would probably start an avalanche.
What he wanted was a sense of this room and of her in it. He wanted
to feel her energy and hear her talking to herself the way she did. He
vaguely remembered from college physics that sound waves didn't dis-
sipate. Not completely, so some of them must still be bouncing around.
He also wanted to reconstruct the day she'd mistaken him for the Chocolate to Go deliveryman and let him into her lair.

Carlie, the reformer, he thought. He had little doubt now that this was
a predominant part of her personality. Even before his revealing peek
at the inside of her house, and her psyche, he'd recognized the traits.
She was driven, perfectionistic, repressed, sensitive to criticism, and a
crusader for the cause of justice. She wanted the predators off the streets,
but did she also want them to suffer the agonies of the damned, and
maybe even pay for their sins with their lives?

He considered the room's chaotic aura, and its underlying precision.
A criminal profiler might say that these were the signs of an orderly
mind disintegrating under the pressure of its own contradictory impulses—rage against the evildoers on the one hand and, on the other,
lofty ideals that didn't allow her to admit her own violent urges. When
reformers broke down they were more likely than any other personality
type to become obsessed with punishment and vengeance. Their sense
of morality became so twisted that they were able to use it to justify
their actions. And they occupied both sides of the spectrum, from mil-
itant religious nuts to skinheads.

He rocked his head back and gazed at the ceiling, wondering if the repressed rage in Carlie Bishop had broken through. And what the hell he was going to do if the answer was yes. Even if he backed off, the Femme Fatale would be caught eventually. The judicial system loved to hate vigilantes, and one way or another, it would make an example out of her. She might even face the death penalty. Could he arrest her knowing that?

There was no answer to that question. He wouldn't know until he got there.

With a heavy sigh, he began to go through the drawers of her desk. The larger file drawer was locked, but a determined two-year-old with a toothpick could have pried it open. Inside were hanging files, most of them empty. Interesting that she preferred piles to filing. It could be another sign of deterioration.

He rifled through the folders, aware that this was taking more time than he'd planned. It was late afternoon, and she didn't seem to keep regular hours at the office, which meant she could show up at any time. As it turned out, the files were mostly personal material—her birth certificate and passport, bank statements and bills. He was curious enough about the workings of her mind to go through some of them, but there wasn't time.

The last file held several journal-type notebooks, all college composition books with dates on the front that confirmed she'd been keeping a daily account of her life since her teenage years. God, he was tempted. He could have devoured the formative years of Carlie Bishop, elusive siren of the hallways of Blue Hills. He would love to have known her thoughts, especially if there'd been any that concerned him. She'd made a lasting impression, even at that age.

He was about to shut the drawer when the edge of another notebook, wedged between the file and the cabinet drawer, caught his eye. He pulled it out. This one was different. It was a slim hard-bound volume with a flowery cover and blank pages. The front wasn't dated, but each entry was, though they didn't start until the middle of the book. The writer had obviously been concerned about concealing them, and Rio could see why.

" 'To the death,' " he read aloud. That was the most current entry, but the others conveyed the same tone, and together they composed a manifesto of revenge. There were also details of the strikes she'd already made and some that were planned. This could mean only one thing.

Rio fell back in the chair. Something had closed off his windpipe. He couldn't get any air into his lungs. It didn't seem to matter that he'd suspected Carlie from the day he saw her on TV, he couldn't believe what he'd found. This was the Femme Fatale's journal. It couldn't be anything else.

What would he do if he had to arrest her?

Now he going to have to answer that question.

TWENTY-THREE

Carlie stood in the silence of her foyer, staring down the hallway in front of her. She'd just picked up her mail and was going through it when the awareness crept up on her. The house was too quiet. There was no movement, no sound, no breath. Even the shower down the hall didn't seem to be dripping.

Do not go investigate by yourself! If you sense something is wrong, call for help. That was her advice to women the world over. But Carlie had never understood before how difficult it was to follow.

She set the mail on the foyer's carved oak chest. Paper rustled and the faint click of her own high heels startled her. The noise resounded in the bottleneck of her entry like the snap of branches against a window, warning of a storm. But there probably wasn't anything that could have stopped Carlie from investigating further, considering what was at stake. A sickening sense of urgency carried her down the hallway toward her office.

The room was dark as she approached it. Another danger sign. She always left the banker's lamp on the credenza burning. Either the bulb had gone out, or someone had turned it off. She had nothing to protect herself with, not even a flashlight. But there was a light switch inside the doorway.

Her fingers touched home. The overhead came on, although just barely. Its dusty glow flickered and grew dim, but it lit her desk enough to assure her that no one was there.

"Thank God," she whispered, and rushed over.

She dropped to her knees in front of the desk's file drawer and pulled it open. Relief made her legs tremble, but she couldn't give in to the urge to collapse until she knew that everything was just as she'd left it, that nothing had been tampered with. The jammed drawer didn't leave much working room, but she pulled the files forward and reached into the empty space behind them.

It's not there, Carlie.

Carlie's knee hit the drawer. She jerked back so hard she banged it shut, and the clatter drowned out whatever it was she'd heard. It sounded as if someone had spoken. Still crouched behind the desk, she edged up to look over the top, wondering if she'd imagined the voice.

"Who is it?" she asked.

The silence frightened her more. There was an echo when you spoke into an empty room. You knew you were alone. This wasn't like that. It was tense, pregnant. Someone was there, hidden. After a moment she rose high enough to scan the area.

"Is this what you're looking for?"

His voice told her where he was. And the tone of it told her to be afraid. It was flat and cold and terrifying. Devoid of all emotion. It didn't sound like Rio Walker at all.

He was sitting in the darkest corner of her office, in an armchair that had been piled high with reference material. She could barely make out the expression on his face, but his eyes reflected the detachment she'd heard. They were cold points of light, visible even in the dark. Most frightening of all was what he was holding. He had the journal.

Dear God, she thought, it was all over.

Now her legs were truly shaking. She could hardly stand. "What are you doing here?" she asked.

"Looking for evidence . . . for this."

He held up the book with such calculated slowness that Carlie could see he meant to use it against her. The realization rocked her. All along, this was what he'd wanted, to catch her. She'd issued a challenge, yes, but they'd been words of anger. Words of hurt. She hadn't expected this kind of retaliation. That he would break into her home in search of things to incriminate her with? That he would violate her privacy with such unfeeling premeditation?

Maybe it was the height of naïveté, but her sense of betrayal was enormous. He had never cared about her. And what galled most was her own stupidity in imagining that he had.

"That's against the law unless you have a search warrant," she got out. "Do you? Do you *have* a search warrant?"

He rose out of the chair, suddenly propelled by some kind of fury, and thrust the book at her. "What the hell *is* this, Carlie? If I had a search warrant, you'd be in handcuffs now."

"It's not what you're thinking."

"I'm thinking you're a cold-blooded murderer!"

She caught hold of her arms, shocked. "No, it's not like that." All she could do was shake her head. There was no way to explain what she was trying to do, not to someone this hostile. She was struggling to understand it herself.

"Then what is it? There are accounts of her crimes here, Carlie, in morbid fucking detail. The men who are dead, they're all in here. She even identifies her next victim."

He hesitated, shaking his head, seemingly stunned by what he'd just said. His eyes were hard, searching. His voice like gravel. "Did you write this?"

She was torn, not sure what she dared admit. A part of her wanted to tell him everything and blow the lid off all the secrets, no matter who might be hurt by them. But she also knew now that he could not be trusted to help or protect her. She doubted he would even understand. On some level she must have wanted desperately to think that he would be her champion, or at least her friend. But he was neither.

"Carlie, this isn't boarding-school drama club. You've got to tell me the truth."

"And what would you do if I did, Rio? Would it be our secret? Would you let me go free?"

He stood there, staring at her, his whole countenance ablaze. Obviously he didn't have an answer for that one, and for some inexplicable reason, his hesitation was crushingly hard to accept. Everything he did hurt her terribly, though she could barely make sense of the pain herself. She hardly knew this man. The childhood infatuation didn't count. Nothing before this moment counted.

He had just smashed dreams she didn't know she had.

She felt as if a weight had been dropped on her. It was suffocating the life out of her, and all she wanted was to be able to breathe again. Surely she couldn't have expected him to set aside his ethical beliefs for her, or risk his career. That was absurd. If he really believed she'd done those things in the journal, he would have to arrest her. That was his sworn duty. But still, some part of her clung to the belief that people came before professions, and there was no sacrifice too great when you cared about someone. Maybe she wanted to believe that because she'd never had it. Maybe that was the stubborn dream he'd smashed.

He walked to her desk, his trench coat filling like an opaque black sail. "Last chance, Carlie. Are you going to tell me what this is about?"

"No," she whispered, "never."

He said nothing, just stared at her as if he didn't know who she was.

Finally, he dropped the book on her desk, walked past her without even looking at her, and left.

Carlie hardly knew what to take with her. She pulled blue jeans from her dresser drawer, several sweaters, her snow boots and down jacket, and something to sleep in. She would need warm gear where she was going. Luck, too, as much of that as she could get.

It wasn't until she had the case nearly full that she remembered food. "There's bottled water in the garage, and I'll get supplies on the way," she told herself, then glanced searchingly around the room. If he really meant to arrest her, the house could be bugged. It felt like a foolish, paranoid thought, but it was even more foolish not to be careful.

She made a promise not to have any more incriminating conversations with herself as she pulled a heavy hooded sweatshirt over her head. She would also have to be careful with her cellular phone. It was traceable, and should only be used as a last resort. She would have to make her calls from a pay phone on the way.

She took one last look around the cottage she loved so much and had toiled to make her own—nearly every piece of furniture had been hand-restored by her, every flower in the garden planted and tended—and then she left quickly, her heart heavy with fear and sadness. She hoped her African violets wouldn't die. It was too late to call the housekeeper who cleaned and watered for her when she traveled. And it wouldn't have been safe anyway.

An ironic thought kept the heartache at bay as she backed the Explorer from her garage moments later. At least she was finally going to get to the tree house, even if she hated the circumstances.

Earlier that evening . . .

Jo Emily couldn't do it. She just couldn't get her scheming, dreaming mind off the packages Danny brought home after work tonight. He'd squirreled them away on a shelf in the front closet, probably figuring she hadn't seen him do it. But she'd been dashing from the bathroom, barefoot and wrapped in nothing but a terry towel, when she'd spotted him coming through the front door with his arms full. Curious, she'd crept back up the hallway and peeked.

Maybe because it was Danny doing the squirreling she'd assumed the best rather than the worst, that it was a surprise for her. She'd never been the type men showered with gifts. She'd always attracted the takers, men who didn't care if they used you up and left you to die as long as they got what they wanted. But Danny was different. Old-fashioned and protective. She had the feeling he would pride himself on his ability to make a woman happy. She just wished she knew what was bothering him the last couple of days.

And why he hadn't given her the present.

It was hours ago he'd hidden it. They'd had dinner by candlelight—which she considered to be the perfect opportunity for gift giving—and cleared the table since then. Either he wasn't going to spring the surprise on her tonight, or she was wrong about it being for her.

"Know my secret for tuna casserole?" she asked him as they stood at the sink, doing the dishes. "I make it with macaroni and cheese, you know, the good kind with Velveeta? It cuts the fishy flavor."

He happened to be drying the casserole dish at that moment, and when he set it down, he patted his tummy. He looked awfully cute in the apron she'd tied around him. It covered his khaki Dockers to mid-thigh and everything but the collar and sleeves of his green polo shirt.

"I had three helpings," he said.

She had to purse her lips, or otherwise they would have stretched into a huge grin. *Boing.* She'd never been good at cooking or anything to do with housework, but she'd been making a concerted effort in the two days she'd been at his place, and he did seem to appreciate it, although he was still keeping his distance. Sometimes she wondered if he'd had his heart broken or been jerked around a lot by evil women. Nice guys were always getting walked on, and from all appearances, he was one of the casualties.

"How was work today?" she asked him. The question made her feel very wifely, and she really did kind of love that. If they were playing house, it was a game she could go on enjoying for a lifetime.

He took one of the glasses she'd just rinsed and set it in the drainer. "I've been working on some self-defense stuff that would protect a woman without her having to fight off the guy, you know, like you had to? I'm calling it a panic patch. It's worn under the clothing and it transmits any major change in vital signs, like heart rate, blood pressure, or galvanic skin response. She wouldn't even have to scream for whoever's monitoring the signals to know she's in trouble. But the trick is to come up with a remote receiver."

"That's a great idea! Maybe I could help you brainstorm. Two heads are better than one."

"When you're feeling better," he said.

"I'm feeling fine," she exclaimed. "I went out shopping today and got the food and the candles and that apron you're wearing. I even got this."

With a soapy hand, she pointed at the shell-pink angora sweater she'd bought. It had a sweetheart neckline that filled out her slender figure, and she'd drawn her hair back with a matching ribbon. He hadn't mentioned it yet, but she'd noticed him noticing.

"That's pretty," he said. "I was going to tell you at dinner."

She smiled and averted her eyes, aware that he was admiring her in his own shy way. She had openly invited him to, but she didn't necessarily want him to see what was happening to *her* vital signs. Thank God she wasn't wearing a panic patch.

They weren't done with the dishes yet, but she set down her scrubber sponge. "If I were the Femme Fatale," she said, her hands gloved in bubbles, "this is what *I'd* write in soapsuds."

Impulsively she swirled her forefinger across the granite countertop, spelling out three little words with the residue.

He couldn't have read them from where he was, but he blushed anyway. "I guess you must mean the South Beach case," he said, "but that wasn't the Femme Fatale, remember."

"I know. I just wanted to write something in soapsuds."

"What does it say?"

"Can't you read it?"

He tried. He even came around her to the other side. " 'I love . . .' " His mouth formed the letters, but the word didn't come out. "I can't read what's next, but it starts with a 'D'?"

"A capital 'D,' " she prompted.

"Dentyne gum?"

She wanted to shake him. Nobody could be that dense. She plopped her hands back in the sink. Frustration made her plunge the sponge in a glass and soapy water exploded all over her. She had it on her face and her sweater. In her hair. She could even taste it in her mouth.

"Just look at me," she moaned. "Ruined m'damn sweater."

"Come here." He gave her the towel for her hands and turned her toward him. "Let me."

She sniffed at her own clumsiness as he used a dishrag to blot the dampness from her hair and her face. She shook her head and silently berated herself. Dummy! You couldn't have a simple snit without wetting yourself?

Danny quietly did his thing while she fumed. He'd started at the top, blotting her cheeks and her lips, her throat and collarbone, and working his way down her person until finally he hesitated. There was nothing left but her breasts, and given their promixity to the basin, they were the wettest parts of all.

She glanced up at him.

A charge went straight through her when she saw the expression on his face. He was flushed, but it looked like pleasure more than embarrassment, and his eyes had that sweet kinda wild-blue-yonder look to them. Definitely a man who enjoyed his work. Jo Emily's mouth fell open but no sound came out, not that she would have had anything brilliant to say at that moment.

He patted and touched her with the rag. He wasn't paying much attention to what he was doing, but neither was she at that point. They weren't even looking at each other. They were connected by their senses and by a buzz of excitement that lit both their nerve endings. Their bodies were communicating better than words ever could. Simple flesh understood at the cellular level what the mind couldn't. It understood the promise of pleasure.

Was he actually fondling her breast?

Freshman biology aside, Jo Emily was honestly surprised by the intensity of Danny's reaction. One of them always seemed to be rushing it, moving too fast, only this time it wasn't her. He was staring at her like he was frozen in place, except that his hand was making up for the rest of him.

A gentle squeeze made her gasp. He *was* fondling. That was fondling. "Danny, I . . ."

Jo Emily might have laughed if she hadn't been so startled. She'd been waiting all this time for him to start the car, but she hadn't expected him to floor it. It was a little like being a swooning girl again, only it wasn't, because this wasn't how they did it at Robert E. Lee Junior High in Knoxville. They might be slower than mud drying on a rock where she came from, but there they started with holding hands, then kissing, and then, maaaybe, petting. This nice, shy boy was coming at it backward. And hers was the dilemma of conveying it to him.

"Danny, could we maybe . . . ?"

His answer was an absent nod. He seemed to be in some kind of a trance. "Sure," he said, "sure we could."

"Danny?"

He slipped his hand under her sweater, and as he came into contact with the damp silk of her bra, a strange, glazed look came over him. "You're wet to the skin, girl." His voice was strained, husky. "That's a dangerous thing."

"*Danny?*" Jo Emily couldn't seem to say anything else. His fingers were already working open the hooks of her bra, and part of her wanted to go wherever he was going. Let him get her out of her dangerous clothing. What the heck difference did it make? She liked him, and maybe more, considering what she'd written on the countertop. But something about this didn't feel right. He had that frozen, starry look in his eyes, and staring right back at him, Jo Emily began to see that something was wrong. He was frightened, maybe even more frightened than she was. She had the distinct feeling that he was forcing himself, like dealing with her was some kind of fear he had to conquer.

"I'm not that wet," she said softly. "I'll be all right."

He nodded, but she felt no confidence whatsoever that he'd actually heard her. His hand seemed to have taken possession of the rest of him and the way it was whipping him around made her think of that old saw about the tail wagging the dog. She did a little dance, trying to nudge it out from under her clothing, but in the process she bumped up against him and realized how prodigiously aroused he was.

That seemed to startle both of them.

"Geez," she whispered. The boy couldn't get any harder if he were petrified. Good word, she thought.

An anguished sound slipped out of him and he hauled her into his arms with an urgency that made Jo Emily gasp. Somebody was shaking, probably both of them, but it wasn't her tremors that concerned her. With a sinking heart, she realized that he was going to fight his way through this no matter what. She was Everest and he was going to climb her.

Jo Emily felt a moment of terrible conflict. Maybe if they got it over with this first time, everything would be okay. Like the first kiss, how weird that always was. She wanted things to work out between them. She couldn't remember wanting anything as much, and he was trying so hard. But she'd also had dreams of how it would be with him, and none of them was anything like this. It was supposed to be special with him. Dreamy, romantic, and most of all, she wanted to feel loved and full. Full of Danny Upshaw, everywhere, even her heart.

"Danny—" She tried gently to push him away, but it took an effort to get his attention. "Danny, what's wrong?"

He seemed bewildered. "Nothing. What do you mean? Nothing's wrong."

She wasn't sure what she wanted him to say. Maybe she wanted him to apologize, which was odd, because the last time something like this happened, she was trying to get him to stop apologizing. Jo Emily was so confused her head hurt.

Her heart must have been right there in her eyes as she looked at him. He must have seen the disappointment. Because when he glanced up and read her expression, he began to back away. "This isn't going to work," he said. "It's never going to work. I'm sorry—"

"No, Danny, don't!"

"Maybe you shouldn't stay here, Jo Emily," he blurted. "Maybe it's not a good idea."

She didn't understand. Not stay here? He couldn't mean that. What was she supposed to do? "Couldn't we talk about this, Danny? We need to talk about this."

He turned away, shaking his head. "No . . . it wouldn't do any good. I'm sorry—"

There he went, apologizing again. But the sadness in his voice was profound. It touched into Jo Emily's own sense of loss. She could see the despair in his bowed head, his slumped shoulders, and she wanted to throw up her hands, it made her so confused and sad. What in God's good name was wrong with him?

Jo Emily stood there, staring at him, helpless. And finally her own despair gave away to frustration. As much as she wanted to understand his turmoil, she didn't understand her own. And the pain was choking her. Why wouldn't he talk to her? Why was he sending her away? He'd held on to her like a drowning man, and now he was turning his back on her.

She was starting to feel like an emotional rubber band around him, a yo-yo on a string. Wanting him, afraid to touch him, afraid to let him touch her. Maybe he was doing her a favor by kicking her out, but not because she was concerned for her safety. She was concerned for her *sanity.*

The most sane thought she'd had in some time came to her as she stood there dumbly, staring at him. It was like a message from above. There was nobody in this place going to hurt Jo Emily Pough except herself, *if* she didn't stay away from Danny Upshaw.

TWENTY-FOUR

It wasn't the moaning sounds that woke Carlie up. She'd been lying awake most of the night, listening to the wind shake the trees and the wolves howl. She'd always believed wolves bayed only when the moon was full, but tonight had proved that folklore wrong. The only thing resembling a moon in the star-flecked sky was a mother-of-pearl icicle that looked as if it were hanging from the eaves.

Noises carried better when you were sixty feet high, Carlie had discovered. Once you pulled the rope ladder up, tree houses could protect you from many things, but they couldn't protect you from the eerie call of a wintry night in the mountains. Rustling, howling, and moaning were Carlie's constant companions.

Fortunately, her cedar-shingle hideaway was as large as a small apartment and had all the amenities except central heating and drinking water. It was surrounded by rustic sundecks on three sides, and the rooms were cozily decorated with blue-and-white braided carpets, chantilly-lace curtains, and white pine furniture, heaped with red canvas pillows and cozy, cotton-knit throws to bundle up in.

For heat there were potbelly stoves in the living room and bedroom, and for cooking, a majestic antique wood-burner graced the kitchen. The cabinet-size refrigerator ran nicely off a generator that also provided electricity for other small appliances.

She'd had the house built in the leafy cradle of two massive oaks that had bent toward each other as saplings and grown into the sky that way, their branches intertwined like lovers. She'd picked the trees, not just for their sturdiness, but because it made her feel secure to be cosseted between them like that, a child swaying in a cradle.

She'd missed that feeling, growing up. Of course, there'd been a nanny, but that hardly counted. Nannies were paid and this one hadn't seemed much interested beyond a certain relish for discipline, which was probably why she'd been hired. Carlie could remember being told to get down on her knees beside the kitchen table and stay there until she apologized for saying her overcooked oatmeal tasted like Kibbles'N Bits.

Barely four years old, she was already being taken to task for her "bluntness," the word her parents preferred to honesty. She'd quickly learned the survival value of the little white lie, but sometimes got it confused with the big black ones. And in later years she'd wondered how kids didn't grow up hopelessly confused the way they were taught to fib in one situation and were punished for it in another.

That morning Carlie had learned that apologies could be classified as lies, too. She'd immediately said she was sorry, but the nanny had doubted her sincerity and kept her on her knees until the rough slate tiles left bruises. Ginger was away that weekend, visiting a friend, but Carlie kept expecting her parents to come in and yell at the nanny for being so harsh. It never happened. Over the years they'd studiously overlooked the woman's unique punishments, and eventually Carlie realized it was their way of condoning what was being done. Silence was acceptance. Another lesson learned at a very young age.

She'd planned her escape in those days, imagining a haven in the treetops, but never expecting to have one. And then at twenty-one, some money and this parcel of land had come into her hands through a trust. She was told it was a gift from the Stanfield side of the family, maternal grandparents who died when she was young, but she was never told why they'd bequeathed it to her. It was one of many baffling secrets that permeated her childhood.

Carlie's schedule didn't permit her to visit often, but all she'd ever known of joy and serenity was in this place. She'd felt at peace here, even with the wolves howling. But tonight the house couldn't work its magic on her. She was in too much conflict. Her thoughts kept spinning off in terrifying directions, then froze at every sound. She'd left the stove burning in her bedroom, and she was huddled in a pair of gray workout sweats beneath an arctic goosedown comforter, but she couldn't get warm.

And that moaning noise. God, what was it?

She sat up to listen as it grew louder, and then a rattling thump brought her to her feet. Her heart went weightless with shock. It sounded like a small tree had toppled, but that couldn't be the case. There was something down there on the ground, something big.

Wrapping herself in the comforter, Carlie grabbed the gas lantern she used to save electricity and made her way to the living room, trying not to set fire to the place. The front windows looked out on the deck, but the shadows created by the creaking boughs made it difficult to see.

The six-foot pine deck reached all the way around the house, but the only way up from the ground was a cable rope ladder, a heavy affair on a winch that Carlie rolled up when she was inside. Most tree houses of any size had some form of spiral staircase. Carlie had wanted her place inaccessible, and she'd never forgotten to raise the ladder before tonight, but in her haste, it was possible.

She would have to go out.

Icy air whistled through the crack in the sliding door. Carlie shivered helplessly against the raw, biting wind. The comforter wasn't going to be enough, she knew. It must be well below freezing, and the deck was limned with a glittery layer of frost, but there wasn't time to go back for shoes.

"Damn," she whispered as knives of pain shot up her legs. The surface was a bed of ice needles against her bare soles. A few more steps and her calves began to ache. She felt as if she were trying to walk across a skating rink. There was no way to steady herself, but luckily there were only a few feet to go.

The ladder *was* down. The breath left Carlie's lungs in a white puff cloud as she reached the railing. The gate was latched, but the rope was dangling over the side. She had no idea what happened, unless she hadn't rolled it all the way up and the heaviness had dragged it down.

She held out the lantern and peered at the ground, fully expecting to see a bear or some other wild creature scurry away. What she did see was far more terrifying. There was a man on her rope ladder. He was still on the bottom rungs, but it was clear he was intending to make his way to the top.

"Stop!" she shouted. "Stop or you're dead!"

All she could see was the top of his head, but she could hear every word that came out of his mouth as he hooked his way back down, and they were as steaming hot as his breath.

"How did you find me?" she cried, not knowing whether to be horrified or relieved.

Rio Walker glowered up at her as soon as he had his feet on solid ground. "You told me about this place, genius."

True. He was a detective, but she hadn't seen much sign of his legendary prowess, until recently.

"I'm not going back," she told him, cutting right to the chase. "So you might as well leave. You're wasting your time. I'm serious, Rio. You'll never take me back aliv—"

"Shut up!"

She stared at him blankly. Shocked would not have been too strong a word. Shut up? People tossed that term around all the time, but this had sounded like a drill sergeant barking out an order.

"Could we dispense with the bad-movie scene?" He forced some civility into his voice, but he still sounded like a man close to the edge. "I'm not here to arrest you or take you back. This is personal. All I want to do is talk."

Personal. *Personal?* "Talk about what?"

"About us."

"What does that mean? There is no *us*." Carlie tried to step closer to get a better look at him, but her feet were now officially frozen to the deck. "Have you been drinking?"

"No, but I'm going to need some booze to get up this ladder."

"You don't like ladders?"

He didn't answer, just took a deep breath, grabbed a handful of rope, and hoisted himself up. He was only about four rungs up when he let out a frustrated moan and jumped to the ground.

So that's what she'd been hearing for the last hour. Him, moaning and thumping. "Heights? You don't like heights?"

"I don't like trees."

"Trees? What did a tree ever do to you?"

He shot her a look that said, Don't go there. Just don't. "Think you could come down here? We could talk in my car."

"It's freezing! If I stay out here any longer, they'll have to amputate my toes."

"Then throw a six-pack over the railing." He shrugged, but it was clear he wasn't kidding. "I might make it drunk. I'll never make it sober."

Carlie didn't know whether to believe him or not. If the choice was to get him some booze or to send him packing, that was a no-brainer. But why break her record now. It was a little late to start using gray matter where he was concerned. Besides, she'd never run into a tree-phobic male, and she was mildly curious about that "personal" reference.

"Wait a minute," she told him.

Moments later she was back with a nearly full bottle of brandy and wearing a lot more clothes. This time she had on shoes, an old hat with woolen earmuffs, and a second comforter wrapped around her.

"Drink fast," she said, taking a swig before she lowered it over the rail on a string. "I don't have enough antifreeze for both of us."

Not ten minutes later he sent the brandy bottle back up, half-empty, and was making another assault on the summit.

"Maybe if you took that trench coat off," she suggested as he hesitated halfway, apparently to get his bearings.

"Shut up," he muttered again.

When it looked like he was going to make it, she gingerly backed away to give him plenty of room. But she was probably as relieved as he was when he finally hoisted himself onto the deck. "Not so bad, was it?" she asked.

He was snarling and shaking too hard to do much more than mutter, "Fuck that," and wrest the bottle out of her hand.

"Easy," she cautioned as he chugged it down. "That's one-hundred-proof stuff."

He wiped his mouth and glared at her. "That's the problem. Not strong enough."

He gave the impression of a large caged animal with his dark hair all over the place and his eyes so wintry and wild. A timber wolf, Carlie thought, or something equally fierce. By the look of his deeply shadowed jaw, he hadn't shaved, and Carlie found herself giving some serious thought to his state of mind. And her own safety. He didn't quite finish the bottle, but she would have to remember not to light matches anywhere near him.

Once they were inside, she again attempted to relieve him of his coat, an offer he refused, hugging it around himself like an angry beast. He did say yes to some hot coffee. Carlie couldn't tell if he was frozen or frightened, but she figured it was some of both the way he went straight to the potbelly stove and huddled there, still growling and shivering.

The place seemed small with him in it, probably because the rooms didn't have the height of a regular house, and his head had come close enough to the slope of the ceiling in some places to make her think he was going to hit.

She left him in the living room, warily eyeing the huge tree trunk that impaled the house like a barbecue skewer, and went to fix some sandwiches and coffee. Her goal was to sober him up, but when she returned with the tray it was clear that he had different plans. He was back into the brandy, but at least he'd poured himself a glass and was sipping it now.

You'd have thought the tree trunk was crawling with vermin the way he was looking at it. "Sandwich?" she offered. "I've got ham and Swiss or tuna on dill bread."

He shook his head. "Sure you haven't got any beer?"

She thought about laughing, but was afraid she might get hysterical. It had been a long day. "Sorry, I didn't know you were coming."

Her stomach didn't seem to like the idea of food any more than his did, so she set the tray on the coffee table and poured herself some of the Harp Inn's special grind. Warming her hands on the mug, she drank in the rich aroma, but that was as far as she got. Apparently coffee wasn't what she wanted either. She couldn't tell if it was him or the situation, but she wasn't any steadier than she had been trying to navigate the deck. And that brandy he was hogging looked awfully good to her.

"Pour some of that in here, would you?" She held out her mug, daring him to venture close enough to fill it. "A lot of it," she said.

Carlie nearly choked on the first swallow. He'd taken her at her word. Have a little coffee with your brandy, Bellissima, she thought. They would both be candidates for rehab before she got him out of here.

She kept what liquor she had in a china cabinet that was built into the far corner of the living room. Since Rio had decided to station himself there, Carlie took her favorite spot on the couch next to the fire and tucked one of the wool throws around her. She slept in sweats when she stayed up here, but if she'd been nervous about his reaction to her nightwear, there was no need. Clearly he was still getting used to the fact that he was sixty feet high and surrounded by bark.

"You really *don't* like trees, do you?"

"It's a long story. Remind me not to tell you."

He took another swig of brandy, but Carlie had heard traces of bitterness, and it stirred something inside her that was familiar, yet dangerous. She was fatally curious about Rio Walker, and always had been. All those years ago when Ginger had riveted her with stories of the thrilling man she'd met at work, she'd talked about his having Native American blood. That had seemed to be the source of his mystique even then, and it had fascinated Carlie, too. She'd credited him with special abilities and insights, with instincts long lost to the industrialized races, if they'd ever had them.

But none of that dovetailed with the man about to consume every last drop of her brandy. Weren't Indians supposed to have a special affinity for nature? Weren't they attuned to the woods and the animals and the earth itself? She'd always believed them more intuitive and spiritual, but maybe that was part of the same lore that had wolves baying only at full moons.

Carlie didn't know, but she wanted to.

As for Rio, himself, he shared none of her reverence for his heritage, then or now. He could read it in her expression, in just about everyone's expression who knew anything about him. They all thought him some kind of medicine man. But if he could have drained himself of every drop of his Shoshone blood, however much it was, he would have done it, happily. And being stranded in a tree house with a white woman peering at him, apparently trying to imagine him in war paint, only reminded him how much everything about his ancestry haunted him.

She patted the couch. "It's comfortable," she said.

Interesting that all of a sudden she seemed to want him next to her. She must be getting drunk. He wished he was. If he'd had to choose between booze or a cigarette right now, he'd have taken booze.

"I'm fine where I am," he told her.

She questioned that with a long look. "Are you going to tell me what you're doing here?"

"For starters, I want to know what *you're* doing here."

"Running away from you?"

She tried to hide her smile in the coffee cup, but that wasn't going to happen. Rio couldn't tell whether she was sipping the potent brew or blowing bubbles in it, but he'd seen the smile, and he took it as an encouraging sign. She was letting down her guard, and he doubted that it was his charm, so it had to be the brandy. Maybe, just maybe, if he could keep her drinking, he might get some information out of her.

Finally she came up for air and gazed at him with those leafy, mint julip eyes of hers. A man could get woozy on the color alone. Cool and green and shady. Too shady. What the hell was she hiding?

"Let's make a deal," he said.

She suspiciously regarded him at length. "What kind of a deal? You show me yours, and I'll show you mine?"

Rio hadn't expected her to go for it, much less suggest it. He finished off the brandy and set down the glass. "Works for me."

"I didn't say I'd do it. I was just trying to establish what kind of deal we were talking about."

That smile again, faintly bold. That voice, breathy. This was the other Carlie. The one who had seduced him deaf, dumb, and blind in Florida.

"And now that you know?" he said.

"Got anything I'd want to see?"

It was an innocent enough glance, but Rio felt as if she'd reached over and stroked him in an erogenous zone. *The* erogenous zone. They both knew what she was insinuating, but she continued to hold his gaze, never looking down, and that just made him hotter. She might as well have very politely struck a match against his fly.

She was good. He kept forgetting that, and it wasn't like him to underestimate an opponent. That was the kicker. When he was around her, he didn't think of her in those terms. She was a woman first, a sexual being. She was shoulders and ankles and soft inner thighs. She was delicate collarbones and damn lovely breasts, if memory served him. All of it bundled up in those goddamn sweats.

He'd known she was going to be sexy in gray fleece. But not how sexy.

"Try me," he told her.

She backed off then. Maybe she'd read his intent. It was hard to see, the way she used that mug as a shield.

"I don't want to play," she said, concentrating on her coffee. She swirled it, sniffed it, sipped it, propped her chin delicately on the cup's rim, and sighed.

Then, with heavy-lidded eyes, she glanced up at him again.

She wanted to play. She wanted to scatter a trail of flower petals behind her, maybe snapdragons, and lead him down the garden path, just the way she did in South Beach. Her game was blowing kisses and running away. A wood nymph. But he had a surprise for her.

"How about a different game?" he said. "Did you ever play Nobody Knows when you were a kid."

She shook her head.

"Now's your chance." He grinned. "You pick the topic and I have to reveal something about myself that no one else knows because it's embarrassing, incriminating, or sinful. And it has to be true, of course, not something I've made up."

"And when you're done, you pick a topic and I go?"

"Easy, huh? I'll even let you pick the topic for both of us."

"Both of us?" At his nod, she looked mildly intrigued, at least enough to abandon her deep involvement with her coffee cup. "There would have to be some ground rules," she said.

"As long as you tell me what they are."

She thought about it for a while, then sat up, plunked down the mug, and proceeded to impress him with her grasp of the situation.

"If I do reveal anything incriminating," she said, "I want your word that it won't be used against me in a court of law. Also, nobody's getting taken away from this place in handcuffs, no matter what's said. There will be no arrests, no trips down to the station for questioning, agreed? We're just playing a game. Two consenting adults, slightly tipsy on brandy, amusing themselves on a cold winter's night."

Based on her personality type, Rio had already established her as a control nut, but if there was ever any doubt—

"Is that a deal?" she pressed.

He raised his glass to her. "Who goes first?"

"You." She lifted her mug. "And the topic is trees."

She wasn't going to let him off the hook. But he'd counted on that. At least she'd taken the bait. You couldn't spend as many years as he had in law enforcement and not know the importance of horse trading. Give to get. Something had to be sacrificed, blood had to be spilled. Your own, usually. Now he wondered if he was drunk enough to tell her the truth. Probably not.

"My ground rule is this," he said. "I'm going to finish off that bottle of brandy before I spill my guts. And if you've got another one stashed somewhere, give it up."

"Peppermint schnapps?"

He curled a lip. "I'd rather be sober."

It took the better part of a half hour and the rest of the booze before Rio was ready to take a stab at telling her what "nobody knew" about him. He didn't like talking about himself under any circumstances, and this was no bedtime story. Liquor had a way of lowering the inhibitions and loosening the tongue, but not enough, he feared.

He sat on a stool by the potbelly stove, the empty bottle cradled between his legs. Get this over with as quickly as possible, he thought. Slap a Band-Aid on it, and then it's her turn. She gets to spill *her* guts.

"I was kidnapped when I was nine years old," he said, staring at the brandy bottle rather than at her. "He took me into the San Gabriel Mountains and kept me there for a year. He was crazy on drugs and booze most of time, and he swore the white culture was poisoning the natural resources on reservation land in order to take it back."

"The man who kidnapped you was Indian?"

"He was my father."

It was quiet after that. She was quiet, and Rio hoped she couldn't hear the scraping noise he was making. He'd been working at the label of the brandy bottle. Now it came off in his hand.

"He was a quarter Shoshone. He was also a decorated Korean War vet, but by the time he got out, he couldn't function in the civilian world. Combat duty had screwed him up pretty badly."

Rio set the bottle on the floor. That was the easy part. From now on it would be like taking a knife to the stitches that were holding him together, sutures that had closed wounds and long since become a part of his flesh. He was reasonably certain he couldn't tell her the rest of it, because it involved his mother. . . .

Maybe he could *drink schnapps.*

"Rio, we don't need to play this game."

He looked up, surprised at the concern in her voice. She was sitting forward and looking as if she were about to come over to him, but he didn't want that. He just wanted to get through it.

"I kept telling him my mother was sick," he went on. "She was all alone, and I begged him to let me go, but nothing mattered to him except that she was white. He saw her as one of the enemy."

"Did he hurt you?"

"He didn't beat me, if that's what you mean. I was locked in a shed, but he only did that on the days I was sick and couldn't go hunting with him. He was constantly testing himself against the elements, obsessed with proving how strong he was. Every dawn he climbed an oak tree as big as this one and picked his way out to the end of a branch like a tightrope artist."

Rio leaned forward on his arms. They ached like he was having a heart attack. Sitting only seemed to make it worse, so he wandered the room for a while and ended up at the windows opposite the two couches that flanked the fire. The light was dim there and maybe it would be a little more difficult for her to see him.

"The branches hung over a canyon. There was a white water river a hundred feet below. It was like he was trying to commit suicide."

"But he didn't fall?" she asked.

"No, but I used to pray he would. Even when I was pleading with him to come down, part of me wanted him to slip. The fear and guilt were so bad I couldn't breathe. Imagine a nine-year-old kid waiting for his father to fall to his death, wishing he would because there was no other way to escape him."

An animal howled in the distance. The sound was so forlorn it could have come from inside Rio. He turned to Carlie, waiting for her to stop him. She couldn't want to hear any more. But he could see the horror in her face, and it was like him with his father. She didn't want to hear the rest. She had to.

"One morning I woke up sick," he said, "too sick to get around on my own, so he left me in the cabin instead of locking me in the shed. That was my opening. Somehow I got down the mountain on foot, but I was too late."

"Your mother?"

He nodded. "She was already gone. The death certificate called it cardiopulmonary failure, but her neighbor told me she died of heartbreak. I didn't know what to do. They were going to send me to live with my grandfather, who was blind, but he frightened the hell out of me, so I ran away. I went back up the mountain."

"You wanted to be with your father?"

"I thought I could do something, help him." He shrugged, but only because he didn't want her to know what was going on inside him. He didn't want her to hear the kid who was screaming into the yawning maw of a canyon, screaming for his father to come back, to forgive him.

"I found his body at the bottom. I don't think he suffered. He died on impact. Anyway that's what I keep telling myself."

Carlie's voice sounded very far away when she spoke.

"You were nine," she said. "A nine-year-old can't save adults from certain death, even when they're his parents. You did everything you could, everything humanly possible for a child. More."

Her voice reached out to him. "You were a hero."

That nearly killed him. "Jesus," he whispered, silenced by the strange kind of fire rising up inside him. He knew what it was. Rage at the terrible helplessness that he had never been able to reconcile in his mind or his heart.

"Don't say things like that," he warned her. "Don't use that word. I might as well have shot them both."

She said nothing more. Perhaps because of the way he was looking at her. The rage was still in him. He had spilled blood. Others'. Now his own. It was her turn, and he hoped to God she understood that he would accept nothing less than the truth, no matter how ugly it was.

She pointed to herself, and he nodded.

"Please, I don't want to."

Her voice was faint, but he didn't care if she had to be hooked up to a respirator, she was going to talk.

"You have to," he said.

TWENTY-FIVE

Carlie was sober now. Stone-cold. And struggling to understand what she'd just heard. How much could a nine-year-old endure and not be crushed by it? She had thought her childhood difficult, but his was monstrous. It was a wonder he'd come out of it sane. Surely he didn't want to continue the game, not after this. If she'd had any idea, she wouldn't have put him through it.

"I'm sorry." Her voice was hoarse to the point of breaking, but she had to say something. "I can't tell you how sorry."

He was so quiet it frightened her. In her experience, when a man suddenly sealed himself off, it was to keep something violent from erupting. He could have been a stone figure standing by the window, except that statues didn't radiate tension. Carlie had registered every word he'd said. Bruising words. They'd been like kicks in the stomach, and if she felt beaten up just from hearing them, then he must be hemorrhaging.

She reached for her mug. It was something to do, but the coffee had gone cold, and even holding the cup was no comfort. There had to be a way to help him through this. She'd lost someone she loved in a violent way, too—and felt responsible. She understood the guilt, the grief. He wasn't alone. It might help him to know that, but as she tried to find the words, her nerve failed her. It didn't feel safe. He was wounded, and people lashed out when they were hurting. They struck back blindly, anything to lessen the pain, and when that happened, even a simple offer of help was dangerous.

No, she could not comfort Rio Walker. She didn't dare.

He was a silent, forbidding presence by her window. He looked as if he could bring down the house with an angry toss of his head, although he wasn't doing anything more threatening at the moment than studying her, waiting for her to take her turn.

She didn't know where to begin.

"Trees?" she said. "That was the topic?"

"You picked it."

"True, but other than the fact that I'm sitting in one, I don't recall any deep, dark secrets about trees."

"Think about it," he prompted.

If she'd had her lonely stones, she would have been working them in her hand, calmed by their sound and their smooth, hard surfaces. Odd that they were the first topic she thought of when he mentioned the Nobody Knows game. Not trees. She'd wanted to ask him about those stones, and his reaction to them. But that had seemed too risky.

"Sorry, nothing," she said. "I fell out of a tree once. Want to see my scar?"

He didn't. "What do they make from trees, besides tree houses? Pulp, paper, bindings, *books*. You wouldn't happen to have any deep, dark secrets that involve books, would you?"

She answered him with a head shake.

"What about that journal I found in your office?"

"I don't think books should count as trees, not technically."

"They *were* trees. That's close enough."

Her feet got tangled in the comforter, and it yanked her back down when she tried to get up.

"That's a fallacious line of reasoning if ever I've heard one," she protested. "We agreed on a topic, and I understood it to be trees in their natural state, not some derivation of that. If we followed your logic and the topic were sex, then my deep, dark secret could be about what happens nine months *after* you have sex. Babies, if you get my drift."

He cocked an eyebrow. "What's wrong with that?"

"Well, for starters, I don't have a secret about babies any more than I have one about trees."

"But you do have one about books, the journal being a book, if that's not too derivative for you."

There was no getting out of this. He didn't give a damn about fallacious reasoning, and short of spilling her cold coffee on him, which would have been difficult since he was across the room, she couldn't even think of a way to distract him.

"Carlie, I told you, this is personal. I'm asking for me, not because I want to trap you into a confession. *I need to know.*"

His voice tugged at her. He sounded a little desperate, which probably pleased her as much as it startled her. The way he was looking at her, she could almost make herself believe he was interested in her and not in who he thought she was. She could almost believe he was opening up again, that he wanted something more than information. That he cared. God, she was hopeless.

"We had a deal," he reminded her. "We agreed to reveal something about ourselves that no one else knew. If you weren't going to keep your part of the bargain, then why did you let me keep mine? Why did you let me dig up the dead, Carlie?"

The question touched her like a cold hand resting on her heart. This was logic she couldn't argue with. She'd encouraged him to tell her, asked him questions. And he had shared himself. He'd done nothing less than bare his soul. Now she had to do the same.

"What do you want to know?" she asked.

He walked to the other couch, but didn't sit. She felt the pressure of his presence, his expectations, even his standing height.

"Everything I said was true," he told her. "That's all I want from you, the truth."

The fire crackled. A cozy glow filled the room, but Carlie was aware of the moaning winter night outside, and wondered if she wouldn't have had a better chance against the elements.

"The journal is mine," she told him. "I wrote the entries. The words are mine and only mine. The rage, the vows of retribution, everything you read, it's all mine."

"Then you *are* the Femme Fatale? Is that what you're saying?"

She bowed her head and spoke into the confessional of her blanket, taking on the persona she'd assumed all those many months ago. "I killed those men, yes, I lured the first one into the woods, where he was attacked by wild dogs. I blinded the second with mirrors. Do you know how easy it is to lure stalkers, Rio? Do you know how easy they are to stalk?"

He cut her off. "You drove the diplomat off the road? Rigged his car phone? His radio? You did that?"

"I did it, yes—" She nodded, near tears. "But only in my mind, only for the pages of a book."

"What the hell are you talking about?"

He advanced on her, and she held out a hand to stop him. This was what she'd feared, that she would never make him understand. "You're a detective! Haven't you ever had to get into the mind of a killer in order to catch him? Well, I had to know how the Femme Fatale's mind worked in order to write a book about her. I had to get inside her head, become her, *be* her. That's why I started a journal. *Her* journal."

He hesitated. "You're asking me to believe that the journal is research for the book you're writing? It's research? That's all?"

"Yes, that's all."

"You wrote it in order to understand the Femme Fatale?"

"Yes, and myself—"

"What do you mean, yourself?"

The thickness in her throat was painful. A wild pulse beat made it difficult to speak. "I could have done it, Rio. *Me,* I could have carried out those strikes, killed those men myself. That's what I learned when I wrote the journal, and that's why I have to write the book. I have to—"

She'd expected him to stop her. When he didn't, she went on, rushing to say it all before he did.

"When Ginger died, I promised myself I would do something," she explained. "I made it my goal to educate the public about stalking. I wanted them to know what a heinous crime it was. I still do, Rio, and what better way to do that than to show how a perfectly normal woman is driven to vigilantism? Even someone like me."

"How do you know the Femme Fatale is normal, a woman, or driven to anything? Maybe she's a glory seeker, who likes seeing her name in the news. Why the hell else does she leave the flowers?"

Carlie dismissed the question with a shake of her head. It barely deserved an answer. "The snapdragon symbolizes female vengeance. It warns stalkers who sow fear that they will reap fear, and if the Femme Fatale wants her name in the news, that's the reason. *To remind the bastards she's out there, waiting for them.* She isn't a glory seeker or a bloodthirsty killer. She doesn't want to kill anyone, she wants to stop the killing. In my opinion, she's one of the great heroines of our century, and I want the world to know it."

"So this is a hymn of praise? A paean?"

"It will be as honest a profile as I can make it. It's not meant to be a puff piece, nor is it meant to be inspirational. If anything, it's a tragedy."

"Why is that?"

"Look what she's had to sacrifice—her life, her sanity. You can't outwit a stalker unless you live in his mind. You have to become him, and when you destroy him, you destroy a part of yourself. There is no way to win. There is only staying alive long enough to stop one more of them. With every strike she makes, the odds increase that she will either be caught or killed. That's not a happy ending."

"No, it's not."

She'd held him off before, but she couldn't now. Probably nothing could have. He joined her on the couch, sat down next to her, and surprised her by gripping her hand.

"Listen to me, Carlie. This has to stop, do you understand? There *is* no way to win. No one is above the law, no matter how noble their cause. You *are* going to get caught, and when you do, they'll make an example of you because of who you are and where you come from. They'll hang you high, Carlie. But before that can happen, somebody has to bring you in—"

His fingers left white and red stripes in her flesh. "And I don't want that man to be me," he said.

Carlie was startled at the rawness of the emotion she felt. It caught in her throat at the sound of his voice. It burned. He wasn't trying to trick her into admitting she was the Femme Fatale. He believed she was, and he was doing his best to reason with her, to protect her from herself.

Thank God she hadn't told him everything. Who knew what he might have done. It hadn't occurred to her that he wouldn't believe her story, and the surprise left her reeling. She didn't know whether to be relieved or horrified. Now her hand was nearly hidden in the folds of his trench coat, and she wondered if he could feel the trembling inside her.

Lord, what a tangled mess. It would have been much more convenient if he'd simply believed her. But still, what a strange, sweet thing it was to have someone care enough to try to save her, from anything.

She found herself wanting to thank him, but was afraid it might get awkward. "All this time I thought you were waiting for me to slip up," she said. "The way you kept showing up everywhere, unannounced. You *were* waiting for that, weren't you? When did it change?"

"I don't know . . . but it did."

His hand covered hers, brown fingers curling protectively into the moist warmth of her palm. He smelled like brandy and spiced aftershave. Apples and cloves.

"Carlie, we play a lot of games, you and I. And I like to win as much as the next guy, but not if it's going to be your name engraved on the trophy. Are you telling me the truth?"

"I already told you I was—"

His weary sigh said that he wasn't convinced anyway. Dark hair dropped onto his forehead, concealing his eyes for a moment, and Carlie felt an odd tug. She wanted to brush it back.

"It's two in the morning," he said at last. "We're not going to get this resolved tonight."

Or ever, she thought. *I've said all I can.*

He rose and looked down at her. "It's a long trip back down that mountain, and I won't make it without some sleep. Can you put me up?

The couch would be fine." A smile flickered. "And so will you. I'm not one of the guys in your book."

He must mean *Killer Smile,* she realized. "So I'm safe with you? Is that what you're trying to tell me?"

"Unless you don't want to be."

Carlie swallowed. When he spoke she could almost taste the resonance. It was like rough wine, a delicious burn that nipped at the back of her throat. No, she didn't want to be safe with him. She had never wanted that. She wanted the wine in her mouth and her belly, sparkling through her veins. She could have closed her eyes and felt it happening. That was how badly she wanted it.

"Answering that could be the most incriminating thing I've done all night," she said.

His alert stare made her think better of giving him a chance to respond. "There's a spare bedroom down the hall," she said. "You're welcome to it."

"Thanks." He offered a hand to help her up, and she threw off the blanket. Baggy gray sweats and bare feet. She must look like hell! But he didn't seem to think so. She could have been wearing a sexy negligee by the way he was looking at her. She could have been naked.

"Gray," he said appreciatively.

"No, please! Don't tell me gray is my color."

"Actually, it's mine. Goes with my gun."

She wasn't quite sure where to look when he opened his trench coat. She hoped he was trying to show her his shoulder holster! "Nice weapon," was her only comment.

He didn't let go of her hand right away, which gave Carlie plenty of time to wonder what would happen if he tugged on it. She could feel her body yearning to press against his, to be yanked into his arms, rocked off her feet, and held.

She might even like to feel that gun pressed against her.

"By the way, who won this game?" she asked.

"You. Want your prize?"

She knew better than to fall for that one. His hair was still tumbling into his eyes, a beautiful riptide of dark waves, and she still wanted to brush it away, mother him . . . love him. He didn't look nearly so wild now, but plenty wild enough.

Who would have thought the way things started that this could possibly turn out to be a good evening. Who would have thought he might turn out to be the man who made it good.

* * * *

A tapping sound roused her. It was faintly familiar. Slow and fat, like raindrops. Like one raindrop after another, plinking against a garbage-can lid. Carlie couldn't decide if she was asleep or awake as the steady percussion lulled her. It wasn't one of her winter-night noises, but she had heard it before.

There were other warning signals, too, but they were slower to register. The house was creaky and hushed. She could hear whispering outside her bedroom door. Trees brushing windows. Thieves in the night. She could see shadows, even though her eyes were closed.

And feel him.

He was moving around the tree house, searching for something.

Or she was dreaming. . . .

Gray light filled the room when she woke up next. It was snowing. The windowpanes were iced with glittering patterns, and lacy drifts had formed on the sill. The beauty of it struck her first, and then the silence. This could have been the whispering she heard last night. Snowfall.

She bundled herself in the blankets and sat up. She'd forgotten the extra-log ritual at bedtime, and the potbelly stove in her bedroom had gone out. The whole house had a nippy, chilly feel, but Carlie had other things on her mind. She was pleasantly astir inside, full of delicious expectation.

A thumping noise told her someone was up and around.

"Rio?" She called his name softly, but didn't get an answer. Her houseguest was nowhere to be found when she wandered into the living room moments later, still wrapped in blankets. The door to the spare room was open and the bed had not been slept in.

He was gone? That possibility took her breath away.

She left the blankets behind and made a quick search of the rest of the house, shivering as she looked through every empty, freezing room. "Oh no," she whispered when she realized he really wasn't there. Anywhere. "Oh, God, he is gone."

She didn't know what to think, and she was afraid of the direction her imagination was taking her. Was he lying? About everything? Was she that gullible? Some emotion was cutting her up inside, but she couldn't tell if it was anger or heartache. The mistake was in allowing herself to be so vulnerable to him. That did anger her.

A crystalline fairyland greeted her as she peered out the sliding-glass doors that opened onto the deck. The world was a wedding, veiled in white lace and organza, but Carlie couldn't focus on the beauty. She found it almost impossible to believe Rio would have gone to such lengths to trap her. She'd actually admitted to the crimes before she'd explained. On tape that would have sounded like a confession.

As she stared down the snow-covered road that led to her place, she had an imaginary flash of police cars, a caravan of them, roaring up the mountain, sirens wailing, piling up in her driveway, and shouting her down with bullhorns. 'THE FEMME FATALE TREED!' the headlines would trumpet. It was like a scene from a Hollywood movie. A bad one.

She went back for a blanket and some shoes.

A moment later she stepped outside onto the sparkling white carpet that had covered everything, even the vertical posts of the railing. Fresh snow crunched softly beneath her heels. Her breath froze on her lips. It should have been painfully cold, but Carlie couldn't feel anything.

"Rio!" Besides the Explorer there was only one car below, and it looked like Rio's unmarked sedan. It was possible he'd gone for a walk, but she couldn't imagine why he would have ventured out in this weather. She called his name again, hoping nothing had happened to him. Praying.

Snow flew every which way as she banged the gate and called several more times. "Rio!" There was no answer, and she was about to go back inside for some shoes when she saw movement through the windshield of his car.

A moment later Carlie got part of her wish. He was half-asleep as he let himself out of his car and stretched the kinks from his long, bent frame. He was also bundled up in a mountain of blankets he must have taken from the bedroom.

"I can't sleep in a tree," he called up to her. "Tarzan, I'm not."

Carlie's laughter frosted the air. "You must be a block of ice! Can you get back up here? I'll put some coffee on."

The kitchen was crackling with warmth by the time Rio joined her aloft. She'd managed to stoke up the potbelly stove in the living room and get the kitchen range going. She also had a pot of coffee on and was warming up some cinnamon rolls when he came through the door.

He shed the wet blankets and shook his hair, combing the glossy natural waves back with his fingers. "God, that smells good. What is it?"

Carlie poured him a cup of coffee and set it on the table. "Help yourself," she said. "The rolls won't be ready for a few more minutes."

She stood by the stove and watched him pull out the chair and casually settle into it, stretching his legs alongside a table built too low and bulky for a man his size.

He hooked the mug with three fingers, brought it to his lips, and blew before he took a sip.

His throaty sound of appreciation pleased her. There was still some drowsiness softening his features, and Carlie found it terribly sexy watching him wake up while he drank her coffee. She could see evidence of the heritage he so deeply resented in the tawny skin and slanting cheekbones, but she found those aspects beautiful, especially in the cool morning light.

Rio Walker, a woman could so easily fall in love with you, she thought. And then what would happen to her? What would you do? Love her back? Or make her regret the moment she first laid eyes on you, a phantom in the hallway of her own home?

He looked up, saw her expression, and let out another low male sound. Carlie barely heard it, but it registered in her mind like a gunshot. He had to stop doing that! He was drinking her in like the coffee, savoring her the way he had last night, as if she were dressed for undressing.

A Swiss cuckoo clock hung on the wall next to the pine cabinets. Carlie could see enough of herself in the glass door to know that her hair resembled an old-fashioned rag mop. Well, maybe some men found that sexy. Her features were still a little poufy from sleep, a little pouty. Her eyes were misty green and softly imbued with some kind of yearning. Maybe that was what he liked, willing eyes. *Wanting* eyes. It couldn't be the sweats she was wearing!

But Carlie could not have been more wrong. It was the sweats. Not that Rio didn't love the hurry-up-and-love-me-Daddy look in her eyes. He'd never seen anything sexier than the sparklings of desire hidden in the mountain mists that veiled her gaze. It made him nuts, that look.

But those sweats she wore brought out the animal in him. He'd always had a thing for women hidden in big, baggy clothes, and peeking out from behind them as if they were trying to figure out the lay of the land. Faded fleece, shrunk from too many washings, clingy, but still roomy. Now there was a feast for the male imagination.

He savored the thought of material warmed by a woman's skin and almost as soft as she was, offering up glimpses of ankle and maybe her midriff when she stretched. He had to admit that a huge part of the allure was the idea of Carlie Bishop, the personal-safety expert, using her clothing as a defense mechanism. But if she wanted to wrap herself like a piñata, she wouldn't get any argument from him. He got to imagine the fun of unwrapping her and discovering all the treasures she had tucked away.

She probably didn't know that he could see the heart-shaped curve of her bottom as she bent over the oven and whisked out a pan of bubbling, steaming hot rolls. She damn sure didn't know what that sight was doing to him. It was getting more crowded at this table every minute.

Carlie was blissfully ignorant of the effect she was having on Rio as she set the hot pan on the table and, with her trusty spatula, scooped out several of the oozing rolls.

"Have some?" she asked brightly, offering one of the delicacies on a red-and-white-checkered napkin.

"Oh, yeah—"

His rough, husky laughter made her wonder about the significance of that remark, especially the way his bronze fingers brushed against her pale ones.

The rolls filled the kitchen with the tantalizing richness of cinnamon and raisins, but Carlie didn't seem to have much appetite as she sat across the table from him, except for watching him eat and lick icing off his fingers.

"I came to a decision last night," he told her, once he'd finished off half the pan. "Facing death by freezing in the backseat of a car makes a guy think."

Carlie waited with bated breath as he took a couple of swallows of coffee, wiped his mouth with the napkin, and generally drove her crazy with anticipation.

"I'm going to turn over my files," he said. "Grover wants suspects, he'll get suspects."

She braced herself. "Will I need a lawyer? Do I need one now?"

"Not unless you like threesomes." His wry tilt of a smile vanished as he met her frightened gaze. "There won't be anybody's name on that list you know, Carlie. If that's what you're worried about. I can promise you that."

"Why—" She was shocked, breathless. *Shocked.*

His shrug was perfection, a classic example of masculine understatement. It was a learning experience just watching him gather his shoulders and cock his head.

"Lots of reasons," he said. "Lack of leads, mostly. But I have the feeling the Femme Fatale has made her last strike, and as long as that's true"—his dark eyes bore into Carlie's for one heartstopping moment—"then I don't see much chance of catching her. Or any reason to try."

Carlie bit her lip to keep from crying. The tears welled up so fast and fiercely it took all her power to stop them. She was weak from the effort, weak as she reached over and touched his hand. "Thank you," she said. *Thank you, more than you know.*

His fingers slid around hers, and she nearly stopped breathing. It wasn't their first physical contact, but nothing compared with this moment. Nothing. He had just made an astonishing sacrifice for her, possibly even jeopardized his career, and she felt as if she might come apart right there in the chair, her heart was so full of bewildering emotion.

"You're going to be okay," he assured her.

"No, I'm not," she whispered. *Not if you don't take me in your arms this very second.*

But he seemed fascinated by their intertwined hands, perhaps because of the contrast in size and skin tones. She was as transculent as clouds and he was brown, like the earth. Or maybe it was something else. Longing. The vibrant need in their linked fingers.

She saw it, too, and when he raised those dark lashes of his to look at her, she could feel herself reaching across the space between them, rising out of the chair. And suddenly there was no space between them. It didn't seem real it happened so fast.

He pulled her into his arms with a taut sound, and Carlie went willingly. But when their bodies came together, everything began to slide out of control. They were in a car on rain-slicked pavement. Neither of them could find the brakes, and even if they had, it would have been too late. Too dangerous. They would go careening out of control if they tried to stop. The car would cartwheel, roll over and over, and its occupants would be torn from each other.

"Rio—"

"Shhhh." His hands were lost in her hair, and his head was thrown back as if he'd been struck. "Don't say anything yet. This is too good."

She shuddered softly and clung to him. She would die if they were torn apart now. At any other point in her life being hauled into the arms of such an earthy, powerful man might have frightened her. But it was exactly what she needed at this moment. He was the ultimate safety and the ultimate danger, and she was torn with the sweetness of the choice.

His hands were tangled in her sweatshirt, and he'd drawn up the fleece, exposing a glimpse of pink-and-white curves. "The mystery is solved," he said. "Inside this gray cocoon lies a soft, warm, fragrant female."

Carlie sighed. She laughed. But deep inside, she felt the tiniest quiver of alarm. It was nothing, no more than a whip snap of dread, but within seconds it had cut through everything, even the heat that was melting her, fusing her body to his. *This* was the risk for her, although he couldn't possibly know it. She would have been safer on the witness stand being tried as a murderer than she was letting him undress her, expose her. She had no idea what he might find, what ugliness would make him shudder and back away, but she knew it was there as well as she knew the wild dance of her own heartbeat.

"Gray *is* your color—" He stepped back to look at her, the sentiment catching in his throat. "But I'd still rather see you out of those than in them."

His eyes were so beautifully dark and hungry that Carlie froze with conflict. This should have been exactly what she wanted, but no, it only terrified her. He couldn't seem to see anything but what he wanted to see, a beautiful woman. What was going to happen when he discovered who she really was?

Childish, she told herself. She was being childish. She wasn't seven years old, she was *twenty*-seven, an adult who knew better. But emotional scars ran as deep as physical ones, and berating herself only made it worse. If he tried to undress her now, she would clutch the clothing to her body. She *was* clutching herself.

"What's that all about?" he asked.

"Nothing. Cold, I guess. It's cold in here, isn't it?"

If he'd figured out what was wrong with her, he didn't let on. "It *is* cold," he agreed. That was all he said, but a regretful smile touched his expression as he tucked his hands in the pockets of his jeans.

Carlie didn't know what to do. Thank God, he did.

"Come on back?" he suggested. "Let me hold you?"

It was a moment before he held out his hand. Maybe he was giving her time, but when he did that, there was no decision left. Only a flurry of sighing and shaking her head as she stepped forward and ended up in his arms, back where she belonged.

"I want this, too," he said. "I want to hold you like this and have it be all right."

Her thoughts were fuzzed, but that had seemed awfully close to what she'd always imagined him saying. Engulfed in his embrace, she marveled at how much she wanted to be there. How much she wanted to feel safe. The fears had quieted. She didn't know for how long, but this was new and beautiful, being in a man's arms without fear, and she was going to steal every moment of sweetness she could.

"There is nothing wrong with you, Carlie," he whispered. "I wish to God I knew who made you think there was, because I'd kill them. I would kill them."

She closed her eyes to capture the tears. He probably thought it was bullies from her childhood. He couldn't imagine that it was her own parents who had made her feel this way. Anyone would have had trouble imagining that. Rio may have been through hell, but he was never unwanted. His mother died because she lost her son, and Carlie could imagine that.

She could imagine dying over love of this man.

"Touch me," she whispered.

The breath he took when his hands came into contact with her naked skin was thrilling. It was the sound of a man caught off guard by the gale force of his own feelings. Her sweatshirt lifted and long coppery fingers slipped inside it. He smoothed his palms along her back and up the delicate ladder of her rib cage, bringing Carlie shivers of delight.

Hands. He had the hands of a healer.

She gasped in anticipation. Solely in anticipation. He hadn't yet caught her by the waist and lifted her to his mouth when the breathless sound slipped out of her. But she knew he was going to, and it made her weak with excitement.

It made him wild.

She was astounded at the thrilling swiftness with which he took control. All he did was lift her off the ground like a startled child. Brush her lips with a breath. That was all he did, but the power of it depleted her.

"Carlie, Carlie, you're killing me," he warned. "All this feeling is killing me."

He pulled at the cuffs of her sweatshirt and her arms came out of the sleeves. This was it, the unveiling of Carlie Bishop, fatally flawed human being. She'd lived her whole life with rejection. She'd grown used to it and learned how to guard against it. What she didn't know was how to be naked. Or what made this man worth the risk.

Her sweatsuit offered myriad drawstrings and zippers to choose from, but he started with the one at her neckline. Carlie couln't look as he drew the slide down to its base, but she could feel her stomach make the descent right along with his hand. It fell and then caught, suspended. Cool air touched all the way to her breastbone, where the nylon teeth ended.

He'd exposed the anticipation fluttering in her throat and the delicate cleft between her breasts. Nothing too remarkable, she would have thought, but his gaze was so breathtakingly hard, she had to look. Her pale skin flushed to pink, and her breasts shivered like water as she realized what he saw, a frightened, aroused woman.

His hand had stopped at her breasts, but her stomach took the rest of the journey down. It sank to the bottom of the well like a coin. Lord, if this was how it was starting, she wondered how it would end. It should have taken all of two minutes to get a woman out of an outfit like hers, but clearly that wasn't the point of the exercise. He wanted to take his time, to savor every drawstring he pulled and every elastic band he snapped.

He was unwrapping her like a gift. And when he finally drew the sweatshirt over her head and tossed it aside, when he jerked the last string and let her pants drop to the floor, Carlie didn't know what to do. She'd never been undressed so deliberately or looked at so thoroughly. It made her stomach hurt, but in some sharp, sweet way.

"Now I'm terrified," she said, shivering.

"Now you're naked." His voice was harsh with wonder. "And if I made the laws, you would never be any other way."

She'd angled away from him, her forearms pressed to the fullness of her breasts, and the sight seemed to tighten every cord in his long, tawny frame.

His jaw caught, and he let out a breath that sounded painful. "Jesus. There is *nothing* wrong with you, Carlie. Nothing in this world. What's wrong is that someone could make you feel like you're ugly when you're perfect. That's what I see. Perfection."

She wanted to protest, to list all the things that she knew were imperfect. She had scrutinized herself as a kid, looking for the stigmata, whatever it might be that had damned her, and she found so many things she'd run out of paper. Her eyes were too strange and green, her skin too pale, her nose too long, and her knees too knobby. She looked like a spider monkey huddled behind those knees! But as long as her list got over the years, she knew she had never found the "big" thing, the real reason her own parents couldn't seem to stand the sight of her.

What is it? she asked Rio silently. There must be something. Parents don't reject their kids for no reason, do they?

But the mystic was lost in his flame.

Lost in the beauty, the mystery, that she couldn't see.

He touched her face with his splayed fingers. Rigid with desire, he feathered golden dark eyelashes, her soft, startled mouth. His thumb dragged softly across her lower lip.

She thought the glint in his eyes might be tears, but she knew that couldn't be. There was nothing about her that could evoke such emotion. Whatever he was seeing came from within him. It was his vision, just as he was hers, but she didn't want him to stop. Because if he looked long enough, deep enough, and he saw something good . . . if he still believed there was beauty in her, then she had to believe it, too, didn't she?

He touched her face, and his jaw flexed.

She reached out to caress the muscle, but her hand shook so badly that she laughed, deep in her throat where it hurt. And that sound broke the trance. It transformed *him* from mystic to flame.

She could see the low blaze in his eyes, a fire that came from somewhere inside him, his soul. A spasm of desire rocked him, and he closed his eyes for a moment.

Carlie watched him burn. Silenced.

"God, if you could only see what's going on inside me," he said. "There wouldn't be any doubt in your mind. You would know, Carlie. You would know."

Carlie couldn't say what she needed to say. There weren't words. But he must have seen it in her face when he opened his eyes.

"Thank you," was all she could manage. "Thank you."

"I haven't done anything yet," he said, irony in his voice, pain.

She might have liked to undress him, slowly and with shaking hands. But he'd already pulled off his crumpled white dress shirt and was undoing his jeans before that thought came to her. And then she was glad. It would have taken her forever. They would have died before she got it done.

Once he'd dispensed with his clothing, he swept the table clear and tugged her by the hand, dancing her into his arms. She expected to hear crashing dishes, but there was only the hard crash of his breathing.

"Here?" she whispered as he settled her on the wooden planks. "On the table? This hard table?"

"Shhhh," he said, caressing the tension from her thighs and bending meditatively over her trembling surprise. "The only thing that's hard is me. You'll never feel the table. I promise."

Healer, she thought. Medicine man.

He caught her hand and brought it to his mouth. Softness tickled her palm. Something warm and wet traced her lifeline, and her fingers curled rapturously. He seemed to need to soak it in, this thing they were doing, soak her in, but he also sensed when she was ready. She had fallen back to her elbows, already too spent to do anything but watch him with wonder and disbelief. He opened her legs and his first gentle touches sent desire tumbling through her.

The wooden planks should have hurt, but his mouth was magical. It nearly lifted her off the table. She had never experienced anything so warm or sweet, never known such delicate pressure as the flick of his tongue. Her own nerves cried out for more. They seduced her, stroked her like fingers, and she could feel nothing other than that fiery pleasure. Soaring pleasure. Excitement whined in her ears.

She closed her eyes, trembling with shock.

Lightness whirled around her tingling center with every kiss and pluck of his lips. They drew her into a vibrant surge and suckled so gently she wept. He was a stroking feather between her legs, and as he delved inside her with his mouth, she began to gasp, to buck, to arch with pleasure.

She called for him, and he entered her that way, climbed on top of her, a dark and beautiful beast. Entered her while she was convulsing.

She had no choice but to surrender and be ravished. He was a magnificent thing, the darkness that overtakes you in a running dream, the animal that devours you in your sleep. He was every fear she'd ever had of dying, but she'd never imagined that death could be so radiant with life.

When she cried out, the weight of him silenced her. It crushed her swiftly, sweetly, and she wanted to be smothered. She forgot about elemental things like breathing as he pinned her to the table and moved inside her.

Carlie lost touch with everything outside her own spiraling ecstasy. Nothing existed but her and Rio, sixty feet above the earth, making love while the snow fell softly outside and the wintry brightness glinted off the icy panes.

His name was on her lips. She said it constantly, helplessly, with every quiver and twist of his body. She couldn't say it enough, and Carlie suddenly knew that this couldn't have happened with any other man or at any other time. Only he was powerful and sure enough to silence the fears rising in her throat, yet tender enough to melt her resistance. Only he, who'd awakened her imagination as a child, could awaken her heart as a woman.

He was her first.

TWENTY-SIX

Danny Upshaw slept in his boxer shorts, sprawled on his stomach, and bear-hugging a bed pillow that was no match for his muscular embrace. He wasn't exactly crushing it but nothing was taking that pillow away from him. His forearms were crisscrossed, and his face was burrowed in the softness.

It was maybe one of the saddest things Jo Emily had ever seen. If wishes counted for anything, she would have been his pillow, snuggled close to his heart and breathing easy, with everything to look forward to and nothing to fear, at least for a little while.

Instead Jo Emily was saying good-bye, silently.

She couldn't stand to stay at Danny's any longer. It was too confusing. He was like a kid with a lollipop, wanting it one minute, tossing it aside the next. And when your self-esteem was as shaky as hers, well . . .

"So long, guy," she whispered from the doorway of his bedroom. She knew better than to linger. Her chain purse hung at her side, and she had a shopping bag bulging with the gear she'd brought with her. Within the hour she would be at the women's shelter Carlie had told her about. She'd called and they had space.

The closet where he'd hidden the packages worked some powerful mojo on her mind as she walked through the living room toward the front door. It would have been easy enough to sneak a peek. The boy was dead asleep. He would never find out. But she didn't have the heart for it. She'd lost the desire to know what was in them. She didn't even want to know whether they were for her or not. Either way, it would only be more heartache.

*   *   *

"Coming!" Carlie hadn't been home from the mountains an hour when her doorbell rang. She wasn't even unpacked. She dropped the pile of laundry she was carrying on her bed and headed down the hallway to answer the door.

She wasn't expecting anyone, but doorbells were as much a part of her social conditioning as phones. When one rang, you answered it.

I hope whoever it is has a strong constitution, she thought as she sailed past her own reflection in the hallway mirror. She looked scary, with her longish hair tied up in a spiky ponytail and her face reddened from the elements, as well as a serious case of whisker burn. She'd showered and changed her clothes, but faded blue sweats weren't any more flattering than gray ones.

At least Rio liked them. Her pace slowed involuntarily at the thought of him. Her legs felt weighted, and the breath that slipped out of her wasn't nearly sharp enough to convey her whiplash emotions. The mere suggestion of his reaction to her wardrobe left her weak with feeling. Monster feeling. Longing. That word, that deadly word. She didn't want to feel that word. She didn't even want to think it, but there it was. Nothing else came close, and even longing didn't do it justice.

Unaware that she'd come to a complete stop, she found herself awash in the rivers of memory. They had made love all weekend, incessantly. They hadn't been able to stay away from each other, and it had seemed like each time was more incredible than the last. She'd never made love that much in her whole adult life. It wasn't natural.

Supernatural, she thought, and laughed out loud.

It should have worried her that they hadn't used protection. It should have worried her sick. You would have thought that the personal-safety expert and the LAPD detective would have a condom between them, wouldn't you? But no. She could even be pregnant . . . and the prospect rather thrilled her.

Now she *knew* she was crazy.

Carlie's head came up as she realized her doorbell had not stopping ringing since it started. Someone must be holding it down. Rio would do something like that.

She breezed through the foyer, floating on those air bubbles of his, but came to a stunned halt when she saw the visitor on her stoop. "Mother?"

Carlie had left the outer door open, and the newest U.S. Supreme Court justice was peering through the locked screen with equal amounts of suspicion and impatience. Carlie's cottage was closer in appearance to the gatehouse of a country estate than to anything Frances had ever lived in. Clearly she didn't understand her daughter's taste, and probably thought she was being perverse in exercising it.

"Am I going to be allowed in, Carlie?" Frances asked. "I've come a long way to see you."

The faintly clipped tone brought Carlie out of her trance. It *was* Frances Stanfield Bishop, in the flesh.

"Mother?" she whispered again. "Yes, come in, do!"

Moments later Carlie had her second surprise houseguest of the weekend settled unhappily at her rustic kitchen table, and was brewing her a cup of tea.

"Is that camomile?" Frances wanted to know, tugging at a gray tweed sleeve. "It smells like camomile, but I could use something a good deal stronger, Carlie. Be a dear and splash some sherry in there, would you? This trip was all very last minute, and the airlines put me in coach by mistake. They wanted to bump a first-class passenger, but I wouldn't hear of it, of course."

Oh, coach. The dreaded coach section. That explained her mother's pinched expression. Carlie would have been happy to splash some sherry in the tea, and then she herself would have chugged down the rest of the bottle, if she'd had any sherry.

"Will Amaretto do?" she asked.

Blue-veined eyelids drooped. "Well, of course, if that's all you have."

Normally Carlie kept her liquor in a corner cabinet in the living room, just as she did in the tree house. But the Amaretto was left over from an all-night work session, when coffee alone hadn't been enough to keep her neurons firing. She'd kept it on the kitchen counter for convenience, and it was still there.

Carlie filled her mother's teacup with three fingers of the liqueur and did the same to her own. She hadn't sobered up from the mountains and Rio Walker yet anyway, so she might just as well stay happy. The cupboards were bare, unfortunately. She hadn't been back long enough to get groceries for the house, and she wouldn't have stocked up with the standard teatime fare anyway. There weren't any cucumber or watercress sandwiches for the tray, but she did have a box of chocolate-covered graham crackers, a favorite of hers in the comfort-food category.

Wondering if her mother had ever heard of comfort food, Carlie arranged the crackers in a lovely starburst pattern on the plate. "Amaretto," she announced as she served the tea, "with a splash of camomile."

Frances pointedly pushed a vase of wilting sunflowers out of her way, but otherwise she was quite gracious about the refreshments. "Thank you, dear," she said, helping herself to some lemon and a sugar lump for her tea. Gingerly she broke off a bit of graham cracker, popped it into her mouth.

And did not make a face, Carlie noted.

Fresh-cut flowers were the last thing on Carlie's mind when she'd rushed out of the house on her way to the mountains, and she probably wouldn't have noticed them now, except that they reminded her how preoccupied she'd been. And how like a wilted flower she must look to her perfectly put-together mother.

Frances's gray tweed suit was conservatively smart, and every accessory matched perfectly, down to the silver-and-onyx lapel pin she wore. Tiffany's, probably. Her shoes and bag were soft black calf. Even the streak of gray at her temple was color-coordinated.

"Chocolate, Carlie? I thought chocolate made your skin break out in hives."

Frances made the comment as Carlie was finishing off her second graham cracker. There hadn't been much time for food that weekend, and she'd just realized she was starving.

"The hives are from strawberries," she reminded her mother. "Chocolate makes me sneeze, or used to. Apparently that's one food allergy I've outgrown."

"How nice."

Was this mother-daughter talk? Carlie wondered, resisting a third cracker. They'd done so little of it, she didn't know. She probably ought to initiate their next topic, but she couldn't think of anything to ask except why her mother was there, and she wasn't quite ready to ask that yet. She had a bad feeling about the answer.

The phone rang as they sipped their tea in silence. Too late Carlie realized that she'd turned the volume up on the answering machine because she wanted to be able to hear Rio's voice from anywhere in the house. Just in case he called.

"Green eyes, where are you? God, I'm missing you, girl."

The undisguised sensuality in Rio's voice echoed up and down the halls like horses in a canyon.

"Who is *that*?" Frances asked.

"Probably a wrong number." Carlie held her breath, praying he didn't—

"Are you there, Carlie? Hey, it's Rio! You okay? No sexy little bruises from the kitchen table?"

The throaty question, rich in irony, dashed all hope. He'd just "outed" both of them. Now he was going to say unthinkable things, and her mother would hear every word.

"You're not feeling guilty about what we did, are you?" he wanted to know. "Because if you are, I can fix that, sweetness. I'll give you a reason to feel guilty. Take off your panties and climb up on the kitchen table again. You'll be in a confessional by the time we're done—"

Carlie sprang up and made a dash for the phone, but he'd already hung up by the time she got there.

The room was thunderously silent as she replaced the receiver. She would rather have faced death by lethal injection than her mother at that moment, but there was little choice. Studying the ivy pattern in the floor tiles, she returned to the table, desperately glad Rio hadn't gone into any more detail about what they'd done on the one in the mountains.

Carlie didn't need to ask if Frances was upset. Her mother could have snapped pencils in two with her lips the way they were pursed. Worse, she'd set her teacup down, but missed the saucer, a serious breach of Bishop etiquette.

"Rio?" Frances's voice was faint. "Your sister dated a detective named Rio. For God's sake, Carlie, you must know that he's dangerous. You wouldn't, you couldn't be—"

Carlie would have said it was a prank call if she thought she could get away with it. "Rio Walker is a member of my task force," she explained, "and he refers stalker victims to my support group. It's a professional relationship."

"Professional?" A delicate cough. "What was that remark about the kitchen table, the bruises?"

Carlie sampled her tea. Not enough Amaretto. Not nearly enough. "He's in law enforcement." She offered that bit of information as if it should explain everything. "Well, you know how they are."

"No, I don't. I certainly don't."

"Quirky sense of humor?" Very gently, Carlie added, "I don't think you came here to discuss my personal life, did you?"

"Well, no, but it looks as if we need to."

Carlie rose from the table and picked up her cup, not quite sure what she was going to do with it. Luckily the teakettle was whistling softly on the stove. She'd left the unit on low to keep the water hot. "More tea?" she asked her mother.

"No, thank you, dear. I'm fine."

Dear? Her mother had called her that twice in her entire lifetime, both in the last half hour. Something was up, and the feel of it already had Carlie nervous. When Frances decided to act parental, it was usually because she had bad news to break.

"Why *did* you come all the way out here?" Carlie ventured, again taking care not to offend. "Is the court in recess?"

"I came to see you, just as I said. And as it happens, we are in recess until next week."

Frances had just discovered that her cup was lopsided, and she was putting it right, but Carlie could see that her hands were unsteady. There was very little about any of this that was typical of Frances Bishop, and Carlie was honestly puzzled. She was reasonably sure the visit had to do with their last conversation, but she didn't have the stamina for another fight with her mother. She was still dazed from the last forty-eight hours.

"How long are you going to be here?" Carlie asked.

"Just a night or two, and then I have to be back. These days they don't let Supreme Court justices travel without a U.S. marshal in tow. He's outside in the car, waiting to bring in the luggage."

"You're staying here? You and a U.S. marshal?"

"No, he'll stay somewhere nearby, a motel, I would imagine. Why? Is there a problem with that?"

Carlie was stunned. "Well, no, of course not, but wouldn't you rather—" She'd started to ask if her mother wouldn't prefer to stay at Blue Hills, but Frances cut her off with an imperious wave of her hand.

"I don't much enjoy staying there anymore. The place reminds me of your father, I'm afraid. And your sister, of course. It makes me quite sad."

"I think I'll have some tea," Carlie said. She filled the cup to the brim with Amaretto.

"Carlie, what *did* he mean about the kitchen table?"

"Mother, wouldn't you like to freshen up? Let's have the marshal bring in your luggage so you can get settled."

"That would be nice, but there's something else, darling, that requires a serious discussion. Why don't you have a seat."

There it was. Anything that required Carlie to sit down had to be bad news. The very tone of her mother's voice gave her the chills, especially given some of the doubts Carlie harbored about Frances. Her whole life she had questioned the extremes to which Frances might go to achieve her ends, whatever they were, the harm of which she was capable.

"I think I would like to freshen up first, though—"

Carlie seized upon that. "Certainly," she said. "Take your time. I need to run over to the office anyway. I've been gone all weekend, and there's some work I need to pick up. Maybe you'd like to take a nap? Oh, and before I go I'll give you a short tour of the house, such as it is."

"It's quite lovely, Carlie. Very old-world and charming, not a bit like you."

Which shows how little you know me, Mother, Carlie thought, stung by the comment. She'd just realized that her African violets in the kitchen window garden were alive and well. Some things thrived on benign neglect. African violets and Carlie Bishop. And perhaps she preferred it that way.

Carlie couldn't get into her own offices. The phone was ringing, and she couldn't get in! The key wouldn't work, but Danny hadn't mentioned a problem, so she assumed it was her and not the lock.

The stones on her key chain clinked frantically. Frustrated, Carlie slammed the door with her shoulder. Why hadn't the service picked up? The Stalker Hotline was a separate number, with its own offices and a bank of operators, but Carlie sometimes got emergency calls from group members, and it concerned her that they might not be getting answered.

She jiggled the key, listening, and felt it slide into the groove. Finally! This time something popped when she turned it and the lock released. She made a dash for the reception-desk phone, letting the door bang open behind her. The floor was littered with mail that had come through the door slot, and she nearly slipped, trying to get through it.

"Safe and sound." Carlie leaned over the desk, balancing herself on the heel of her hand as she gripped the receiver. Someone had hidden the phone behind the in-basket, making it an Olympian feat, which was probably the point. Danny was always trying to discourage the support-group members from monopolizing his phone.

"Carlie? Is that you? Oh, God, I hope—"

"Jo Emily? What's wrong?" The other woman's voice shook with urgency. Carlie was jolted by fear. "Where are you?" she asked. The hotline training she'd had was coming back to her. First find out where they are. If you get cut off, you can still get help to them.

"I'm at the apartment," Jo Emily told her. "My place—"

"Is anyone else there?"

"No, I don't think so. I came by for the rest of my things. I'm going to the shelter, Carlie."

"Did something happen? Did you and Danny—"

"Oh, no! No, nothing like that. I just can't stay there. I just can't, Carlie."

"It's okay, Jo Emily, I understand." Actually, Carlie didn't understand at all, but she sensed the other woman was in danger, and not from Danny. "Is it the stalker? Is he there now?"

"No, but he called. He called me, Carlie. The phone rang while I was packing, and I picked it up without thinking. He said I'd never escape him, that he was everywhere. Every phone I answered, every door I opened, every scary face I saw and sound I heard would be him.''

"Did he threaten you?" Credible threat, Carlie was thinking. The California statutes still required tangible proof of intent to harm. It wasn't good enough that a stalker haunt his victim twenty-four hours a day, that he drive her insane with fear. He had to threaten violence, too. And most of them were too smart for that. Stalkers were smart sons of bitches.

"How about breaking my windshield with a baseball bat? Wasn't that bad enough?"

Unfortunately it wasn't, not without evidence. As concerned as Carlie was about Jo Emily, she knew the gargantuan legal hurdles they would have to get over to put away even the most dangerous offenders.

"Are you sure it was the same man?" she asked. "Did he say anything to identify himself?" She still believed Jo Emily's stalker could be the man who lured Ginger to her death. And Carlie had never been more motivated to bring someone to justice, no matter what it took.

"None of the usual stuff, no. Not that song title or anything."

Carlie was sharply disappointed. "Are you sure? Think about it. Was there anything?"

"Oh, wait. Yeah, maybe—I kept hearing a funny clicking noise on the line. Weird, like water dripping in a sink or something. Do you think he was recording the call?"

A clicking sound? Carlie felt a moment of shock. Her mind tried to take her to a terrifying place, but she rejected the thought as completely illogical. Rio made a sound like that when he worked. She'd heard it herself. He was well known for it, but this was something different. It had to be. This was a phone making a noise that such equipment often made, even when it wasn't being tapped. That made a great deal more sense than what she'd been thinking.

"I don't want to call the police," Jo Emily was saying. "I don't want to go through that again. I can't do it, not right now."

Carlie took a steadying breath. She needed to be calm for her friend's sake. "No, don't call the police. Take your things and go to the apartment manager's office. Do you hear me, Jo Emily? Go to the manager's office, and I'll pick you up there and drive you to the shelter, okay?"

"S-sure."

"Good girl. Do it now. I'm on my way."

Carlie hung up the phone and slumped on the desk, completely drained. This was too much. In one weekend she'd had a soul-shattering fling with Rio, her mother had appeared on her doorstep, and now Jo Emily—well, it was tragic what was happening to Jo Emily.

She gathered herself up and noticed the mail scattered all over the floor. Danny was so dedicated he usually dropped by on Saturdays to pick it up and check the messages. Maybe with Jo Emily at his place, he couldn't. This looked like several days' worth, and as Carlie stared at it, she thought of her life, bits and pieces flying every which way, totally out of control, and wondered when it had happened. When *had* she lost control?

Carlie could pinpoint the major turning points in her life. Ginger's death had changed everything, and not entirely for the bad. It had given her a sense of purpose. Since then she'd known what she wanted and been unrelenting about getting it. Perhaps she was like her mother in that way. But now she was confused. The quest for justice no longer felt as compelling for some reason. She would have blamed it on Rio, but she wasn't one of those women who allowed her life to be derailed by a man. She counseled derailed women, helped them get back on track.

As she gathered up the mail and prepared to leave, a premonition touched her thoughts. It might have been a flash into the future, but what she saw in her mind was an executioner in a black hood, and something about him was uncannily familiar. For a moment she wondered if he was known to her, to all of them. Someone close. Somewhere close. No answer came except the pounding force of her pulse. But she did realize that he was the unifying force in all of this. He was the reason she couldn't let herself be derailed.

Frances was tipsy. Carlie would have bet her last chocolate-covered graham cracker on it. When she walked into the living room that night, prepared for the worst, her mother was in the American willow rocker, going at a steady pace, her head tilted back, her eyes closed. And she was humming along with Bruce Springsteen.

That was how Carlie knew. That and the empty bottle of Amaretto. Bruce was singing about being on fire.

"Mother?"

The rocker came to a stop and Frances gave out a little sigh before she opened her eyes. "Oh, there you are," she said, her diction slightly less than precise. "I'd about given up on you."

"Are you all right?"

"I'm . . . well, yes, I am . . . um, relaxed, thank you." She waggled the empty aperitif glass she was holding. "This is quite nice, isn't it, this Ama-ammo—this stuff."

Carlie fought a bemused smile. Oh, Mom, she thought. Why couldn't you be drunk more often? You're almost funny.

Carlie touched her mother's hand reassuringly as she took the glass and set it on the fireplace mantel. It was the most physical contact they'd had in years. They never touched, never hugged.

"Would you like some coffee?" she asked. "Or maybe you'd like to go to bed? It's nearly midnight in Washington."

"Oh, pooh, I'm fine." Frances struggled to sit up in the wicker chair and created a riot of creaking and groaning. "I often stay up, watch Letterman, the silly fool. I like those Stupid Pet Tricks, don't you?"

Carlie was speechless. And quite sure she'd entered the Twilight Zone. Who was this woman?

It was all she could do not to be rude and gape. There had to be some way to keep this conversational ball in the air. She might discover an entirely different person than the one who'd raised her at arm's length. But by the time Carlie got her bearings, Frances had as well. She'd drawn herself up and all but shaken off the effects of the liqueur.

Too bad, Carlie thought.

Frances tugged at her sleeves to straighten them and crossed her legs at the ankle. What she missed were the silvery tendrils that had slipped from her elegant bun and were wisping around her neck and forehead.

Send her to the finest finishing schools, and for what? Carlie thought ironically. Perhaps for the first time she realized that her mother was a stunningly attractive woman, and not quite perfect, thank goodness.

The room was quiet, except for the creaky rocker, which whispered of Frances's continuing efforts to restore some order to her appearance and some dignity to the situation. When she was done smoothing her jacket, and her feathers, she asked Carlie to sit down, using her gravest tone.

"Please," she said, indicating the pillowy cane couch just behind Carlie. "I've something to tell you."

Carlie didn't hesitate, but by now she was becoming concerned. When Frances had broken the news about Ginger's death, she'd done this very thing, arranged for the two of them to be alone and asked Carlie to sit down first. Carlie had refused to sit, or to calm herself, or in any way to be persuaded that her sister's death was for the best, which was one of the platitudes her mother had used.

Carlie had sensed that she was being "handled." They didn't want her to make a fuss and embarrass the family. She had, of course, and still was, making a fuss. But this situation was different. She had no inkling of what was to come. She'd already lost everyone she cared about. Her sister and father were gone. She didn't know what else it could be unless there was a health problem Frances hadn't told her about.

"I'm afraid you and I should have had this talk a long time ago. It concerns your father."

Carlie's first reaction was relief as she listened to her mother reminisce about her "arranged" marriage to Bernard Bishop. At least Frances wasn't ill. Carlie could stop worrying about that, but she had no idea why her mother was making it sound as if her relationship with her late husband was less than ideal. Carlie had always thought them the perfect couple, the perfect family. She'd been the only impediment, the unplanned second child.

"Oh, your father and I looked wonderful on paper," Frances assured her. "Family trees, stock portfolios, P and L statements. But there are other kinds of ledgers, reckonings that have more to do with the heart than with balance sheets, and on those we didn't fare too well."

Carlie made no attempt to hide her surprise. "You and my father weren't happy? Is that what you're saying?"

Frances rose too quickly from the rocker and sent it into a frenzy of creaking. Her distress was evident as she walked to the latticed windows and looked out. "I didn't think this would be so difficult. I really didn't. Are you sure you don't have any sherry?"

That might be the only thing Carlie was sure of. Why did people seem to need to get drunk before they could talk to her? First Rio, now this. She couldn't be that difficult to communicate with.

"You said this was about my father," she prompted.

"Yes." Frances bowed her head. When she turned back to Carlie, her expression was shadowed with regret. "I'm so sorry to have to tell you like this. It's not what I planned. And to be honest, maybe I was hoping I'd never have to tell you."

"Tell me what?"

"Bernard isn't your father, Carlie. Or wasn't. That's what I've been struggling to say all along. I had an affair with another man while Bernard and I were in Washington. My friend was highly placed in the government, greatly respected. Bernard found out, but because of the scandal it would have caused, we all agreed to keep the secret. We were huge supporters of this man, Bernard and I. One of the reasons we were in Washington was to help him with his campaign for national office, and this would have destroyed any chance he had."

"But you were pregnant?"

Frances nodded. "The understanding we had with your natural father was that Bernard would raise you as if you were his. That was difficult, of course, for all of us, and perhaps most of all for you, in ways that none of us understood, I'm sure . . ."

Carlie said nothing while her mother went on, justifying the pact that had been made all those years ago. It was a bombshell, but Carlie couldn't seem to gather her thoughts beyond one primal awareness. This was the reason she'd been shunned. Now she understood. She was illegitimate, a constant reminder to both her mother and father of Frances's infidelity.

"If Bernard wasn't my father, then who is?"

Frances worked her clasped hands. "I can't reveal that, Carlie. There is so much at stake here. You don't understand what could happen if this got out—and the affair is the least of it."

Meaning I'm the least of it, Carlie thought. She'd been rejected by the father who raised her, and now she wasn't even to know who her real father was?

"There's more, I'm afraid—" Frances drew in a breath and lifted her head.

Carlie could see how difficult this was. Her regal mother humbled, admitting a mistake, wringing her hands? It had never happened in Carlie's memory. Still she found it impossible to feel sympathy. If anything, she felt betrayed. She was the dirty little secret. No wonder Frances wanted her out of the limelight, and what an embarrassment she must be to her natural father, whoever he was.

"When it became clear that the police weren't going to find your sister's stalker," Frances explained, "I went to my friend in Washington and asked for his help. At extreme risk to his career, and to everything that he stands for, in fact, he helped me. He did what the law-enforcement agencies couldn't do."

"And what was that?"

"He took care of it, Carlie. That's all I can tell you. That's really all I know. It was taken care of."

Carlie was up and out of the couch. "All along you've known who killed Ginger, and you let me keep searching for someone who didn't exist, a phantom?"

"Oh, he existed all right."

"But he doesn't now? What are you saying, that her stalker is dead?"

"I didn't say he was dead, I said 'taken care of.' That's what I know, Carlie. It's all I know about the man who stalked your sister."

"You can't tell me who he is?" Carlie stared at her mother almost fiercely, demanding an answer, but all Frances would do was shake her head.

"Then can you at least tell me who he's not? Tell me he's *not* the man stalking Jo Emily, and I'll leave the case alone. I'll let the police handle it. Otherwise I have no choice but to—''

"It's not the same man." Frances was sharp, emphatic. "It can't be, Carlie, and you mustn't try to prove it is. You have to leave this alone. You'll ruin us all. I swear you'll ruin us all."

Carlie's CD player was built into some beautiful old oak cabinetry beside the fireplace. She walked over there and turned off the music. She needed quiet to think. She needed to be alone.

"Carlie, you do understand how important this is, don't you? You're going to cooperate?"

Carlie didn't know what she was going to do. She'd had too many upheavals in too short a time, and her brain felt close to short-circuiting. A veil had been jerked away, and some of the most imperative questions of her life had been answered, but it was too much to handle all at once.

Still, through all of it, one detail had stayed with her, one tiny thing that she'd been able to focus on because the rest of it was too big to grasp. Her mother had used the word *stalker* rather than *murderer,* and as far as Carlie could recollect, she had always done that. It could have been simple denial, but she never spoke of her Ginger as having been a murder victim.

TWENTY-SEVEN
꧁ꕥ꧂

He wasn't her father?

Carlie had done little more than sit in the dark and stare into space since her mother went to bed. Frances had decided to fly back first thing in the morning, and Carlie was honestly relieved. She and her mother had reached an impasse, and Carlie was a jumble of thoughts and emotions that couldn't be sorted out. It was two in the morning and she'd been trying to collect herself all night, but her mind was going in too many bewildering directions. None of it made sense. She didn't even know how she felt about what her mother'd told her.

She'd had several disturbing shocks today, too many for one person alone to bear, but the worst of it was, she *was* alone. Who could she dare tell? There was no safe sounding board for this kind of craziness. Her real father was a man she'd never met, a figure so powerful he couldn't even acknowledge that Carlie existed, according to Frances, and it seemed possible that the two of them were involved in a conspiracy to cover up the truth about Ginger's death.

Carlie could hardly imagine that, but it only got worse. Her sister's stalker had been "taken care of." That was all her mother would tell her. But now Jo Emily was being stalked by a man with the same signature behavior, yet Frances adamantly denied that it could be the same man.

There was some connection in all of this, some link that held it together, but what?

She arched her head back and steepled her hands at her throat, then rested her elbows on the desk. She needed to think. Clearly. She needed . . . something, insight. A breakthrough. After a moment she closed her eyes, but wasn't sure how long she stayed that way. Perhaps she even dozed off.

The *plink* of dripping water carried from down the hall.

She felt haunted by the sound. It seemed to permeate her life as well as her senses, and she had begun to think of it as the drumbeat of disaster. Its steady tapping symbolized some immutable impulse, a dark river that ran below the surface, beyond the reach of conscious order.

It was the beat of a human heart, an evil heart.

Carlie sensed that, just as she knew the sound had something to tell her. But she was afraid to hear what it said.

Rio . . .

She bent forward, shivering, bent so deeply that her forehead came to rest on the desk. Why did he keep materializing out of the shadows? He was always there, in the darkness that preyed on her thoughts. And it felt as if he'd always been there. It didn't count that her mother thought of him as dangerous. Frances would have warned her against anyone who was from a background as different from hers as Rio's.

The clicking on Jo Emily's phone was even easier to explain, but Carlie was puzzled by the apprehensiveness she sensed in Jo Emily. Rio was the one who'd referred her to the group and he seemed concerned about her welfare. It didn't make sense that Jo Emily would fear him. But she was a quirky little thing, and Carlie suspected she'd had troubles with the police in the past. It might be authority she feared.

The tapping sound bore into her thoughts again, and this time Carlie listened. It was like water on a rock, unrelenting. And perhaps the strongest force in nature, she realized. A rock could displace the water it was thrown into, but water in any form, even a slow drip, could erode a rock to nothing.

Water was powerful.

He was water.

Rio meant river.

Carlie sat up too quickly. Her head spun dizzily. It felt as if she'd discovered something. She must have, the way her heart was pounding, but she didn't know what it meant. She didn't know what any of it meant . . . *except that she wanted to be with him again.*

How ironic that it was him she wanted to turn to in all of this. Wanted that despite her doubts. It felt like he was her island, her port of refuge, and perhaps the only one she had. The signals telling her it was unsafe didn't make sense to her. She had never felt more cherished and protected than when she was with him. And whole. Her entire life had been a search to discover what was wrong with her, that vital missing part.

He'd helped her see that there was nothing wrong. Nothing missing. That counted for something. It counted for everything.

He'd left several messages for her, at work and here, and one of them was to persuade her to let him give her a personal tour of his "secret Los Angeles." He hadn't explained, except to say that L.A. was a city of unsolved mysteries, and he'd uncovered some he wanted to share with her.

His hushed, sexy laughter had dared her to join him. "I've seen your hideaway. Come see mine," he'd said.

She rolled back her shoulders, wondering if she would ever feel sane again. She had wanted to believe she was beyond the clutches of grand passion, a clean and sober adult, cured of obsessional love by her college anthro professor. That affair had felt like the pinnacle, and in its wake it seemed as if she could never be that vulnerable to a man again, but she was wrong.

Rio was in her thoughts, her dreams, her blood. If it was possible for an experience to take a woman prisoner, her weekend with him had. There was no way to stop thinking about him, or *them* together. He was part of her nervous system now, the electrical impulses that fed her brain.

He came up from behind her, always behind her ... suddenly. His shadow engulfed her and his hand covered her mouth. She was swept up against him, held in thrall by a prison she couldn't escape—had no desire to escape—and from that point on, she was spinning, drowning in mad, helpless sexual surrender. Afterward she could hardly breathe for the guilt and confusion. She didn't understand it, any of it. Or him. And especially, herself.

Why did that fantasy still haunt her so? In some ways the thought of being with him again frightened her terribly. Her life was caught up in a web of confusion, and he was part of it. But that wasn't going to stop her from seeing him, she'd decided. Or from going on this tour. She didn't know who was evil. Or dangerous. She didn't know whose heart it was that beat with dark, frightening impulses. But maybe it was time to listen to her own heart. At least when she did that, she knew where she wanted to be. Where she felt safe.

"How could you have grown up in the area and not known the bridge is haunted?" Rio asked as he and Carlie looked out over the yawning Arroyo Seco, a natural canyon, overgrown with willow, smoke trees, and sage, that ran beneath the Colorado Street Bridge.

"I must have been hanging out with the wrong people." She met his inquisitive gaze with a faint smile. She wasn't crazy about heights, particularly haunted ones.

The bridge was one of the oldest historical landmarks in Pasadena, but the early Bishops had actually settled in the area in 1862, predating its construction by fifty years. In a now legendary poker game at the Slippery Rock Saloon, Bernard Bishop's great-great-grandfather had walked away from the table with a fourteen-thousand-acre parcel of land, won with nothing more than steel nerve and a good face for bluffing.

The land had belonged to an heir to one of the original Spanish land-grant families, and the windfall had prompted the entire Bishop clan to emigrate from Maryland, where they'd grown McIntosh and Winesap apples. California agriculture and real estate had turned their modest fortune into an empire, and since then the Bishop women had all been active members of the historical society, as had the Stanfields. But Carlie had never heard of this apparition of Rio's.

"Is it a friendly ghost?" she asked.

The sun was setting to the south of them, and it had turned Rio's dark hair golden. It did nothing to lighten the irony in his tone. "If you mean like Casper, I wouldn't bet on it."

It was late afternoon, but the rush-hour traffic was still light and moving swiftly in both directions. Carlie was grateful for the guardrail that separated the bridge's walking path from its four-lane highway.

"Did someone jump?" she asked. A feeling came over her as she braced herself on the concrete stanchion and peered over.

"It was a woman, wasn't it? Driven mad by some irresistible man."

A light breeze, already chilly with the promise of evening, teased her hair, feathering it around her face as she turned to Rio for the answer. The long skirt of her apricot silk georgette dress whispered around her ankles.

"It wasn't quite that romantic," he said, gazing at her pastel countenance as if *she* was the irresistible one, a mouthwatering confection he couldn't wait to sample.

"The bridge is haunted by a migrant worker who lost his balance," he explained. "He fell into a chute of wet concrete that was being poured into one of those supporting pillars."

He pointed out the massive columns that lifted the bridge from below. "No one noticed he was missing until the concrete had hardened, and by then it was too late. He was sealed inside."

"God, that's creepy." Carlie scanned the superstructure with a wary eye. At the other end of the bridge she spotted a pillar etched with a tilting cross that looked like a huge X. "Is it that one?"

"According to the legend."

"And now his spirit haunts the bridge?" At his nod Carlie took a step back. Creepy was too mild a word. If this was the first stop on his tour, what was coming next? "Didn't they try to rescue him?"

"They couldn't, not without bringing down the bridge."

Rio had parked the car on the nearest cross street and they'd walked to the structure. Carlie was well on her way back to that street when he caught up with her.

"Where are you going?" he panted.

"Somewhere else."

He whisked her around and pressed her to the iron spires of the railing, capturing her with powerful arms locked on either side of her head. The way the wind filled his black coat and blew his dark hair put her in mind of the infamous robber barons who'd arrived in sunny California just after her ancestors did.

"Want to tell me what's wrong?" he said. "You've been acting oddly all evening."

"I have not." She pretended indignation, but it was probably true that she'd withdrawn. She was apprehensive, not so much for physical as for emotional reasons. She'd read somewhere that when you loved a man, you gave him power, and she had already given this man so much power. Did that mean she loved him?

He scrutinized her with those all-seeing eyes of his, but she turned her head away. Let him decipher the code on his own. She wasn't giving him any help on this one. None at all, thank you.

"You don't want to be holding out on me, girl." He tilted his head warningly. "I'm trained to extract confessions from hardened criminals. Extracting one from you would be the high point of my whole day."

Carlie wasn't a thrill seeker. Her rule of thumb was, Don't jump unless *you* packed the parachute, and with that in mind, she had no intention of playing cringing suspect to his bad cop when *he'd* written the lines. She escaped him by beating him to the car and locking him out until he agreed to continue the tour, which didn't take long since the sun was rapidly falling and the next stop required exactly the right amount of light.

Sunset Strip was famous for its billboards, and the one Rio had in mind promoted a national chain of hardware stores. It was rumored to flash a message when the sun touched the tops of the palm trees. According to Rio, it had been designed that way, but the ad agency behind it was smart enough to leave it a mystery, and everyone saw something different. Carlie couldn't see anything at all, but Rio swore there were words arranged diagonally across the board.

"Don't hold out on me," was what he claimed it said.

Slightly more serene than bridges and billboards, their next stop was a circular garden on the fringes of the Los Angeles Zoo that reminded Carlie of the solar system. The place was a small galaxy of bushes and blossoms with a wizard's door at one end and a glass ball in the center that captured and reflected everything on its surface. Larger than most globes of the earth, the ball sat on a marble pedestal and Carlie, who knew her flowers, walked around it, silently identifying each bloom.

"Any snapdragons?" Rio wanted to know.

She just looked at him and smiled. Let that be his mystery. Her mystery was to wonder who had created this celestial haven in the middle of one of the world's most congested cities.

When the light was low and orangy, Rio took her to the Spanish Kitchen, a boarded-up restaurant on Beverly Boulevard that was steeped in folklore, both chilling and romantic.

"I could tell you stories about this place," he assured Carlie as he let her out of the car.

"Just tell me it's not haunted," she quipped. Shadowed in waning light, the two-story adobe structure had a forbidding look about it. But at the same time, with its iron grillwork, pink facade, and arched windows, it seemed to be frozen in another era, a deserted hacienda wedged in between the thriving businesses that surrounded it, and lost in the shuffle.

"In the thirties," Rio was saying, "there was supposed to have been a young couple whose lifelong dream was to own and operate this restaurant. She wanted to make it a hideaway for lovers, similar to the place in Matzalán where she and her husband met. But on opening night, someone murdered him. She was so distraught she made a will and then she laced their favorite dish with deadly nightshade and ate it so that she could be with him."

Carlie studied the shabby facade with its broken neon sign and peeling paint, thinking about her own penchant for hideaways and trying to imagine the excitement of its opening night, and the tragedy. "What did the woman's will say?"

"That she didn't want anything touched until the killer was caught. That's why the place settings and menus are still on the tables, just the way they were the night he died."

"The murder was never solved?" The restaurant didn't look as if it had been touched in all that time.

"If the story is true, it *was* solved. He was shot by a business rival. The mystery is why the place was never reopened or sold. Rumor has it that the wife didn't die, and she's living in one of the rooms above the restaurant, waiting for some young couple to buy the place and make her dreams come true.''

"But that was over sixty years ago."

"True." Rio was reflective. "Time is running out."

Carlie'd had enough of ghosts and hoary landmarks, and she really wasn't up for going inside, but Rio insisted he knew a way, and there was something she had to see.

He pulled free a corroded padlock and let her in a back door that took them through the kitchen. The interior was dark and musty. It smelled like old newsprint to Carlie, and was illuminated only by what fading pink light could penetrate the window boards. Things were very much as Rio had described, except that some of the dishes were broken on the floor, probably from earthquakes. Vandals would have stolen them, Carlie imagined.

She'd expected to be frightened. Instead she experienced a vastly different emotion as she took in an abandoned dining room, memorable for its heavy brass torch sconces and wrought-iron flourishes. Heartbreak. It was palpable. Sharp as a knife, it could have been her own. It *was* her own. For a moment she was overcome with grief for everything she'd lost, parents who couldn't bring themselves to love her, the man who betrayed her, the sister who died.

"That's why vandals haven't touched this place," she murmured, her voice ringing hollow in the emptiness. "It isn't fear of ghosts that stops them, it's sadness. To see this desolation is to remember that your heart is breaking, too. Everyone's heart is breaking."

She'd been speaking to herself, talking out loud again. But Rio seemed to know what she meant.

His hand was at the small of her back, in that sensitive place where the slightest pressure could be felt.

"Come on," he said. "Maybe this will help."

One of the tables, a small octagon in the corner, just big enough for two, was covered with a dusty dropcloth. He whisked the cloth away with the deftness of a magician, revealing glittering crystal goblets, rimmed in gold, and white china place settings. There was even a handwritten menu on the table.

Carlie picked it up. The date at the top was January 10, 1933, over sixty-five years earlier, and that night's entrée was "savory rock shrimp paella." The dessert was flan in orange sauce, the wine was Madeira, and there was a choice of *tapas, ensalada,* or *albondigas* soup.

Rio lit the candles with a silver lighter he took from the table, and pulled out a chair for Carlie to sit on.

Carlie resisted. One of the crystal candleholders was wobbling a little. She steadied it with a touch.

"Did you do this?" she asked him, meaning the table.

He said that he hadn't, as far as he knew it had always been that way. It wasn't that Carlie didn't believe him, but she was still off balance.

"I don't want to disturb the memories someone's taken such care to preserve," she told him. It felt very much like they were intruding on another couple's private moment. Whether it was past or present didn't seem to matter. These people were alive for her. Their love was alive.

"You don't believe she's here somewhere, waiting?" The empty dining room echoed Rio's question.

"Even if she were, we're not the couple she's waiting for. We'd only disappoint her."

Rio picked up his goblet.

"Let's make sure we don't," he said.

Carlie's response was silence. The room was so still she could have counted her heartbeats to a hundred. His. Someone was counting. Heartbeats didn't go unregistered. Someone knew their speed, their volume, even their weight. Whether they kicked, skipped. Or stopped forever. There had to be a place where they kept every one on record. Maybe it was this room.

Finally, recklessly, she picked up her glass. The rims touched, and the musical clink of crystal sounded hopeful and bright. She could almost imagine the gaiety that must have filled this place for a brief time that night. If she could just bring it back, if she could freeze that moment before happiness stopped for all time. She didn't even know the couple and she wanted to do that. She understood heartbreak.

A bandstand and a small wooden dance floor occupied one corner of the huge room. "Do you think they danced that night? Over there?"

The moment she said it, Carlie saw herself dancing with Rio. She knew what that would be like because she'd done it a million times in her mind. But she also understood how little it would take to unravel her. Once you'd been on a thrill ride, you craved that high again and again. Fear was no longer a deterrent. It was the attraction.

The thought of dancing filled her with fear.

So did he. Irresistible fear.

They started toward the dance floor, and Carlie realized that the point of no return could be anything, a glancing touch as they walked. He might not even mean to touch her, but the results would be the same. A sigh could be her undoing, no matter which one of them uttered it, and surely if he released a breath that was rough with passion—

She stopped, had to stop.

Heartbeats. No one could count that fast.

Rio slowed up. "Are you all right?"

"Fine," she said, making an effort to keep her tone conversational. "It's hard to imagine that a couple could be so deeply in love, I guess. That's the mystery to me."

"It's not hard at all."

"Even a man?" She searched his face, his eyes. They were as impenetrable as the sea at night. Black water eyes.

"That deeply?" she repeated.

"What? Do you think we don't lose our hearts, too? Do you think we don't bleed when we're cut?"

The small shoulder bag Carlie carried was beaded with pastel glass in blue and peach to match the floral pattern on her dress. She rolled the delicate orbs in her fingers and looked around the vast shadowy room. What she wanted was a moment to recover, but the arches and dark passages that branched off in various directions captured her attention and spirited it away to another part of the old hacienda.

One archway in particular revealed a passage so shadowed Carlie couldn't see to the end. What she could see was herself, running down it, crying out in surprise. . . .

"If I were to hide," she said, "could you find me in the dark?"

She turned because he hadn't answered.

He just smiled and studied her flushed face. "I'll give you a ten-second lead," he said.

"Only ten seconds?"

"One . . . two . . . three . . ."

"Rio, wait!"

"Four . . . five . . . six . . ."

"Rio!" With a tiny utterance that was more squeak than anything else, she spun around and ran for the darkness of the hallway. Ran hard.

It was a wild flight to freedom. Grasping handfuls of her skirt, she dashed from one blind alley to another, through archways, and finally up a short flight of stairs to a landing dominated by huge carved doors. Gasping for breath, she heaved the doors open and entered a room even larger than the one she'd left.

Her heartbeats had blurred into one sound, a soft roar.

A ballroom, she realized, turning dizzily to take it all in. The ceiling glittered with a sphere that at one time must have rotated and sprinkled the room with diamonds of light. The wall opposite her was mostly mirrors, and there was no furniture beyond dust-skirted tables that ran the length of both walls and several towering stacks of chairs that dotted the hardwood floor.

Quickly Carlie slipped behind one of the stacks. She had no idea what Rio might do, and that was what frightened her. She couldn't imagine that he would play fair, based on what she knew about him. What she didn't know concerned her more.

As far as she could see, there wasn't a way out other than the way she came in, and she'd forgotten to close the doors. The thought of being trapped in the room brought a wave of panic. But this was not a search-and-destroy mission, she reminded herself. He was not the enemy.

Her beaded bag felt like a security blanket, except that it was icy cold. Shivering, she clutched it against her and waited. The building was oddly laid out, and it might take him some time to find this place at night. She wasn't sure she could have found it in daylight.

What brought her head up was a faint tapping sound.

The measured beats continued as she listened, a sound as compelling as footsteps. Carlie found herself anticipating them, counting them over the wild ticking of her senses.

A form appeared in the archway. She ducked back as it unfurled like a dark apparition, snuffing out the meager light. It would have been a terrifying sight if she hadn't recognized the full wing cut of his coat and the black-as-sin hair.

His movements were filled with sinister grace and his instincts were infallible. Blindfolded, he could have found her almost as quickly, she was sure. And whether he admitted it or not, some of that ability must have come from his bloodlines.

Fleetingly she wondered what went through a man's mind when he pursued a woman. If he concentrated on the moment of capture. Or if he fantasized what he would do once he had her in his arms. It didn't seem possible that a man could chase a woman and not imagine the wild rush of her blood. That he could bear down on her without inhaling the sweet frenzy of her flushed and trembling body.

Was he imagining her cries when he caught her?

Would his heart beat as wildly as hers was beating now?

The tapping had stopped, she realized. Even over the pounding in her ears, something caught her attention and forced her to listen. Silence. The room had gone silent.

She drew back, straining to pick up anything that might tell her where he was. The waiting felt more ominous with every second that passed. He was somewhere near, she knew it, and bent on taking her unawares. Finally she could stand it no longer. She edged forward to look. And heard the floor creak behind her.

It was the only warning she got.

There wasn't time for anything, not even to turn.

A hand slid over her mouth, smothering the wild gasp in her throat. Her head dropped back as she was drawn against him. Her body arched like a bow, but she didn't fight. She couldn't.

It was the way he touched her.

He seemed to know where the wildness was thrumming inside her. Her throat was exposed, and his hand dropped to its taut curve, covering the frantic tick. It whispered down her body like the wind, his hand. It touched the places where she throbbed, startling her senses as it lulled them. She didn't know whether to moan or scream. It felt as if she were being violated and caressed at the same time.

"You can't hide from me."

The sound of his voice startled her, too. It was everywhere. It couldn't have come from him. It filled the room like an echo.

She tried to get a look at him, but he wouldn't let her. He held her hostage while the wind had its way with her, whispering up and down her thighs. It touched her where she quivered and where she clutched. It touched her where she yearned to be touched, where she was soft and open.

She nearly staggered when his hands fell away.

For some reason he'd released her, and her first thought was to run. But she couldn't make her legs work. She stumbled into the open room and stopped. A gasp broke from her as she looked up. That couldn't have been him behind her. He was still in the doorway, huge and forbidding. His dark head nearly brushed the top of the archway.

"But you were behind me! You touched me."

His coat lifted like wings as he walked toward her. Carlie wanted to scream. This couldn't be happening. She was seeing things, night-blind. But he'd reached her before anything could come of her confusion, and his swiftness silenced her.

"Touched you like this?" he asked.

She didn't know what he meant until she felt his hand caressing her face. His fingers danced beneath her chin and lifted it. "Was this how he touched you Carlie? Was this how it felt?"

God, it *felt* wonderful, his caress. Her head lolled back and her throat arched as he stroked her there. She closed her eyes and gave out an involuntary sound, a sigh.

"Was it?" he asked.

The question had barely registered before he spun her around.

"Or like this?"

Now he was behind her, holding her around the waist, holding her tight to his body. She could feel the rise and fall of his chest and the muscles of his thighs. She could feel the rest of him, too. Dark. Virile. Unyielding.

"Yes," she whispered. "Like that."

His hand curved itself to the front of her throat for a moment, holding her that way, savoring the bow string tension. And then it clamped over her mouth.

Her spine arched. It trembled exquisitely. She felt as if she were going to break with pleasure.

"Don't say a word," he whispered. The georgette dress dropped off her shoulders with very little help from him. It slid to the floor, cool silk around her ankles. She wore nothing else except a slip and panties, which fell next.

I'm terrified.

You're naked. And if I made the laws you would never be any other way.

She shook her head frantically, muzzled by his hand. Her legs went weak as he locked his forearm to her belly, supporting her as he bent her forward. She could feel his erection pressing against the curve of her hip, and it was huge.

"There are two ways to make people behave—"

Something shuddered inside him and went taut. She could hear it in his voice, feel it in the hands that held her.

"Love and fear," he breathed out softly, savagely. "You're about to know which it is."

Carlie's heart burst like a tiny star. She tried to scream. She tried to struggle, but she didn't have the strength. The fear he mentioned was rocketing through her, but at the same time her body was soaring with anticipation. She didn't understand the wild rush of it, the flooding weakness. Was this love? Whatever it was, it burned so brightly she was blinded by it.

The last thing she saw as she tumbled forward, her body draped wantonly over the bracing strength of his arm, was her beaded bag on the floor, its contents spilled out. The last thing she felt was Rio touching her, stroking her, whispering her name like a prayer, and entering her in the most thrilling way imaginable.

The last thing she heard was her own scream of ecstasy.

TWENTY-EIGHT

Carlie had no choice but to use the mirrored wall to steady herself. It was the only thing holding her up. Rio's reflection shimmered by her feet as he knelt to clean up the mess her bag had made on the floor. Her key chain was part of the contents that spilled out when the purse fell, but it was the last thing he scooped up. He was careful not to touch the stones, she noticed. He'd gripped the chain by the keys and was staring at the charms as if they could burn him.

Carlie's legs were too shaky to think about anything other than how not to collapse. With his help she'd managed to get her dress back on after they made love. But she hadn't been able to stop trembling, even when he held her and spoke to her, trying to calm her. He hadn't wanted to let go of her, but she'd insisted. Finally he'd draped his coat around her to keep her warm and brought over a chair from one of the stacks.

It was a miracle she wasn't on the floor in a heap: The shivering he'd seen was nothing compared with what was happening inside her. The sex had been too much, too raw. It had left her emotionally devastated. There'd been that moment when they'd crossed the line, some point of no return when she'd given it all—her control, her power, her ability to stop him. And worse, to stop herself.

She'd never felt so naked. So helpless.

She couldn't deny that it had sprung from her own fantasy. Or that, in some way, it was thrilling and primitive. But it had shaken her to the core, and left her wondering about everything, about him, who he was. About herself. Now, more than ever, she needed to test her strength and reassure herself that she could stand on her own, even walk out of this place if she had to.

"You look like an accident victim," he said when he came back with her purse. "A beautiful accident victim, but—"

A victim, nonetheless.

I feel like one, Carlie thought as she took the bag. She started to thank him, then realized he still had her key chain. The stones were cradled in his palm, and when she saw them, he closed his fist over them.

Carlie waited for him to explain. Finally she said, "What are you doing?"

"Trying to decide whether to give them back. They may belong to me more than to you."

She had no idea what he was talking about unless Ginger had promised them to him at one time. "They were my sister's," she said, trying to remember if she'd told him the story before. "The stones were part of her rock collection."

"Yes, I know."

"Did she want you to have them, Rio? Is that why you reacted so strangely the first time you saw them?"

Even in the low light, Carlie could see the way the stones glistened in his palm. The one carved from jet had always reminded her of an animal, and the other, a black-and-amber cat's eye, looked as if it belonged there, cradled in the earthy, coppery tones of his skin.

Perhaps he noticed that, too, as he studied them. They held some special meaning for him, she could tell.

"They were never intended for me," he said clearing the hoarseness from his voice as he handed them back to her. "They're yours."

Carlie took the keys and the conversation was over. She'd heard the emotion, but now it was gone, locked away somewhere. A door had been closed, and he wasn't willing to open it again. He might as well have left the room.

"I think we should get you home," he said. "It's late, and you're cold."

He got no argument from her on that. Even with his coat clutched around her, she was shivering from the chill. Their inescapable reflections in the mirror were constant reminders of what they'd done. Carlie could still hear her own echoing cries and gasps, and the room's flickering shadows left her feeling unsettled and wanting to be somewhere else.

She wondered when it had changed. At some point in the evening, it had stopped being a game. They'd truly been hunter and hunted, watching, waiting, circling each other. Intimate enemies. Odd that it wasn't when she ran away. Or when he found her. That wasn't what had come between them and left her feeling this way, alone. Confused. It was when he saw the stones.

"What are we doing here?" Carlie glanced up as Rio pulled over to the curb. She'd been absorbed in her own thoughts and hadn't realized that he'd stopped in front of the gated entrance of Blue Hills, the Bishop estate in San Marino.

"This is home, isn't it?"

"Not anymore," she said, giving him a look. The tone of his remark was sardonic enough to tell her that it was not an idle one. "If it ever was home."

Only the gabled roof of the regal English manor house could be seen from the road. Carlie hadn't been to the estate since her mother moved to Georgetown. But faced with its forbidding size and the rock walls that resembled battlements, she could understand why Frances hadn't wanted to stay there, even for a night. Neither the memories nor the pain had dulled at all.

"Is this about Ginger?" she asked, pressing Rio to talk.

"It's about the stones on your key chain, Carlie," he said. "The stones your sister found on this land—dug them up in her own backyard, so to speak."

The key chain was in Carlie's purse now, and it would stay there. She'd picked up enough iciness in his tone to tell her that he was talking about something deep-rooted, just as she'd suspected. They'd never discussed his feelings for her sister, but Carlie remembered their conversation in South Beach. He'd said Ginger wanted out of the glory game her parents had created for her, and implied she might not be the innocent victim everyone thought she was.

Carlie had been furious, but now his remarks took on another meaning. They could have been the words of a rejected lover, and that possibility rocked her. It pierced her with envy, a feeling virtually unknown where her sister was concerned. Ginger had always had favored status, but Carlie hadn't envied her for that; she'd admired her. Now Carlie had to face the fact that this might be about unrequited love on Rio's part.

"How did you feel about my sister?" She asked the question under her breath, quickly, desperate to get it over with.

"Are you asking if I was in love with her?"

"Were you? Are you still?"

He wouldn't answer, other than to say, "That's one of those questions that gets you in trouble either way."

Carlie's envy had become despair. He wouldn't answer because he *was*, not that it should have surprised her. Everyone loved Ginger.

"This has nothing to do with your sister, except that she was the one who found the fetishes."

"Fetishes?"

"Those charms of yours," he said. "They're Indian fetishes, stone carvings used for hunting, healing, initiations."

Carlie touched her bag. "How could they be? Ginger's entire collection came from our property. She combed the place, looking for rocks. Sometimes she dragged me along with her through ravines and streambeds."

"Your land didn't always belong to the Bishops, did it?"

"Well, no, of course not, but—"

He silenced her with a look. "It was Indian land, Carlie. Your people settled an area that originally belonged to the natives. Thousands of acres of it. Most of the Shoshone are out in the desert now, along with the other indigenous tribes, forced out there by the land-grabbers."

Carlie needed a moment to digest that. She could feel the stones now, lumped under her hand. "It sounds like you're saying that we, my ancestors, took your land. *Stole* your land."

"Technically the Spaniards got to it first. But are you denying that the land was taken? Stolen? Use whichever word you like."

"I'm denying that *we* stole it. This has been Bishop land since the mid-1800s. We have legal title."

Carlie wasn't as sure as she pretended about the legal title, since the land had been won in a poker game. Or why she was so vehemently defending the Bishops, since she wasn't one by birthright. But neither did she understand why Rio was arguing on behalf of the ancestry he'd always shunned.

Still, as she looked at him, she realized it wasn't his Shoshone blood he'd rejected, it was the past, his memories. He didn't know how to deal with the pain, so he'd sealed it off inside him, along with all reminders of his heritage. And perhaps only now was realizing what he'd lost: a part of himself.

Rio's fingers moved against the console, slowly now, an echo of some primordial drumbeat.

"My father carried fetishes like the ones on your chain," he said. "Exactly like them. I watched him chant over them every night. And I listened to him rant about how the white man had stolen our land and desecrated our hunting grounds and burial sites. How wealthy settlers robbed the graves of our ancestors and sold the sacred icons for profit, how much money the white man had made off our land, and our backs. . . ."

He went on, describing the nightmarish ordeal his father had put him through. Carlie didn't know how to respond when he was finished. She wondered why he'd told her in this way, and if he intended to hold her responsible for a crime that was centuries old, appalling as it was.

"I could tell you I'm sorry for what happened," she said. "But I know how that sounds, like a silly, empty gesture. If it were up to me, I'd give the land back, Rio. I swear I would. It's brought me nothing but heartbreak."

"Then give it back," he said coldly.

"It's not mine to give." She didn't go into what she'd been through recently, how she'd been, as it were, disenfranchised herself. That was complicated enough, and she doubted he would be terribly sympathetic.

"Maybe there's something I can do," she said. "I'll give the stones back, of course. To the Antelope Valley Indian Museum, or wherever you think best. I could donate some of the proceeds from my book, too, or maybe sponsor a women's group on the reservation—"

He didn't respond. He wouldn't even look at her, and finally Carlie gave up. It all did sound empty, futile. She might as well have been talking to the stone walls of the estate. They were immovable, immutable. They cared about nothing. For her those walls had represented the impossibility of ever being acknowledged or accepted. On a daily basis they'd reminded her that in the great scheme of things, she counted for nothing.

It was beginning to feel as if she were doomed to care about people who didn't care back. She could hardly bear the thought that he was one of them.

"I want to go home now," she said. "*My* home."

Carlie flung out an arm, reaching groggily for something. Rio. It must be him she was searching for, but he wasn't there. She opened her eyes to darkness so thick and dense she couldn't see her own hands.

"Rio?" Her voice was soft, breathy, concerned. "Is that you?"

A raspy, choked sob came back to her. It was the same sound that had awakened her, but she had no idea what it was. It couldn't be what it sounded like. He couldn't be crying.

She cocked her head, listening.

After a moment Carlie realized the sound had stopped. His name was on the tip of her tongue again, but the silence made her hesitate. Out of habit, she reached alongside the bed, patting the length of a hard surface until her fingers hit a switch in the base of a table lamp.

The sudden flare of light made her eyes ache. The pain was so sharp she groaned impatiently, and hid beneath her hand. When, finally, she could deal with the brightness, she was struck with a moment of total disorientation. She was in her bedroom. It wasn't the Spanish Kitchen with Rio. That was the night before.

Do not go investigate by yourself. If you hear something, get help. Carlie was still finding it hellishly hard to live with her own advice. It seemed premature to call the police, which left Rio, the wall of silence. They hadn't resolved their differences yet, and she still needed some time. No, she would handle this herself. She knew self-defense, and she'd certainly had plenty of practice with pepper spray. Her new security system had some bugs, but there was a master switch in the bedroom that turned on the lights throughout the house.

She could lock the bedroom door—and probably be up all night, waiting for the next sob, cough, or whatever it was—or she could take a calculated risk and check it out.

Nothing ventured, nothing gained, she thought.

And got out of bed.

The house was chilly, but she had on a pair of fleecy new sweats, and she was used to running around in bare feet, even when the weather turned colder. The gooseflesh rippling down her arms was from nerves. Sometimes silence was more frightening than noise.

Everything looked clear as she went from room to room. There were no signs of forced entry, no one lying in wait behind doors or in closets. She was beginning to think, hope, that it was a false alarm. If there was anything her life needed right now, it was normalcy, some order.

But when she got to the last room, she saw instantly that she was wrong. There was someone in her kitchen. A pair of shoes was visible from the far side of the refrigerator, and it looked like the tips of black boots. Everything else was hidden by the big appliance.

They were heavy enough to be a man's, Carlie realized. The only clues that they weren't were the laces and the style. Now was the time to call the police. This was an intruder. But still she kept inching toward the exposed feet, approaching in a wide, cautious loop until she could see who was hiding in her tiny kitchen.

Her head snapped back in shock. "Oh, my God!" she whispered. "Jo Emily—"

Carlie dropped to the floor, horrified at the sight of her friend. Jo Emily's clothes were savagely ripped, and there were oozing lacerations on her arms and face. A deep bruise had turned her jaw purple. It looked as if it might be dislocated.

"He got me again—" It was all Jo Emily could choke out before she began to cough. Blood oozed from her mouth.

Carlie turned to the phone on the far wall, torn. If there was any chance Jo Emily was bleeding internally, the paramedics would have to be called. But maybe she could check the wounds first.

"There really is a stalker after me," Jo Emily rasped. "You believe me, don't you?"

"Of course I do!" Carlie tried to keep her voice soothing as she brushed blood-soaked hair from the stricken woman's face. "Of course I do, Jo Emily. You're safe now. There's nothing to be frightened of. I just want to see how bad these injuries are."

Carlie went to the sink for a damp cloth. It took her only a moment, but Jo Emily had stopped coughing and seemed to be resting a little easier when she returned. The blood was coming from a gash inside her lip, Carlie discovered with great relief. The jaw looked gruesome, but it wasn't causing Jo Emily pain to move it, which meant it probably wasn't broken. As for the rest, there were some nasty cuts and bruises, but nothing that couldn't be washed and dressed with bandages.

Carlie moved quickly but reassuringly to get her friend cleaned up and into the spare bedroom. She helped her into the only gown and robe she still owned, cushioned her on the bed with pillows, and then brought in a pot of goldenseal tea and some chicken broth she'd warmed.

But watching Jo Emily try to eat with her mouth so swollen and banged up made Carlie's heart ache. It enraged her, too. Who could have done this? she asked herself. She'd posed the question countless times in her work with victims, but it never lessened her enmity toward the brutes whose sole purpose seemed to be to terrorize. She would never understand how one human being could savage another one this way, just for the sick pleasure of it. It was like abusing a child.

Carlie's fists were clenched beneath her crossed arms, but the fury seething in her soul could not be hidden. It glinted in her eyes and fired a nerve near her lip. She saw her own reflection and lifted her head, accentuating the effect. One woman's murderous outrage, she thought, caught like a Polaroid snapshot, in the vanity mirror.

Carlie rather liked the she-devil look, but didn't want to frighten Jo Emily. She had something in mind, more an idea than a plan at this stage. But there was a great deal she needed to know from Jo Emily before anyone else, like the authorities, were notified, and it was always easier to get difficult questions answered in a calm, safe atmosphere.

"How did you get in the house?" she asked when Jo Emily had finished a cup of tea and taken some of the soup.

"You gave me the key, 'member? Said I should come over whenever I wanted and look through those clothes you were going to give away."

"Of course." Carlie had been so distracted with Rio, it had slipped her mind. She'd given her the key the night she took her to the shelter. Carlie was getting ready to donate some clothing that no longer fit, but she'd wanted Jo Emily to look through the items first and pick out anything she liked. She'd also wanted her to know there was a place she could come if she wanted some privacy, or a change of pace.

Jo Emily settled back in the pillows, and Carlie took it as a sign that she was done eating. She moved the tray aside and sat on the bed. "Do you feel up to talking about what happened?" she asked.

A jerky little nod, and then Jo Emily squeezed her eyes shut. "He must have been waiting in the laundry room out back. My clothes, they were flying all over the place. I never even got to set the basket down, he grabbed me so fast. Clamped his hand over my mouth and snapped my neck back like he was going to twist it off, yeah, twist my damn head off—"

Whoever attacked her knew the location of the shelter, Carlie realized as Jo Emily went on. She was no longer safe there, but Carlie already had a solution to that problem. She would keep Jo Emily here, if she agreed. She could have this room, and stay as long as she wanted to. *I'll keep her here and protect her myself, goddammit, since no one else seems to be able to.*

"He kept telling me I'd never escape him, and if I tried, he'd break my hands so I couldn't do manicures anymore—" Jo Emily shook her head, a sob in her throat. "He said he was going to take a bat to my hands the way he did my windshield—"

She couldn't go on. Carlie wanted to hug her close and promise her that everything would be all right, but she couldn't do that just yet. She had a bad feeling, and she didn't want Jo Emily to sense what was going on inside her. Carlie also had something troubling to tell her friend, and she didn't know how to do it. They were going to have to call the police again. The attacks were escalating. This one was worse than the other two, and it was important to document all contact with a stalker.

He'd also threatened her with physical harm, although they still had no proof. It would be Jo Emily's word against his.

"No more talking now," Carlie said. "You need to rest. Think you could sleep?"

"I think so—" Jo Emily's head jerked up. There was a terrified look in her eyes. "What's that? That sound?"

Carlie hadn't heard anything, and couldn't imagine what she was talking about. "What sound?"

"Someone's tapping, can't you hear it?" Her finger stabbed the air. She was pointing toward the hallway, and Carlie realized she must have heard the leaky faucet in the bathroom.

"Oh, that's the shower," she explained. "It's just the shower. It drips."

Jo Emily looked as if she weren't sure she wanted to believe that. Blue veins streaked her temple, and a pulse leaped in the hollow of her cheek. But finally she gave an exhausted sigh and sank back. "Scared me half to death," she said. "That's the sound he makes."

Now it was Carlie trying to calm herself. She felt as if she were going to be sick, the way her stomach had turned over. Jo Emily had brought this up the other day. The phone, she'd said something about the line clicking, but that wasn't what she meant now.

"How does he make the sound?" Carlie's voice was faint. "Could it be his shoes? Or his keys? Change in his pocket? Maybe there was water dripping in the laundry room."

She wondered if Jo Emily knew about the technique Rio used. If Carlie remembered correctly, he'd been written up in the local papers because of his unusual abilities. It had to do with the high-profile cases he'd solved, but that was a few years back, and Jo Emily was new in this area. It wasn't likely she would have seen the articles.

Carlie felt a moment's guilt at the thought that Jo Emily might want to implicate Rio for some reason. It was hard to imagine a stalker victim being that devious. Those cuts and bruises were real. Her torment was real.

"Maybe . . ." Jo Emily was thinking about the question. "Except that I woke up one night hearing that sound, my first night in the shelter. I couldn't see him anywhere, but I had the feeling he was there."

Carlie was determined to stay calm. She needed more information if she were to make sense of this. "Did you see him this time?" she asked. "Are you sure it's the same man every time?"

"I think so. He always wears the same black ski mask and he says that same thing—you know, the song."

Carlie didn't understand how it all fit together—the clicking sound, the song lyric, the ski mask. But the truth couldn't be any more disturbing than what she was thinking, and she wasn't sure how much longer she could bear the suspense. She had to know who the stalker was.

"Jo Emily," she said pleadingly, "we have to tell the police. Or let me call Rio at least—"

But Jo Emily was already shaking her head, frantically shaking her head, and confirming Carlie's worst fears. For some reason she was frightened of Rio, and Carlie could only think of one explanation. She still couldn't bring herself to ask the question. Perhaps it was denial, but she needed more evidence before she could even entertain such an idea.

She rose from the bed and walked to the doorway, listening to the plink of water across the hall and wondering why she hadn't had that faucet fixed. Wretched thing was driving her nuts. Tomorrow. She would get someone in here tomorrow, the moment she woke up.

"All right," she said at last, speaking to the open doorway, to the walls, everywhere but to the woman on the bed. "I won't call the police. I won't call anyone, but you have to tell me what happened. Will you? Will you tell me in detail? Everything he said, everything he did."

Carlie turned, and Jo Emily nodded, her eyes bright with fear. "I can't exactly remember everything. I told you how he nearly took my head off, and then he slammed me up against the washing machine, like he wanted to knock the wind out of me. That's when I hit my face on the coin feed, damn thing just about ripped my lip off." She laughed, but tears filled her eyes.

Carlie had never seen a face so fraught with pain. "That's enough," she said. But it was Carlie who'd heard enough.

Jo Emily couldn't seem to stop herself. "I thought if I pretended to be unconscious, he might ease up, but he kept ramming me against that machine, and then he tried to drag me out of there, out of the laundry room, so I bit him, real hard, bit the piss out of his hand, 'cuz I knew if he got me alone . . ."

A veil of stillness dropped around Carlie as Jo Emily went on, describing her escape. She wasn't sick anymore. There was no nausea churning in the pit of her belly. She was numb. She felt nothing. Something in her had sealed off from the distant voice that was shouting at her, trying to tell her that some hideous truth awaited her, lurked just around the corner, ready to engulf her whole life in pain and darkness.

It wasn't possible that the man who had made love to her with such sweet fury in the mountains, the man she was undoubtedly falling in love with, could have done the things Jo Emily was describing. He couldn't have. She didn't even need to ask herself why because it wasn't Rio. It wasn't him, and Carlie would find some way to prove that.

She was trembling as she returned to the bed and sat down. "I'm going to catch this man, Jo Emily, I promise you that. I'm going to do it for both of us. But you can't tell anyone, do you undertand? You can't repeat a word of this conversation."

She took her friend's hand. "Are you with me?"

For some reason Jo Emily wouldn't look at her, and when Carlie bent over her, and gently brought her head around, she saw a terrifying glint in her friend's eyes. It wasn't fear that lit them now. It was rage, the same emotion that was sealed off inside Carlie. Blind, unreasoning rage.

"Carlie," she said, a sob in her voice, "there's something I need to tell you. Carlie—"

But Carlie was afraid of what Jo Emily was going to say and cut her off. She grabbed her and hugged her close, as she'd wanted to do before. And this time she did utter the words she'd been unable to say then. She whispered them fiercely. "It will be all right, Jo Emily. It will. You have my promise."

TWENTY-NINE

Peggy Sykes was not what Carlie expected. All Carlie knew about her was that she was Rio's partner. He'd never described her or gone into any detail about their relationship, except to mention that they'd worked together before she became ill. But Carlie had sensed that it was an important relationship to Rio, and perhaps she'd had a moment or two of concern, wondering what kind of bond they had. But whatever she'd imagined, it wasn't the woman she encountered when she walked into Peggy's hospital room that morning.

Most of the policewomen Carlie dealt with had a brisk military efficiency about them that seemed to go with the territory. It was a tough job commanding respect in the male-dominated world of law enforcement, not to mention crime. Carlie had always envied their self-command, and had probably thought Peggy would be the epitome of that, a sleek Emma Peel with an enigmatic smile, a genius IQ, and of course, enough icy beauty for ten women.

Now Carlie wondered if she had the right room as she watched the tall, sturdy, fortyish woman finish speed-packing her weekender suitcase. Carlie had a peek at the chart on the door. It was Peggy, all right, but she didn't look sick as she wedged a travel alarm clock between a slender book of proverbs and a brown leather shoulder holster. Nor, thank goodness, did she look like Emma Peel. But she was formidable in the efficiency department, plenty brisk and military.

Carlie liked her on sight.

"You here already?" Peggy glanced over her shoulder as she slammed the case shut. Apparently all LAPD detectives were wired like sonar, and she'd heard someone come in. "Hold on until I get this other thing packed."

Carlie observed with interest as Peggy shoveled typical hospital-patient contraband into a police duffel bag. She struck Carlie as someone who could have whipped her entire squad into shape, including Rio, with one hand tied behind her back. The boy would have been strung up by that noose of a tie of his if he'd given her grief.

Even Peggy's outfit seemed to reflect a desire for order and perfection. Her bright red turtleneck and matching socks were set off by gray wool slacks and unblemished suede loafers, all of which complemented her trim figure and brought out the sparkling threads of silver in her dark hair.

Carlie felt fairly shabby in her jeans and scuffed ankle boots. At least she was wearing a black blazer with a little crest on the pocket.

"Tootsie Roll?" Peggy offered Carlie one from a huge transparent candy cane. "The originals, not those bite-size things."

Carlie shook her head, and Peggy went back to her chore. She tossed in several packs of Stim-U-Dents, a plastic Baggie full of Q-Tips, Chap Sticks in assorted fruit flavors, the usual oral-hygiene gear, a crumpled pack of Camels that she swore were under her pillow for the entire hospital stay, and a desk calendar of sayings, one for each day of the year.

" 'In order to cover a hole you've got to dig a new one.' " She yanked the duffel shut and tied off the strings. "Thought for today."

"Works for me," was Carlie's only comment. Brisk, efficient, *and* a kook, Carlie decided. She was certain they'd never met, but Peggy was acting as if they knew each other.

At last, packed bags on the floor by the bed, she turned to Carlie and said, "All right, where do I sign?"

"Excuse me?" Carlie couldn't help but laugh. "Maybe I should introduce myself? I'm Carlie Bishop."

Peggy did a classic double take. "No kidding? I thought you were one of those hospital-administrator people, up here to bid me a fond farewell."

She crossed her arms and tilted her head, as if for a better look. "Carlie Bishop, as I live and breathe. I've seen you on those talk shows, teaching women how to kick men in the groin." She winked. "Tell 'em to wear football cleats."

Carlie would have been hard-pressed not to call Peggy's expression warm and friendly. There was something guarded about her eyes, but that wasn't uncommon in her line of work either. Like military efficiency, it was part of the territory. Now Carlie wondered how sick Peggy actually was, and if she was going to be okay.

"You must be glad to be going home," Carlie said.

"You could say that. After two weeks of poking and prodding, they decided I had a mildly infected heart valve, pumped me full of antibiotics, and sent me packing."

"Another medical miracle."

Peggy grinned at Carlie's remark. She picked up a sweating blue plastic pitcher from the wheeled tray. "Sorry, I don't have anything more interesting than ice water to offer you. How is it you happen to be on the sixth floor of the UCLA Medical Center? Not visiting friends or relatives, I hope."

"Actually, I'm here to see you," Carlie hastened to explain. "Rio Walker's a friend, and he told me you two were partners. I've been worried about him lately."

No lie there, Carlie realized, except maybe one of context. She'd been avoiding his calls since the private "tour" he'd taken her on because she needed time to sort things out, and to ask questions of people like Peggy. Carlie was now investigating him, as difficult as that was to admit, just as he'd investigated her. At least she knew he wasn't one of those guys who didn't call after sex.

"Is there something wrong with Rio?" Peggy was no longer warm and friendly. She was a bristling mother cat.

"No, not like that. It's hard to explain—"

"If you're going to tell me he's a working fool, I already know. He's obsessed with that damn Fatale case. Nobody can convince him to back off, and he still won't, even now that Grover's on his ass—"

Carlie felt a swooping emptiness, as if her lungs had been punctured and drained of air. "The Femme Fatale case?"

But Peggy had already caught herself. And Carlie could only assume that the policewoman had just realized she might be speaking to one of Rio's suspects.

"I talk too much," was all Peggy would say.

"Not at all," Carlie assured her. "Rio's on my task force, and we've become friends. At least I'd like to think we have."

Carlie wouldn't have been able to pull off the breezy nonchalance if she hadn't had some actress in her. Not a chance. It felt like she was the one who'd been hit with a baseball bat, smashed like Jo Emily's car window. She was shattering inside. Rio was worse than guys who didn't call. He was despicable, a liar and a cheat. He'd told her he was putting the case on the back burner. God, he lied. He lied about *that*.

Peggy had gone back to her bags. "I can't help you where Rio's concerned. I haven't seen him in a while."

Carlie wasn't too stunned to realize she'd been dismissed. She wanted out of there, and would have left without another word if she hadn't noticed the newspapers. A stack of them sat on the windowsill, and the top one was folded over to what looked like the most recent article on stalker victims. Gabe Quiñones's series, she realized, with a pang of guilt. He'd been calling, too, and leaving threatening messages that he'd already missed one deadline and was going to cancel the series if he didn't get some input from Carlie. Jo Emily hadn't returned his calls either, he'd complained.

Publicity was the last thing Carlie wanted right now. Going with the series had been a risk that seemed to have backfired. It had probably brought the stalker out of hiding and put Jo Emily in mortal danger. That was another reason Carlie had to find the man, the *only* reason that mattered.

Carlie wore her shoulder bag looped over her head for safety purposes. Her fingers tightened on the straps as she realized that Gabe Quiñones might be helpful to her. The series had brought the stalker back. Why couldn't it flush him out, expose him? Admittedly it was a reckless idea that could even involve publishing false information as bait. But what a professional coup it would be for Quiñones. He'd been passed over for a Pulitzer several times. Surely he would win for this one, something on the order of the Unibomber story, but on a smaller scale. He would be part of solving a heinous crime.

Carlie's fingers were white knots at the knuckle, and it struck her that she must look as desperate as she felt. Gabe was a reporter, and a driven one. She would have to take him into her confidence, at least partially, and there was no guarantee he wouldn't expose her. She could become a sacrificial lamb for the story, just as Jo Emily already had been, and Carlie couldn't take another chance like that.

Peggy was watching her now, she realized. She had to leave before the other woman started asking questions. Peggy was a veteran investigator, and if she'd been following Gabe's series, it might not be difficult to put things together and figure out what Carlie was up to. But for one crazy second Carlie wished Peggy *would* figure it out. She had been carrying this burden alone, and the temptation to reach out was tremendous.

She couldn't succumb to desperation now. She'd set up a scenario that had put another woman in terrible peril. It was the extreme opposite of the cause she'd dedicated her life to, and there was no one she could turn to but herself to solve it. She couldn't appeal to Rio or Gabe, and certainly not to Peggy, a woman she didn't even know. There was no one. Carlie was alone. And she alone was responsible.

In order to cover one hole you had to dig another. How true that was, Carlie thought. "Thank you," she mumbled to Peggy, wondering what she was thanking the other woman for as she turned to leave, and having no idea how prophetic that parting remark would turn out to be.

A crisis of national proportions awaited Carlie when she got to Safe and Sound later that morning. The congressional hearings on funding cuts for victims' assistance programs had been moved up and Carlie had been called to testify. Danny was waiting for her with the news when she walked in the door.

"Me?" she said, stopped in her tracks.

"You," Danny confirmed. "The president's chief of staff called on behalf of the big guy himself to ask that you speak before the full Senate Judicial Committee tomorrow afternoon. You're scheduled for four P.M. No telling when they'll get you on, but you've got to be there."

"Tomorrow?" It was almost too many syllables for Carlie to manage. It wasn't that she hadn't been expecting this. But the hearings were originally scheduled for later that month, and Carlie had arranged for a task-force member who lived and worked in Washington, D.C., to testify.

Whoever spoke would have to be armed and ready to make the most compelling case of her life to keep the legislators from slashing the budget. It was a daunting prospect, and yet Carlie knew that she might be the best person for the job. She had passion to spare. What she didn't have was a presentation. Several of the task-force members had submitted the sections of the report for which they were responsible, but Carlie hadn't finished her own, and she was also the one charged with putting the entire report together, complete with recommendations.

Her assistant was tilted back in his chair, watching her as if he might be about to witness a human being crack like the Liberty Bell. But Carlie's head was already whirling with ways to accomplish the impossible.

The breath she exhaled was part laughter and part disbelief. "Twenty-four hours, Danny? Can we get me ready?"

He lifted his shoulders, but Carlie could feel the effort from across the room. Danny wasn't himself these days. The situation with Jo Emily had left him moody and dejected, even withdrawn. He didn't seem to want to talk about it, and Carlie wasn't sure how to help. She'd never seen him like this, and she was honestly a little frightened. Frightened for everyone in her life, it seemed. And wondering if she ought to be for herself.

"Danny, we have to try," she said. "Our own funding is at stake."

Her heartfelt entreaty brought his head up.

"Sure, definitely, we'll do it," he said. "We'll have to break down every sector report we've got for the data, but we'll do it."

"Good, good! Can you get started on it now? I'll get my own report together, and then we can work on the presentation. Oh, Danny, thank you."

He brightened at that. Maybe this project would distract him from his concerns about Jo Emily. Carlie hoped so. She missed the old Danny.

Actually, Carlie was hoping the same thing for herself. An emergency like this was the perfect excuse not to deal with her personal problems, or face the pain of what was happening with Rio. She could push it all away, push *him* away. There were times when you had to give your heart a rest.

Carlie had started for her office, and was thinking through the logistics of her trip, when it hit her. "Oh, God! I can't leave Jo Emily."

Danny was clearly startled. "I thought she was at the shelter."

"She is, or was—" It had slipped Carlie's mind that Danny knew nothing about the last attack. Carlie hadn't revealed Jo Emily's whereabouts to anyone except the shelter director and the security firm she used. That morning she'd had her home system upgraded with an automatic armed-guard response so that someone would be sent to her house if the alarm was triggered. It was the only way she could leave and know, with any confidence, that Jo Emily would be safe there.

"She wasn't comfortable at the shelter," Carlie explained.

"Yeah?" Suddenly he was alert, hopeful. "Do you think it would help if I called her?"

This was one of the hardest things Carlie had ever had to do. Telling Danny the truth was painful enough, but not being able to take him into her confidence was worse. It went against the bond they'd built over the years. He was her buddy, her rock. She'd always been able to turn to him, even when there was no one else. God. There had been no one but Danny for so long she couldn't remember when there was anyone else. There hadn't been, except Ginger.

"I'm sorry," she said. "I really am, Danny, but calling Jo Emily wouldn't be a good idea."

"Why? She doesn't even want to talk to me? That makes me feel like some kind of monster."

He turned away from her, and Carlie had some fears about what he might do if she went to him. Men generally needed to be left alone when they were this vulnerable, and Danny had been acting odd. She went anyway. He was a friend, worth the risk. Worth any risk.

"Please, Danny—you shouldn't feel that way." She gave his brawny shoulder a gentle pat.

"I know this must hurt like hell," she said, "but it's not about you. Jo Emily's in a bad way right now. I'm not sure she trusts anyone, including me."

"If it's not about me, why did she sneak out while I was sleeping? She didn't even leave a note."

Carlie sat herself on the edge of his desk and studied his slumped shoulders for a moment, wishing she could tell him there was nothing wrong with him, just the way Rio had told her.

Danny Upshaw, you are a stand-up guy and a credit to your sex. I don't know why Jo Emily took a powder, but she's missing out big time. You have a good heart, and there are so many women who would love to love you, who would feel privileged just to know you. . . .

Carlie meant every word of it, but she didn't say it. Instead, she grabbed his hand and gave it a little shake, as if they'd just been introduced. It was a bold move where Danny was concerned, but she probably needed the contact as much as he did.

"Let's think positive," she said. "Maybe when things calm down and this bastard who's stalking her is caught, Jo Emily will feel differently. If you could be a little patient. Give her some time. Do you think you could, Danny? You two seemed perfect together. I was really hoping—"

His jaw clenched, and he seemed to be fighting some lacerating emotion. "We were all hoping," he said bitterly. "I guess we're always hoping for things that can't be."

"I guess we are." Carlie sighed as if it were her last, and then hoped he wouldn't hear the weight of it. She didn't want to make him feel responsible for her anguish, too.

His mouth twisted as he struggled to grin. "Life sucks." His eyes brimmed and he squeezed her hand. "It really does, you know."

That much Carlie did know.

It was three in the morning and the view of the city from Mulholland Drive was spectacular, but Rio Scott Walker was not enjoying the vista. His tiny bungalow sat atop the world-famous hills like the highest car on the Ferris wheel, swinging over a carnival of jeweled and sparkling lights. It was a rare, crystalline night in the city of angels, a time for reflecting on the wants and needs of the inner man.

There was only one hitch in that idea. What Rio needed tonight was a crime punishable by death in at least forty states. He wanted a piece of Carlie Bishop. Nothing else would assuage the darkness eating away at his soul.

He turned from the window with a low sound of displeasure and settled back at the kitchen table, where he'd been "reflecting" for most of the night. It was actually a vintage dinette booth, rumored to have been pulled out of the now demolished Brown Derby restaurant on Hollywood and Vine. That was long before Rio moved into the bungalow, but it was part of what had sold him on the place. The other was the view.

There was a time he could gaze out the window and see the future. Now he could see nothing but traffic lights.

And her face.

A pack of Marlboro Lights lay on the dinette table. It was the same pack he'd had with him in South Beach. And the one he'd taken a cigarette from the day he looked up at the TV set in his office and saw the world's most beautiful pair of green eyes.

He'd been carrying the Marlboros around with him ever since that day in his office, and the pack was still just one cigarette short of full. He'd vowed not to smoke until he cracked the case, and he'd been a model of restraint. Not smoking, not shooting up post offices, but not cracking the damn case.

"Fuck that." He picked up the pack, fished out a cigarette, and held it under his nose, inhaling deeply.

Either he smoked or somebody was going to die.

She'd done another disappearing act. He'd been trying to reach her for the last forty-eight hours. He'd been by her place a dozen times, but no one answered the bell. And when he got her assistant on the phone at her office, the kid had blown him off with some story about her being called out of town on an emergency.

Rio hadn't known whether to believe him or not, but Carlie's elusiveness had triggered all kinds of nasty suspicions. The trip could be an excuse to disappear and carry out another strike. Grover had been right to take him off the case. Rio had grown careless because of his personal relationship with her, and at the first opportunity she'd disappeared.

It wouldn't be that hard to track her down. But he'd made the mistake of becoming emotionally involved, and he was torn about how to proceed. It was Peggy who told him he had tunnel vison, that he was obsessed with Carlie, and blinded to the possibility of the Femme Fatale being anyone other than her.

Not entirely true. He had a laundry list of suspects for Frank Grover that included her Supreme Court justice mother, Carlie's entire support group, her assistant, Danny Upshaw, and even Jo Emily Pough.

She looked fragile and helpless, but no one had a stronger motive, and Jo Emily had a serious crazy streak in her. Not too many people knew she'd been a prostitute once, but Rio had gotten her out of trouble, and he knew what she was capable of better than most.

As for Upshaw, he had the opportunity, the ability, the motive, and more importantly, the perfect cover, his gender. Carlie's support group was a gene pool of potential suspects. One of the charter members, Dorrie Springer, had a rap sheet that included manslaughter. She'd killed her abusive boyfriend and walked on a self-defense. All the members had either been victimized by stalkers or were dealing with loved ones who had been.

Fuck the suspects. Grover could have them. Rio was going after her. From now on he was going to dog Carlie Bishop's every step. Watch her every move. He was going to watch her dress and undress, watch her eat and sleep.

Go fucking nuts watching her.

There was one cigarette lying on his desk. He lit it up and let it burn until it was a glowing coal, then he ground it out on the tabletop. He wanted the satisfaction of pain, the atavistic anger that pain would bring. He wanted rage. But all he felt was heat.

She'd stolen his soul.

Her family had taken the rest.

Yeah, he wanted a piece of her.

He had that coming.

THIRTY

It was anonymous.

It was unreal.

It was the most naked moment of Danny Upshaw's life.

Shivering like a kid, he stood next to a low-slung dresser that looked like every other cheap, wood-laminate stick of furniture in every other cut-rate motel room across America, and wondered if he could go through with it.

He felt as if he'd stepped into someone else's life. But it was his own life he'd stepped into. His own self. He couldn't hide from it any longer. Or avoid it by avoiding Jo Emily. This no-frills, hourly-rate room was where he would come face-to-face with who he was. A man. Or something less than human.

The woman posed on the end of the twin bed had already kicked off her stiletto heels. Now she was undoing a shiny wraparound dress, and Danny could see there was nothing underneath it. Watching her made him profoundly uncomfortable, but she seemed to expect it, and she had looked pretty in a weary, blowsy kind of way when he opened the door.

"I could undress you," she offered, warmth in her voice.

He shook his head. The thought made him nearly sick with apprehension, with shame. "Open the box."

She turned to do it, and he watched her in the mirrored closet doors. She wasn't unattractive. Her body lacked tone and was probably too fleshy for some men, but Danny forced himself to concentrate on the pale light of her bare shoulders and the silky veil of blond hair she'd tucked behind one ear to keep it from falling in her face. Her mouth was hard and her posture careless, but he ignored all that. In his mind she was as gauzy and graceful as an angel.

He could see what it had cost her, trying to please men like him, and that saddened him. The irony was that she would never know what it had cost him to come here, to confront his darkest fears. Sex was violent. That had been true as far back as he could remember. It was why he'd given his life to teaching women how to defend themselves. They needed protection against men like him, the Danny Upshaws of this world.

He had a gut-deep fear of this nameless woman, of himself, of being in the same room with her. If she'd given him an opportunity, he would have cut and run. All she would have to do was visit the bathroom, and he'd be out the door. He wished she would, for both their sakes. He didn't want to hurt her. But, God, he had to know the truth.

"It's beautiful." She took the red silk lingerie from the box and held it up. The room's only light, a table lamp by the bed, flickered like a candle, playing shadows across the far wall.

"I love the color," she exclaimed. "Did you pick it out yourself?"

Danny saw her looking at him in the mirror, and he struggled to control a simple nod. He was finding it hard to breathe, finding it hard to do anything at all, except make himself stay there.

She turned to him, all smiles, and brought the gown to her face, nuzzling it like a kitten. "It's beautiful," she said. "You're beautiful."

Surprise ripped through him like a pair of sharp scissors, cutting and snipping, burying itself in his groin. There was easily as much pain as pleasure in it. Probably more. Sexual desire had been a nightmare for him since he was young enough to experience it for the first time. He was easy to arouse, perhaps too easy, because his own urges created hellish conflict.

"You're going to want to get those jeans off before you bust 'em," she said, with a knowing glance at his crotch. "Sure you don't need any help?"

"No, I can—shit!" He fumbled out of his shirt and got his pants unzipped, swearing at his own awkwardness.

He could hardly look at her when he was done. It wasn't his body he was ashamed of. Women had always liked his build, but they read him wrong. They confused his reluctance with shyness and tried to coax him. That was what triggered the monsters.

Finally she stopped nuzzling the gown, and held it up again, admiring it. "Would you like me to wear it?" she asked. "I can be whatever you want. Do you like sluts? Virgins?"

Sluts. The word made him sick.

By the time she had the gown on, Danny was soaked with sweat. His hands balled into fists as she came toward him. The sensation that pierced him could have been rage or it could have been need, simple human need. He didn't know anymore, but he had to find out.

"Hey, it's all right," she said soothingly. "Just tell me what you want. I aim to please."

"If you don't mind—" He didn't want to offend her. "I'd like to call you Joey."

Carlie needn't have worried about Jo Emily. She was having herself a fine time in Carlie's absence. She'd been born in a trailer, and lived most of her adult life in seedy rented rooms and tiny apartments. Carlie's was the closest thing to a "nice" place she'd ever spent any amount of time in, and she was loving every minute. The quaint Cape Code–style house felt like an enchanted cottage to her.

She admired the elegant cane-and-wrought-iron furniture, heaped high with cushions, the Bombay chests and Oriental carpets, and especially the window gardens. Feeling very much the genteel lady, she meandered appreciatively from room to room, openly wishing the place belonged to her.

And snapping her gum. Genteel ladies probably didn't snap their gum quite as vociferously as she did. But it *was* Dentyne, not Juicy Fruit or anything, and the way Jo Emily had it figured, they secretly wished they could. When she was little—all of eleven or twelve maybe—and still living on the church grounds with her folks, she promised herself that even if she got filthy rich someday, she would always lean a little toward the flashy side. That way she wouldn't have to be frustrated and cry every time the vacuum cleaner broke, like her mama. Or speak in tongues and handle poisonous snakes, like her daddy.

Her folks were the custodians at Miracle of the Bread and Fishes nondenominational church near Knoxville, and they still lived in an old silver Air Stream on church grounds. They were good people, and Jo Emily loved them dearly, but she did not share their enthusiasm for snakes and such.

She'd left home at fifteen, and felt guilty every day since that she hadn't stayed in touch. She wished she could call them now, tell them how she was a houseguest of someone almost famous, but she'd probably only worry them when they found out why she was here.

On that dispiriting thought Jo Emily resumed her snooping. Carlie had locked up her office, so she left that room alone, but nothing else was sacred. She searched the closets and found all kinds of treasures, among them a velour robe with an emblem on the breast pocket that she figured must be the official family crest.

Jo Emily couldn't imagine anything better than being a Bishop and would have worn the robe to bed if she hadn't been afraid of wrinkling it. Instead she settled for a pair of Carlie's sweats that were as green as her friend's eyes. She found them tucked in a basket of freshly washed clothes, and once she had them on, she went to the kitchen to make herself a bedtime snack, as she imagined Carlie might do.

She wanted to carry that wonderful wicker tea tray, laden with delicious tidbits, into Carlie's room. But most of all, she wanted to sleep in the lacy wrought-iron bed. Carlie had told her it would be all right, and even though it was early evening, Jo Emily couldn't wait.

She found Spanish olives and marinated mushrooms in the refrigerator. She sliced some jalapeño-pepper cheese to go with them, broke a fist-size chunk from a crusty baguette, and made *mmm-mmm-mmmmm* noises in her throat. For the finishing touch, she poured a glass of white zinfandel, grabbed a bunch of seedless grapes and a handful of Pecan Sandies, and congratulated herself on the spread.

Jo Emily popped her gum one last time as she walked down the creaky hallway to the bedroom. She was really just reminding herself to get rid of it before she ate. There was nothing worse than mixing gum and food. She didn't even plan to save it this time, although Dentyne held its flavor well, and would be good for another long while. Unlike Juicy Fruit, which was one big splat, and then it was gone.

"Don't you just love it," she murmured, stopping in the doorway to admire the bed.

Moments later, when she had everything arranged just so, she began sampling the delicacies one at a time and clearing her palate with grapes, like she'd seen Martha Stewart do on TV. That was the only thing missing in Carlie's bedroom, a television set. Jo Emily liked falling asleep to reruns of *Designing Women,* and she'd always enjoyed *Oprah.*

Suddenly stuffed, she moved the tray aside, fell backward, and closed her eyes. Carlie had told her not to worry about the alarm system, that everything was automatic. There was a remote panic button on the night table, which either turned everything off. Or on. Jo Emily couldn't quite remember. . . .

Birds were singing when she opened her eyes the next morning. *California had birds.* Funny that hadn't occurred to her before now, but maybe this place was the reason why. They were all hanging out in Carlie's sweet little flowerpot of a backyard.

Jo Emily stretched, luxuriated, and contemplated her day. Since she had nowhere to be and no one to see, she could loll around in bed and be as lazy as she wanted. And loll she did, most of the damn morning, reading magazines and picking at what was left of the grapes. Carlie had a great selection of fashion rags, although why there wasn't a *Cosmo* in the bunch, Jo Emily couldn't fathom.

She spent the afternoon going through the clothing Carlie had boxed up to give away, and found herself the prettiest little navy-and-white coatdress imaginable and a pair of spectator pumps that might fit with some stretching at the shoe shop. It was a good day, all in all, but by late afternoon she was restless, and by sunset, she was on the phone to her folks, desperate to talk to someone.

Her mama cried and her daddy sent up prayers, but Jo Emily was just glad to hear their voices. By the time she convinced them she would be fine, she'd begun to think about Danny Upshaw for some darn reason. She would have given anything to have told her folks about some wonderful man in her life. Instead she had to tell them about some sicko, son-of-a-bitch stalker.

The minute she hung up she made herself another big ol' tray of food. This time she went for the deli chicken salad with almonds, the Santa Fe pasta, which was swimming in artichokes, and something called tabouli, that looked like it was made out of little bits of round brown rice.

She stayed away from the wine because it made her sleepy, but a big plastic bottle of Diet Pepsi caught her eye, and some fancy bottled water. There was cheesecake, too, rum raisin, of all things. Everything looked yummy as she headed for the bedroom, but for some reason, Jo Emily was craving a Jumbo Jack in the worst way.

The tray was loaded, and the only thing on her mind was not dropping it. Even so, she sensed something different about the bedroom when she walked in. She paused in the middle of the room, confused, and thinking maybe the furniture was out of place. A slow turn brought her all the way around, but it wasn't until she stared hard at the latticed windows that she detected something.

"Now, what is that?" she wondered, studying the beam of light that hit the window. It didn't occur to her to be frightened, even though she had a vague notion it might be a flashlight. This was Carlie's place. People who lived in enchanted cottages didn't get hurt. She was safe here. Anyone would be safe here.

She was looking for a spot to set the tray when she heard someone tapping on the pane. With a little bleat of surprise, she turned. "Who's there?"

The bleat became a bloodcurdling scream.

The tray of food crashed to the ground as a freakish image appeared in the window. His eyes peered at Jo Emily through the holes of a black executioner's hood. God's eyes. Black with loathing and contempt. It was the man who'd beaten her nearly senseless. He'd come back to finish the job. He was going to smash her hands. Kill her!

As she backed away, her mind froze on some inner cry of recognition. She knew who this monster was. Her nervous system had flashed the identity of her attacker the way a signal flag flashes semaphore. But it was there only for an instant before the curtain dropped, not long enough for her conscious mind to grab hold.

God in heaven, who was he?

She ducked out of the room, still screaming inside, and ran for the kitchen phone. But it had already begun to ring when she got there, and she knew that it was him. He was closing in, blocking all the exits. "No, please!"

She ripped the receiver from its cradle and reared back to heave it. He was coming for her. She could hear his footsteps, hear his breathing. The image locked in her mind was of a snarling beast with a baseball bat. The drip from the shower across the hall sounded like glass shattering. Each sharp plink was a flying piece.

She strained to see down the hallway, expecting him to be there. She had no idea where he was now. Or which way he might come from, but it felt like there wasn't any safe place to hide. She didn't know how to protect herself.

The panic button was in the other room. Her purse was, too, where she kept the revolver. Frantically she hit the phone's disconnect button, trying to get a dial tone. A sharp buzz droned in her ear and she sobbed with relief. Press 911! But she couldn't make her fingers work.

The walls shook around her, thud after thud. Jo Emily had no idea what was making the terrible noise, but it came from the front of the house, the living room. It sounded like someone was pounding on the door. She dropped the phone and ran there, halting as she saw what it was. The knob on the front door wrenched back and forth. He was trying to get in.

"The police are on their way!" She could barely get the words out. Her voice was going. Carlie told her there was a security system, but she couldn't hear an alarm. Maybe she was supposed to have pressed the panic button. Or he'd found a way to disconnect it!

The door bent and creaked under a barrage of brute strength. When it finally gave way, Jo Emily dropped to her knees. She had no protection now. There was no one coming to help her.

She turned away, but not before catching a glimpse of the man who burst into the room, and the mere sight of him terrified her into helpless bursts of shrieking. "Go away!" she screamed, curling into a ball. "Go away, Danny!"

She turned her head into the wall and huddled there, refusing to talk to him, even when he knelt next to her and pleaded with her. He called her "Joey" and he kept telling her he'd heard her screaming, that's why he broke down the door. But Jo Emily was in shock and barely knew what he was saying.

"I was only trying to help," he told her.

Sometime later a security guard showed up, and Jo Emily realized the alarm must have been a silent one. She heard him calmly backing Danny off and Danny protesting. The guard wanted to talk to her, but she wouldn't—couldn't—talk. And it wasn't until a policewoman arrived and gently began to question her that she was able to respond.

Jo Emily's shivering eased a little as she sipped at the whiskey the policewoman had given her to calm her.

"I'm not really supposed to do this," the officer had admitted when she'd slipped the glass into Jo Emily's hands. "But you won't tell anyone, will you?"

The woman had such a kind way about her that Jo Emily found herself opening up. She told her everything she knew about the stalker, even things she'd forgotten over the years and were coming back to her now for the first time. But just beyond Jo Emily's reach was that elusive moment when she'd known who he was. *She had known.*

"I want you to call me if it comes back to you," the policewoman urged.

Jo Emily promised she would, and when they were done, and the policewoman was getting ready to leave, she did something that shocked Jo Emily. She leaned down and whispered, "We're going to catch the bastard, honey. He's never going to do this to you or to anyone else again."

Jo Emily looked up in surprise, taking in the woman's short-cropped graying hair and friendly smile for the first time. "What's your name?" she asked.

"Detective Peggy Sykes, at your service." The older woman patted Jo Emily's hand. "And you're going to be fine. Meanwhile I believe that young man over there wants to talk to you."

She meant Danny, who'd been nearby the whole time, quietly waiting for Jo Emily to acknowledge his presence. But Jo Emily couldn't do it. She couldn't talk to him, not tonight. There was a time when she could have loved Danny Upshaw. But she didn't know anymore. She just didn't know.

Jo Emily shook her head and the tears began to flow. "Tell him to go away," she said.

*   *   *

"Ladies and gentlemen, if you believe in liberty, if you believe in the revolution we fought to guarantee our freedom as Americans, then how can you let over a million Americans, honest, law-abiding people, be hunted down like animals?"

Wake up! Carlie wanted to shout. Listen to me! This was her first Senate hearing. The topic was close to her heart, and she could have gone all night, but the session had run late and she had the great bad luck to be the last speaker of the day. The only thing on the distinguished senators' minds now was going home.

She raised her voice, refusing to give up. "That is what's happening in our country. A million people—"

Carlie felt a tug at her sleeve. Startled, she turned to see a young woman in Senate blue handing her a folded note. A page, Carlie realized as she took it. She scanned the brief message and caught her breath.

When she looked up, she saw that every eye was now riveted on her. "Ladies, gentlemen, they're telling me that a member of my support group was attacked tonight by the man who's been stalking her. She's a personal friend, and there aren't words to tell you how devastating this is. They're holding a flight for me so that I can get back, but I thank you all for your—"

The buzzing and shuffling made Carlie hesitate. Now that she was leaving she had their full attention. This was what she'd been waiting for all evening, the entire day. How could she afford not to take advantage of it?

Hurriedly she began to speak, hoping she could still make the flight. "Please understand that there is nowhere my friend is safe from this man, nowhere *any* of us are safe if someone decides to stalk us. She's run the length of this country to escape him, cut herself off from her family and friends, attempted to change her identity and her profession. Those of us trying to help her have used all of our limited resources, but even if we caught the stalker tonight, there's a good chance he'd go free. He's made her life a living hell, but she has no legal recourse until he threatens or *takes* violent action. That's too late!"

She threw her hands up in despair and spoke to them as human beings, not senators, not politicians. "We need laws that protect *us,* not them! We need better enforcement and harsher sentences. There is nowhere my friend is safe. Nowhere she can hide, including a government-run safe house, and now, my own home. I have a state-of-the-art security system with an armed-guard response and still he managed to get to her.

"My friend is lucky to be alive." Carlie drew a breath before she continued. "But maybe she'd rather be dead than live like a hunted animal, waiting for the moment when this man, who calls himself the Executioner, tires of the game and decides to take her life, simply because he can.''

She left the dais to enthusiastic applause. Before she reached the doors, she was in tears, and before those doors had closed behind her, she'd made a decision. *Hang on, Jo Emily,* she thought, *I'm on my way, and we're going to get that bastard. He's done all the damage he's going to do. Now it's my turn.*

THIRTY-ONE

❧❦❧

January 25, Nine P.M.

He lured with sex. He killed with sex. And he will die by it. His torture devices will torture him.

He is a man of dark beauty and grace, the kind every woman wants and none can resist. Now he won't be able to resist me.

I will be the quiver that excites his blood, the gasp that excites his mind. The butterfly that flits away every time he reaches for the net. I will be his perfect prey.

And he will be mine.

He had the advantage of shadows. Now I have them.

He hid behind doors. Now I will.

I know who he is. He does not know me. He will.

I am the last living thing he will ever see.

The last eyes he will peer into.

His executioner's eyes.

Carlie stepped out of the shower and wrapped a towel around her shivering nakedness. A draft whipped from down the hall. The bedroom windows were open, and the house cold. She stared in the vanity mirror, marveling at the icy composure she saw there. It seemed to come from within. An aura of serenity had enveloped the remote, sharp-angled creature she gazed at, and Carlie wondered if she could make that woman beautiful. More beautiful than she had ever been in her life. Irresistible.

The answer had to be yes.

Her sister had loved fables and fairy tales. Ginger's favorites were

about handsome princes and happy endings, but Carlie had secretly preferred a dark little tale about water witches who lured unwary travelers
into their lily-scented ponds with nothing more than limpid eyes and
rose-red lips. This woman in the glass had luminous eyes and a succulent mouth. But the answer hidden deep in Carlie's heart was no. She
was too eerie and remote to be irresistible. Too deadly.

A fifth of *grande cuvée* brut chilled in a bucket on the vanity. Carlie
lifted the bottle, dripping from the ice, and refilled her flute. She'd
already drunk a glass with the full intention of becoming intoxicated.
She needed the liquor's wildness. Its fire. She would finish the entire
thing if it became necessary.

The answer *had* to be yes.

She turned the latch on her makeup case. Witch's brew.

Moments later her eyes had a haunting veil of purple shadow around
them and her hair was falling and tumbling from a mother-of-pearl clip.
Rapunzel's ladder. To her mouth she had applied a glaze of ruby lip
rouge. To her cheeks a feathering of petal pink. And the effect was
stunning. Where she had angles before, she had curves now. Her gaze
was softly misted and fetching. The image in the mirror was perfection
in every feature. But no less chilling. It came from deep within, that
coldness. She was a cameo portrait with no soul.

Carlie wondered if she were looking at a stranger. She couldn't be
sure who this creature was. It felt as if she were playing out a role, but
the script had been written for someone else. Written by him? The
stalker?

She drank more champagne. Drank down the glass.

With every attack on Jo Emily, she was more convinced that they
were dealing with Ginger's killer. There were too many parallels in their
signature behavior for it to be coincidence, and Carlie needed it to be
the same man. Her entire plan depended on it. She had secreted Jo Emily
away, knowing the stalker would think she was still here and try to get
to her. Only it was Carlie he would get to.

There was only one way to catch a predator.

Become the prey.

The trap was set and baited. No one had to disable the alarm system
tonight. It was already off. She was using another kind of surveillance,
a closed-circuit video camera she'd had the security company install in
the bedroom. The only thing left was for her to slip into the crimson
kimono she'd draped over the back of the vanity chair, and everything
would be ready.

Ginger's favorite fragrance was violets and Carlie had lightly sprayed
the pulse points on the inside of her wrists with the scent. She was

setting the perfume atomizer on the mirrored tray when she heard the floorboards creak in the hallway. Her hand froze.

He'd come.

The ticking of the shower told her it was him. It sounded as if he'd entered through the front door and was walking toward the bathroom. The boards creaked again. They moaned. She clutched at the terrycloth towel, securing it. When the door opened, she turned toward the sound.

"You?" she whispered.

The black tie hung around his neck like a noose. Darkly lowered lashes masked his expression as he studied her. But she saw it all, felt it all. Suspicion and wonder and male rage. He hadn't expected this. Hadn't expected her to be waiting for him, ready for him. Whatever he'd planned to do, she'd rocked him. Rocked every twisted male impulse that lived inside him.

"What is this?"

His voice was harsh. It scoured her naked skin like pumice. She felt drunk. She was drunk. The fire rose in her belly and fanned high into her throat. It filled her nostrils with the scent of wildness. She *was* ready for him.

"I'm surprised you didn't come up behind me and drag me into a dark room," she said. "That is the way you usually work."

Fiend. I should know.

He stared her up and down, saw the flute in her hand, the half-empty bottle of champagne. "What are you doing?"

"Having a li-little party."

"Your front door was unlocked."

"That's right," she said defiantly. "It *is* my house."

"Are you alone here?"

"What do you mean?"

"Jo Emily left the shelter. I thought maybe she came here."

"Why do you want to know?" She reached for the brut to pour herself some more, but her hand was shaking, and she couldn't manage it. An actress. She was an actress. Even if her nerve deserted her, she could get through this. She had to.

Champagne splashed into her glass and foamed over.

God, how could this be happening? It was a bad dream.

She had never allowed herself to believe that it could be him. She still didn't believe it. But how did she explain the horror that had risen up inside her at the mere sight of him? She wanted to close her eyes and deny his existence. She wanted to die. She would never understand how a man could make her believe in herself, as he had done, and then negate everything that had happened between them. It was like letting her glimpse perfection before he destroyed it.

"Is Jo Emily all right?" he asked.

"Bastard," she said under her breath. "You don't care about her."

"Carlie, whatever it is you're doing, *stop*. This isn't worthy of you."

"Worthy?" She spat the words at him. "What would you know about that?" Now wonder and rage and suspicion were pouring out of her. What was worthy about the way he'd invaded her life and stalked her from the beginning? Or tried to make her believe he'd set aside the case. Jo Emily was terrified of him. Carlie's own mother had warned her against him.

"Carlie, don't make me—"

"Don't make you what?"

The bottle rocked on the countertop as Carlie carelessly dropped it there. The flute hit the porcelain sink and cracked down the middle. She barely knew what she was doing anymore. She tried to get past him, but he grabbed her and dragged her into his arms.

"What's wrong with you?"

"What's wrong with *you*?" she shrieked at him. "What have you done to Jo Emily? What?"

"What do you think I've done? Stalked her? Smashed her windshield? Terrorized her? You think that's me?"

No, not you! It can't be you. I'll die if it is.

"Rio, oh, Rio," she cried softly. God, this charade was killing her, destroying her. She couldn't do it.

She pressed herself against him, her naked breasts and thighs white against his black canvas trench. The towel had fallen away, but she was oblivious. She'd drunk too much, risked too much. She wanted only comfort, solace. Escape. She couldn't think beyond that. If he would hold her, take her in his arms and make her forget everything, it could be what it was before. They could have it again. She could have it. Wholeness. Healing.

"Make love to me—"

"Carlie, what are you doing?"

He tried to hold her away, but she fought him. "No, please, I need you!"

"Carlie, don't—"

He didn't want her? It stunned her to think that he didn't understand what she needed, especially when it had been so humiliating to ask. He was the one who had helped her see herself as she really was. If he didn't know what his efforts to reach her meant, then they must have meant nothing. She ducked her head in confusion and something went cold inside her. Ice cold.

"What did you do to Ginger?" she whispered. "What did you do to my sister?"

"Carlie, for Christ's sake!" He stepped behind her and got the kimono from the chair. "Put this on."

The robe went flying. She ripped it from his hand and tossed it away. "Get out," she said. "Get out of my house."

"I'm not going anywhere."

"Get out or I'll—"

"What? Call the *cops*?"

His cynical tone pushed Carlie to the breaking point. She swung at him. Her palm hit his jaw with a sharp crack, but before she could pull away, he had her hand. Had her by the wrist.

"Is this what you want?" He pulled her close, jerked her right up against his mouth. "You like it rough, the way your sister did? You want me to knock you around?"

"Get out!"

His eyes darkened. Black water. Deadly. He was angry now, and it was a paralyzing sight. He combed his hands into her hair and drew her head back. Her mother-of-pearl clip clattered to the floor. He whispered something incoherent, and then his mouth touched hers with a scalding kiss.

"Is this what you want?" he whispered. "Is it?"

She heard the shake in his voice as he pushed her back against the vanity. He moved to undo his belt.

"Tell me, Carlie. *Tell me, godammit.*"

The kimono lay on the floor by Carlie's feet. She scooped it up, but couldn't get it on. Her hands were shaking too hard. Everything was shaking. Her body was giving her such chaotic signals, she didn't know what they meant. Her heart was wild, a flood, but her thighs still ached with the pain of wanting, and the truth of her body's craziness amazed her. She couldn't want him, not this way. She must still be drunk.

"Not rough enough for you yet?" he said.

The pain flared into her belly as she remembered how it had been with him. But when she looked up she saw a demon, not a man. She saw her own destruction. If she let him make love to her, it would be all over. She wouldn't be able to go through with any of it, and Jo Emily would never be safe. No one would ever be safe.

"Carlie—"

"Stop," she whispered as he reached for her. She heaved at him with all her strength. "Stop!"

He rocked back, and she grabbed the bottle of champagne and broke it against the countertop. A sob choked her throat as she menaced him with the jagged edges. And then she saw it, the blood. His hand was bleeding! She stared at him in shock. Had she cut him, or was it something else? Jo Emily had bitten her attacker on the hand. Dear God.

"Leave her alone!" Carlie cried. "Do you hear me? Leave her alone, *please.*"

"Who? Jo Emily?"

"If you have to hurt someone, hurt me!"

It wasn't passion that darkened his expression now. It was fury. He was done with her, through. "You're as crazy as she was," he said. "As fucking crazy as she was."

Carlie sank to the floor, oblivious to the shards that had flown everywhere. As she watched him go, her hopes exploded like the glittering glass. There was nothing left. In her mind the stalker was an amorphous figure in black, a symbol of evil. It was not Rio Walker. Whoever she'd expected to show up, it wasn't him, and she had not been prepared in any way.

But there was blood. Blood on his hand.

Carlie didn't know what that meant. She didn't understand anything, not even her own heart and mind. There was only confusion, deafening confusion, with no way to know what was real. Her plan had failed, and worse, she'd failed. She'd abandoned her teachings and principles, taken a huge risk to gratify her own need for vengeance. This was not a time for vigilantism. She had to call the police.

It didn't matter who he was anymore. She told herself that repeatedly, mentally shouted it over the pain and confusion, as she walked to the bedroom. But moments later, staring at the phone, she knew it was impossible. She couldn't make the call. She could no longer deny the possibility that it might be him, no matter how slight. If there was any doubt in her mind, any at all, then she had to do this herself, regardless of what she faced in bringing him to justice, regardless of who he was. He'd brutalized her sister and terrorized her friend.

He was the Executioner.

It was a ritual, talking to herself. She voiced her thoughts and it was like speaking with someone, sharing her fears. She wasn't alone anymore. She didn't have to be strong, the safety expert, the group leader, the respected author. She could pace and ramble aloud. She could sit with the stones her sister gave her and go on as if Ginger were there.

Tonight it was Rio she talked about, searching her soul in an effort to understand. She stayed up well into the night, pacing, going over the details of their relationship, repeating them to herself, word for word, and wondering if they'd actually happened. His tour of L.A., the bridge, the billboard, the Spanish Kitchen. She dug for every word he'd ever said to her . . . and said them to herself.

Roused from sleep by the telephone, Carlie grabbed it without thinking. "Hello?" she mumbled.

The silence brought her awake.

"Who is it?" she asked. "Hello? Is anyone there?"

No one answered, even when she repeated the question. And finally she went quiet, too, dreading what she would hear.

At first it was so faint it sounded like his breath. Tapping. He was tapping on the mouthpiece.

Carlie hung up the phone, afraid she was going to be sick. She didn't want to play this game, not this one, not with him. But it had only begun. Every hour he called back, sometimes holding off just long enough to make her think it was over, that he'd quit. That's when the phone would ring. When the silence would start, and her heart would stop.

It was the tapping, always the tapping that made her wince and hang up the phone. It wasn't him. It was *not*. Someone knew what he did, how he worked. A lot of people knew.

Now, twelve hours later, she was sitting in the same spot where she'd found Jo Emily that night, on the floor next to the refrigerator in the kitchen. There were probably better hiding places, but it was warm here, and the brightness made her feel protected, especially now that it was dark outside.

Huddled in her gray sweats and surrounded by the newspaper clippings of Ginger's ordeal, she waited for the ringing to start. She'd told Danny she was working at home, and she knew it wasn't Jo Emily or anyone else who would normally leave a message, because Carlie had stopped answering the phone after the first call. She'd set the machine to pick up, but whoever it was wouldn't respond.

He didn't want the machine.

He wanted her.

Breathing on the other end of the line.

God, she could see him in her mind. By now he was all she *could* see. The billowing trench coat, the sinister grace. He was there, always there. He stalked her thoughts.

The images her mind flashed were terrifyingly real. She had evidence now. It was piling up that he was somehow involved. His own behavior condemned him, and she herself had accused him of stalking both Jo Emily and her sister. But she couldn't make herself believe it.

He'd left in a dark fury the night before, and hadn't called since. She couldn't explain that any more than she could account for her horror when she heard the tapping sound. She lived with a soul-deep fear that it was him, except for this seed, this mustard seed, that stubbornly said it wasn't.

Which did she trust?

She closed her eyes and leaned her head against the soft rumbling of the refrigerator. What frightened her most was the possibility that this was a calculated move on his part and he was still trying to trap her in some way. Peggy had let it out that he was investigating the Femme Fatale, but Carlie didn't think that could account for his actions now. Anger didn't make sense either, even though her accusations seemed to have enraged him.

"Oh!" She jumped back as if the phone had leaped at her. The jangle of bells ceased as she picked up the receiver, but her head was thundering. "Who's there?"

Silence. Someone was trying to drive her insane, and what better way than the telephone? Who knew about her love-hate relationship with phones? She almost laughed. Her agent?

She was about to hang up when the caller suddenly clicked on.

"Carlie? Is that you?"

She sagged forward with relief. "Yes," she whispered. Her mother. It was her mother.

"Speak up, then," Frances snapped. "I can't hear you."

Carlie had never been so glad to hear that sharp, demanding tone. Still, it took a massive effort to sound normal. "Why did you call, Mother?"

"Why don't *you* answer your *phone*? I've been trying to reach you all day."

That was her mother? No, she'd heard the tapping.

"I don't understand you, Carlie. I don't understand you at all. You might have warned me that you'd be speaking in front of a Senate investigating committee. My aide saw you on C-SPAN and alerted me."

"It was a hearing, not an investigation. I was called to speak against budget cuts for victim assistance."

"I don't care what it was, you should have told me. You know how I feel about surprises. I don't like them."

If it hadn't been for the refrigerator, Carlie would have been on the floor. She didn't have the energy to defend herself, and mostly, bizarre as it seemed, what she wanted to do was laugh. To laugh so hard she sobbed. It had to be nerves. She shouldn't have picked up the phone.

"I heard your speech, Carlie."

Carlie racked her brain. She couldn't remember having mentioned Ginger, or the Bishop name, or anything else that would have upset her mother.

"It was quite wonderful."

"What?"

"Your speech. They're saying you turned the hearings around, even at that late hour. I understand they were all quite impressed . . . and so was I."

Carlie had no idea what to say. Her mother was paying her a compliment and she didn't know how to respond.

"Are you there, Carlie? Are you all right?"

"Yes . . . fine."

It might be the first genuine compliment she'd ever received from Frances. If her mother was reaching out, Carlie was tempted to respond. She couldn't remember a time when she'd needed to talk with someone the way she did now. But whoever she confided in had to possess the most rational of minds, be infinitely wise and steady, and most of all, make her believe that she was crazy to think it might be Rio, that she had to get help, call the police, do the sensible thing instead of this dangerous game she was playing.

It had never occurred to her that person might be her own mother.

"Thank you for telling me," Carlie said woodenly. "I must have sounded pretty desperate up on that dais. The victims' advocacy program is very important to me."

"Not desperate at all—passionate. And yes, I think I'm beginning to see how important your work is."

"Mother, there's a reason I didn't answer the phone." *I was afraid it was him. I have to stop him, and I don't know how.* Carlie was on the brink of pouring out all her fears when something told her to hold back. It was a premonition of disaster. Her mother wouldn't be supportive. She'd be aghast. Frances Stanfield Bishop would be furious if Carlie admitted that she was trying to trap Ginger's stalker.

Her mother had her own secrets, possibly some terrible ones.

She knew who killed Ginger.

She knew who he was.

That hit Carlie so hard she had to fight to hang on to the phone. It was another flash of intuition that defied logic. It went against everything Carlie believed to be sane and reasonable.

"Why didn't you answer the phone, dear?"

"Oh, I—I didn't hear it. I turned off the bell so I could get some work done."

"Carlie, you don't sound like yourself. Is there something wrong? I have time if you'd like to talk."

"No, I'm fine. Just busy. Terribly busy."

With that, Carlie made her excuses, wondering if she'd done the right thing as she set the receiver in its cradle. She struggled to get up from the floor, but before she could do it, the phone was ringing again, and she accidentally kicked it over.

It was probably her mother, calling back to insist on knowing what was wrong. Carlie almost hoped it was, but she could hear someone else speaking before she got the receiver to her ear.

"So," a muffled voice said, "you decided to answer."

Carlie froze at the sound. Every word was hushed and sinister, cold with menace. This was him, she knew. The call she'd been terrified to take. She could not hang up on him again. She had to go through with it this time.

She covered the mouthpiece with her hand and brought the phone to her ear, afraid he would hear the shake in her breathing. She couldn't have spoken if she'd tried.

"What are you wearing?" he whispered.

His voice hissed like steam. It could have been Rio. *It could have been anyone.* Carlie didn't know who it was, and right now she couldn't concentrate on anything but what she had to do. It was crucial that she speak to him, keep him on the line, lure him into a false sense of intimacy.

"What would you like me to wear?" she whispered through her closed fingers.

"Red . . . snapdragon red."

She hesitated until the silence made her fear he might hang up. "I'm wearing a silk kimono . . . and nothing else."

"Describe it to me."

"It's short and it ties at the waist. The silk is heavy and soft. It's red, of course—"

He cut her off with a snort of derision. "You're wearing gray, Carlie. Ugly gray sweats. The same ones you wore in the tree house."

The phone went dead, and Carlie let it fall from her hands. She had closed all the doors and windows, all the blinds and shutters and curtains. There was no way he could know what she was wearing now. Or in the mountains.

After that he called back every hour on the hour, all night long, jarring Carlie out of a stupor each time she began to doze off. He never spoke, nor did he hang up. The silence rang on forever, a high-pitched whine that played inside her mind like the deafening screak of a microphone.

Finally, near dawn, Carlie decided not to hang up either. She listened to the icy stillness until something turned over inside her, turned from cringing dread to fury. Blind fury.

"Fuck you," she whispered.

He didn't call back, and it was the most profound relief Carlie could imagine. But as the hours wore on, another kind of silence set in. Day blurred into night, and the machine didn't ring at all. A full twenty-four hours passed before it blared to life again, and by that time she was nearly incoherent with fatigue.

She'd managed to get herself to bed, but she hadn't slept, hadn't eaten. She couldn't focus her thoughts.

"Ginger liked it rough." His whisper-soft voice sounded like waves, crashing against the receiver. "What do you say, Carlie?"

Filled with revulsion, she rocked backward, holding herself. The pile of bed pillows broke her fall. She wanted to shriek at him never to mention her sister again. Filth like him, he had no right! But she had to play along, had to say that yes, she liked it that way, too. Rough. Anything to get him to show himself.

"Don't hold out on me, Carlie."

She went still, confused.

"What do you mean?" she asked him.

"You don't think we bleed when we're cut? You don't think we lose our hearts, too?"

She sucked in a breath, and he began to laugh. Rio had said those things the night of the tour. He'd been talking about men loving as deeply as women did, but they were inside the restaurant, the Spanish Kitchen.

She sprang up. "Who are you? How do you know what he said?"

The stuttering dial tone told her he'd hung up.

"Shit!" She flung the phone across the room. "Stay on the fucking line, you bastard!"

The stress of being at his mercy was destroying her. And not knowing who she was dealing with was worse, especially since he was tormenting her with some of the most private and precious details of her life. Denial was tearing her apart, but no matter what he said or did, he would never make her believe he was Rio. She'd built a fortress against the possibility and it was taking all her strength to hold off the doubts and fears.

The room tilted beneath her feet as she got out of bed. She pulled on her old chenille robe and held the bedpost to steady herself. From there she went straight to the bathroom sink. She had one of those sick headaches that come with hunger and exhaustion, and the sight of her pale, pinched features in the mirror bent her over the bowl.

He'd consumed every second of her life since the first call. There was no escape, no relief. He'd even taken control of her vital functions. He could make her heart lurch painfully and her mouth go dry. He could let her catch a breath, and then jolt her again, harder. He was the man at the switch. He controlled the voltage, and she was helpless.

She fell forward and a sob shook her.

This was what she hated most, that one person could have so much destructive power over another. Stalkers crippled their victims by turning them against themselves, and that was what he'd done to her, crippled her. She felt paralyzed, yet he hadn't touched her.

Her head throbbed as if it were about to split open. She cradled it in her hands, still too queasy to move.

But a moment later she reared up dizzily.

"His phone number," she whispered. There was something she'd forgotten in all the confusion. When she'd disabled the alarm system, she'd asked the security service to trace all her incoming calls. They used a program much like Caller ID that allowed them to capture the caller's phone number. If the stalker hadn't put a block on his, they may have caught it.

It took every bit of concentration Carlie had to tap out the service's simple three-digit code. Only one phone number had been captured, they told her, and inexplicably it turned out to belong to her former home, Blue Hills. But when Carlie heard the time of the call, she realized what had happened. Her mother had not been in the nation's capital when she called. She'd been at the family mansion in San Marino.

Her mother was here in California.

Carlie couldn't be sure what that meant, but it touched into one of her deepest fears that her mother was involved in all of this in some way. Her stomach pitched, and she fought back another wave of nausea. When would it stop? It felt like a carnival sideshow, with one trapdoor after another flying open.

She had to learn for herself what she'd always taught her students, that fear had become her own worst enemy. It was all a game, a cruel psychological one. But if she didn't harness the fear, it would destroy her faster than he would.

The first step was to take back control of her life in whatever way she could. Do the small things, she told herself. Do what you *can* do, and the rest will fall into place.

Later that morning she found the strength to shower and wash her hair, and the noise of the water gave her a respite from the phone. Let him call and hang up on himself. She would talk to him when she was ready to lay out the bait again, and this time he would take it.

She might have to wade into the slime with him, but so be it. That didn't put them in the same camp. Her motives were the opposite of his. The moral opposite. They were good. They were right. There was no doubt in her mind that he was the same man who murdered her sister; now he was after Jo Emily, Carlie herself, and maybe others. She wanted the reign of terror to end. Forever. *Even if it was Rio.*

THIRTY-TWO

Frances stood at the grand piano in the music room, trying to remember the one piece that Carlie had excelled at playing, "Heart and Soul." Ginger had been the virtuoso. She could play anything, including the Schubert concertos Frances loved, and she'd come by the skill almost effortlessly, as she had most everything she attempted.

Every now and then a paragon was born into this world. Her eldest daughter had been one of those—gifted, loving, luminous. But maybe that kind of perfection was doomed. Maybe it couldn't exist. When a light burned too brightly, it drew the darkness, and everything the darkness concealed.

And then there was Carlie, awkward child that she was, plinking away at the keys and struggling mightily to master the same pieces that Ginger dashed off. Carlie had been hopeless at music lessons and recitals, but she'd tried. She'd tried so hard. Of the two of them, Frances might easily have loved her more, if she'd been free to.

There were flowers on the piano, an arrangement of white silk lilies, surrounded by a collection of framed photographs. Frances went to the picture that had always drawn her in times of reflection, and picked it up. She'd looked young and fresh and starry-eyed all those years ago, nearly thirty years to be exact. She'd been at the country club with Bernard when the photo was taken. They were relaxing on the patio in their tennis whites, following a heated doubles match.

Bernard sat on her left, but it was the man on her right, with his perfect smile and dark gold hair, that made her draw a breath. Even now. He was so good he'd played alone against the two of them, she and Bernard. And he'd won. He was still that good. Another paragon. It was why she'd had to give him up.

Frances's smile was wistful as she set the picture back. One could have been forgiven for mistaking him for Ginger's father rather than Carlie's. Although when all was said and done, it might well be his flesh and blood who was the luminary. His daughter's light had been hidden all these years, and was just beginning to shine.

With a little shiver, Frances walked across the room to the fireplace. The house was chilly. The heat had been turned down and the staff dismissed, except for the gardeners and the housekeeper, who came in once a week. The mansion was so old and full of ghosts that Frances found it difficult staying even a night, but she was deeply concerned about her daughter.

Carlie hadn't convinced her that nothing was wrong. Frances did not yet know the extent of it, but there was a great deal that could go wrong, terribly wrong, and she was the only one who could stop it. The only one who could stop *him*. But what frightened her most was Carlie's naïveté. If Frances was right, her daughter had no idea how much danger she was in.

It was her life at stake, nothing less than that.

Frances pulled her cardigan sweater close around her shoulders and stared into the fire. It was all there in the leaping flames, her memories, her losses, the excruciating choices she'd had to make. Now she was faced with another one. She had sacrificed a great many things to achieve what she had, and one of them was her relationship with her daughter. It looked as if those achievements would have to be sacrificed *for* her daughter.

There was a trunk sitting in the entryway. The limo driver who'd left it there probably assumed it was packed with Frances's clothing. She wondered what he would have thought of the gleaming weapon she'd brought cross-country. He might not have given a second thought to a fencing saber. Fortunately no one else had, considering Frances's enthusiasm for the sport.

A stake through the monster's heart.

She lifted her head, and felt the rightness of her choice. It might not be the most efficient way to eliminate evil, but it was fitting in this case.

The world would be shocked, she imagined. Frances Stanfield Bishop had always wanted to see her name in the history books while she was still alive, but she hadn't thought it would be this way, the newest Supreme Court justice, impeached in the first year of her term, tried for high crimes. It was the darkest irony she could imagine. But also fitting. Things had come full circle.

*   *   *

If I made the laws, you'd be dead.

That was what he'd said when he called earlier that evening. The primal quiver of fear that lived inside Carlie had turned to ice at the reference. He knew about that, too. *He knew about everything.*

She'd closed her eyes, forced herself to breathe, and within moments she'd regained control. Somewhere along the line she'd ceased being shocked by his intimate knowledge of her life. She'd refused to be shocked. It gave him too much power.

It was time they met. That was what he told her, and then he'd given her directions to an old movie lot in Van Nuys. His last words had been, "Be there in half an hour, wear the red kimono. And Carlie, come *alone.*"

She'd followed his instructions to the letter. If he wouldn't come to the bait, then the bait would come to him. This was the last thing she would ever have advised a stalker victim to do. It was insanely dangerous. She was playing right into his hands, but there was no other way to unmask him. And it wasn't just a question of identification. She had to get him back here, get him on tape. She wanted proof. Indisputable proof.

As it turned out, the studio was on a poorly lit side street in an exceptionally bad area. Carlie had pulled the Explorer to the curb and killed the engine, grateful to be in the large, sturdy car. She'd had no intention of getting out until she'd caught sight of who she was dealing with. But now, after a half hour of peering through the windshield and checking the rearview mirror, she saw that she'd underestimated him. A smart stalker would never show himself.

This one would be waiting for her somewhere inside the lot, she suspected. Unfortunately he hadn't given her any clues as to where that might be, and the thought of wandering around a deserted movie lot in the dark, looking for a killer, was more than a little terrifying.

But as much as she wanted to call it off and go home, she couldn't. Leaving would mean he'd won, and the stakes were too high for that now. This had stopped being about her a long time ago. It was about a nameless, faceless evil that threatened them all, everything she loved.

The entrance gate she pushed open was sagging off its hinges and badly rusted. It gave out a groan that would have made a sound-effects team proud. She'd brought a purse-size flashlight that was also a pepper-spray container, but the moon was nearly full and very bright. Carrying a flashlight would have looked odd, so she tucked it in a pocket of her full-length canvas coat.

Her shadow raced ahead of her, jet-black against the moonlit pavement, as she walked through a parking area. There were some trailers that must have housed offices or stars, a few weather-beaten props, including a mechanical monster that looked as if it had been scavanged for parts, and a ghost town set that was eerily authentic.

Carlie gave it a wide berth. She also avoided the haunted house, deciding to wait in front of Thomas Alva Edison High School, which was in plain view of the entrance, but looked suspiciously like a set for slasher movies. With very little effort one could imagine empty halls, echoing with the screams of teenage girls.

An hour later, chilled to the bone, she was angry. "Where is he?" The coat she'd worn wasn't warm enough to ward off the bitterly cold night for very long, and the kimono he'd demanded she wear meant she had on virtually nothing underneath the coat.

The brightness was a mixed blessing. It could blind you if you weren't careful, and it made for the blackest shadows Carlie had ever seen. They dropped unexpectedly, danced grotesquely, and every one of them brought her a painful start.

The sounds were worse. The old buildings seemed to be infested with crawling and flying things. Carlie couldn't see what they were. They moved too fast, but she heard their skittering feet and whipping wings, and every once in a while, she caught a glimpse of something slithering near her feet.

It filled her with disgust. Her empty stomach rolled and pitched, and it was all she could do not to retch. As the adrenaline of the past several days wore off, exhaustion caught up with her. The flying things became demons. Ghouls hid in the shadows, and every snap of sound was a breaking bone.

God, how she wanted to leave, but she forced herself to stand there, teeth chattering and fighting off waves of nausea, until finally it began to dawn on her that she'd been set up. It had been three hours. If he hadn't shown by now, he wasn't going to. Obviously he'd never intended to.

Stiff with cold, Carlie walked to her car.

Jo Emily had ridden in damn few taxis in her life, which was why she wished she could have enjoyed this one more. It was probably going to cost her a mint before she got where she was going, but she hadn't thought it would be smart, carrying a loaded gun in her bag on the RTD.

She nudged her elbow into the purse she'd cradled in her lap and felt the metal object nestled against her pelvis. She only hoped she had the chance to use it. But meanwhile she probably ought to stop playing with it. If the damn thing went off, she'd be the one dead as dirt.

Headlights flashed through the back window, strobing the interior of the taxi. Jo Emily ducked down, then peeked back up near the edge of the window to see who was following them. The double lamps and cab lights made it out to be some kind of delivery truck. She sank back down. That had scared her so bad she didn't have enough spit to swallow.

The folks at Freedom Road were going to be worried when they found her gone. Carlie had put her into the hands of an underground network that hid victims of stalking and abuse when all else failed. It was a temporary situation while the network took steps to get the victim a new identity and relocate her, but the location was so secret no one knew where it was, not the police, not even Carlie.

She hoped everyone still thought she was sleeping. She'd left by the bedroom window of the safe house, and it was easy getting out, but she felt bad about having to do it. The people who ran the network gave their lives to it, and sometimes risked them. The last thing she wanted was to make their job more difficult.

After tonight she would probably need them to ship her out of the damn country, but there was one last thing she had to do, one last thing before she could go peaceably into that dark night of the soul, as some big-deal writer had once called it. If she'd told the people at Freedom Road what she was up to, they would have locked her up for her own good, and thrown away the key. They would have thought she was squirrel-bait crazy. And maybe she was.

The deep breath she took felt like it could pierce her. She stared at the lights snaking along the roof of the cab and blinked, blurring them into a pale stream. The tears started slowly, then poured down her face, soaking it, but she never batted an eyelash. Maybe she was.

The telephone was ringing when Carlie got back. Instead of answering it, she began to laugh. Laugh hysterically. Laugh until she dropped to her knees and doubled over. Even if she'd had the strength to pull the unit out of the wall, that wouldn't have stopped it. The portable phone was ringing, too.

When the screams came, it felt as if they were being ripped from her throat by force.

"C-coward—" She struggled to her feet, cursing him. "You're nothing but a fucking coward!"

Floorboards creaked in the hallway behind her.

Carlie whirled on a man in black, a man with a ski mask over his head. A cry caught in her throat. She was too stunned to scream. She'd had no idea anyone was there. She'd stopped believing that he would ever show himself, and now the only thing she could see were his ungodly staring eyes.

They were as black as the hood, unrelieved evil.

"Let's see how brave you are, bitch," he whispered.

He lunged at her, and Carlie narrowly evaded him. But there was nowhere to go. He had her trapped in the kitchen.

"I'm wearing the kimono—" She fought to get out of the raincoat. "Don't you want to see it?"

"I have seen it."

He was garbed like a SWAT-team sniper, and as he reached into his flak vest, she flung the coat at him and tried to get past him. The coat fell to the floor, and a cloud of netting dropped over her, cinching tight. It happened so fast the room began to swim. She was trapped in a black mesh prison that wouldn't let her move or speak or breathe.

He dragged her like netted prey into her own bedroom and forced her to watch him assemble a bizarre device. It looked like a huge white mummy case, and when he had it ready, he hung it from one of four large steel hooks that he must have pounded into the ceiling while she was gone.

The floor shifted beneath Carlie's feet as she realized what it was. Drenched in sweat, she fought against passing out. This was how Ginger died, in a suspension bondage device that suffocated her. The lassolike loop of cable on the floor was rigged to close around the victim's legs and whip her into the air, upside down.

Carlie forced herself to watch him, but nothing he did gave any clues to his identity, though there was something familiar about the methodical way he worked. He was at least six feet and muscular, unless his clothing was padded, and he was still disguising his voice in a raspy whisper.

"Love or fear? What does it for you, Carlie? I hope for your sake it's fear."

He was going to kill her. As the realization hit home, Carlie began to look for a way to escape. He was strong enough to kill her with his bare hands, and struggling could trigger that kind of violence. Her only hope was to disable him, too. If she could trip him and bring him down with enough force to stun him, then heave herself to the window and break it—

It was a suicidal plan, but she didn't see any other way. He was going to kill her whether she tried to escape or not.

She sank quietly to the floor as he continued to work. Now was the time, she realized. He was too engrossed in his task to keep an eye on her. It would be easy to go limp and feign unconsciousness. She was almost there already. The rest of it would be hell.

Rigging the device gradually brought him nearer to her. Carlie steeled herself. *No mistakes. Even one and you're dead. Instantly.* When he was close enough, she made a battering ram out of her legs and slammed them against his as hard as she could. The blow staggered him. She'd prayed he would fall over her and crack his head on the iron footboard, but the railing caught him and snapped his neck in a whiplash motion. A bone-crunching thud shook the room as he landed on the floor.

Carlie began to shove herself toward the window with her feet. Raw terror propelled her. The carpet flayed her skin through the mesh, but she couldn't feel anything except a frantic need to survive. She glanced back as she neared the window and saw that he'd already come to. He was getting up.

No! Her mind screamed for help as he dropped over her and held a cloth to her nose. Chloroform. He was going to put her under. She would be unconscious when he restrained her in the bondage device. She was dead already.

As she slumped forward, any hope of survival slipped away, along with consciousness.

The first sound she heard was the slice of a sharp blade through fabric. Carlie felt herself being jerked forward. Pain pierced her arm, and she screamed inside the mask that covered her face. She'd been cut with a knife. He was stabbing her.

She doubled over, trying to protect her vital organs.

"Hold still," he snarled under his breath. "Shut up and hold still."

She gasped for air as the mask was ripped off her face. The bedroom light stung her eyes, and the silver blade flashed paralyzingly close to her bare flesh. The blur of motion confused her, but she could focus enough to see that he was cutting her free with the knife, not stabbing her. He wasn't going to kill her?

The black hood and clothing concealed him totally as he wielded the knife. Carlie didn't move as he hacked at the netting and peeled it away. She barely breathed. He had her on the bedroom floor, propped up against the wall, and all she could imagine was that he wanted her to have a brief, punishing taste of freedom before he sealed her up in the bondage device. If she was conscious when she died, her last thought, her last emotion, would be terror.

She would never give him that. She would die at peace, no matter what he did to her. He could mutilate her body and torment her mind, but he couldn't touch her spirit. There was a place beyond the reach of human cruelty, and she would find it. There was nothing this dark monster of a man could do to hurt her then.

Watching him, Carlie realized that she had one last wish. She didn't want to die without knowing who he was. He'd killed her sister and terrorized her friend. His identity might help her to understand how that could have happened, and why she was about to be his third victim.

He moved swiftly down her body, freeing her arms. Her hands felt numb, but she could move them. As he began to work on her legs, she heaved herself up and grabbed for the black hood. Her nails sank into the knit material, and she wrenched it off, tumbling backward as it came free in her hands.

Carlie stared at her tormentor's startled face in total shock. Whatever she expected, *whoever* she expected, it wasn't Peggy Sykes, Rio's partner.

"You're the Executioner?" she whispered.

Peggy clamped a hand over Carlie's mouth and forced her back against the wall. She bent over Carlie, hissing fiercely.

"I'm not your stalker," she said. "I'm here to stop him. At least I'll get to kill this sick bastard in the line of duty."

Carlie shook her head. She didn't understand.

"He's in the bathroom, taking a leak," Peggy explained. "He'll be back any minute, and when he walks through that door, you're the first thing he's going to see, so sit tight. I'll get to him before he gets to you."

Carlie's mind had been stunned so many times, it couldn't absorb another shock. But this was an entirely different kind of blow. Peggy had given her a glimpse of survival, and it hit Carlie harder than anything the stalker could have done. She had inured herself to torture. She had no defenses against this, against hope. Tears filled her eyes and she sagged against the wall.

"Hey, don't pass out of me," Peggy whispered. "There isn't much time."

Carlie nodded to let the other woman know she would cooperate, and Peggy released her.

A toilet flushed down the hall. Creaking floorboards warned that he was on his way back. Peggy leaped up, and Carlie braced herself. The bedroom door flew open just seconds after Peggy hid behind it.

He hesitated on the threshold, peering at Carlie. "How'd you get loose?"

"Bastard!" Carlie struggled to her knees. She had to get him to come to her, even if it meant confronting him.

"Oouufff!" A terrible blow to the ribs slammed her up against the bedroom wall. He'd kicked her, and he was coming at her again, but Carlie couldn't move. She choked on the blood filling her mouth. The pain was so agonizing it made her gag.

The bedroom door creaked, and Peggy emerged, her nine-millimeter Beretta trained on the stalker.

"Get away from her!" she shouted at him. "I'll blow your fucking balls to hell!"

The stalker dropped to the floor and rolled. Peggy fired repeatedly, savagely, screaming at him to stop. But she missed him, and when he came up he had a gun on her.

Carlie fought not to black out. She knew Peggy was in trouble, but she was swaying in and out of consciousness, and the stalker was well out of her reach. She could hear him, but she couldn't see him.

"Shoot, bitch," he taunted Peggy. "Let's see who has the fastest bullets."

"Drop the gun, *asshole*! You don't want to kill an officer of the law. That'll get you death row in this state."

"Then I'll see you in hell, pig!"

"You fast enough to get her and me, too?"

Carlie thought she recognized the man's voice. It wasn't the stalker who'd spoken. She looked up, afraid to believe, her heart pounding wildly. Her vision was spotty, but she couldn't be imagining him. That had to be Rio in the doorway.

"Take him out, Rio," Peggy said.

Carlie shuddered with relief. It was all she could do not to collapse. "Thank you, God," she breathed.

But Peggy had begun to scream at Rio to shoot the stalker, and that's when Carlie realized it wasn't over. People could still die. Rio could die.

"Take him out!" Peggy cried. "Kill the bastard now or I will!"

The stalker snarled at Peggy to shut up.

Rio's eyes flickered with a horrible light, and it looked like he might risk everything, even his partner's life, just for the satisfaction of blowing the deviant away.

"He ain't going to shoot me!" the stalker crowed. He started to laugh and the sound of it seemed to drive Peggy insane.

"Peggy, no!" Rio shouted. But there was no way to stop her.

Carlie smelled the stench of burned sulfur almost before she saw the crack of light. Peggy lunged at the stalker and got blown backward by the lethal force of his .357 Magnum.

Rio pumped three bullets into the stalker's heart, and then he rammed a flying boot into the man's ribs and lifted him with such force that his body flipped in the air and landed at Carlie's feet.

Blood flew everywhere, spattering Carlie. She gasped in surprise, but held Rio off when he rushed over to her.

"I'm all right," she told him. "Go help Peggy. I'll call 911."

By the time Carlie had crawled over the stalker and pulled the phone down from the bedside table, Rio had Peggy's head cradled in his lap,

and he was using his coat to absorb the bleeding. Carlie couldn't see
how serious her injury was, but it looked like a stomach wound.

"What the hell were you doing, Sykes?" Rio chided gently. "Trying
to make me look bad?"

"Try, Walker? With you it's easy."

As Carlie pressed out the numbers, she could hear the two of them
bantering, and that gave her hope. She didn't want to think about what
it would do to Rio if anything happened to Peggy. He was a loner with
very few friends. To lose even one would be devastating.

A dispatcher came on the line, and Carlie answered the woman's
questions, begging her to get an ambulance there quickly. "There's an
officer down," she said. "Detective Sykes has been shot. Please hurry!"

When she hung up the phone, Carlie realized Peggy and Rio weren't
bantering anymore. Peggy looked as if she'd taken a turn for the worse,
and she was struggling to tell him something. Carlie went quiet, listening. She didn't want to intrude, but Peggy had said something to her
earlier that hadn't made sense. She'd talked about killing this stalker.

Carlie couldn't remember the words exactly, but she remembered the
gist. *At least I'll get to kill this one in the line of duty.*

"Shut up for a minute, will you?" she was exhorting Rio.

Rio clearly didn't want her to get emotional, but Peggy ignored him,
as she probably aways had.

"You didn't finish one damn report the entire time we worked together," she said, her voice weak but determined, "and you let a little
nurse with a big needle run you out of my room, but other than that
you're a decent partner . . . which is why I'm about to hand you your
nemesis—"

He tried to laugh, but it came out grainy and hoarse. "Did you get
shot in the head? What are you talking about?"

"The Femme Fatale," Peggy said. "You're looking at her."

"What?" He didn't move for all of a minute, just stared at her, and
then he began to shake his head slowly. It wasn't confusion, it was
denial. He didn't want to believe her. He wasn't going to no matter
what she said.

"Case closed," she said. "I'm the one you want, although why the
press stuck me with that ridiculous label, I'll never know."

Carlie was trembling as she pushed to her feet and put the phone
back on the table. It was shock as much as exertion. It was Peggy? The
woman Carlie revered and was writing a book about was Rio's partner?
Carlie had thought it was Frances, her own mother.

There'd never been a specific incident that had made her suspect
Frances, it was intuition more than anything else—and her mother's odd

behavior. Frances's insistence on secrecy and her attempts to back Carlie off were too strident. She'd refused to discuss Ginger's death or reveal the murderer when she'd admitted knowing his identity. She'd even tried to mollify Carlie by saying that it had been "dealt with."

That was what Frances did. She "dealt with" things. She was a full-blown control freak, and Carlie had sensed that her mother's bottled-up rage was deep-rooted enough to be pathological. The idea for Carlie's book on the Femme Fatale case had come partly from her need to explain and justify her mother's behavior. Of course she could tell no one that at the time.

Peggy tried to move, but gasped in pain.

"Christ, Peggy," Rio said. "I don't care who you are, just don't die on me." Awkwardly, he patted her face with his hand. "I should have shot the bastard. I shouldn't have waited. Jesus, I'm sorry."

Peggy grabbed him by his tie. "You never could apologize worth a shit, remember? Don't start now."

Carlie had sagged back to the floor, unable to stand any longer. She closed her eyes, swimming in dizziness. She could hear Rio imploring his partner to hang on, and she was praying that the paramedics got there soon. But when she opened her eyes, it was another frightening sight that filled her field of vision. The stalker was lying at her feet, and she was mesmerized by his dead, staring eyes inside the hood.

With some effort, she pulled the black ski mask off him and stared in bewilderment at the chiseled features, the face that was handsome, even in death. The man she was looking at was Gabe Quiñones, the crime reporter. If she had really believed it would help her to know the stalker's identity, she'd been wrong. She had no idea why Quiñones would have killed her sister and gone after her. None. Or Jo Emily, was he stalking her, too?

"How is she?" Carlie asked Rio a moment later as she painfully made her way over to where he sat with Peggy.

"Bad," was all he could get out.

"The paramedics are on their way," she assured him. "They should be here any minute."

"Case closed—" Those were the words on Peggy's breath as her eyes drifted shut.

Carlie touched Rio's arm and felt him shaking. Oh, dear God, she thought. This will destroy him. If she dies, he will hold himself responsible.

THIRTY-THREE
༶ༀ༈༶

Jo Emily should not have opened the door without knocking. She'd been taught better manners. Her mama'd been pretty specific about keeping your nose out of other people's business, not that Jo Emily had always listened. This time she was wishing she had.

At first she thought she had the wrong place. Clothes and leftover pizza and Bud Lite empties were scattered like fertilizer on a field of crops. As far as she could tell, the purple-and-black pretzel by the fireplace was one of those Abdominizers they advertised on TV for three low payments, and the broken table lamp must have been target practice for a barbell lying on the floor.

She was staring at the remains of Danny Upshaw's living room, and what she saw frightened her. Danny himself was sitting on the couch in the middle of it all, wearing boxers that looked familiar enough to be the ones he had on when she left. Only he wasn't hugging a pillow now. He was bent over and hugging the top of his head like it would crack if he let go of it.

Jo Emily was at a loss. One of those Wild John weekends, maybe? Where men reclaimed their primitive selves? That stuff was done in groups, and this looked like a personal thing. Secretly she wondered if it could be about her, then chided herself for being foolish. Men didn't suffer over the Jo Emily Poughs of this world.

The gift box confirmed it. She spotted what could only be the present she'd agonized over, lying by the entertainment center as if someone had opened it and left it there. Something red and ruffly was spilling out, and Jo Emily found herself moving toward it as if in a trance.

Please don't let that be what I think it is.

But it was. A peignoir set, she realized, kneeling down.

"Jo Emily . . . ?"

Danny had just noticed she was there, but she couldn't look at him. A heavy floral fragrance saturated the lingerie. It was perfume, and that could mean only one thing.

"I guess this was intended for someone else all along," she said.

"No—not the way you're thinking."

Finally she looked up, dizzy with pain. She would never have believed it could hurt this much, not after all the blows her heart had taken, all the bastards. Weren't you supposed to be numb after all that?

"What way am I thinking?" she asked him.

His bright blue eyes beseeched her to understand, but they were red around the edges, and his ruddy complexion was as pale as death. Hungover, she thought unhappily. He looked like a man coming off a serious bender.

"You're probably thinking I bought it for someone else," he said, "but I didn't. I bought it for you."

"For me? But why didn't you—"

"I couldn't give it to you. I was afraid." His jaw knotted up, and he let out a heavy sound. "Afraid I'd hurt you."

Jo Emily stared at him in confusion, afraid to believe what her intuition was telling her, that he wasn't talking about emotional pain. He meant "hurt" in the physical sense.

"All my life I've had this gut fear of losing control and going insane, like my dad. . . ."

She had another look at his living room, at the mangled fitness equipment and the broken lamp, as he went on talking, revealing that his father had been an alcoholic. When she turned back, he was massaging his temples and staring soberly at the same wreckage she was.

She'd been brutalized in every possible way, stalked and assaulted, terrorized. The thought of a man going insane, this man—

"Danny, you're going to have to explain what you just said, and you're going to have to do it fast, because—well, I think you know why."

"Explain?"

It sounded hopeless the way he said it. But finally he told her what he meant, all of it, while Jo Emily sat on the floor of his living room in welling silence.

He'd grown up in a house where his father beat his mother with terrifying frequency, where sex was rape and love was torment, a house where his mother was killed in front of his eyes, and his father swore it was an accident.

He'd been in grade school when it happened, and he'd dealt with it the only way he could, by forcing it from his mind. He managed to suppress the worst of the memories and bury them in some dark, inaccessible place. But he couldn't suppress his mother's voice, begging him not to hurt women the way his father had, warning him that men were animals by nature, their urges violent and bestial. She'd whispered to him from the cradle that he was his father's son and would always have to battle his violent nature.

"She begged me to be a priest," he told Jo Emily. "She thought it was the only way to save me from myself. I was there at the hospital when she died, and I swore to her that I would never be like him. She didn't hear me, but I swore it anyway."

His eyes were squeezed shut now, and his temples were red where he'd been massaging them. Jo Emily knew this must be difficult for him. She didn't want to intrude, but she found herself wondering if he'd believed his mother, if he was still a virgin. That would explain a lot.

Finally she asked, "Did you keep the promise?"

"No," he admitted, "the furthest thing from it. They put me in a foster home with some good people, but the damage was done, I guess. When I hit my teens, I had sex with every girl who'd let me, until I found myself in the act of forcing one of them. When I saw the blood, I knew my mother was right. I was my father, a carbon copy."

"Blood, Danny? You hurt the girl?"

He nodded, his eyes squeezed shut. "It was her first time, only she didn't tell me that until later. I offered to marry her, but her family had money and they wanted no part of me. They even tried to bribe me not to talk about it."

His next breath seemed to rip him apart. "That was the last time I ever touched a woman. It was easy keeping my 'urges' under control. All I had to do was resurrect the past. I forced myself to hear my mother's pleas for forgiveness while my father raped her, to remember the way he slammed her head against the wall and then made the police believe she'd fallen. My own memories crippled me. I couldn't do anything but shake when I got those feelings."

Jo Emily was horrified. If she'd known she wouldn't have come onto him that way. She would have been more sensitive to his ordeal. Working with Carlie must have been his salvation, she realized. It had allowed him to help women like his mother and to focus his rage on the men who abused them. The tragedy was that he was still paying for his father's sins, as well as his own.

Saddened, she wondered if he could ever work it out. The wounds suffered in childhood were the worst, the deepest. Sometimes they never healed quite right.

She rose to go to the couch and her shoe hit the gift box. The smell of gardenias wafted up.

"Danny, I don't understand, whose perfume is that?"

She pointed to the lingerie, which he seemed to have forgotten. He shook his head and swiftly turned the same shade as the red silk material. Jo Emily had never seen a guiltier soul, and that was going some, considering her past.

"God, Jo Emily, don't make me tell you about that, too."

"Danny, you can't hold back now."

He seemed to understand the logic in that, or maybe it was the desperation in her voice.

Still unable to meet her gaze, he said: "I had to find out if I was capable of normal sex. How else would I know if I could function, and if it was safe for me to be with someone I cared about?"

Someone he cared about. Jo Emily felt something inside her unfurl and lift its head for the first time.

He glanced up and, with a man-going-under sigh, admitted the rest of it. "I don't know her name. She was a prostitute. I made sure we were both protected, but I guess that doesn't help much, does it?"

"Prostitute?" If Jo Emily hadn't been kneeling on the carpet, she might have tumbled over. She didn't know whether to be devastated or relieved. It seemed as if their lives were connected in so many ways, both good and bad.

"Oh my, God, Danny," was all she could say. "Oh, my God."

"I'm sorry," he whispered. "I really am."

He clearly didn't know what to make of her reaction, but she was already on her feet, and the only barrier between them now was his coffee table, a sleek wood-and-glass beauty she'd admired the night he brought her here.

"I'm okay," she told him as she joined him on the couch. "I just can't believe it, that's all."

He was still in the dark, even when she explained that she'd almost been one of those nameless women he visited.

Finally she grabbed his hands and shook them. "I worked in a massage parlor, Danny. I couldn't tell you before. I was so afraid you wouldn't understand how somebody could be driven to that."

"A massage parlor? When?"

"When I first got here. I couldn't get a job without using my own name and references, but the stalker would have found me, so I created a new identity, and I took a job at a place called the One Stop Love Shop."

She gave a little shudder, remembering, and wishing she hadn't. "I'd

still be there if it weren't for Rio. He's the one who helped me when
the cops busted the shop and took everybody in. He found out about
my situation, that I was being stalked and all, and he made them let me
go."

"The One Stop—"

She hushed him up, actually flattened her hand to his mouth. "I know
how awful that sounds, but I never did much of anything besides massage the customers. I was supposed to, but I couldn't. I couldn't go
through with it."

His lips formed a surprised grin beneath her fingertips. "Me, either,"
he got out.

"Danny?"

"I couldn't do it, either," he admitted. "I even tried to pretend she
was you."

"Oh, my God." It seemed that was all Jo Emily could say. She
wanted desperately to hug him. The closeness, the reassurance of his
gentle male strength, would have given her so much comfort, but it was
too soon to allow herself that respite. Everything could change in a
minute. The next minute. She had another confession to make, and this
was the one she dreaded.

Searching his sturdy, clean-cut features, she wondered if it was com-
passion she saw in his piercing blue eyes. She rushed to tell him the
rest.

"Rio and I had a deal. When he referred me to the support group,
he asked me to keep an eye on Carlie. He thought she was the Femme
Fatale, I swear he did. He said she was breaking the law, hurting people,
maybe even innocent people. He wanted me to help him flush her out
by saying I was being stalked—"

She stopped to catch her breath. "And to tell you the truth, I was
afraid not to do it. I mean, him being the police and all."

"You aren't being stalked?"

"No, I am. It's just like I told you. Back in Tennessee somebody
took a baseball bat to my car. I *was* being stalked, but I lost him when
I came out here. Rio wanted me to say the stalker had hunted me down,
so I did. I made that up and I talked about it in group, but then my
windshield got smashed, and that's the God's truth. Danny. I thought it
was the same guy, that he *had* found me, and I was terrified. You know
I was terrified. I went into hiding, even from Rio."

He was staring at her so hard she concentrated on her nails, afraid of
what she might see in his expression. Disgust or something worse. It
felt as if she'd brought this down on all of them, that she'd lied, and to
punish her, the gods had made her lie come true.

Finally she risked a glance.

He looked sad more than anything else, she realized. He wasn't hunched over the way he had been, but his arms were crisscrossed like he was protecting his midsection.

All he said was, "I wish to God you hadn't had to go through all that."

"Oh, same here," she blurted softly. "I wish the same for you, Danny, I do."

She couldn't find his hand. It was tucked away in the knot of his arms, so she gave his knee a quick little pat, and marveled that such a big man could look so bereft.

There was a catch in her throat that made her voice even huskier than usual. "I know you wouldn't hurt me, Danny," she said, hoping he believed her. "I've always known that. You have a good heart. Matter of fact, you have about the best heart I've ever encountered. And women like me can tell about things like that."

Right before her eyes he seemed to crumble. The bluff and glowing features of his rugged face contorted with grief, and his chin trembled.

Jo Emily was overcome. She touched him again, gingerly, and he hauled her into his arms.

"I'd put a bullet through my brain before I'd hurt you," he said. "All I want is to take care of you."

The sweetest words she'd ever heard. No contest.

She could feel him shake with relief, and it brought tears to her eyes. When she tilted her head to look at him, she was touched by his effort to smile. It made her sad to think that he'd been imprisoned by his fears all these years. Such a waste that anyone would spend so much precious time building walls, prisons of their own making. Not that she didn't understand the need. She'd done it too, walled herself in to fend off anything that could hurt her, even emotionally. A body could wither up and die in one of those prisons.

"I think you could use some taking care of yourself," she told him. "If we were to stick together awhile, you and I, and give this thing half a chance, it might could turn into something good."

"Stick with me, kid—" He forced the roughness from his voice. "I'll keep you supplied in Dentyne gum."

She was going to tell him he had a deal, but he hushed her with his fingers. "And *love*," he said. "I can keep you supplied in that, too."

He was making her fight like hell not to cry, and she bristled in self-defense. "Now that's a promise you'd be smart to keep, because I just happen to know a wrestling move or two. Ever heard of the Cross-Face Chicken Wing?"

"Now I'm scared."

He mocked her with a tender grin, and Jo Emily realized for the first time since she met him that he wasn't afraid anymore. The prison doors were open, and he was about to walk through them, a free man. That was when she knew that they might have a chance at something real and fine, her and Danny Upshaw. They just might.

THIRTY-FOUR

Warmed by the crackling fireplace in the music room, Carlie listened with a sense of regret and resignation to her mother's words. After thirty years of silence Frances had decided to unlock the chest that held the family secrets. The ghosts were loose, and the air smelled faintly of cedar and cobwebs, of yesterday.

Some of what Frances told her, Carlie already knew, but wouldn't let herself believe. Her sister had been bent on self-destruction at the end. Rio had tried to make her see that, but Carlie had refused. Now there was no way to escape the frightening abyss that Ginger Bishop's life had become. The hard part was making sense of it.

Carlie still didn't understand how Gabe Quiñones fit into it all. She'd been startled to hear her mother admit that she had been wrestling with the thought of confronting Quiñones herself. Carlie had always believed that Frances was capable of taking up arms to defend the family. She hadn't imagined her mother would take up arms to defend her.

"Tell me about Quiñones," Carlie said.

Frances was standing by the grand piano, and she had a photograph cradled in her arms, one she'd taken from the piano top. "Ginger was fatally drawn to him, although I knew nothing about it at the time. She'd become secretive about her relationships, but she'd promised me she wasn't seeing, well—your friend anymore, and I was so relieved to hear it, I didn't question her about anything else. She'd become completely obsessed with him."

Her mother was referring to Rio. But Carlie still didn't understand. According to Frances, it was the relationship with Quiñones that had led to Ginger's death. "There must have been signs she was in an abusive relationship, even if you didn't know who it was."

"There were signs, yes, but it wasn't the kind of abuse you're thinking of. She'd grown terribly thin, and she was agitated at times, but there weren't any visible marks or bruises on her. I thought it was nerves. There was always tremendous pressure on her to perform."

Frances seemed reluctant to go on. "Are you sure you want to hear this, Carlie? It's not pleasant."

Carlie had to hear it. Quiñones had tormented her with references to Ginger, and Carlie had almost become his second victim.

At her nod, Frances said, "It was rough sex that turned deadly. But it was consensual. Ginger not only went along with it, I have the feeling she may have sought it out. It's quite clear to me now that she was deteriorating, even suicidal, but I couldn't see it then."

Or didn't want to see it. Like me.

"Quiñones wasn't stalking her?" Carlie asked.

"No one was stalking her. Her death was an accident, caused by one of the perverse sex games they played. Quiñones restrained her and then he left the room they'd rented, as he often did, apparently for hours. But this time a cleaning lady found Ginger before he came back, and something had gone wrong. Ginger was dead, smothered by the contraption he put her in."

Frances grimaced, and Carlie felt it inside. Her stomach tightened with the same abhorrence her mother must be feeling.

"You're sure Quiñones didn't plan it that way? That he didn't intend to kill her? He was a sick, demented man, Mother. I can vouch for that."

Frances shook her head as if to say she didn't know. "I didn't even know he was involved until I found the letters hidden in Ginger's jewelry box. And to be honest, I thought Ginger was the sick one. Of course, I blamed myself, although I had no idea what I'd done to make her want to die in such a horrible way. I still don't, but the letters made it very clear that your sister was. . . ."

She struggled with the rest of it. "She was obsessed with sex and death."

Rio had suggested that Ginger knew no other way to escape her parents' "glory game" than to self-destruct. Carlie still couldn't imagine that Ginger had consciously planned to die, but at some point a death wish must have taken root. She was drawn to everything dark, the angel seduced by evil.

Ginger had been chosen from the womb to live out someone else's dreams. She never had a chance. It comforted Carlie to think that her sister had escaped and gone back to that time before everything went wrong, that she was happily combing the grounds of some magical estate, looking for rocks and fossils, and wondering what life held in store. Dreaming her own dreams.

Carlie spared her mother those thoughts. It wouldn't serve any purpose to heap more guilt on her now. Given who Frances was, and how she'd been raised, Carlie was surprised she'd revealed this much. Frances had spent her life upholding and defending the family name. For her to have risked bringing scandal down on their heads was nothing short of revolutionary.

Besides Carlie had an even more troubling concern. "Whose idea was it to say that Ginger had been stalked and murdered?"

Frances hugged the photograph to her. "Everything Quiñones and Ginger did was in her journal. When I found it, I called him, hoping he would tell me what had really happened to her. I knew his career was at stake, but I had no idea how far he'd go to avoid being connected with her death. He's a very resourceful man, as you know. The stalker story was his idea. He coached me on what to say to the authorities, how to handle the media and the public scrutiny. What he wanted in return was an exclusive on Ginger, her life and death."

She shook her head wearily, as if too exhausted to go on. "At the time it didn't seem as if there was any choice."

Carlie would never have called Quiñones resourceful. Sick, perhaps. Depraved. She'd learned from her own security company that Quiñones had recently hired on there under another name. He'd been the one who installed the video camera in her bedroom, which he'd then used to spy on her. He'd also bugged her house and heard every word of her diatribe about Rio, most of which he'd repeated back to her. He'd almost convinced her he was Rio.

"Odd that I never saw what a monster he was," Frances said.

Carlie wasn't surprised. She hadn't seen it either. Even now it was difficult to believe the man who visited her group could have been that twisted. "He was obsessed with pathology, with sickness," she said. "And with fame to the point of being delusional. He was so sure the series with my group could win him a Pulitzer, he started faking attacks on Jo Emily. That way he could say that her stalker had found her. When I stepped in, he turned on me. Even a better story, I suppose."

"Last I heard they weren't awarding Pulitzers in hell," Frances said.

The house was cold. Carlie held her hands to the fire, trying to remember the last time she'd stood in this room and warmed herself at the hearth. Whenever that was, she knew it had been a very different experience. This was the first time it felt as if she might have a right to be here.

It saddened her that it had taken so long. Unnecessary pain, she thought. That was the greatest crime, and they were all guilty of it. Quiñones's crimes were monstrous, almost beyond the human imagination, but there had been so much unnecessary pain in her own family. So very much.

"There's something I'd like you to see," Frances said.

It was the picture she was holding. She crossed the room and relinquished it from the shield of her arms.

Carlie felt a twinge as she reached out to take it. Quiñones had cracked two of her ribs when he'd kicked her, and she'd had to have them taped. That was just two days ago, and she was still tender.

"Why did you want me to see this?" Carlie asked. She'd expected a picture of Ginger. But this was her mother, Bernard, and another man—young and handsome, commanding attention with a smile as dazzling as his tennis whites. The picture must have been thirty years old, but Carlie recognized him as the country's chief executive.

"The president?" She glanced up at Frances, aware that something more than time had separated her mother from the laughing woman in the picture, surrounded by attentive men. She'd been carefree then, a completely different spirit.

Frances's voice was soft, almost lilting. "I think it's time you met your real father. I'm sorry he can't be here in person, but he knows I'm telling you this, and he's given me his blessing."

My father? Carlie studied the man's engaging smile and sandy mop of hair. He looked like a happy-go-lucky college kid. She'd met him on various occasions over the years, mostly political functions that had come about because of her family's connections. The Bishops had been friends as well as staunch supporters of the president, although it had never occurred to Carlie that her encounters with her real father were anything more than random events.

As she thought about it now, she realized that he'd sought her out with questions about her future, causing her fits of blushing shyness. Naturally she'd dismissed his interest as a mere courtesy, a gesture of thanks to her parents. She'd thought so little of herself she couldn't have imagined someone like him taking a genuine interest. But many things were beginning to make more sense now, including her presidential appointment.

"The mountain acreage was a gift from him," her mother said. "And there's a trust fund that will mature when you're thirty. Of course, one must take the bad with the good. He also passed on his allergies."

"He's allergic to almonds?"

"And strawberries, just like his daughter."

Carlie's ribs gave her a sharp jab as she realized the president and first lady had their own child, a twenty-one-year-old son. "I have a little brother," she exclaimed softly.

Frances nodded, but her anxious expression made Carlie hurry to reassure her that she wasn't going to rush out and tell the world. "I wouldn't think of embarrassing either of you that way. I know how sensitive this is, and there's his family to consider, too. It's enough for me to know."

It *was* enough for now. She hadn't yet absorbed the full impact. The future would take care of itself, and yet she couldn't help but think that someday it would come out, not to the world, but surely within the small circle that was linked by blood ties and secret pacts and whatever else they shared in common. Allergies, she thought, smiling.

She returned the picture to her mother. "Were you very much in love with him?" she asked.

Frances seemed startled, and Carlie realized she'd stepped over one of the lines that defined their relationship. Her mother quickly retreated to the piano, where she returned the picture to its place of honor.

She stepped back, rubbing her arms.

"I was," she admitted, "desperately, I'm afraid. And he loved me, too. But when I found out I was pregnant, it was over."

"Why?"

"His future, of course. They were already talking about him as president someday. Bernard and others had spent millions building support. When I told Johnny I was pregnant, he convinced me that the two of us should go to Bernard. I thought he was going to fight for me, whisk me away from my husband. But somehow Bernard convinced us both that our feelings had to be set aside for the good of the country. It ended up being a strategy session."

She tried to clear her throat of its raspiness. "You can't imagine what it's like to have your love, your unborn child, reduced to damage control."

Frances fell silent, and Carlie could feel the radiating pain. Her mother was still full of questions and regrets. You didn't recover from that kind of heartbreak, or that kind of love, not completely, not ever, especially when it had been wrenched away from you. You lived with the memories, bittersweet, and if you were smart, you were grateful life had given you the opportunity to feel that deeply.

Carlie glanced at her watch and saw that she was late.

"Do you have to go?" Frances asked. She seemed genuinely disappointed.

"It's a memorial service for the officer who saved my life, Peggy Sykes."

"The LAPD detective? Isn't she the one the papers are saying was the Femme Fatale?"

Carlie tried not to give anything away with her expression. The department had decided to ignore all the speculation and give Peggy a burial befitting a fallen officer, with full honors. There would probably be an investigation later, but for now they were proceeding as if she'd been killed in the line of duty.

"You know how the media seizes on these things," Carlie said. Neither she nor Rio had mentioned Peggy's confession when the backup units arrived at Carlie's place that night. Nothing had been discussed between them, but clearly they'd both wanted to protect Peggy. It was her disguise that had caused speculation among the press, along with a breaking story that Peggy's ex-husband might have been the first Femme Fatale victim.

Few people knew there was a husband. Someone from Peggy's past had come forward with a sensational story about her brief teenage marriage with a high-school boyfriend who'd abused drugs and beaten her. The informant claimed Peggy left him when he caused the baby she was carrying to be stillborn, but he stalked her for years, backing off only after she joined the police force. He had a string of other victims after Peggy, but it wasn't until he brutally killed one of them, and was set free on a technicality, that Peggy retaliated.

"I really must go," Carlie said.

"Carlie . . ."

Frances looked as if she were going to open her arms, and Carlie didn't know what to do. There had never been any physical affection between them, and Carlie didn't feel ready for that now. Things were happening too fast to know how she felt. But of one thing she was certain. They'd all been hurt too much. She had been rejected by this woman throughout her life, and perhaps it was only natural to want to rebuff her now, to turn her away as she'd been turned away. But what would that accomplish except to cause more pain?

Unnecessary pain, she thought.

Carlie went straight to her mother and took her hand, warming its chilliness, rubbing it away. "I'll come back," she said.

Frances smiled through a sparkle of tears. "I'll keep the fire burning."

The funeral service for Detective Peggy Sykes was as memorable an occasion as it was solemn and heartfelt. Over a hundred law-enforcement officers from around the country attended the graveside service, gathering at the burial park to pay their last respects. As the large crowd congregated, a phalanx of Los Angeles Police Department helicopters flew overhead, and an honor guard stood at attention, symbolically guarding the body of the fallen warrior.

It was a moving tribute. Even the case-hardened veterans were visibly affected as the helicopters performed the missing-man formation, and the last chopper pulled away from the others.

Carlie's throat tightened as she watched. She stood apart from the mostly uniformed crowd, not wanting to intrude on their loss. It was their time to say good-bye to one of their own. She'd barely known Peggy, but it was still difficult. She could only imagine how it was for Peggy's fellow officers. It was clear that she was greatly loved.

Rio stood next to the flag-draped casket, his head bowed. Carlie could hardly bring herself to look at him. He showed little outward emotion, but looked as if he'd aged overnight, and she knew what must be going on inside him. She was glad when the chaplain distracted her and began to speak of Peggy's dedication and her uncommon bravery.

"To lose your life in the line of duty," he said, "is the ultimate sacrifice. Peggy Sykes made that sacrifice. She was a warrior, and she died a warrior's death. She left us as she lived, safeguarding those she was sworn to protect. Today we mourn her passing, but we also celebrate her life, her exemplary service, and especially, her courage. She leaves a great hole in our ranks, but we will struggle to fill it, because she would expect nothing less."

As he finished his remarks, a four-man color guard presented the flags, resplendent against the brilliant blue sky, while a dozen buglers played "Taps."

Carlie glanced at Rio and saw his eyes close briefly behind his gold-rimmed aviator sunglasses. The cords of his neck stood out, perhaps locked in an attempt to swallow. She hadn't seen him since the day Peggy died in his arms, and it was all she could do now to witness his private struggle.

When the buglers were done, Rio stepped forward. Since Peggy had no family and Rio was her partner, the honor of saying the last words fell to him. Carlie couldn't imagine what they would be, but she prayed he wouldn't break down. She wasn't sure she could bear that.

He pulled a small leather-bound book from inside his coat jacket and turned to a marked page. His hesitation brought a hush to the crowd. Finally he cleared his throat.

"Many of you knew that Peggy liked proverbs," he said. "I asked her once what her favorite saying was, and she laughed and told me not to get sappy on her. But when I was going through her things, I found this passage marked in her book, and I'd like to believe it was one of her favorites . . . because every word is the Peggy I knew.

" 'Never look down to test the ground before taking your next step,' " he read aloud. " 'Only he who keeps his eye fixed on the far horizon will find his right road.' "

Dry-eyed, his features shattered with sorrow, Rio closed the book and set it atop the casket. In another voice, much quieter, he said, "Peggy found her right road."

Carlie turned away, her eyes swimming. It was too much. She couldn't watch any longer, and she didn't want Rio to see her this way. She knew she ought to slip away now, leave before the service was over.

But moments later, as the crowd began to make their way around her and leave, she realized she was still standing there, unable to find the strength to walk away.

"I'm glad you came."

It was him. She turned. "You are?" Her voice shook.

Stony-faced, he took off his sunglasses and slipped them in the pocket of his suit jacket. His tie was neatly knotted, but when Carlie met his gaze, she saw the man she'd encountered that first night in the grocery-store parking lot. The beautiful kohl lashes, the eyes that had seen every heartbreak known to man. All she wanted now was to make those eyes stop hurting.

"You couldn't have saved her," she said.

His head reared up, and it frightened her. He was going to tell her she had no right, to go away.

"You don't know that," he said.

"But I do. I may not have known Peggy, but I knew the Femme Fatale. I made an exhaustive study of her, and there was only one thing she wanted—to prove that no one was above the law, even her. She went after the most heinous offenders, the ones who'd slipped through the legal cracks, knowing that she would pay the same price they did. She was willing to die, and she knew that's how it would end. We talked about that in the mountains, you and I."

He studied her as if he were trying to decide whether he could believe her or not, whether he could let go the weight of the world. It was a burden he'd undoubtedly been carrying since childhood.

She hammered away, sensing she had him on the run. "You're no good at apologies, Rio. Peggy told you that herself. So stop apologizing. She would have hated it."

He almost smiled. "She would have, wouldn't she?"

"It was her last wish. You ought to honor it, don't you think?"

Grief brought his head back down for a moment. His jaw flexed so hard the tendons were visible. He glanced around at the grave site, at the book he'd set on her casket.

Finally, when he could, he nodded. "At least let me apologize to you, then," he said to Carlie.

She didn't understand.

"For what happened that night, for the things I said before I left your place."

He was talking about the night she'd menaced him with a broken bottle, she realized. Surely it was she who should be apologizing. She'd accused him of stalking Jo Emily and Ginger.

"Really, there's no need." She stepped toward him, suddenly awkward in her simple black dress and pearls. Her high heels sank in the lush green lawn of the memorial park.

His hand steadied her and kept her from tumbling into him. She was going to explain that they were both upset when it happened, that she'd been drinking, but she could tell by the strength of his grip and the look on his face that he needed to do this.

"I had you under surveillance," he told her. "You were acting oddly that night, so I staked out your place. I even followed you to the movie lot the next night. By then I'd figured out that you were trying to lure the stalker, and I thought it might work, so I let you go ahead with it."

He sounded weary with regret. "I thought I could protect you."

"And you did," she said.

"No, I wasn't even at the scene when it happened. I got a call that Peggy needed backup on a possible homicide. Now I know it was Peggy who set me up. She sent me off on a wild goose chase so she could have a clear shot at the stalker. But none of that excuses my putting you in that kind of jeopardy."

So she was part of his burden, too. "Please, Rio, forgive yourself so that I can stop hurting."

"What?" He stared at her, his voice roughened by surprise.

"It hurts me when someone I love hurts. It hurts me when he can't, or won't, forgive himself."

He must have heard what she said, yet he stood there for the longest time, squinting at her with disbelief in his eyes.

"You meant that? You love me?"

She laughed helplessly. "Duh."

He let out a ragged sound, half sigh, half moan. It sounded like the release of some great burden. Carlie hoped she was right. She hoped he was free of the weight, even if only for this moment, one perfect moment. No one ever knew how many of those they were allotted in a lifetime, she realized, those perfect moments of clarity, of happiness. They had to be cherished.

Some new and burning mystery seemed to take hold of him as he studied her. It was as if she were his reflecting pool and by looking deeply into her eyes, he could map out the future, or as much of it as he needed to know.

Sunlight broke through the trees, striking them both. It was as hot and bright as the smile that slowly lit his handsome face. He ripped his necktie loose.

"Let's get out of here," he said. "Or I may do something crazy and get us both thrown in jail."

"Crazy like . . . ?"

"Crazy like have my way with you in a cemetery, crazy like marry you and have a half-dozen kids and spend the rest of my life loving you back, if you'll let me."

"A *half dozen?*"

"Run," he said, "run for your life, Carlie. I'll give you a head start."

Carlie's heart did a somersault. She'd seen that look in his eyes before, that thrilling darkness. This was the apparition of the Spanish Kitchen, the man who'd found her in the the ballroom.

"Rio, wait—"

"One . . . two . . . three . . ."

"Rio!"

"Four . . . five . . . six . . ."

Carlie caught hold of her skirt. She whirled and started to run, not into the darkness of a hallway this time, but into the shimmering splendor of a new day, a new life. Her heels sank into the grass, and she had no idea where she was going as she darted away from Rio.

But just as suddenly she stopped. Stopped and turned back, her hair flying. Brushing the strands from her face, she drank him in, breathless, and her heart told her which way to go.

A smile burned through Rio's surprise as she started toward him, first walking, then running, flinging out her arms. Her delighted shrieks could surely be heard across the green hills and shaded dales of the tranquil memorial park as she propelled herself headlong at the cop with the beautiful lashes, headlong at the future. And Detective Peggy Sykes must surely be laughing, too.

Carlie's perfect moments were only beginning.